This is a work of fiction. Names, characters, places and incidents either are the product of imagination or are used fictitiously. Any resemblance to actual persons, living or dead, events or locales, is entirely coincidental.

RELAY PUBLISHING EDITION, NOVEMBER 2020
Copyright © 2020 Relay Publishing Ltd.

Jo Crow is a pen name created by Relay Publishing for co-authored Psychological Thriller projects. Relay Publishing works with incredible teams of writers and editors to collaboratively create the very best stories for our readers.

www.relaypub.com

D1526442

# MOTHERS DON'T LIE

## JO CROW

# BLURB

**The perfect life becomes the perfect lie.**

Molly Burke has it all. With the help of medication to control her borderline personality disorder, she's become a successful real estate agent with a loving husband who treats her four-year-old son as if he were his own. The emotional highs and lows from a difficult childhood have smoothed out but are still best concealed with little white lies to protect loved ones from her troubled history. Until Molly's past returns to shatter her idyllic life.

Molly's son, Colin, is discovered injured and covered in his grandfather's blood—and her father-in-law is nowhere to be found. The police suspect foul play. Longstanding bitterness erupts between Molly and her mother-in-law, exacerbating Molly's feelings of inadequacy and triggering fierce reactions that can no longer be contained.

A hallucination of her missing father-in-law only increases Molly's paranoia over the sins of the past. Deceit lies around every corner and embroils everyone in the growing madness. Someone knows what she did. And someone is trying to expose the truth.

And if the truth is revealed, her family will pay the price.

# CONTENTS

# 1

My palms were clammy. Beneath them, the steering wheel felt cold and heavy. I was driving too fast. Every now and then, the car jittered and threatened to swerve into a dark crevice at the side of the road. And with it, my heart hammered hard against my rib cage. I wanted to stop, to turn around and slide back into the life I was living yesterday. Before I made the decision to run. Before I realized that everything was not *okay*.

Yesterday, the promise of a happy future had still glimmered on the horizon. If I'd stayed, in just a few months, I'd have had the money to clear my debts and start fresh; scrub out all the mistakes from my past and focus on truly turning things around. But now, in the dead of the night, with the inky sky squeezing the sides of my battered old Civic as it hurtled down the freeway, I knew I couldn't go back.

In the rearview mirror, headlights appeared in the distance. At first, they were just pin pricks—a good way behind me on the road—but as I watched, they drew closer. In the dark, I couldn't tell what kind of car they were attached to, but whoever was driving was moving quickly, catching up with me, closing the gap between us. I pressed my foot on the accelerator, but the Civic groaned and refused to go any faster.

I shuffled in my seat, shaking my head so that my long red hair fell back from my face, I tried to keep looking ahead. On the passenger seat, my phone began to ring, and my body jolted as if it were a police siren cutting through the silence. The ringing filled the car. Behind me, the headlights were drawing nearer. I swiped the phone into the footwell, and it clattered hard, but whoever was trying to call me hadn't stopped. The glow of the incoming call was leaking out from its facedown screen. Finally, it went quiet.

I looked up. The headlights were so close and bright that their reflection made me wince and narrow my eyes. I was holding my breath. The car behind me beeped its horn, and then it swung out of its lane. It was pulling up next to me, driving alongside me. Still beeping.

I tried not to look at it. I didn't know whether to slow down and stop or keep going. It was still level with me, too close, trying to make me pull over. Finally, I turned my head, expecting to see Tracy's desperate and bruised face screaming at me not to leave.

But it wasn't her.

It was a middle-aged guy with thick shoulders and a long, wiry beard and, even though I didn't know what Tracy's partner, Andy, looked like, I knew that this man was not him. "Speed up or get off the fucking road! Stupid bitch!" he yelled through his open car window.

Tears started to roll down my cheeks. Relieved tears, scared tears. He slammed his fist on his horn a few more times, raised his middle finger at me, then sped off, his tires screeching as he accelerated away.

A hot wave of nausea flooded my limbs. My breath was coming quick and shallow, warning signs that a panic attack was about to take hold of me. *Calm down, Molly, it's not good for the baby. Think of the baby. Think of the baby.*

Eventually, I saw the exit I needed. As I pulled off the freeway, the wide empty road I'd been traveling on began to narrow; I was nearing the beach. By the time I stopped the car, my legs were trembling, and my arms felt like they were made of lead. I tried to slow my breathing. *Five, four, three, two, one*, the way Carol had taught me to when we were hiding beneath the stairs and praying our foster parents didn't find us. I closed my eyes and counted until my breath returned to normal.

The spot I'd arrived at was somewhere I'd been many times before. It was the place I retreated to when I needed to be alone with my thoughts. The place I came to after my parents died, after Jack died, when I dropped out of college, and when I discovered that I was pregnant. That day, the day I saw those two fateful blue lines at the end of a white plastic stick, all I felt was panic. But all these months later, for the first time, I felt the way expectant mothers are supposed to feel—like the little person growing inside me was the most important thing in the world. Like I'd rather die than let anything happen to him. And that was how I knew I was doing the right thing by getting him away from Tracy and Andy.

Even if they hunted me down. Even if they found me, hired fancy lawyers, made me do what I'd promised. At least I'd know I'd tried to be a good mom. The best mom. The kind of mom who takes care of her kid.

I breathed out slowly and turned off the engine. Pressing my palms against my stomach, I leaned down and whispered, "You have nothing to be afraid of. I'll never let anyone hurt you. I'm your mom." The words caught in my throat, and I blinked back my tears. "I'm your mom, and no one will ever, *ever*, take you away from me. It's just you and me now, little buddy. You and me. Forever."

As I spoke, I felt a tiny flutter beneath my hands.

"Oh," I said. "There you are."

I smiled a shaky smile and tried to tell myself that it would be hours before anyone noticed I was gone. It was the middle of the night. I wasn't due to see Tracy until the weekend and, by the time she realized what had happened, I'd be miles away. My phone had stopped ringing. We were alone. Just me and my son.

There were two dusky orange streetlights over towards the steps that led to the beach. But nothing else. No one else. I reached over to the glove compartment and flicked it open. I took out the handful of papers that I'd wedged in there weeks ago. Papers that promised my baby to another couple. Papers that would have given us both an entirely different life.

I took the matches I'd shoved into my purse, got out of the car, and strode down to the water. Letting the cool waves bite my toes, I lit a match. Then I held it beneath the neatly typed contract and let the flame engulf it.

When it was nothing but a fiery torch clenched in my fist with the heat scalding my skin, I dropped it into the water. And I let the ocean carry it away.

Taking one last look at my faithful old car, I slung my bag over my shoulder and walked away. Away from the life I thought I'd be living. Away from Portland. Away from the promises I'd made.

I took the unborn child I was never supposed to keep, and I left.

## 2

_____

*FOUR AND A HALF YEARS LATER*

B ryan was due home any minute, and I'd been fizzing with excitement all day. The letter had arrived just after he left for work and I'd tried to catch him, but he'd already been halfway down the street. So, I'd decided to wait and make the announcement special.

Beside me, Colin was standing on a small set of wooden steps, grinning excitedly at the cake on the kitchen countertop.

"Can we do chocolate sprinkles, Mommy?" He grinned a gap-toothed smile at me, and I tousled his hair. Red, like mine, it had gotten too long lately and needed a trim. But Bryan liked it longer; he said boys were supposed to be a little scruffy around the edges.

After clapping my hands, I started rummaging through the cupboard where I kept the baking supplies. "Of *course,* we can do sprinkles. They're Dad's favorite. I have some in here somewhere..."

I'd just dug some out from the back of the shelf when my phone rang.

"Col, can you manage while Mommy answers the phone?"

Colin nodded, thrilled to be trusted with the most important job.

Wiping my hands on a dishcloth, I grabbed my cell and held it up to my ear. "Hello?"

"Hey, it's me."

"Carol..." I smiled at the familiar sound of my sister's voice and leaned back against the worktop, watching Colin as he began to smother Bryan's cake in far too many sprinkles.

"How are you?" Carol sounded relaxed, the way she always did when she was calling 'just to talk.'

"Good." I bit my lower lip. I shouldn't tell her. Bryan should be the first to know. But then, before I could stop myself, I said, "The adoption papers came through—Bryan is officially Colin's dad."

From his wooden stool, Colin grinned at me and made an excited bunched-fist movement.

"Oh, Molly, that's great news."

"We haven't told him yet. The letter came this morning. We've made a cake and we've decorated the house. He'll be home soon, actually. I can't wait to see his face." I was speaking quickly, aware that my voice was louder and bouncier than usual.

Carol paused and I heard her take a deep breath in. "Sounds lovely."

Laughing, to hide the fact that her tone had raised my hackles a little, I replied, "Once more, with feeling?"

"Sorry," Carol replied curtly.

Standing up a little straighter, I stifled a sigh; Carol and I had always been close, but lately we seemed to be falling into disagreements at the drop of a hat. Surely, she couldn't be annoyed at me for celebrating the adoption?

"Carol, is everything okay?" I was trying to be sympathetic towards her. But I'd been trying for a long time and was starting to wonder if she'd ever get over her compulsive need to dampen everyone's good news with her own sourness.

"Fine. Why wouldn't it be? I just don't think you need a mother and a father to make your family whole, you know? Look at Jack; he had both and look at what happened to him."

At the mention of Jack, my shoulders tensed. I began to tap my fingernails on the back of the phone. "This isn't about Jack. And besides, his parents are hardly a great example, are they?"

"I know that, Molly. I'm just saying—"

This time, I couldn't stop myself—I breathed out heavily and clicked my tongue in frustration. I shouldn't have; I should have reminded myself what Carol had been through over the past two years. But I'd spent months going easy on her, and it was starting to wear thin. "I know what you're saying but..." I moved away from Colin and lowered my voice. "Carol, I understand how you feel. You've been to hell and back. Rick's death and then the

8

miscarriage... I can't even imagine." I paused. "But you can't keep on being so—"

"So..?" I could picture Carol folding her arms in front of her chest and scowling at the phone.

"Frosty."

I almost winced as I waited for her reply. Bryan was always telling me to just bite my tongue and keep the peace, like he did with his family, but Carol and I had been through too much together to play that game.

Finally, she spoke. "It's okay for you to say that, Molly. Your life turned out just perfect in the end, didn't it? Despite everything. Despite what you went through to keep Colin. You still ended up with a perfect kid, a perfect husband, a perfect job."

With a sharp intake of breath, I turned my back to Colin as if somehow he'd hear what Carol was saying and put the pieces together. She was the only one who knew the truth about where he came from, and until now, she'd kept her promise not to make me talk about it. There was silence on the other end of the phone; she knew she'd gone too far. Trying desperately to listen to the voice in my head that was telling me it wasn't worth getting into an argument over, through gritted teeth I said calmly, "Come on, Carol, that's not fair. It hasn't always been easy for me. You know that."

No reply.

"Things will get better. Trust me." I tried to lighten my voice to show her that I was smiling into the phone and hadn't taken what she said personally. "Let's not fight. We're sisters."

"*Foster* sisters," Carol snapped back at me. But then her voice changed. It sounded shaky, like she was about to cry. "Molly, I'm sorry. I didn't mean—"

"It's fine. I know what you meant." Over by the cake, Colin was waving his sticky fingers at me; he'd finished decorating and was growing impatient. "Listen, I've got to go. Colin's about to smear chocolate frosting all over himself. I'll talk to you later."

"I—"

"Bye, Carol."

After hanging up, I couldn't get Carol out of my mind. Even as I finished decorating the house and set the cake down on the dark, wood table in the middle of the lounge, I felt like the stuffing had been knocked out of me. I hated arguing with her. We'd always looked out for one another. Since we were children, thrown together in the grimmest of circumstances, we'd been best friends. Sisters. She had *never* told me I wasn't her sister before, and she'd certainly never used my past against me, which meant she must really be hurting.

For so long, Carol was the closest thing to family that I'd had. We were a matching pair—both just as dark and twisty as each other. Carol had her shit to deal with and I had mine, and somehow we got through it together. Then she met Rick, I met Bryan, and everything looked like it was going to be okay for us both. Since Rick died, though, there had been an unspoken tension between us, as if she just couldn't stand the fact that I was still happy and she wasn't.

Watching Colin run off to change into the new T-shirt I'd bought him, I shook my head at myself.

My life could have been so different. It could have been full of sadness and grief, like Carol's. But somehow, I'd ended up with a beautiful family, a beautiful home, and a great job.

Perhaps I should have invited Carol over to celebrate with us; maybe that would have made her feel part of things. I thought about calling her back. But, selfishly, I wanted the evening to just be the three of us.

The adoption process had taken so long. There had been moments when we thought it would never happen. And now, finally, Bryan was officially Colin's father. We were a real family, and it felt right that we'd celebrate it together. The Three Musketeers. Just us.

Bryan's car pulled onto the drive just after six. He was a little later than usual, so both Colin and I were almost beside ourselves with anticipation.

As we watched him get out of the car and walk up to the front door, I held tight onto Colin's shoulders. But as soon as Bryan entered, I let go and Colin flung himself forwards yelling, "SUR-PRISE!" while throwing his arms around his dad's legs and squeezing him tight.

Bryan frowned down at Colin with an amused smile on his face. "Hey, dude. What's going on?"

Tugging at Colin's arm, I whispered, "Show him," and Colin stood back, proudly jutting out his chest so that Bryan could see what he was wearing.

For a moment, Bryan's expression froze. His brow wrinkled as he stared at it and mouthed, "I love my dad..." Then he looked up at me.

From behind my back, I took the letter and handed it to him. My hands were trembling. Tears were threatening to spill onto my cheeks and make them red and blotchy.

Bryan's eyes scanned the letter.

"It's official," I said, grinning.

Colin was grinning too. "You're my dad. It says so right there." He tugged at the letter.

"Ha!" Bryan let out a loud, ecstatic laugh. Then he swooped Colin up in his arms and pulled me to him. As I tucked myself under his chin, I felt him breathe in the smell of my shampoo, the way he always did when he was about to say something that was guaranteed to make my heart ache. "I'm the luckiest man in the world," he shouted. "The very luckiest... and look at this!" Bryan let go of me and carried Colin through to the lounge, waving his hands at the decorations and the cake.

"I did the sprinkles, Dad," said Colin proudly. He'd been calling Bryan "Dad" for as long as I could remember. We got married when he was just a toddler, so he'd never known anything different. But suddenly, hearing him say it took on a whole new meaning.

"Good on you, Col. Great job." Bryan set Colin down and took out his cell phone. "Molly, this is amazing. I've got to call my folks. They'll be thrilled. Really."

"Sure, I'll open the champagne," I said, drifting over to the kitchen and taking two long-stemmed glasses from the cupboard above the wine fridge.

As I poured, I watched Bryan pacing up and down and waiting for his parents to answer. I loved our open-plan lounge-diner for that exact reason; it was so family-friendly. Perfect for cooking together, eating together, entertaining.

"Mom, you'll never believe it... the adoption papers came through. I am one hundred percent, officially, legally, Colin's father."

Bryan was grinning into the phone. Even after three years of marriage, every time I looked at him, his piercing blue eyes and chiseled chin made me feel a little flutter in the pit of my stomach. He adjusted his glasses on his nose and nodded. "Mmm. Ah ha. Great idea. Sure, come now. See you soon."

As he hung up, I blinked twice and tried to stop my smile from faltering.

"Mol," he called over. "Leave the champagne in the cooler for now. Mom and Dad are coming over to celebrate."

Immediately, my heart sank. I wanted to say, *No, Bryan, why?* But he looked so excited that I couldn't bring myself to ruin it.

"I told them we can get takeout." Bryan sat down on the couch and pulled Colin onto his lap. "A proper party, hey, little guy? What do you fancy? Pizza?"

With wide eyes, Colin turned to me. It was almost his bedtime. "Can we, Mommy?"

"Sure." My voice came out a little strained. "Sure. Of course." I sat down beside them and leaned in towards Bryan. "Although, I had kind of hoped it would just be the three of us this evening..."

Bryan looked at me, then his eyes softened as if he'd just realized what he'd done. "Oh, Molly, I'm sorry, sweetheart. I can call them back, tell them—"

"No, no. It's fine. I'm being silly. It'll be lovely to celebrate with your folks."

Bryan put his arm around me and squeezed. "You're the best. Best wife. Best mom. Best everything."

I leaned onto his shoulder. "I know," I said, smiling. "I know."

# 3

Bryan's parents, Kathy and Frank Burke, arrived so quickly that I barely had time to whiz around the lounge with the vacuum before escaping to the restroom to calm myself down. Ever since Bryan and I had made the decision to leave Chicago and return to Portland, I'd tried my best to be the perfect daughter-in-law.

Before we'd gotten married, Bryan hadn't seen or spoken to his parents for years. He'd left Maine in his early twenties and had returned only a couple of times since to see his mother—not his father. When we met, it was one of the things we bonded over; a shared resolve never to return to our hometown. But then something changed. Being with me, Bryan said, and having Colin to think about, had made him want to reconnect with Kathy and Frank. To meet Carol. To give Colin a real family. And, eventually, I said yes.

Tucking my long red hair behind my ears and wiping off a smudge of eyeshadow that had migrated to my cheek, I swallowed hard. Despite the fact that we'd been back in Portland for three whole years, seeing Kathy and Frank always made me think of the *time before*. The way I was when I first left town in the middle of the night. The way I was when I met Bryan. The way I was when he saved me from myself, wrapped me in a cocoon, and promised to always take care of me and Colin.

I let out a shaky breath. From the hallway came the sound of the front door clicking shut as Bryan ushered his parents inside. Right from the very first time I met them, I'd put on my best smile and tried to be warm, engaging, funny. For years, every time Bryan flared up at his father or things grew tense at a family dinner, I'd tried to persuade him that he was doing the right thing by letting them into our life; family is important. If you have family, you don't let them slip away. You make an effort to keep them close.

I'd cooked them meals, made it clear that I wanted them to be like real grandparents to Colin, and encouraged Bryan to allow his mother to take care of Colin once a week. But, for whatever reason, they *still* didn't like me. It simmered in his mother's eyes every time she looked at me. Where Frank was apathetic and indifferent towards me, Kathy actively disapproved of Bryan's decision to marry me. And she didn't try to hide it.

Maybe it was because I was a former foster kid with no parents. Maybe it was because I came with 'baggage.' Or maybe she'd simply have preferred Bryan to marry a nice, wholesome girl and have a child of his own. She loved Colin, and always played the dutiful grandmother, but sometimes I'd catch a glimpse of her staring at him—at his red hair and freckles, which were a mirror image of mine—as if she was wishing that he looked like Bryan instead. Whatever the reason, their attitude towards me had recently begun to grate. I tried not to let Bryan see it. But it was becoming increasingly difficult.

Brushing down my jeans and wishing it wasn't so darn hot outside, I unbolted the door and braced myself. For one evening, I was determined to ignore my in-laws' withering looks and their snide comments. This was a celebration. A celebration for Bryan. And he wanted his parents there. So, stepping into the hall, I plastered a grin on my face and said, "Kathy, Frank, thanks so much for coming."

Putting down her purse on the console table beside the front door, Kathy turned to me and smiled thinly. "Well, it was lovely of Bryan to invite us." She emphasized her son's name as if she knew that I'd hoped it would just be me, Bryan, and Colin that evening, and narrowed her eyes slightly.

I didn't reply, just walked through to the lounge and stood awkwardly by the edge of the couch.

"Mom, Dad. We thought we'd get pizza. Is that okay with you?" Bryan already had his phone in his hand, ready to order.

"Of course, dear." Kathy sat down in the armchair by the window and beckoned for Colin to give her a hug. He ran over and let her wrap her arms around him but turned his head so that her kiss landed on his cheek instead of his lips. At the grand old age of four, Colin was already too grown up for lip kisses. Kathy shook her head at him. "You used to be such an affectionate little boy," she said dolefully.

I bit my lip; it wasn't the first time Kathy had implied that I'd somehow persuaded Colin not to allow her to smother him with kisses. "He's still affectionate, Kathy. It just has to be on his terms. Isn't that right, Bryan?" I looked over at Bryan, who was on hold to the pizza place. He frowned, clearly totally unaware of what we were talking about, then nodded and made an *mmm* sound. Trying to change the subject, I unfolded my arms and waved towards the kitchen. "Would everyone like champagne? Frank?"

Bryan's dad was standing by the window, looking out at the street. He was a thin man, wiry, tall and angular. Bryan said that he remembered a time when his dad had been the life and soul of the party. But somehow, I couldn't picture it; the Frank I knew was sullen, quiet, and either watched me a little too closely or refused to acknowledge me at all. When I said his name, he turned and raised his eyebrows at me.

"Champagne?" I repeated.

Frank simply nodded, and I bit the inside of my cheek to stop myself from saying something snippy like, *Smile, Frank. It's supposed to be a party.*

Sometimes, when Frank was like this, I felt guilty for encouraging Bryan to make amends with his father. The only person he smiled for was Colin. Certainly not me, or Bryan, and barely ever his wife.

Pouring champagne into the glasses that I'd lined up on the worktop in the kitchen, I watched as, finally, Frank walked over and patted Bryan on the arm.

"Well done, son."

I tried to breathe away the tight tangle of nerves that had formed in my belly. Frank rarely congratulated Bryan about anything, so those words, no matter how lacking in emotion, would have meant a lot. Beaming and trying to remind myself why we were all gathered together in the first place, I called everyone over to take their glasses.

"Mommy, can I have some?"

"Well..." I looked up at Bryan and he shrugged. "Just a sip."

Bending down, I held the glass to Colin's lips and let him take the tiniest mouthful of champagne. Instantly, he wrinkled his nose and made an exaggerated spluttering sound.

Beside me, Kathy tutted loudly. I wanted to tell her that it was just a sip and that, besides, it was none of her business what I gave *my* son to drink. But I didn't. I looked at Bryan and his proud, smiling face as he scooped Colin up into his arms, and I told myself to let it go. *Let it go, Molly. Just ignore her.*

———

By the time dinner was almost over, my attempts to let Kathy's snide remarks and Frank's sullenness glide over me were beginning to falter.

Clearing away the dishes and the pizza boxes, I beckoned for Colin to come help me with the cake. But when we set it down proudly in the center of the table, Kathy widened her eyes and said, "Oh, how silly of me. I forgot. I brought a dessert... just a little something I had in the freezer. It should be defrosted by now—Frank, dear, would you go fetch it from the car?"

Obediently, Frank stood up and took his car keys from his pocket.

I clenched my hands in my lap. "Colin and I spent a long time on this, Kathy. Maybe we could save your dessert for another day?"

"Oh, I'm sorry, dear. I didn't know you'd made anything—it's so unlike you to cook from scratch."

I breathed in and looked at Bryan, hoping he would step in and save me from saying something I'd regret.

Kathy reached over and patted my knee. "Now it's been defrosted, we really do need to eat it today. Yours will keep."

I opened my mouth to speak, but Bryan pursed his lips at me and gave a little shake of his head. "Molly, we can have yours tomorrow, can't we, sweetheart?" He was trying to diffuse the tension, but sometimes the way he refused to stand up to his mother when she was *clearly* goading me made my blood boil.

"Sure." I gritted my teeth and looked at Colin. His smile had been replaced by a disappointed frown, and he was pursing his lips tightly. "Cake for breakfast tomorrow, hey, buddy?" I said brightly, waiting for his eyes to light up.

Colin paused for a moment, then grinned and bunched his fists. What better for a four-year-old than the thought of chocolate cake for breakfast?

When Frank returned, he placed an elaborate cake dish in the middle of the table, nudging mine to one side.

"Looks great, Mom. What is it?" Bryan was already lifting the lid and getting ready to cut it into slices.

Kathy stood up, leaning over to take the knife from him. "Here, dear. I'll serve. It's tricky with the thick frosting." She cut a larger than normal slice and handed me the first plate. "It's coffee cake with cream cheese frosting. My signature recipe."

Taking a fork, I smiled and watched as the others all began to dive in. I'd never liked cream cheese frosting, but if I said so, then Kathy and I would be at war for the rest of the evening. So, I took a large scoopful and lifted it to my lips. I was just about to bite into it when I noticed Colin picking at his plate.

"What's wrong, Colin?"

Colin frowned at his cake. "What are these bits, Mommy?"

I leaned over and squinted at the small chunky bits that he'd weeded out with his fork. Beside me, Kathy continued to chew slowly and loudly. "They're..." I frowned, looked at my own plate, then as if something had given me an electric shock, pushed it away. "Walnuts?" I turned to Kathy, my mouth hanging open.

Kathy looked at me with a blank expression.

"Kathy, I'm *allergic*. You know I'm allergic."

"Are you?" Kathy widened her eyes as if she'd genuinely forgotten.

Opposite me, Bryan's smile faltered. "Mom. How could you forget? That could have been really dangerous."

Kathy's cheeks began to redden. "I'm very sorry, dear. Really. It was an accident." She reached over and dramatically moved my plate to the other side of the table. "Clearly, I would never do anything to hurt you, Molly. But..." She trailed off and glanced at Frank, who was watching us with a steely expression on his face.

"But?" I asked, aware that my pale, freckled skin would be turning pink across my cheekbones.

"Well…" Kathy shrugged. "It's hard to keep track sometimes. You know, with how you used to be."

I was about to stand up from the table and start yelling at her, but Bryan interjected.

"Mom, Molly used to have a bit of a problem, we know that. But she's totally fine now."

"Are you sure?" Kathy lowered her voice, as if whispering would prevent Colin from hearing what was going on.

Exasperated, I sat back in my chair and shook my head. "Kathy, I had some problems after Colin was born, but I'm *fine* now. I wouldn't *lie* about having an allergy."

"Well, I'm sorry, dear, but how am I supposed to know that? When you were *ill*, you lied about a lot of things."

Bryan's jaw was twitching. "Mom, that's enough."

"Alright." Kathy raised her hands. "I'm sorry." Then she turned to me. "I'm sorry, Molly."

Looking at Bryan, I tried to cool the simmering fury that was building in my chest. What I really wanted to do was shoo Colin from the room and let rip at Kathy for being so fucking insensitive and judgmental. But if Bryan was willing to stick up for me, then I should be willing to keep things civil. So, I tightened my lips into a grimace, bit the inside of my cheek, and served myself a huge piece of chocolate cake.

# 4

A little while later, with Colin tucked safely up in bed, I made coffee and suggested we sit out on the deck to drink it. Usually, coffee was a sign that the evening was drawing to a close, and I hoped that the chill in the air might hurry things along a little. Unfortunately, it was still unseasonably warm out, and no one showed any signs of moving. As I stepped outside, I paused and tried to feel pleased that Bryan was chatting amicably with his parents. For once, Kathy and Frank looked relaxed and comfortable as Bryan told them about his upcoming promotion at work. Frank, in particular, looked the most animated I'd seen him all evening; he was a car fanatic, so the fact that Bryan worked in a fancy showroom was something he just loved to brag about to his friends. And now that Bryan was heading for promotion, no doubt Frank would be hoping for a family discount on something flashy.

As the conversation lulled, I walked over and handed out the coffees. Kathy nodded approvingly. "Thank you, Molly."

"You're welcome." I sat down in the deck chair beside her and crossed one leg over the other. Instinctively, I rubbed at my ankle, pulling down my jeans' leg to cover the small, silvery scar that was nestled there.

"By the way..." Kathy turned away from me and looked at Bryan as she raised her coffee cup to her lips. "Did I mention that Robert Davidson has just moved back home?"

Bryan frowned. "Robert Davidson?"

"You know." Kathy waved her manicured nails in the air. "Peggy Davidson's son. He used to babysit you when you were little. He's a psychiatrist now." Kathy glanced at me then looked quickly back at Bryan. Sipping her coffee, she raised her eyebrows. "I hear he's *very* good."

I was holding my coffee cup with both hands, my fingers wrapped around the warmth of it, and they now paused midway to my lips.

"Kathy—" Frank leaned over and put a hand on his wife's knee. "I don't think now is the time—"

"I'm just *saying* Frank—"

Beside me, Bryan began to blush. He knew exactly why she'd mentioned a psychiatrist; she still thought I needed fixing. "Mom. Molly is fine. We're fine. We don't need a shrink."

"I was just trying to—"

Finally, Bryan's patience snapped. I could feel it happening. His muscles tensed and the air quivered. For a moment, he was deathly quiet. But then he stood up and walked towards his mother. Gesturing to the house, he said curtly, "Mom, I think it's time for you to go. Forgetting Molly's allergy is one thing. But sitting here

24

in our backyard and talking about psychiatrists, trying to belittle her, I'm not going to accept it. Especially not when we invited you over to celebrate with us. I don't want to argue. I just think it's time you left."

Quickly, I looked down into my coffee and tried to bite back a triumphant smile. When I glanced up, Kathy's mouth was hanging open. Standing up, she shakily put her coffee cup down on the arm of her chair and straightened her shoulders. "Alright," she said, her lower lip trembling. "I'll go."

As she flounced back into the house, I saw Bryan's steely gaze waver as he looked at his father. Slowly, Frank got up from his chair, shook his head at his son, then followed Kathy inside.

As soon as they were gone, I put my hand on Bryan's arm and pulled him close to me. I wrapped my arms around his waist and felt him lean into me. "I'm so sorry, Molly. They're impossible sometimes."

Standing back and taking a deep breath, I smiled up at him. "Thank you for sticking up for me. I don't think I'll ever understand why they can't just accept me. I got it when we first started dating, but we've been married for three years. From today, you're legally Colin's *father*. I thought they'd..." I trailed off and shook my head. Then closed my eyes. When I opened them, I said resolutely, "I'll go after them. If they leave on a bad note, it'll take weeks to make it up with them."

"I'll go." Bryan's lips were pursed, and he'd started to move towards the kitchen.

Catching his arm, I shook my head at him. "No, it's okay. I will. You just stay here and enjoy your coffee. This is supposed to be *your* celebration, remember?" I reached up on tiptoes and kissed his cheek. "I'll be right back."

Inside, I could hear Kathy and Frank in the hallway. I was muttering to myself, trying to figure out what to say to smooth things over for Bryan's sake, when I heard my name.

"Typical Molly." Kathy spat.

"It's not just her. You shouldn't let Bryan bully you like that. It's not right. You weren't trying to poison the girl, for God's sake. And as for the shrink? Well, it's pretty clear to me that she's not over her *problems*. Seems like a shrink is a damn good idea."

"Bryan should never have married her."

"Well, we knew that from the beginning." The door clicked and the tone of their words changed as air bled into the hallway from outside. "It's the lying that gets me." Frank's voice began to fade. "Trust our son to marry a compulsive liar. Sometimes, I think he chose her just to spite us."

"It's not just the lying that worries me, Frank." I could barely hear what Kathy was saying. Straining my ears, I moved closer and peered around the corner. They were standing in the doorway. Kathy was shaking her head, her neat blonde hair barely moving with all the spray that was holding it in place. "It's the way she tries to turn Colin against us."

"She'll never do that, Kathy. I won't let it happen. I won't let her steal our grandson away from us."

Kathy nodded, swiped at an invisible tear on her cheek, then looped her arm through Frank's. Before Frank could turn to pull the door closed behind them, I ducked back into my hiding place.

Another click. Silence. They were gone.

Shaking, I pressed my palm to my chest. My heart was hammering, and a queasy seasick feeling gripped my stomach. *Steal him away. Steal him away.*

I was fighting the urge to cry when Bryan appeared behind me. "Did you talk to them?"

Trying to blink away my feelings, I shook my head. "They'd already gone. We'll call them tomorrow."

"I really am sorry about them, Molly."

Still trying not to cry, in a small voice I said, "Do you think they'll ever accept me?"

Bryan frowned, then cupped my face in his hands and smiled. "They do accept you, of course they do." He rolled his eyes. "You know what they're like. It's nothing personal."

"It feels personal. I thought they understood that I'm better now. Everything is under control." I searched his face, desperate not to see the same shadow of doubt that I saw in his parents' eyes.

"Of course, it is." Bryan placed his big, strong hands on my shoulders and held my gaze with his. As always, I saw nothing but love. "You are too hard on yourself, sweetheart. After everything that happened with Colin's father, is it any surprise that you had a difficult time after he was born?" He smiled and squeezed me with his fingers. "But we fixed it, didn't we? You and me."

I nodded. We did fix it. The pair of us.

Bryan reached forward and kissed me on the forehead. "Listen, Mom and Dad will always be hard work. But they love Colin. And that's why we moved back here, right? To give Colin a proper family."

I nodded and pictured Colin, sleeping soundly upstairs.

*Steal him away. Steal him away.*

I blinked hard and tried to smile.

Bryan kissed me again. "Thank you for trying to make this evening so special." Then he drew back and smiled at me. His eyes were twinkling, the way they had when we first met. The same twinkle that made my knees feel weak and my skin dance with electricity. "Maybe," he said, tucking a loose strand of my long red hair behind my ear. "We could continue the celebration upstairs." He glanced up towards our bedroom. "And I'll take your mind off everything. Now it's just you and me…"

Pushing all thoughts of Kathy and Frank from my head, I leaned into Bryan's embrace. "That sounds wonderful."

---

Later, close to midnight, Bryan was sleeping soundly, but I was still staring at the ceiling. Kathy and Frank's words were looping round and round and round in my head, and every time I closed my eyes their voices got louder.

Slipping out from under the covers, I walked softly to Colin's bedroom and pushed open the door. In the corner of the room sat the rocking chair that Bryan had made for me on our first anniversary. Curling into it, I pulled a blanket around my shoulders and tucked my knees up under my chin. In bed, Colin was sleeping with one arm over his eyes—the way Bryan sometimes did—and his mouth wide open.

I smiled and wrapped my arms around my legs. My ankle was aching, as it often did at night. Usually, I was able to ignore it. But tonight, along with the pain, came a memory that I'd locked away a long time ago. It was before Colin was born. I was almost eight months pregnant and had been living in Chicago ever since I burned my adoption contract and ran away from Portland. All that time, I'd been alone. I'd called Carol only once to reassure her I was okay but was terrified that if I told her where I was—somehow—the information would make its way back to Tracy and Andy.

I'd moved from part-time job to part-time job, constantly being let go for "daydreaming" or missing shifts. Waitressing was especially difficult because every customer who walked in sent my heart racing, my brain tricking me into seeing Tracy or a man who could be Andy ready to grab me by the arm and drag me away.

Finally, I found a job where I wasn't required to interact with anyone—washing pots at a roadside diner. I was out back, stretching my legs and looking down at my swollen pregnant feet when I heard shouting from inside. I braced my hand on the wall and tried not to panic, tried to tell myself it was just an angry customer. But then I heard someone yell, "Where is she?!" and someone else saying, "You can't go back there." Heavy, angry footsteps pounded into the kitchen. A flash of red hair through the frosted glass door. The handle moving.

And I ran.

I hurtled to the back of the fenced-in yard, scrambled up onto a pile of disused palettes and stood on top, swaying back and forth.

"Molly? What the hell?" It was my manager's voice, but I didn't dare look back. "Molly, don't!"

But I grabbed hold of my belly and jumped.

If I hadn't been pregnant, I probably would have tried to fall on my side. But I was. So, I landed feet-first. Pain splintered through my ankle and I fell to the ground. I was crawling, crying, desperate to make it to my car and shut myself in, when it all became too much. Everything went black. And when I woke up in hospital, with pins in my ankle and my distraught boss Margaret hovering over me, she told me that the red head was our chef Tony's wife. Convinced he was having an affair, she'd barged in and demanded to see him, refusing to accept that he wasn't even on shift that day.

As Margaret told me the truth, she watched me start to cry and put her hand softly on my shoulder. "Molly, perhaps you should talk to someone..."

But I grabbed hold of her hand and told her what I told everyone else—that I was scared because my ex was violent. That I just needed time. And then I'd be okay.

Of course, I wasn't okay. After that, it got worse. I saw Tracy everywhere. And Andy too. Until I could no longer trust my own mind.

Sitting in Colin's calm, beautiful bedroom, I reached down and massaged the scar on my foot. "You were worth it." I sighed, staring at him. "You're worth all of it."

## 5

---

*TWO DAYS LATER*

L eaving the office, I tried to tell myself that I had no reason to feel nervous. Bryan had made up with Kathy and Frank, and he had dropped Colin off with them early that morning.

For the first half of the day, work had been full-on. I'd never dreamed of being a realtor. In fact, when Bryan and I got married, all I wanted was to be a homemaker. To take care of Bryan and Colin, and the house. But when Colin turned two, Bryan tentatively suggested that a part-time job might be good for me. He didn't say as much, but I knew it worried him that I didn't have many female friends to connect with. I spent all my time with Colin. And I didn't see anything wrong with that. But Bryan knew someone, who knew someone, who found me a small receptionist's job at Proctor & Sons, one of the best realtors in town. Just a couple of hours a week. So, I said I'd give it a try.

The first two weeks, leaving Colin was such a wrench that I spent every single day feeling sick to my stomach. But then I started to realize that, actually, the comings and goings of the office weren't as dull as I'd expected them to be. After a while, I approached the manager, Graham, about working my way up to become a qualified agent. He agreed, and it wasn't long before he was telling me that I was one of his best assets.

But the past few months, my talent for securing clients had been slipping. My figures had been the lowest six weeks in a row. And Graham wasn't happy. Still being part time, it was hard to compete with the others. So, I'd started to book back-to-back meetings on my days in the office in the hope of turning things around—proving to Graham that my prior successes hadn't just been beginner's luck.

Up to lunch time, I'd barely even had time to pee or drink a glass of water. But then two bookings canceled, and the downturn gave me time to start overthinking things again. I'd been due to collect Colin at two, but by one thirty I was so wound up that I texted Kathy and asked if she'd have him a little longer. She'd said yes, but even as I asked, I knew it was probably a stupid thing to do— yet more ammunition for her "Molly is unreliable" theory.

Usually, being on the way to collect Colin after such a long day made me feel light and excited; the way he jumped into my arms and yelled, "Mommy!" never got old. But today all I could think about was how *not* to keep thinking about what Kathy and Frank had said about me and what I could do to show them that I wasn't the person they seemed to think I was.

Part of me wanted to be open with them about it. Part of me wanted to try to reason with them, make them see that I'm good for

Bryan and a great mom to Colin, and that things would be so much better if we all just got along. But a bigger part couldn't bear the thought of confronting them.

For years, I'd relied on being quiet and unassuming. I couldn't stand the thought of people being mad at me, and I'd never been very good at sticking up for myself. Even in foster care, Carol was the one who did all of that stuff. Or Jack. So, the idea of challenging Kathy and Frank about what they'd said filled me with dread.

Pulling into their pristine driveway, I shuddered.

Their house was the kind I'd always dreamed of when I was younger. Sometimes, Carol and I had walked through these upper-class neighborhoods and pretended we lived in one of them. Often, we'd pick a house with a child's swing out front and a long brick-paved driveway. We'd hang out on the sidewalk talking about what we'd have for dinner when Mom and Dad got home, about going to the beach on the weekend, or to Rhode Island on holiday. I'd often wondered whether, perhaps, we had even stood outside Bryan's house once. Whether he'd been inside, just as miserable with his two-parent family as we were with our foster parents. And how things might have been if we'd met back then, instead of years later in Chicago. But I always stopped myself from wondering too much, because if it had happened that way, we wouldn't have Colin. And that was unthinkable.

If someone had told me before Colin was born that this was the life I'd end up with—that someone like Bryan would fall in love with me when I was at my lowest, pay off my debts, help me get well, and adopt my son—I wouldn't have believed them. It would have seemed impossible. So, to keep the peace, and because I couldn't stand the idea of doing something that would cause problems for Bryan, I took a deep breath, smoothed my skirt and my blouse, and walked up to Kathy and Frank's door with my head held high, determined to act as if absolutely nothing had happened.

When Kathy answered, she was wearing jeans and a pale pink sweater. Her hair was smoothed into a neat blonde bob that made me wonder whether I should think about changing mine again. I'd let it grow back but every time it reached a certain length, I got the urge to cut it shorter; a habit I'd picked up when I first moved to Chicago and was trying to remain untraceable.

"Molly. How was work?" Kathy ushered me in, smiling as she usually did.

"Busy," I replied, slipping off my shoes because I knew how much she hated high heels on her wooden floors.

"Would you like a glass of lemonade? Or iced tea?"

"No, thank you, Kathy." I glanced over her shoulder towards the lounge. Usually, Colin came running as soon as he heard me arrive. "I better get Colin home and start on dinner. Are he and Frank out back?"

Kathy folded her arms across her chest. Her lips tightened. "Actually, no. They're not home yet. But I'm sure they'll be here soon. Shall we wait in the kitchen?"

Kathy strode off past the stairs towards her large sparkling kitchen. I followed, frowning. "Not back? Where'd they go?"

Kathy waved a hand at me, opening the fridge and taking out a bottle of lemonade. "Just a hike."

"A hike?" My breath started to catch in my throat. Colin was far too young for hiking. "Kathy, really? Why wouldn't you ask me about it? He doesn't have the right shoes for hiking. And it's *dangerous*. Where'd they go?"

Kathy shrugged as if it was no big deal and handed me a glass of lemonade that I refused to accept. Putting it down on the counter-top, she said smoothly, "It's fine, Molly. Frank knows this area like the back of his hand. Stop worrying. They'll be back any minute."

"Kathy, listen to me." I stepped forward. The sickening heat that I always felt when I was away from Colin for too long was begin-ning to creep up my arms towards my throat. I tried to speak slowly, meeting her eyes and not letting go. "Where exactly did they go?"

Kathy's cheeks began to flush. "Frank didn't say. They quite often go hiking. It's not a big deal."

"They've done this before? Why have you never told me and Bryan about it?"

Kathy began to tap her nails on the kitchen worktop. Quietly, and unexpectedly, she said, "I'm sorry, Molly. I—"

Ignoring the fact that she'd apologized when usually she'd simply stiffen and start rolling her eyes at me, I took my phone from my purse. "What time are they usually back? I'm calling Frank."

Kathy, for probably the first time since I'd known her, looked nervous. She glanced at the clock that hung above her enormous glistening range cooker. "Well, I'd expected them to be back by now. Frank doesn't take him far."

"When did they leave?"

"Just after two."

"Two? Well, how long do they usually hike for? Have you called Frank's cell?"

Kathy took a deep breath. "I suppose they're usually gone a couple of hours. They don't walk far. Colin's too little for that."

I was rapidly losing my patience and folded my arms in front of my chest so that I didn't start gesticulating wildly. "Did you *call*, Kathy?"

"Frank doesn't carry his phone when he hikes. There's no signal. He says it's pointless."

I let out a half-laugh, half exasperated groan. "Right. Then I'm calling Bryan. And the cops."

"Molly, please..." Kathy stepped towards me and moved as if she was about to rest her hands on my arms, but I backed away.

"I'm calling them, Kathy."

---

Bryan arrived at the exact same time as the police. In the half hour that we'd waited, I had paced up and down Kathy's kitchen and refused to even look at her.

Now, as I tried to calm down enough to tell the police that she'd allowed her husband to take my four-year-old son on a *hike* with no means of contacting anyone if they got in trouble, Kathy was visibly shaking. "They've been gone for hours," I said, wide-eyed, staring at Bryan and expecting him to be as furious as I was. "And she didn't even bother to call anyone!"

"Ma'am, try to calm down." The female police officer nodded at me sympathetically. "We're here now, and we'll head up to the trail to look for your father-in-law and your son."

"You will? Good. Thank you." I glared pointedly at Kathy and was about to add, *At least someone is taking this seriously*, when Bryan stepped up beside his mother and put his arm around her shoulder.

"Molly, Mom and Dad would never do anything to hurt Colin. You know that. They love him just as much as we do—"

I opened my mouth to yell, *No one loves him as much as I do! I'm his mother!* when Bryan reached out and took my hand.

"It's going to be okay. The cops will find them. Dad probably tripped and hurt his bad hip." Bryan smiled at me and, just as it always did, my anxiety started to plateau. "The officers will find them sitting on a bench waiting to be rescued. Just you wait." Bryan glanced over at the female police officer, who was radioing her colleagues to request another car. "I'll go with them. You wait here with Mom, okay?"

"No, absolutely not, Bryan. Colin is my son—"

"He's my son too, Molly. And someone needs to be here in case they come back. Alright?" Bryan's tone was soft but forceful—the way he sounded when he didn't want me to disagree with him.

I nibbled at the inside of my cheek. "Alright."

When they left, Kathy fired up the coffee machine and offered me a cup, but I refused it. I felt sick to my stomach, and I didn't want to be anywhere near her.

By the large bay window in the lounge, I leaned on Kathy's magnolia wall and tried not to fall apart. When Colin was a baby, I had spent every single day terrified that he would be taken away from me. But when I met Bryan, even though I didn't tell him why I was so scared, he helped me get better. He made me feel safe. Even when we moved back to Portland and I expected to see Tracy and Andy in every shadow or around every corner, I didn't. I stayed *okay*. But now, fear was ripping through my insides and I was struggling to stay upright.

A hand rested on my shoulder. When I looked up, Kathy was smiling a thin smile at me. "It's going to be alright, Molly."

I wanted to shrug her away, but the warmth of her hand had made me feel ever-so-slightly less shaky. So I let her leave it there. "I hope so. I really hope so."

For two hours, we waited.

Kathy made four mugs of coffee, which all went cold and undrunk. And I paced up and down until my ankle began to throb. With every pulse of pain, the question, *What if they've finally caught up with you?* echoed in my ears until, finally, I pressed my palms to the side of my head and shouted, "No! No, no, no."

Over by the window, Kathy looked up at me. She was pale and frowning and watching me as if I were unravelling before her eyes. "Molly?"

At last, my cell phone rang.

"Molly, we've got Colin. He's okay, but we're taking him to the ER to be sure." Bryan was breathing heavily but sounded relieved.

"The ER?"

"He's *okay*, Molly. I promise. Meet us there, yeah?"

I turned to Kathy. "They've got him. They've got Colin."

"And Frank?" Kathy leaned in towards the phone.

"And your dad?" I asked.

On the other end of the line, Bryan was silent. Then he said, "No. We didn't find him."

## 6

As soon as I hung up, Kathy dialed a cab. In a surprisingly calm, authoritative voice, she demanded that they come very quickly as there had been a family emergency, and it was important we got to the hospital immediately.

"I can drive," I said as she put the phone down.

"No, you can't. You're in no fit state, and neither am I." She looked around the room as if she'd forgotten something, then said, "We'll wait on the porch."

Outside, I shifted impatiently from one foot to the other. It was cold and I didn't have a jacket. Beside me, Kathy was silent.

"I'm sure they'll find Frank," I said. "He might even be there by the time we get to the hospital."

Kathy nodded but didn't reply.

Finally, the cab arrived. I hurtled down the steps, into the back, and had already given the driver instructions when Kathy slid in next to me.

Portland Central was a fifteen-minute drive from the house. When we arrived, the ER was surprisingly quiet and my heels clip-clopped loudly as I ran up to the reception desk. "My son's here. Colin Burke. With my husband and…"

"Straight through there, Mrs. Burke. Bay three."

Pulling back the curtain, as soon as I saw Colin, air rushed back into my lungs, and I heard myself whisper, "Oh, thank God."

But then I noticed his T-shirt. I swallowed hard and looked at Bryan, who was standing with his hand on Colin's shoulder while a nurse peered at Colin's head. "Is that?" A red, ugly stain was covering the small dinosaur motif on the right-hand side of Colin's shirt.

The nurse looked up at me and smiled sweetly, glancing at the blood and then at me. "Colin's had a bit of a bump on the head. But he's going to be just fine. We'll clean him up and keep him in tonight for observation. But he's doing great. Aren't you, Colin?"

Colin nodded slowly but when I reached out, desperate to hold him close to me, he flinched.

Letting go of Colin's shoulder, Bryan asked the nurse if it was okay for us to step out for a moment.

"Of course," she said softly.

My eyes widened. "I don't want to leave him," I whispered, trying not to let Colin hear the panic that still laced my voice.

"I know, sweetheart. But I think the police will need to…" Bryan trailed off. The police. Shit.

Reluctantly, I followed him outside. Kathy was standing by the reception desk with the female police officer from the house. She was crying, but when she saw us she wiped her eyes with the back of her hand and smiled shakily.

"Officer Daniels was just explaining to me that they're going to have to wait until morning to resume the search for your father," she said to Bryan.

Instinctively, I reached for Bryan's hand and squeezed it. He squeezed back. "I know," he said slowly. "I'm sorry, Mom. There was no sign…"

Before he could say any more, Daniels raised her hand and interrupted. "The hospital has a family room just over here, perhaps we could…?" Then started to lead us towards it before waiting for a reply.

While Kathy and Bryan sat down, I lingered by the door. "Do we really need to do this now?" I asked, picturing Colin alone in that cubicle, wincing as the nurse cleaned his wound. "I mean… I don't mean to sound…"

"I understand, Mrs Burke. You want to be with your son," the police officer said gently. "But my boss will be here in a moment, and he'd like to talk to you. It won't take long."

I glanced at Bryan. He was holding his mother's hand now, but she was staring blankly ahead as if what was happening was just a bad dream that she was about to wake up from. Finally, the door opened, and a smartly dressed man with a beard and a notebook walked in. Brusquely, he shook my hand, then Bryan's, then

Kathy's, introducing himself curtly as, "Detective Monroe." Then he stood in the middle of the room and flipped open his notepad.

"A detective?" Kathy's voice was small. "Do we really need...?" She looked from Bryan to the policewoman, then let out a short high-pitched laugh. "Surely, you don't call a detective every time someone gets lost on a hike?"

Detective Monroe nodded. "Ordinarily, no. But under these circumstances, your husband's disappearance has been handed over to me."

"Disappearance?" A hint of Kathy's usual tenacity had returned to her voice. "He's only been gone a few hours, Detective. Isn't it a little premature—"

"Mrs. Burke," Monroe cut in. "Your grandson was found with a head wound. He says someone attacked him and your husband, but he didn't see who."

Kathy inhaled sharply. "Attacked?"

My knees had begun to tremble. Screwing my eyes shut, I counted. *Five, four, three, two—*

"Molly?" Bryan was standing in front of me, holding my upper arms tightly.

"Colin and Frank were *attacked*?" The words felt thick and unnatural on my tongue. "But why? How? Were they mugged? Who would possibly want to...?" I looked past Bryan at the detective.

"I'm afraid we don't know why, or who, just yet. Right now, our priority is finding Frank. There was a lot of blood at the scene. Colin's wound is relatively minor, but at this point we're concerned that Frank could be injured and in need of medical assistance."

I opened my mouth to speak, but nothing came out. In her chair, Kathy released a small mewing sound and began to fan her face with her hands.

Bryan stepped forward, his voice stern and deep. "Perhaps, Detective, you could be a little more sensitive with the details? For my mother's sake."

Detective Monroe studied Bryan's face for a moment, then smiled thinly. "My apologies. I'll leave you all for now. I'm sure you want to be with Colin." He was at the door when he turned and added, "But I'll need you to bring him down to the station when he's well enough so that we can take a statement. And, Mrs. Burke, if you could accompany Officer Daniels back to your home and provide an item of Frank's clothing that we can use in the search? At first light, we'll be sending the dogs out."

That night, I insisted on sleeping on a cot in Colin's hospital room. At first, Bryan tried to persuade me not to stay. But when he caught the wild, ready to yell, look in my eyes, he backed down and said he'd come back in the morning.

Before Detective Monroe left, I asked him if he could station an officer outside Colin's room. But when he asked me, with an expression that gave away no hint of what he was thinking, if I had reason to believe someone that might want to hurt Colin, I said no. I couldn't think of anyone who would want to do that. I said it firmly, convincingly. And it was true; there was no one who would want to hurt him. But there were two people, people who I'd refused to think about for nearly three whole years, who might want to take him. To punish me. To put right what I did…

By midnight, my eyes were starting to droop and my head was thick with exhaustion. But I refused to sleep. Every time my head started to drop or my eyelids began to close, I pinched my thigh—hard—and jolted myself awake. I stayed up all night, watching Colin, watching the door and the window and the nurse's station outside for anyone who looked out of place—who might be there to snatch him from me. Sometime before 3 a.m., a nurse came by to check on Colin and asked if I was okay. She put her hand gently on my arm and ducked her head to meet my eyes. "Mrs. Burke," she said quietly, "you really should try to rest."

"I'm not leaving my baby," I snapped, pulling my arm back. But then I saw her worried expression, and the way she was looking at Colin, and I corrected myself. "My son. I'm not leaving my son."

"Mrs. Burke?" The nurse was older than me. Perhaps Kathy's age. She was short, with a rounded stomach and large cheeks. She gestured for me to sit down, and, for some reason, I did. "Are you alright?" she asked, perching on a chair beside me.

Sighing, I buried my head in my hands. When I looked up, the nurse was still there, waiting for me to answer her. "After my son was born, I had some mental health problems," I said. It came out of nowhere. A sudden and unexpected truth. "The birth wasn't easy, and we were kept in hospital a while."

I was about to continue, to tell this stranger something I'd never really discussed with anyone—even Bryan—but she put her hand on my knee and said softly, "I understand. All this has brought back some bad memories."

"Yes," I said weakly.

The nurse glanced at the clock. "Well, it'll be getting light soon. How about I bring you a coffee?"

She handed me a tissue, and I realized that I was crying. "Yes, please. Thank you."

As she disappeared through the door, I tried to settle back into my chair and ignore the voice in my head telling me to check the window one more time. But eventually, I gave in. It was still sealed, locked tightly like all the other windows on the children's ward, and on the horizon the sun was finally starting to creep back up into the sky.

*In daylight*, I told myself, *everything will feel better.*

When daylight finally came, things did not feel better. The buzzing of the ward as it sprang to life made my head throb. But as Colin started to wake up, I painted a smile on my face and tried to snuggle in beside him on the bed.

At home, ever since he was tiny, if Colin was sick, he and I would cuddle up in "Mommy's grown-up bed" and watch movies together. We'd wrap ourselves in the duvet and shut out the world until he felt better. But as I patted his head and tried to slip my arm around his shoulders, he pulled away.

"Colin?" I said, squeezing his hand. "You okay, buddy?"

Before he could answer, someone appeared in the doorway and when I looked up, Bryan was standing there with a great big stuffed giraffe in his arms and a balloon that said Get Well Soon. Colin grinned, and I stood up to make room for the giraffe.

46

In the corner of the room, Bryan handed me a coffee and said quietly, "How has he been? Did he have an okay night?"

"He's fine. He slept fine. But he seems a little jumpy around me."

"Not surprising, after what he went through." Bryan squeezed my upper arm then kissed my forehead. "You need to rest when we get home."

"I'm fine, Bryan. How's your mom? Is there any news?"

Bryan fiddled with his glasses and shook his head. "No news yet, but they're starting to search again, so maybe soon. I said Mom could stay with us until we know more."

"Of course," I said, ignoring the sinking sensation in my stomach. "Of course, she should stay."

Bryan pulled me closer. "You wait, by this time tomorrow it'll probably all be sorted. Dad'll be home and the whole thing will seem like nothing more than a bad dream."

## 7
---

Above me, dappled sunlight broke through the trees. Looking up, I raised my hand to shield my eyes from the brightness. As I moved my head, it felt heavy. There was no sound. No birds, no people. It was like I was underwater—everything soft, out of focus, quiet, peaceful.

Up ahead, Colin and Frank were walking hand in hand. Frank leaned down and whispered something to him. I could see his lips moving, but no sound came out. Colin turned, waved at me, and laughed. I tried to wave back, but my arms wouldn't move from my sides. Frank turned too. But he was wearing a baseball cap, and it was casting a dark shadow over his features. I couldn't tell whether he was smiling at me or staring.

I tried to run to catch up with them. I started to jog. The thud-thud-thud of my feet as they pounded against the dirt track jolted my body. I tripped. Stumbled. And when I looked down, my feet were bare. I shouted for Frank, "Frank! I've lost my shoes. I can't keep up!" But he didn't turn around. Neither did Colin.

As I watched, my son's tousled red hair grew darker. He and Frank became silhouetted against a now furiously burning sunlight that was swallowing them up. I ran. The ground beneath me scratched at the soles of my feet. When I looked down, they were bleeding, but I couldn't stop.

I kept running, past a tall twisted tree and another, around a corner. And then there they were—lying on the floor, side by side. Frank's hat was beside him. Colin's shirt was covered in blood. His face was pale. He wasn't moving. I bent down and shook him, but he wouldn't open his eyes. I tried to pick him up, cradle him in my arms. But he was too heavy. I couldn't lift him. I stumbled, fell. My hand landed in something hot and wet.

When I looked down, my palm was slick with blood. I tried to scream. I could feel it building in my chest. Fear. Pure fear. But when I opened my mouth, nothing came out. I tried again. I tried to call for Bryan. But I had no voice. No one could hear me.

"Molly," Bryan's voice, barely a whisper, filled the air. "Molly, wake up."

---

I sat bolt upright in bed. The bedroom was pitch dark and as I leaned back, the headboard was icy cold against my bare shoulders. A shiver crept from my neck to the base of my spine. I put my palm on my chest. My heart was hammering so hard it felt like it might break right open. I couldn't catch my breath. It was coming thick and fast, and I was trembling. I grappled for the bedside table, desperately seeking the lamp. When I found it, soft warm light filled the room. Beside me, Bryan covered his eyes with his arm, groaned, and turned over, towards the window.

"Bryan?"

"You had a bad dream, sweetheart. Go back to sleep."

I opened my mouth to reply but nothing came out.

"Mol? Turn out the light, yeah?" Bryan's voice was deep and laced with sleep. Beside him, his glasses, watch, and phone were neatly arranged side by side in the wooden organizer I'd bought him for Christmas. I grabbed my own phone and tapped it. Three a.m. "Mol, please..." Bryan pulled a pillow over his head and shrugged himself further under the sheets.

"Sorry, sorry," I said quickly, flicking off the light and holding my phone close to my chest. I lay down and closed my eyes, but fear was still lingering beneath the surface of my skin. I hadn't had a nightmare like that for years and had forgotten the pure terror that they left me with; a feeling that would stay with me the rest of the night and into the next day if I didn't do something to shift it.

Gingerly, I sat back up and swung my feet onto the floor. "I'm going to go downstairs for a while," I whispered.

Bryan let out a grumble that sounded like *Hmmm* and waved his hand at me. During the day, he was the most attentive man alive. But to him, sleep was precious and nothing in the world would break him away from it. "A good night's sleep means you can tackle anything, Mol," he'd say to me when I asked if we could stay up and watch a movie, or if I woke in the early hours and wanted someone to talk to.

Grabbing my long gray cardigan from the hook behind the door, I gently padded into the hallway. Moving slowly through the shadows of the house, I tried to remind myself that it was my house. My safe haven. The first place that ever truly felt like home. But in the dark, and with my pulse still throbbing in my ears, it was foreign. Foreboding. Different.

In the guest room, Kathy was snoring. A deep, rumbling snore that sounded like something a man twice her age and size would make. When I reached Colin's room, I paused. He was a light sleeper and I didn't want to disturb him, but I needed to see his face. His beautiful, perfect face. Not the ghostly image I'd seen in my dream.

As the door opened, it creaked a little and Colin let out a small mewing sound. He pulled his stuffed elephant closer and nuzzled into it. I leaned against the doorframe, desperate to walk over and kiss his forehead but aware that if I did, his eyes would flutter open and he'd be unable to get back to sleep; in that respect, he certainly took after his mother.

Watching him, taking in his tiny perfect hands and his shock of auburn hair, just like mine, my heartbeat began to settle back into a normal rhythm. He was home, in his own bed, in the room we made so perfect for him. I smiled. From the ceiling, Bryan had hung a glow-in-the-dark solar system. The planets weren't the right color—they were eerie greens and muted purples—but Colin adored them. And from the small dresser in the corner of the room, a night-light was spinning pale white stars in a slow-moving circle on the ceiling. Those stars were so calming that, sometimes, when Colin was at day care or with Kathy, I'd come in here, close the curtains, lay on his bed and just watch them going round and round and round.

I sighed and wrapped my arms around myself. I was about to leave when an almost imperceptible breeze drifted across the room. I narrowed my eyes at the curtains. They fluttered ever so slightly, and I bit the corner of my lip, hard. When Bryan and I first moved in together, I insisted on just one rule: Colin never, ever sleeps with the window open. Bryan thought it was ridiculous but agreed. With the window open, it would be too easy for someone to sneak in, snatch Colin away, and make off with him in the middle of the night. We could be fast asleep and not even know he was gone. We could wake up one day, find his bed empty, and never see him again.

Usually, I kept it locked. The key was in a jar on top of his wardrobe. Glancing at Colin, I tiptoed over to the window and nudged open the curtains. I was right; it was open. Not wide, but wide enough. Fighting the urge to slam it shut, I pulled it gently closed. The key was still in the lock. I turned it, checked it three times and, instead of returning it to its usual resting place, shoved it into my pocket.

Downstairs, using the light from my phone to reach the kitchen, I found the trash can and threw the key into it. It landed with a thud on top of the remnants of last night's dinner. No one had eaten properly. It was late when we finally returned from the hospital and, while she waited, Kathy had raided our cupboards and thrown together a lasagna. Colin wouldn't eat it, so I'd given him a bowl of chocolate covered cereal—which Kathy tutted at—and let him go straight up to his room. Bryan made a good effort, but Kathy and I had both moved our food slowly around our plates until, finally, we gave up.

Now, my stomach growled angrily at the thought of food. I could dampen the pangs with coffee, but then I wouldn't stand a chance of getting to sleep. Instead, I settled on what Carol had always done for me when we couldn't sleep as children—a cup of steaming hot milk with honey. Now, without anyone to yell at me the next morning for using too much of either ingredient, I was generous with both. I took the largest mug I could find from an overhead cupboard and set a pan on the stove—because the ritual wasn't quite the same if I used the microwave—and while the milk began to simmer, I added a huge glob of honey to the bottom of my mug.

When we first moved to 44 Maple Drive, I would often find myself awake at night. While Colin and Bryan slept soundly upstairs, I'd be completely unable to settle. I'd move from room to room, gently brushing my fingers against our brand-new furniture, the shiny frames that proudly displayed our wedding pictures, the pillows on the couch, the drapes in the windows. It had all seemed too good to be true.

Three years later, I'd almost stopped noticing it. But with the memory of the first bad dream I'd had in years still pressing down on my shoulders, I forced myself to stop and take it all in. Five, four, three, two, one. Everything is okay. Your baby is safe.

These were the words I used to utter to myself all day every day back in Chicago. For such a long time now, I'd had no need for them. But standing in Kathy's kitchen yesterday, not knowing where Colin was or what had happened to him, and in the hospital last night, it felt like the bottom was falling out of the world all over again.

With my hands wrapped tightly around my mug of hot, sweet milk, I padded over to the large bay windows that looked out onto our beautiful street. Large houses, green lawns, brick driveways, and kindly neighbors were everything I'd ever wanted. *Five, four, three, two…* I exhaled deeply and nudged the drapes to one side.

Stepping back, I settled into the armchair beside the window and pulled a pillow onto my lap. Resting my mug on top of it, I let my eyes rest on the Davieses' house opposite. It was just like ours— white timber, boxed hedges around the perimeter of the property, a large tree out front, and small sash windows at the top of the house. I smiled; I'd always loved looking at this mirror image of our life. The Davieses were about the same age as us with two small children, a girl Colin's age and a boy a little older. One day, I'd invite them for dinner.

A little too soon, I took a sip of milk and winced as it scalded my top lip. Reaching forward, I set it down on the coffee table and when I looked back to the window, something flickered in the distance. I narrowed my eyes. Someone was standing beneath the Davieses' big, old Maple tree. My fingers tightened on the arm of the chair. I looked at the clock. Almost midnight. No one should be about at this time.

Standing up and stepping sideways, I pressed myself against the wall beside the window. Then, slowly, I nudged the drapes to the side and peered through the gap. The figure was still there. And they weren't moving. Images of Colin's open window, and his bloodied T-shirt, and his deathly pale face as he lay beside Frank, flashed across my mind.

With my breath trapped in my throat, I hurried to the front door and flung it open. Charging down the steps and brandishing my phone like a weapon, I heard myself yell, "Who are you?! What do you want?!"

In bare feet, I strode across the road, blood pumping fast and hot through my veins. "Who are you?!" I yelled, louder. So loud that, inside, the Davieses' dog began to yap. With fury contorting my features, I was about to reach out, grab the figure's arm, and shine my phone's bright white light straight into their face.

But then I paused. I stumbled backwards. The person wasn't a person at all. Just the small, dark red maple that Arthur Davies had planted a few weeks back. My legs began to tremble. I wavered on the spot, pushing my hands through my hair.

Behind the tree, the Davieses' porch light flickered on and flooded the front lawn. "Molly?" Arthur Davies was holding a baseball bat. At his side, the family beagle, Ronnie, was growling. Patting the dog's head, Arthur soothed, "It's okay, boy. Go back inside."

He let Ronnie go then walked gingerly down his front steps, still holding the baseball bat. "Molly? Are you alright?" He was wearing light gray sweat pants and a thick blue robe but no shirt. As he approached, he pulled the robe tight around his chest and cleared his throat nervously, glancing back at the house as if Lucy might appear and ask what on earth was going on.

"I'm so sorry, Arthur. I thought I saw someone."

Immediately, Arthur stood up a little straighter and tightened his grip on the bat.

"It was no one," I said quickly, trying to laugh. "Just the tree." I nodded towards it and Arthur narrowed his eyes as if he was trying to figure out whether I'd been drinking.

"Oh," he said, his shoulders relaxing a little then looking awkwardly back at the house as if he was wondering whether I was planning on leaving or staying for a chat.

"I'm sorry." I bit my lower lip. Bryan had told me not to say anything to anyone yet, until the police knew more. But I needed to say it out loud. "You probably haven't heard. Bryan's father is missing. He and Colin were…" I shuddered. "They were attacked when they were out hiking. The police found Colin and he's okay. He stayed at the hospital last night and we brought him home this afternoon, but they still haven't found Frank. They were searching all day. Bryan thought it would all be sorted out by now but—"

"My God." Arthur stepped forward, wide-eyed. "Molly, I'm so sorry. Is Colin okay?"

"He's fine. Fine. I'm just… a little jittery."

"Of course," Arthur nodded. "Of course, you are. Any parent would be."

I released the breath I'd been holding and smiled weakly. "I'm sorry I woke you."

"Don't be. Not at all. We'll keep an extra eye out on everything for you."

"Thank you, thank you so much," I said, suddenly noticing the dew beneath my naked feet.

"If there's anything we can do—"

I waved, already starting back towards the house. Safety. Colin. "Thanks Arthur. Thank you."

Inside, I pushed the door closed, locked it and slid across the bolts on the top and bottom of the frame, then sank down onto the floor and wrapped my arms around my knees.

*Five, four, three, two, one.*

*It's normal to be scared. Any parent would be. It's not happening again. You're not falling apart. Everything is okay.*

## 8

*TWO WEEKS LATER*

"Bryan, of course I feel bad for her. But it was supposed to be a couple of days and..." I pushed the bedroom door shut and lowered my voice. "And all I'm saying is that maybe she'd be better off back home? I'm worried about your dad too, and I know Kathy's nervous to be alone, but she doesn't exactly seem happy here with us."

Bryan was sitting at the foot of the bed. As always, he was dressed as if he was going to work, even though the showroom was closed on Sundays. "She's my mother, Molly. And of course she's not happy. My father has been declared *missing*. It's all over the news. Reporters are swarming around her house. People are saying he could be..." Bryan shook his head at me, deliberately not repeating what the local news had been saying. "What do you want me to do? Kick her out?"

Sighing, I knelt down in front of him and put my hands on his knees. "Bryan, honey. Of course, I don't want you to kick her out. I'm so sorry for what she's going through. What *we're* going through. But..." I sighed and nibbled the corner of my lower lip. "I'm not sure how much longer I can cope with her monopolizing you the way she does. The amount of attention she demands from you, it's like she's forgotten that I'm even here, let alone that I'm your wife." I was trying to keep my voice calm and reasonable, but it was becoming increasingly difficult; Bryan had always found it hard to confront his mother. And while he would stick up for me if he was pushed into it, mostly he just couldn't see the things that I could. "I haven't slept properly in days, Bryan. Colin's still not himself. And the anxiety of having her here isn't helping."

Bryan rested his elbows on his thighs and rubbed his temples. "Molly, you've got to understand. This whole thing, it's bringing back a lot of bad memories for my mom. Memories of my brother." He widened his beautiful blue eyes at me, and instantly, I felt a thud of guilt in the pit of my stomach. "When Greg died, she barely made it through. If Dad..." Bryan sucked in a gulp of air and put his head in his hands.

"Alright. Okay. I get it. I'm sorry." I knew how badly it had affected Bryan's family when his brother died. My heart had almost clean broken in two when Bryan had told me about it. But after two weeks of Kathy's overbearing presence, I was struggling to remain sympathetic. Neither Bryan nor I had been to work since the attack. In fact, we'd barely left the house at all. And in those fourteen long days, it had become a toxic melting pot of emotion. I was still having bad dreams and waking up exhausted every night, pacing the house, checking the windows to make sure no one could get in and steal Colin away from me. In daylight, it seemed ridiculous. But in those small, dark hours, I couldn't rest until I knew everything was secure.

Bryan spent most of his time on the phone to the police or scouring the Facebook page he'd set up to see if there were any new leads. And Kathy? Kathy watched me. Every move I made; she was there to scrutinize it. She watched me making coffee, doing dishes, fetching Colin's breakfast. She watched me iron Bryan's shirts, put in the laundry, mop the floors. And every time I did something she didn't approve of, she tutted. A tiny, almost inaudible clicking sound with the tip of her tongue.

If I heard that clicking sound one more time, I might not be able to restrain myself from running over to borrow Arthur Davies's baseball bat.

It was awful that Frank was missing, but I knew what might happen if I didn't look after myself. The warning signs were there already, and I needed my house back. My family. My son. Kathy's presence was too much, and I didn't know how much longer I could keep pretending that it wasn't.

Bryan looked up at me and tilted his head. For a second—just one, tiny flash of a second—I thought he was going to start yelling. But instead, he pushed my hands away and stood up. "Sometimes, Molly, I wonder if you'll ever grow up and start thinking of other people." He stalked over towards the window and turned his back to me.

Blinking back tears and kicking myself for bringing up Kathy in the first place, I walked slowly to the door. "I know you don't mean that, Bryan. And I'm sorry I hurt your feelings. I'll give you some space."

In the hall, I closed the door behind me and sighed, scraping my fingers through my hair and letting my nails release some of the tension in my scalp. When Bryan was like that—simmering with frustration or anger—it was best to let him calm down. Usually, it only happened when he was stressed about something at work; if a big sale fell through or someone beat him to the post of salesman of the month. Since Frank disappeared, however, it was like he was ready to explode at any second.

In a few hours he'd apologize for what he'd said, I'd apologize for what I said, and we'd make up. But, for now, I needed to find a way *not* to spend the entire day under Kathy's withering gaze or in Bryan's way.

Padding past Colin's room, I paused. He'd been spending more and more time alone the past few days, and it was starting to worry me. Although I didn't love the idea of him going on secret hikes with Frank, it was nice that he was an outdoors kind of kid. Usually, he'd much rather be playing around in the woods or on the beach than indoors watching TV.

So, deciding to try to be "spontaneous" Mom for once, I rapped on his door and entered with a grin on my face. "Hey buddy, I have an idea."

Colin was sitting in the middle of his bedroom floor, playing quietly with his dinosaurs. He looked up but didn't smile.

"I was thinking," I said, trying to sound super excited, "that me and you could go do something fun today. Just the two of us." I crouched down in front of him and ruffled his hair. "What do you say?"

Colin shrugged and wrinkled his nose the way he did when I'd piqued his interest. "Maybe," he said hesitantly.

"Great. Grab your shoes and meet me downstairs in five minutes. Okay?" I was already bounding towards the door, mentally running through a list of the things I needed to grab before we left.

Downstairs, Kathy was in the sunroom. As I hurried past on the way to the kitchen, I saw her look up, but I didn't go in. Grabbing a backpack from the cupboard where we kept all our junk, I started putting in snacks and water bottles and sun lotion. And then a few minutes later Colin appeared. He'd put on his dinosaur sneakers and was standing with his hands behind his back, swaying slightly from foot to foot as he watched me.

"What's your idea, Mom?"

I blinked. He usually called me "Mommy." But I didn't make a big deal of it. "Well, my idea is..." I drum rolled my fingers on the kitchen worktop. "To go canoeing on the lake!" I grinned and waved my hands as if I was revealing that we'd won the lottery.

Colin's shoulders tensed. He paused and looked back into the hall. "That's okay. I'll stay here."

I frowned at him, my smile faltering. "But you've always wanted to try canoeing."

I was waiting for Colin's answer when Kathy and Bryan appeared simultaneously behind him. Kathy nudged past, patting his head and walking over to pour herself a glass of mineral water from the fancy glass bottles she'd insisted on stocking the fridge with. But Bryan remained behind Colin. "What's going on, Col?" he said playfully.

62

"Mom wants to go canoeing, but I don't want to."

Bryan looked at me questioningly. "Canoeing?" He sounded surprised but no longer mad.

I shrugged. "I wanted to do something fun to take his mind off things." I glanced over at Kathy and lowered my voice. "It's been very hard for him the last few days, and I thought doing something he's always wanted to do would cheer him up."

By the sink, where she was standing sipping her water—her little finger protruding in the air as if she was holding a wineglass—Kathy tutted.

Despite myself, I turned around and snapped, "Kathy? Is there a problem?"

Kathy paused, looking at Bryan as if she wasn't sure whether to say what she wanted to say. But then she breathed in and turned back to me. "Frankly, Molly, I think it's *disgraceful* that you're thinking about having fun when Frank is…" she glanced at Colin, choosing her words carefully, "missing. And I also think it's enormously hypocritical of you to reprimand Frank and me for allowing Colin to go hiking and then to turn around and suggest something even more dangerous. Colin's four, for heaven's sake. He can barely swim. Do you really think canoeing is appropriate?"

I looked at Bryan, expecting him to back me up the way he had when Kathy had tried to poison me with walnuts but, instead, he shrugged.

"Mom does have a point, Molly. I'm not sure now is the time. And if Colin doesn't want to—"

"You're siding with her?!" I was close to yelling. I knew I shouldn't. Not in front of Colin. But I couldn't help it. After two weeks of living with Kathy breathing down my neck, Colin avoiding me, and with dreams from my past taunting me every night, I felt like I was on the edge of losing my mind.

Bryan nudged past Colin and pulled me to one side, gripping my elbow tightly. "Molly. Come on. He doesn't want to go. Just leave it."

Pulling away from him, I grabbed my backpack from the counter and shook my head at the pair of them. "You're both being ridiculous. He'll love it when we're there. Come on, sweetheart." I reached for Colin's arm and started to lead him down the hallway.

"Mom, I don't like being outside anymore. I want to stay here."

I stopped and sucked in a deep breath, trying to make my face lighter and my voice more singsong. "Colin. You love being outdoors. What happened with Grandpa scared you and that's fine, but you can't stay cooped up forever. Now, come on." I continued towards the door, but Colin started to drag his feet.

As I snatched the car keys from the hook, Kathy and Bryan appeared behind me. Colin was struggling against me, but I didn't want to let him go. He was starting to cry.

"Colin, come on. Don't be so silly." I was tugging at him, trying to inch him towards the door when Kathy suddenly erupted.

Storming forwards, she wrapped both arms around Colin and pulled him into her chest as if she were protecting him from a kidnapper. "Molly get a grip on yourself. Colin is *scared*. Surely, a mother should recognize when her child needs love and protection, not forcing him into situations that he clearly doesn't want to be in.

Whatever happened to Frank *traumatized* the poor child. And you expect him to be okay after just a couple of weeks?" Kathy's eyes were wide and furious. "*You* might not care about what's happened to my husband, but the rest of us do."

My hands were shaking.

Colin was crying.

But Bryan wasn't moving. As I looked at him pleadingly, willing him to come to my aid, he simply shook his head at me. When Colin finally looked up from his grandmother's arms, Bryan bobbed down and Colin ran towards him.

"It's okay, buddy. Mom was just trying to help you, that's all. But, hey, I tell you what. Why don't you go on into the lounge, and I'll download that new movie you wanted to watch? Grandma can make us popcorn. What do you say?"

Through teary eyes, Colin nodded, and Bryan swiped the moisture from his cheeks.

"Okay, bud. Go on in." He stood up. "Mom?"

Kathy had been standing between us and now turned her back to me, flicking her hair and patting Bryan's arm as she followed Colin into the lounge.

Watching them, I felt like someone had kicked the air from my stomach. Like I was a stranger in my own house. "Bryan?" I shook my head, leaning back against the wall and fighting the urge to cry.

Slowly, Bryan walked over and stood in front of me. "Molly. What's going on with you?"

"You sided with her *again*." I looked up at him, searching his face for a clue, any clue, as to why in the world he would stand there and let his mother speak to me like that.

"Colin didn't want to go. I wasn't siding with her. I was siding with him."

"She called me a bad mother, Bryan." As I said the words, my voice cracked.

Bryan made a small tutting sound but reached out to gently rub my upper arm. "No, she didn't, Molly. Look. Emotions are high. Don't take things so personally."

Feeling my lip start to tremble, I blinked furiously and looked up at the ceiling, willing myself not to cry. "You..." I sniffed and slipped my hands into Bryan's. "You don't think I'm a bad mom, do you? Because you know that Colin is my world, Bryan. You know that I'd do anything for him..." I trailed off.

Bryan breathed in slowly. He was looking at me in a way that I didn't recognize, and it made my skin begin to prickle. But then he pulled me closer and wrapped his arms around me. "Of course not," he said. "I could never think that."

# 9

Less than forty-eight hours after coming to blows with Kathy, I found myself piling into the office of Bryan's old babysitter—now psychiatrist—Doctor Robert Davidson along with Bryan, Kathy, and Colin. The room was almost exactly how I'd pictured it—white walls, a few abstract paintings, a big leafy house plant, a couch, two armchairs, and a coffee table. But as he smiled and ushered us inside, I still couldn't quite believe that I'd agreed to it.

"Good morning everyone." He motioned towards the couch. "Take a seat, take a seat."

Bryan, Colin and I squeezed onto the couch. But before sitting in the armchair beside us, Kathy gripped the doctor's hands between hers and said effusively, "Robert, it is so wonderful to see you. Haven't you done well?"

I winced. Robert Davidson was a grown man—a professional, forty-something-year-old with broad shoulders and a small, neat beard—no longer the scrawny teen who'd babysat for Bryan all those years ago.

"Mom. I think it's *Doctor* now, not Robert," Bryan chided softly. But Dr. Davidson shook his head and smiled.

"It's fine," he said politely. "But we do need to remember, Kathy, that I'm seeing you as a doctor, not a friend in these sessions. It's important I remain..." He paused, searching for the word. "Impartial."

Kathy smiled and nodded. "Of course, *doctor.* Of course." Then, as if she'd remembered that we were there because her husband was missing, she let her expression drop and sighed. Sitting down, she poured herself a glass of water from the jug on the coffee table and sipped it loudly.

In the other armchair, Robert balanced a notepad on his knee and looked at us. Colin was sitting on the other side of Bryan, and I wished that I could put my arm around him. Thankfully, Bryan reached out and patted him on the shoulder. "Okay, bud?"

Colin nodded, but he looked scared, and the expression in his eyes made a lump form in my throat. Swallowing hard, I copied Kathy and poured myself a drink.

"Right," said Robert, patting his notepad with the palm of his hand. "Now, first things first, thank you all for coming. It's a big step and it's great that you want to do this together, to help each other through what I know must be a very difficult time."

"Thank you for fitting us in, Robert, at such short notice," Kathy said solemnly. "I know you're extremely busy."

"It's not a problem, Mrs. Burke, really." Robert looked from Kathy to Bryan and me. "Molly, Bryan, I've heard from Kathy what she hopes to get out of our session. But could I ask what this means for you? How are you hoping I can help you today? And what triggered you to make the appointment?"

A twinge of panic gripped my chest. I felt like I was in school again, being asked a question I didn't know the answer to. I looked at Bryan with wide eyes. He squeezed my hand.

"Well, I guess we'd like some advice about how to cope with things going forward." Bryan lowered his gaze and cleared his throat. He'd never seen a psychiatrist in his life and talking about his feelings didn't come easy at the best of times. Sticking to the facts, he added, "We don't know when, or if, my father will be found. It's been a couple of weeks now, and no one seems to know anything." His jaw twitched and he straightened his shoulders. "So, we need to stick together. We need to be strong and help each other. But at the moment, well, there's a lot of tension in the house."

I shuffled uncomfortably. Tension between me and Kathy. Tension between me and Colin... what was the common denominator there?

"I see." Robert nodded. "Well, that's completely understandable. It's a very tense situation you've found yourselves in. And..." He looked down at his notes. "Kathy, you're living with Bryan and Molly right now, is that correct?"

Kathy sniffed as if she was close to tears. "Yes. Bryan very kindly asked me to stay with him. I probably should have returned home by now but, to be honest, I'm afraid. Someone *attacked* my husband and grandson. Until a few days ago, the neighbors said that reporters kept turning up, knocking on doors, asking questions." Kathy leaned forward as if she were recounting a grizzly episode of some trashy TV crime show rather than something that had happened in real life. In a hushed voice, she added, "The police tested Colin's shirt. It wasn't his blood. It was *Frank's*. It was on the ground too. A trail of it leading off into the under-growth." She swallowed hard and fanned her face with her hands as if she might be about to start crying. "They sent dogs. They had search parties up there. But he's gone. No one can find him. And knowing that something so terrible happened to him, and that he's out there somewhere, how am I supposed to feel comfortable at home? Alone?"

Dr. Davidson nodded sympathetically. "It's completely normal to feel afraid in this kind of situation, Kathy. You're going through something very traumatic. And I think it might be worth making an appointment to discuss how you're coping individually with all of this."

Kathy swallowed hard but didn't reply. On a daily basis, she swung wildly from being calm and stoic to being a quivering wreck, but clearly—while a whole family session with Dr. Davidson was fine —she didn't appreciate the implication that she might need more help than anyone else.

Accepting her silence as a 'no comment,' Dr. Davidson looked at each of us in turn. "So, let's talk about your living situation. How is it going? Living together? Has it been helpful to you?"

"It's been a challenge, Robert. I'll be honest." Kathy sighed, still using his first name, and avoided looking in my direction.

"Would you agree with that, Molly and Bryan?"

We nodded. "Yes," I said. "It's not easy when you've got your own routines and ways of doing things, and then someone else comes into your space. It was a complete change overnight. And, obviously, it's a very emotional situation for everyone."

Kathy made a *pah* sound and Robert turned to her. "Kathy?"

"I agree that it's been difficult. But I've done my best to fit in with the way Molly and Bryan live. I have made a true effort not to be a burden. To just fade into the background. But I've never experienced anything like this before. I'm bereft. I'm without my partner, my confidant, my *husband*. And, I'll be honest, there have been times when I've felt that not everyone understands that."

Feeling my cheeks begin to flush, I sipped my water and put it back down with a thud on the table.

"It has been very difficult for Colin too." Kathy looked over at Colin and smiled at him. Wearing his headphones and immersed in his iPad, he was blissfully unaware of what we were saying. "He needs time to process what's happened, but Molly seems to want to push him." Kathy waved her hand as if she'd suddenly obtained a master's degree in psychology. "Take the other day, for example, when she wanted to take him canoeing. Colin didn't want to go, but Molly became *very* agitated about it." She glanced at me then straightened her back and put her hands primly in her lap. "And, well, like I said. It's not helping."

I opened my mouth to speak, but Bryan patted my arm and shook his head.

"There have been several incidents like that," Kathy said, exaggerating the word "incidents" as if what I'd done was a criminal offence.

"Kathy. Come on. It wasn't an *incident*, was it? It was just a misunderstanding. I'm Colin's mother. I was just trying to help him." I could hear my voice getting louder and more high-pitched, but I couldn't seem to stop it.

"Help him?" Kathy *huffed* with her nostrils. "Molly, dear, you manhandled Colin in the hallway. You practically dragged the poor child out of the house when he begged you not to. When he *told* you he didn't want to go. All to prove a point to me, I suspect."

"A point?"

"Well." She glanced at Robert again in a way that said he really should only be listening to her because *her* version was the credible one. "Since Frank disappeared, Colin has gravitated towards me and his father. He seems *upset* around his mother. But Molly was determined to win him back, so she concocted some elaborate idea about going canoeing." Kathy laughed a little. "Ironic, really, considering the way she reacted when I told her Frank had taken him for a simple little hike."

"Kathy, I was mad about that because you didn't tell us about it." I looked at Bryan, expecting him to step in and back me up. But he didn't. "You let them go off without a cell phone. You didn't even know precisely where they'd gone."

Patting at her pearls, Kathy narrowed her eyes at me. "Well, quite frankly, Molly, none of us would be in this situation if you hadn't switched your day around at the last minute." Pausing for breath, Kathy turned so that she was facing me head-on. "You didn't even see her, did you? You said you did. But you didn't."

I cleared my throat. My palms felt suddenly slick with moisture. "Of course, I did! Why would I lie about seeing Carol?!" My voice came out far too loud and high-pitched. Beside Bryan, Colin looked up from his iPad and frowned at me. I smiled at him and shuffled in my seat, trying to compose myself.

Kathy opened her mouth to reply, and I was certain she was going to say something awful. Something that would make me look like the worst mother in the world. But before she could, Robert stepped in.

"Okay, ladies, let's stop there, shall we? I don't want us to get into who said what to who and why and when. That's just going to get us all worked up." Opening his arms at us and speaking very slowly, Robert continued, "What we're trying to do here is develop some coping strategies that will help you all deal with your complex feelings. To do that, we need to foster a sense of openness and empathy. If we're honest about how we're feeling, if we're transparent and make an effort to communicate with one another, then that will help us navigate this very difficult time. How does that sound?"

"Very sensible indeed," said Bryan, clearly embarrassed by my and Kathy's spat.

"Good," I said, exhaling loudly, even though the way Robert said "honest" had made my skin start to prickle. Had Kathy told him that I used to have problems? Had she already whispered in his ear and convinced him that I was a compulsive liar? Because that *used* to be an issue. It wasn't anymore. And I was getting sick and tired of it continually coming back to haunt me.

"Yes. Fine. That's precisely what I wanted from this visit. Thank you, Robert." Kathy sipped her water and straightened her shoulders.

"Let's start with Colin, then. Shall we?" Robert ducked his head to try to meet Colin's eyes. Until now, he'd been ignoring all of us, but Bryan lifted his headphones gently off his head and said, "The doctor's talking to you, buddy."

Colin shuffled closer to Bryan and squirmed as if he didn't want anyone to look at him.

"Colin, it must have been very upsetting, what happened to your grandfather."

Colin nodded. "I was hit on the head. When I woke up, Grandpa was gone."

Robert widened his eyes sympathetically. "And how have you been feeling since then? Do you think you could describe it? Sad? Worried? Angry?"

"Yes."

"All of those things?" Robert was speaking very softly.

"Mm hmm." Colin's voice was tiny and thin and so full of hurt that it made my heart flip over in my chest. I reached out, across Bryan, and patted his knee. "It's okay, Col. The doctor's going to help us to help you feel better." I stood up and shuffled Bryan out of the way. Sitting down next to him, I put my arm around Colin's shoulders and for a moment he let himself relax into me. I stroked his hair. But then he took a deep breath and jolted as if I'd given him an electric shock.

"Don't!" he shouted, jumping up from the couch. "Don't do that!"

I sat back in my seat. "What is it, Col? Did I hurt your head?" Looking past him at Dr. Davidson, I added, "The ER kept him in overnight for monitoring, but they said he's fine."

"It's not my head. Just leave me alone." Colin's face was turning red and his fists were bunched together. Tears sprang to his eyes.

"Colin…" I stood up and reached for him.

"I said don't! Just leave me alone! Leave me alone!" He started to yell. Louder and louder. "Get away from me! I hate you! Don't touch me!"

# 10

I couldn't move. For the first time in my life, I didn't know what to do to help my son. Colin was shouting and shaking and looking at me as if I were some kind of monster. Finally, Bryan stepped in. Guiding Colin towards the door, he bent down in front of him and said, "Okay, bud. Big deep breaths. Count to five. One, two, three..."

Colin copied him and I bit my lower lip. I should have known that. I should have helped him.

After a few minutes, Colin's complexion returned to normal, and Bryan ushered him back to the couch. Sitting in between us, he handed Colin some water, and we all watched him as he sipped at it.

Opposite us, Robert smiled and nodded approvingly at Bryan. "Great work, Dad."

Dipping his head to meet Colin's eyes, Bryan smiled. "Can you tell us what made you feel so upset, Col? Was it when Mom touched your head?"

"No." Colin glanced up at me but then took his eyes away. I gripped the arm of the couch. "It's Mom's smell."

"Smell?" Bryan frowned and looked at Robert.

I felt sick.

"Your mom's perfume made you feel upset, Colin?" Robert was scribbling something on his notepad. Kathy was watching me. In the corner of the room, a small standing fan was whirring round and round and pushing the smallest hint of a breeze in our direction. I shuffled in my seat. It was hot. Too hot.

Colin nodded slowly and sniffed, wiping his nose on his bare forearm. "Before I got hit. I smelled the same smell. The exact same smell."

---

"I just don't know why he'd say that." I poured myself another glass of wine and sank back into the curved leather armchair. We were in our favorite bar—the one with loud music and sticky floors —and opposite me, Carol did the same.

"He's a kid, Molly. Don't read anything into it."

"But he said that whoever hit him smelled like me. I mean—"

Carol waved her wineglass at me. "He's a *kid*. He's got things muddled up. Didn't Dr. Davidson have anything to say about it?"

I was turning my glass slowly between my fingers and looked up guiltily. "I sort of stormed out."

"Stormed out?"

"I was upset."

Carol shook her head, typical Molly, then took a large drink of red wine. "Okay, well, do you want Doc Carol's opinion instead?"

She was brushing down her shirt and had sat up straight, crossing her legs as if she were waiting to take notes. I laughed, a short sharp snort that made me nearly choke on my wine. "Go on then…"

Carol leaned forward and slowly repeated, "He's a kid. He went through something traumatic. Don't read too much into it."

"I'm pretty sure 'reading things into stuff' is exactly what shrinks *love* to do," I retorted as she settled back into her usual pose. "But I get what you're saying."

Carol started examining our now-empty wine bottle and asked if I'd like another. We'd been drinking since seven thirty and my head was starting to swim, but I didn't want to go home. Even though Kathy had finally agreed to leave, she'd asked for "one last night," and I'd politely excused myself from it. At first, I was worried that Carol wouldn't come; we hadn't spoken properly since the day of Colin's adoption party. But as always, in a crisis, any petty disagreement we were in the middle of was forgotten.

Despite knowing I should go home, I nodded. "Sure. Why not?"

Carol started to stand, but then sat back down and cleared her throat awkwardly. "Listen, Molly. I know we're over it, but I just wanted to say that I'm sorry for what I said the other day. I was out of order. In a lot of ways. And—"

Putting my glass down, I reached out and took her hand between mine. "Stop it. You don't ever have to apologize to me. You know that."

"I know. But what I said about Jack and Colin's—"

I squeezed her hands, stopping her before she could say anything out loud that I wouldn't be able to unhear. "I said forget it."

"You're sure?" She was analyzing my face, trying to fish out an answer.

"Yes. I am." I sat back and folded my arms. "I just don't really want to talk about any of that stuff. This thing with Frank, it's…" I reached down to rub my ankle but stopped myself and instead adjusted the cuff of my jeans. "It's just bringing back some old feelings, you know."

Carol was well and truly sitting back down now and had shuffled her chair closer so that she could hear me properly over the thud thud of the music. "Molly, are you okay?"

"I'm fine. Can we please talk about something else?"

Carol bit her lower lip. She was older than me but didn't look it. Her face was plump and smooth, and she had only the smallest of worry lines at the corners of her eyes.

Instead of speaking, she just continued to look at me until finally I said, "Let's forget the wine. I need some fresh air."

Outside, walking arm in arm past our favorite bars and restaurants, I leaned my head onto Carol's shoulder and finally said, "It's been difficult the last few weeks. When I thought that Colin was missing, and afterwards, it brought back all these feelings from…" I trailed off. I still hated saying it out loud.

"From when you ran away?" Carol asked quietly.

"Yes." We stopped beside a bench, and Carol gestured for us to sit down. Beside her, I shoved my hands into my jacket pockets and hunched my shoulders up under my ears. Glancing sideways at her, I added, "I haven't thought about Andy and Tracy for years. Before I said yes to moving back home, I looked them up. She sold her store, and I couldn't find any record of them living in the city. So, I told myself that they'd moved on. That they'd probably got another kid from someone else. Or split up and married other people. Or just stopped caring about what I did. But as soon as Kathy told me that Colin and Frank had been gone too long, it hit me—the same feelings I had after Colin was born."

"What feelings?" Carol was speaking softly, as if she was worried that she might frighten me into clamming up again.

"Feelings that someone was going to take him from me. Steal him away. Feelings that *they* were going to steal him. Track me down. Take him back."

For a moment, Carol didn't say anything. But then she angled herself so that she was facing me and said, "You took Colin because you wanted to keep him safe. Because you thought Tracy and her partner would be bad parents. Right?"

I nodded. "Right."

"So, then you've got to stop beating yourself up. Andy might be Colin's biological dad, but you're Colin's mother. By blood *and* by your actions. And Bryan is a wonderful father. Colin is happy. He's safe. What happened with Frank is awful, but it's not related. You did the right thing, Molly. And there is no reason to think that anyone is after you."

I was starting to cry and blinked up at the starry sky above us. "Thank you."

"Perhaps," Carol added tentatively, "if you were honest with Bryan about what happened? If you finally told him the truth about Tracy and Andy, it would take away this *paranoia* that eats away at you sometimes?"

A moment ago, I'd been relaxed, soothed by Carol's kind words. But suddenly every muscle in my body was tense. "No," I said firmly. "Bryan can't ever know." I grabbed Carol's hands between mine and squeezed them tightly. "Promise me. You'll never tell him."

"Of course, I won't. I just thought—"

"No." I let go of her hands and tried to smile. "No, I can't. But you're right. Everything is fine. I'm fine."

---

After changing the subject and talking mindlessly about work for a few minutes, Carol and I parted ways. She hailed a cab, but I said I wanted to take a walk first to clear my head.

I was nearing the more affluent range of bars near the movie theater where Bryan and I used to go on occasional date nights, in the middle of texting Bryan to tell him that I would be back soon, when a firm hand thudded onto my shoulder. "Molly Brown?" It was a man's voice. Deep and gruff, and the hand was heavy. I froze.

Brown. Molly Brown. I'd been a Burke for three years. *No one* called me by that name anymore.

I turned around slowly, reaching my right hand into my pocket for the pepper spray that I religiously kept on me. A tall, slim man with dark-rimmed glasses was smiling at me. "It is you," he said, extending his hand to shake mine. As he spoke, the thick stale odor of cigarette smoke wafted out from between his teeth.

When I didn't return the gesture, and noticing me flinch at the cigarette he was holding, he stubbed it out on the ground and laughed nervously. "Sorry, it's been a while. You probably don't—"

"Who are you?" I stepped back, whirling through my memory. Tracy had described Andy as tall, broad, and traditionally handsome. This man was none of those things. But still, my heart was pounding.

"Greg, Greg Garcia? We were in college together. We took the same class, but you disappeared after the first year, that's probably why you don't..." He trailed off then added, "I always meant to ask you out, back then."

"And you just recognized me? Walking past you on the street?" My fingers curled around the spray. This wasn't right.

Greg smiled and gestured to my hair. "You're easy to spot."

"Is that supposed to be funny?"

"No, gosh, no. I..." He rubbed the back of his neck, looking down. Then he spotted my wedding band. "Oh, I'm sorry. You're married. Of course, you are."

"Yes. I am," I said, waving my phone at him. "And I'm calling my husband now to come pick me up, so…"

Greg was saying something, but I couldn't hear him. I was walking away, my heart pounding so hard that its beat filled my ears. I didn't remember Greg. His face wasn't even a little familiar. But then, a lot of my short time at college was unfamiliar.

I looked back. Greg was still watching me. And he was lighting another cigarette. Turning the corner, finally out of sight, I pressed myself against the side of the building behind me and tried to catch my breath. I could still smell the smoke. It was on my clothes, and it made me want to rip them off and burn them.

Twenty minutes later, as the cab that had driven me home disappeared at the end of our street, I let myself back into the house and before I'd even left the doormat, I began peeling off my shirt.

Bryan staggered into the hallway, blinking at the light. His hair was sticking up in tufts that told me he'd fallen asleep on the couch. When he realized I was taking my clothes off, his eyes widened, and he started to smile. "Good night?" he said, sidling over to me and slipping his hand around my waist.

"Bryan, don't," I said, ducking away. "I stink of smoke."

"Smoke?" Bryan's nostrils twitched. "No, you don't."

"Yes, I do. Some asshole was puffing it in my face for at least ten minutes." An exaggeration. But it had *felt* like ten minutes.

Bryan raised an eyebrow, then followed me through to the kitchen and watched me shoving my things into the washer.

"Molly…" Bryan took my hand and pulled me away from the laundry. Rubbing my shoulders, he said, "You're freezing. Are you okay?"

Leaning into his chest, I closed my eyes. "I just hate cigarette smoke. My foster mom used to…" I trailed off and nuzzled his neck. "It doesn't matter. I'm fine. I'll be fine."

# 11

---

*THREE DAYS LATER*

"I think she's trying to make it up to us, Molly. Give her a chance, yeah?" Bryan put his hands on my upper arms and kissed my forehead.

After our disastrous appointment with Dr. Davidson, Kathy had finally agreed to return home. Much to her disapproval, Robert had suggested that perhaps some space was what we all needed. He didn't offer an explanation for Colin's reaction to my perfume. But I knew what he was thinking, what they were all thinking— whoever attacked Colin and Frank smelled like me. So much like me that it had triggered Colin to go into utter meltdown.

Now, standing in the hallway and trying to smile back at Bryan, I shuddered at the thought of it; that my own son would be afraid of me. "Okay. I'll try."

For two days, Kathy had sulked and ignored our calls. But then finally she called Bryan and offered to watch Colin if we wanted to go out together. I was reluctant, not just because I didn't want Kathy in the house again so soon after getting her to leave, but because Colin still seemed so fragile. I didn't want him to see his dad and I going off for a date night when he was still feeling anxious and sad about his grandfather. But Bryan persuaded me. "It's been far too long since I had you to myself," he'd said with his twinkling eyes and dimpled cheeks. So, I'd agreed.

Kathy arrived at 7 p.m. Colin was already in his pajamas, settled on the couch with a new movie and a bucket of popcorn. "Ooh, movie night?" Kathy said, shuffling up beside him.

Colin rested his head on her shoulder and snuggled in close.

Usually, the closeness between Colin and his grandparents was the only thing that softened my attitude towards them; whenever they did something to annoy or upset me, I reasoned that I needed to keep the peace for Bryan, and that they couldn't be such terrible people really if Colin loved them so much.

But now, seeing them cuddled up like that, I felt overwhelmingly jealous. Colin and I had always been so close. A team. Him and me. We'd let Bryan into our club and become the Three Musketeers. But I'd always felt that the bond between a mother and her son was the strongest that there was. Since Frank's disappearance, that bond was strained to breaking point.

Returning from Robert Davidson's office, I'd immediately showered and scrubbed my skin until it was sore to get rid of even the smallest hint of my lilac perfume. I'd washed all my clothes, even changed the bed sheets, and thrown two whole bottles into the trash. I'd woken the next morning absolutely certain that Colin would run up to me and wrap his arms around my legs, and that we'd eat breakfast together the way we used to. But he didn't.

And three days later, he was still avoiding me.

"Ready to go, sweetheart?" Bryan put his hand on my shoulder and nuzzled into my neck.

"Yes," I said, turning to kiss him on the cheek. "Of course."

Usually, on date nights, we took it in turns to drive so that the other could drink. But tonight, Bryan had ordered a cab.

"Wow," I said, stepping out onto the front porch. "What did I do to deserve this?"

"I just felt like we needed a treat." Bryan slid his hand around my waist and squeezed. I was wearing the black tight-fitting dress that he liked so much, my red heels, and my silver locket. I felt a little odd without any perfume but hadn't had a chance to replace what I'd thrown away. As we slid into the cab, however, Bryan smiled at me and said, "Have I told you lately how ridiculously beautiful you are, Molly Burke?"

Trying not to glance up at the cab driver's rearview mirror to see if he was watching us, I blushed and tucked my hair coyly behind my ear. "You haven't, actually."

Bryan reached over and took my hand in his. Despite everything, he knew how upset I was about Colin, and he was trying to make me forget it all for the night. "Well, then I'll make sure to tell you several times this evening to make up for it."

---

At the restaurant, a little Italian place with soft lighting and incredible pasta, Bryan pulled out my chair and ordered us a bottle of wine.

When it arrived, he told the waiter he'd pour it himself and offered me a large glass.

Taking my first sip, I sighed and leaned back. "It feels good to be out of the house," I said, noticing the tension drop from my shoulders.

"It really does."

"Are you doing okay?" I asked him gingerly. Bryan and I had spoken very little about his feelings over what had happened. Finding Colin like that, covered in blood, and not knowing when or if he'd see his father again must be eating him up inside. But he was refusing to let me see it. Whenever I asked, he shrugged it off and insisted he was fine and just focusing on helping me, and Kathy, and Colin. But I knew what happened to people if they kept their emotions bottled up inside. I knew that Bryan needed to talk, whether he wanted to or not.

"Yeah. I love this place, don't you?" Bryan looked at our surroundings and nodded approvingly.

"I'm talking about your dad, Bryan." I spoke softly and reached out to put my hand on top of his.

Bryan took his hand back and picked up his wineglass. "I'm okay, Molly, really. Nothing sinister going on in here." He tapped his forehead and then repositioned his glasses on the bridge of his nose. "I'm fine."

Reaching for my locket, I shook my head. "Sweetheart, I don't see how you can be *fine.* Your dad—"

Bryan waved his hand to cut me off. "To be honest, Molly, I'm more worried about you than I am about me. I can deal with my feelings."

I flinched, trying to ignore the sharp twist in my belly. "And I'm not?"

"I didn't mean it like that. But things with you and Colin... I know how much you adore him. I know it's killing you that he doesn't want to be near you."

I swallowed hard and reached up to pull on the end of the French braid that I'd spent half an hour getting just right before we left the house. Quietly, I said, "It's like he thinks I caused this somehow. It's like he thinks..." I could barely bring myself to say it. I couldn't look up. "It's like he thinks I did it."

When I raised my eyes, for a moment, Bryan just looked at me, taking in my features and blinking slowly. But then he said, "Of course he doesn't. He's a little kid, Molly. He's just taking out his feelings on the person closest to him—his mom."

I was about to say, *Really? Do you think so?* When the sound of a familiar laugh caught my attention. Turning, I spotted Carol and, relieved to have an excuse to bring a stop to our melancholy conversation, I got up out of my seat. "Bryan, sorry, it's Carol. Just let me go say hi." It wasn't until I was standing in front of her table that I noticed who she was with—a slim, younger looking guy with glasses and a thin layer of stubble.

As soon as she saw me, Carol began to blush. She was dressed up, in an uncharacteristically floral blouse and heavy makeup. Her hair looked like it had been professionally styled—still short, but smooth and neat—and I tried to keep my expression neutral as I noticed she'd removed her wedding ring. "Molly," she said, looking nervously from me to her dining companion. "What are you doing here?"

I gestured towards our table. "Bryan and I are on a date. What are you doing here?"

"Oh, us too," the guy with glasses cut in, standing up and reaching out to shake my hand. "I'm Steve. Carol and I have been chatting online for a while. This is our first date."

I raised my eyebrows. Steve was very chatty. Not at all Carol's type.

Carol looked like she wanted the ground to swallow her up. But eventually, as Steve sat back down, she said, "Steve, this is my foster sister Molly."

"Wow, Molly. How amazing to meet you. Carol has told me so much."

"Has she? Good things I hope." I met Carol's eyes and smiled at her softly, hoping she would see I was genuinely pleased that she was out on a date, even though she hadn't *ever* mentioned Steve to me before. "Listen," I added, "why don't you guys join us? A double date?"

Carol shuffled awkwardly in her chair. "Maybe another time," she said stiffly.

"Okay, sure." I smiled at Steve, trying not to mind that I'd poured my heart out to Carol a few days ago and she hadn't thought to bring up her new love interest. "Have a good night, you guys."

When I sat back down opposite Bryan, I glanced over my shoulder then whispered, "Okay, so first of all, Carol's on a date and apparently she's been talking to that guy online for *ages* and hasn't told me."

Bryan smiled wryly at me. "And second of all?"

"I invited them to come sit with us, and she didn't want to. It's like she's embarrassed of me or something."

"Embarrassed? Molly, come on. She's your sister. That's ridiculous. Would you want to share a date with another couple?"

Bristling at the implication that I was overreacting, I folded my arms in front of my chest. "It's not ridiculous, Bryan. We're nice people to hang out with. Why wouldn't she want Steve to meet us?"

"Her husband died, Molly. Be a little more sympathetic, can't you?" Bryan almost sounded annoyed with me, which made me sigh and suck in my cheeks. "Maybe she doesn't want to put pressure on something that may or may not go somewhere."

"I am sympathetic."

"Are you?" Bryan was looking at me the way he did when he was behaving more like a ticked-off professor than a husband. It made me feel silly and flustered, and like I didn't quite trust my own instincts. Bryan shook his head. "Listen, can we forget Carol? Call her tomorrow, have coffee, and you'll realize everything's absolutely fine. But for now..." Bryan reached out and took both of my hands between his. "I'd very much like to enjoy dinner with my wife. Is that okay?"

Tucking my hair behind my ear, I wrinkled my nose at him. "Yes. I think it is."

# 12

After dinner, instead of going straight home, Bryan suggested we take a stroll. Outside, the air was cool. As the evening wore on, the restaurant had become stuffy and full of noise. But now, in the stillness of the street, I finally felt relaxed. I'd only just looped my arm through Bryan's and nuzzled into his shoulder when he stopped abruptly and started patting at his pants pockets. "Shit. Sorry, Mol. I left my cell."

Turning back towards the restaurant, I waved my hand and said, "Go get it. I'll wait here." Then I leaned back against the cool glass storefront of the fancy jewelry store I always dreamed of splurging in and watched until Bryan disappeared from sight. Brushing down the front of my black dress and wishing I hadn't eaten so much pasta, I let my eyes settle on the park gates on the opposite side of the street. I glanced at my watch. They'd be locked by now. But with several glasses of white wine swilling through my system, I wondered whether Bryan would agree to sneaking in and taking a late-night forbidden walk.

It was the sort of thing we did when we first moved back to the city. It was the sort of thing that had helped me forget who I was when I ran away in the middle of the night to start a new life, when I broke my promise to Tracy and Andy, when I first started to fall apart.

At first, when Bryan had suggested we leave Chicago and move home to Maine, I'd said no. Absolutely not. Never. I couldn't risk returning to a place where people could be looking for me. Waiting to jump out of the shadows and snatch my child. But Bryan kept on asking. As far as he knew, Colin's father was a tourist who'd visited the restaurant I worked at, stuck around long enough to sleep with me and beat me up a few times, and who left town as soon as I got pregnant.

He didn't know that Colin's biological father was actually a respectable guy called Andy whose partner Tracy had a hysterectomy in her mid-twenties and couldn't have children. He didn't know that Andy and Tracy had promised to clear all my debts in return for me carrying their child—using my egg and Andy's sperm to create a perfect baby boy. And he didn't know that I stole the baby I was supposed to give up and ran away when it was still inside me. Took away their happy ending.

All Bryan knew was that he was desperate to reconnect with his parents. And that he couldn't understand why I wouldn't want to be closer to Carol so that Colin could grow up with a loving family around him. I'd spent months in turmoil over it. But eventually, I said yes. I searched and searched and couldn't find any record of Tracy O'Conner. None. The bookstore she'd owned and had returned to Portland from Rhode Island each weekend to manage, now belonged to someone else. So, we had packed up our things and returned to a place that, for both of us, held so many memories.

I exhaled slowly and closed my eyes. A few weeks ago, the nervousness I'd felt in those early days back in the city had been hard to recall. A few weeks ago, when I walked down the street with Colin on our way to buy ice cream or play in the park, I felt totally safe. But when Frank disappeared, things started to change. Since then, since the very moment I thought Colin might have slipped away from me, I'd been feeling anything *but* safe. Perhaps Carol was right. Perhaps if I told Bryan, he'd take me in his arms and make me feel better. Perhaps he'd understand. But that wasn't a risk I was willing to take.

I looked at my watch. Bryan was taking a long time. A slight breeze whipped around the corner of the jewelry store, and I rubbed my upper arms against the sudden chill. I turned to look at the window display—gold and silver and platinum sparkled back at me. But then I felt something. A sensation I hadn't felt for a very long time—like someone was watching me. I chewed my lower lip. It was my mind playing tricks. Memories wriggling their way to the surface. Not real. But as I let my eyes drift over trinkets that I'd never be able to afford, I still couldn't shift it. In the window, the park gates were dimly reflected. I narrowed my eyes. There was someone there.

I swallowed hard and braced my palm on the glass as my legs started to tremble. It was a woman. A tall, slim, woman with fire-red hair. Just like mine. Just like Tracy's.

I whirled around, clutching my purse to my chest as though somehow it would protect me. Ready to run back to the restaurant, screaming for Bryan and for help.

"Molly?"

Wide-eyed, I turned to see Bryan looking at me with a perplexed expression on his face. "There was someone there. Did you see?" I pointed towards the park and looked frantically up and down the street. But the woman was gone.

Bryan frowned and laughed a little. "Ah. Maybe. Can't say I was paying any attention, Mol. I was watching you and thinking about how beautiful you look." Bryan leaned in, slipping his hands around my waist and pressing his lips against mine. For a moment, I resisted. But then I gave in. I let myself melt into him. And by the time we got home, I'd almost managed to convince myself that the woman I'd seen was nothing more than a figment of my imagination.

---

The next morning, I woke early and scurried downstairs to fix breakfast for Bryan and Colin.

Kathy was back home, where she belonged, and I had the boys to myself again. The specter of Frank's disappearance was still lingering in the background. It was there when I turned on the TV or looked at Facebook or saw the posters plastered all over town. But at least now I could start trying to reconnect with my family. And, although I felt guilty for waking with a smile on my face, I also felt optimistic. Things would sort themselves out. Frank would turn up. Carol and I would get back on speaking terms, and Kathy would remain a respectable distance away from my house. Whatever I saw, or thought I saw, last night was simply the culmination of all the stress and tension from the past two weeks. Nothing more.

Humming to myself, I made Colin's favorite—dinosaur shaped pancakes with maple syrup—and Bryan's too—an elaborate breakfast sandwich with bacon, sausage, egg, and tomato. I poured orange juice into the luscious glass jug we'd been given as a wedding gift, made a fresh pot of coffee, then called them both down.

When Bryan appeared holding Colin's hand, he was dressed smartly despite the fact it was Saturday. Colin was still in his pajamas, and I grinned as he wiped his eyes sleepily and noticed the pancakes on the table. I loved the way he looked in the mornings—ruffled hair, sleep-filled eyes, and flushed cheeks—and I longed to scoop him up and snuggle into him. But I didn't. Reminding myself to give him space, I stepped back and waved at the table.

"A special Saturday breakfast for my two favorite fellas."

Bryan licked his lower lip and went straight for the coffee. When he noticed the breakfast sandwiches, he grinned. "Molly, you are officially the best wife in the world. You know that?"

I blushed, his compliments still somehow making me feel like a schoolgirl with a crush.

"And the best mom too, right, Colin?" Bryan patted Colin's shoulder and pulled out a chair for him.

Colin looked up at me and smiled. A little warmer than yesterday. Not a grin. But not a grimace either.

I slid into the chair opposite him and poured him some juice. "Eat up, honey, before they get cold."

Colin tucked in, the way he always did, leaving the dinosaurs' heads until last and eating their limbs and tails first. Beside me, Bryan squeezed my thigh and nodded. "This is great, Molly."

I winced a little at his touch and rubbed at my leg. For some reason, it was sore, but I shrugged it off and kissed Bryan's cheek. "I wanted to say thank you for last night. And that I'm sorry things were so tough while your mom was here. I'll make an effort to check in on her and smooth things over. I really think it'll be so much easier now we're not under the same roof."

Bryan took a bite of his sandwich. Tomato juice dribbled down his chin and he nodded. And then the phone rang.

"I'll get it," I told him. "It's probably Carol."

Hurrying over to pick up the landline, I smiled as I said, "Hello, Molly Burke speaking."

"Mrs. Burke. Good morning." A stern voice that was not Carol's replied. "This is Detective Monroe."

"Oh," I said, my face falling. "You'll want my husband, Bryan. Do you have news about his father?"

At the table, both Bryan and Colin looked up at me. Bryan was pushing his plate away, ready to stand up.

"No, Mrs Burke. Actually, I'm calling to talk to you. Are you able to make it down to the station today?"

"Me? The station?" A prickly heat started to build in my belly. I tried to lighten my voice, as if it was no big deal, but it came out forced and too close to laughter. "What do you want to talk to me about?"

"It's easier if we discuss it here at the station. Can you make it for ten thirty?" The detective paused, then added, "I can send a car to collect you if that's easier."

"No, there's no need for that. Ten thirty is fine." I looked up at the clock in the kitchen. It was already nine fifteen. "I'll see you then."

Sitting back down, I swallowed hard and tried to smile.

"The police want to talk to you?" Bryan lowered his voice, as if this would stop Colin from hearing what he'd said.

Nudging my sandwich around my plate, I poured myself some coffee and drank without waiting for it to cool down. I winced as it stung the roof of my mouth but kept drinking.

"What about?" Bryan had stopped eating.

"I'm not sure. It didn't sound like a big deal." Pushing my chair back, I swigged the last of my coffee and looked down at my clothes. "I better get changed. It'll be busy downtown at this time, might take a while to park."

Leaning down, I kissed Colin's forehead and said, "Dad's going to take care of you this morning, Col. I'll be back soon, though. Maybe this afternoon we could all do something. A picnic? Or go for pizza?"

Colin shrugged. I thought Bryan might step in and say, *Sounds great*. But he didn't. And he was watching me in a way that made my skin feel too tight and too hot.

Upstairs, I opened up my wardrobe. What does one wear to a police station? I decided on the same outfit I'd worn to Dr. Davidson's then jumped quickly into the shower. As the warm water touched my skin and began to splash down my legs, I winced. I

99

looked down and stumbled backwards, jutting up against the cold glass door of the shower cubicle.

Blood was swirling around the shower tray. I could barely breathe. I followed it up, up, up. It was coming from my thighs. Deep, raw, scratch marks. The kind I used to leave on myself when my illness was at its worst. After Jack died. After Colin was born. But they couldn't have been there last night; Bryan would have seen. He would have mentioned them.

Turning off the water, I stepped out and grabbed a wad of toilet paper, pressing it against the scratches. I reached for my phone. Nine forty-five—I was running out of time. So, forcing myself not to think about why I'd started scratching again and why I didn't remember doing it to myself, I pulled my jeans over the toilet paper and left for the police station.

Leaving our street, I patted my hair, calmed my breathing, and told myself it was no big deal; they probably just wanted to check some details about Colin. When I'd dropped him off? What time I'd arranged to collect him? That sort of thing.

Yes. That would be it. Just clarifying details. That's all.

# 13

---

D etective Monroe was wearing a crisp pinstriped shirt and navy jacket, but was no more amenable than he had been when we met at the hospital. As I entered the room, I expected him to smile and tell me there was nothing to worry about. But he didn't. He simply ushered me into the chair opposite and sat drumming his fingers on the table.

"My colleague will be here in a moment, then we'll get started."

"Sure," I said, looking around at the sparse white room and wishing he'd offered me a glass of water or a coffee like they do in the movies.

A few moments later, while Detective Monroe sat shuffling his papers, Officer Daniels, who I remembered from the hospital, entered and sat down. She didn't smile either.

Detective Monroe pressed record on the machine at the end of the table and asked me to state my name for the tape.

"Okay, Mrs. Burke. Thank you for coming in today. As I'm sure you're aware, we have some questions relating to the disappearance of your father-in-law—Frank Burke." Detective Monroe looked up and closed the file he'd been reading. "Mrs. Burke." He repeated my name a second time, sternly. "Could you confirm for me what your movements were on the day that Frank Burke disappeared."

Swallowing hard, I nodded. "Of course. But, I mean, we already went through this when Frank first went missing…"

The detective didn't move, just waited for me to continue.

Clearing my throat, I repeated what I'd said the first time they'd asked. "I left work about five thirty and arrived at my in-laws around six."

Detective Monroe held up his hand. "From the beginning of your day, please, Mrs. Burke. I'd like you to take me through your movements from when you woke up to when you arrived at your in-laws' house."

Movements? I shuffled in my chair. "Okay. Sure. I got up the same time as usual. Six thirty. We always eat breakfast together. I was supposed to have Colin all day, but my boss had called the night before and asked me to meet a new client. I'm a realtor…" I looked from the policewoman to the detective, but their expressions didn't change. "I'd asked Kathy and Frank if they'd have Colin, and they'd said yes. They love having him. So, I left for work early—seven thirty—and then Bryan dropped Colin round to their house on his way to work."

"So, you arrived at your office at what time?" Officer Daniels was making notes on a small flip pad.

"If I left at seven thirty, I guess eight?"

"You're not certain?"

Tucking my hair behind my ear, I wet my dry lips with my tongue and tried to ignore the way my heart was beating about ten times too fast. "I know I left home at seven thirty because the Jeremy Ray show was on the radio. Just starting. I didn't make a note of when *exactly* I arrived at the office because—well—who does? But it usually takes half an hour to get through the morning traffic. So, I'd guess eight. I arrived at eight." I sat back and folded my arms in front of my chest, feeling a little indignant. Who kept an exact record of their movements on any given day? Certainly not normal people with normal lives. Certainly not me.

"And you stayed at the office all day?" Detective Monroe was watching me expectantly.

"Yes." I nodded.

"All day?" He flipped open his folder and moved some pieces of paper around. "Because when we spoke to your boss, he said that you left around ten, came back at twelve, then left again at two."

"I..." I looped back through my memories, shuffling them and sliding them around in my mind. Had I left at ten? "Yes. You're right. I'm sorry. I met my new client at ten over on Johnson. You can call her. Mrs. Rebecca Kline. She's interested in commercial properties for a new salon she's opening and—"

"We've already spoken to Mrs. Kline. Thank you." Officer Daniels tapped her pen on her notepad.

"If you've already..." I breathed in sharply and closed my eyes. When I opened them, I said very slowly and deliberately, "Detective, I thought this was just a chat. But should I have a lawyer present?"

Detective Monroe tilted his head to one side. He had piercing blue eyes that didn't give away even a hint of what he was thinking. "That depends, Mrs. Burke. Do you think you need one?"

Blinking and trying to slow my thoughts down, I was about to reply when Officer Daniels added, "And after seeing Rebecca Kline, you returned to your office. Then left again at two? Where did you go then?"

For a moment, I didn't reply. I nibbled my lower lip and felt my foot tap-tapping on the sticky linoleum beneath the table. *Tell the truth, Molly. Tell the truth.* "I met another client."

"Another client? By the name of?"

"No, I mean. Not another client. I met my sister, Carol. My foster sister. Carol Nielson."

Detective Monroe put both palms on the table and narrowed his eyes at me. "Mrs. Burke, we're aware that you've had problems in the past. You were diagnosed with..." He looked down at ran his finger along his sheet of paper until it reached a highlighted section. "Borderline personality disorder."

Trying not to let moisture cloud my eyes, I nodded. "After my son was born. Yes. I went through a very difficult time. But I take medication for it now. It's under control."

"It says here, in notes from your doctor, that your personality disorder manifested in one particular trait that you found very hard to get a hold of. Even when you did start taking medication."

My head was swimming. How had they gotten access to my medical records? I should have requested a lawyer. Bryan would be so mad. If he were here, he'd have insisted on a lawyer. Right away. He wouldn't let them twist my words and talk to me about things that had absolutely nothing to do with Frank's disappearance. I shifted in my chair. My thighs were uncomfortable, grating against the paper I'd used to stop them bleeding beneath my jeans.

"You were a compulsive liar, were you not, Mrs. Burke?" Detective Monroe was watching me very carefully. I felt dizzy. Like I might pass out and fall to the floor right then and there. "Now, I have to admit," he continued, "I didn't really know much about the term 'compulsive liar.' Most people tell little white lies every now and then. But I did some research. With *your* kind of lying, it seems it's pathological. Some kind of stress reaction a lot of the time. Self-preservation maybe." He tapped at his highlighted paragraph and read aloud. "The compulsive liar responds instinctively with an untruth to any question asked and often tells elaborate and fanciful stories, going into so much detail they almost come to believe the lies themselves."

I forced myself to exhale. I'd been holding my breath the entire time the detective had been speaking. "It was a problem. Yes. But it's under control now."

And then, to my surprise, Detective Monroe smiled. "You can see my problem, though, can't you, Mrs. Burke? Because you've already lied to me twice. You told me you were at your office all day. We know you weren't. You told me you met a second client. We know you didn't."

"No, I told you I met Carol," I said indignantly, tapping my hand on the table.

"But you didn't meet Carol. We checked with her. She was at work all day, and her colleagues have confirmed that she never left the office."

"I..."

"But you also told Frank and Kathy that you were meeting Carol. Originally, you were supposed to collect Colin at midday, but you told them you'd arranged to meet your sister. So, they kept him longer, and Frank took him out on the hike to keep him occupied."

"I..."

"Why did you lie, Molly? Where did you go?"

"I don't remember," I muttered, reaching up to rub my temples. My mind was swimming. I could picture meeting Carol. I could see it so clearly. But the image was fading.

"Did you follow Frank and Colin on their hike, Molly?"

Suddenly, the fuzziness in the room dissipated. The sounds came back, crisp and sharp, and I blinked at the detective in disbelief. "Follow them? Why would I follow them? I had no idea they even were up there. When Kathy told me that Colin and Frank were out hiking, I was so mad I thought I'd explode. I wouldn't have felt that way if I already knew, would I?"

"Molly..." Officer Daniels had lowered her voice and was looking at me gently. "I should tell you that we have a witness."

"A witness?"

"A witness who says they saw a woman fitting your description acting suspiciously on the path where Frank and Colin were attacked."

"Suspiciously? That's crazy. Perhaps they saw someone. But it wasn't me." Instantly, my mind flashed back to last night. The woman on the street who looked like Tracy. The redhead.

"So, then, where were you?"

"I..."

"Okay, let me ask you another question. The night your son Colin was kept in for observation at the hospital, the night of the incident, you asked me to station a police officer outside his door. Why is that?"

"I'm sorry?" I leaned forward, as if I hadn't heard what he'd said.

"Why did you feel unsafe?"

I frowned, then tried not to laugh. "Because my son had just been attacked, Detective. That's why I felt unsafe."

"But when I asked if you could think of anyone who might have a reason to hurt your son, you said no. If it was a random attack, why would you be afraid that someone would come to the hospital and hurt Colin?" Monroe was tapping his pen on the table and Daniels was watching me closely.

"I didn't *think*... I was just a little scared. Which I think is completely normal under the circumstances. Isn't it?"

"Yes, I suppose it is."

Folding my arms, I let a steely expression settle on my face. "Why don't you just say whatever it is that you're trying to say, Detective? And stop playing games."

Monroe blinked at me. Then laced his fingers together and leaned forward onto his elbows. "Alright. I have a theory."

I blinked back.

"The theory is this: We have a mother with known mental health problems. Life has been good for a while, but she's not been performing well at work, perhaps she's not getting the attention she had in the past from her husband. She used to have people fawning all over her when she was sick. But now she's better, all that has gone away. So, she needs to do something. She needs that feeling back. The feeling of being looked after. Of having people worry about her and wrap her up in cotton wool." Monroe cleared his throat and flipped back through his notes. "Perhaps this mother came up with a plan. Perhaps it was a spur-of-the-moment thing, I don't know. But what I think is that she followed her son and his grandfather, knocked them over the head, and ran away, knowing that they'd be okay but that when they were found, she'd have the sympathy of all her friends, and family, the police, the doctors."

I opened my mouth to speak, but no words came out.

"Perhaps the reason this mother wanted police stationed outside her son's hospital room was because she was afraid her plan had gone wrong—that her father-in-law knew what she did and would come tell everyone. He wasn't supposed to wake up and run off. He was supposed to stay with Colin, wasn't he Molly?"

Finally, I found my voice. Standing up and scraping my chair back against the floor, I said loudly, "I would *never* hurt my son."

Detective Monroe nodded, then closed his notebook. "Like I said. Just a theory. I'm open to being proved wrong, Mrs. Burke." He gestured to the door. "You're free to leave. But next time we speak, you probably should bring a lawyer."

## 14

Outside, the sun was too bright. I'd been at the police station for over four hours and it was approaching late afternoon. Taking my phone from my purse, I texted Bryan. *It was rough. Need some time. Back soon.*

I couldn't face a family meal, or a movie, or anything that would require me to put on a brave face and pretend I wasn't freaking out.

Bryan would ask me why the police wanted to speak to me. And I didn't know what I'd tell him. Did they honestly think I had something to do with Frank's disappearance? Or was Detective Monroe simply enjoying torturing me?

I should have asked for a lawyer. Were the police allowed to access to people's medical records like that? Surely, they shouldn't have been able to use them against me? To treat me like a criminal? It was wrong. It was immoral.

And the more they'd confused me, and pressed, and asked questions, the more I'd been unable to tell them the truth. Detective Monroe had been right about that, at least. Lying had always been my defense mechanism. After I was diagnosed and had counselling and got the right medications, it had stopped. Pretty much. It only reared its head when I was stressed. So, what did they expect? They'd got me so tied in knots that I genuinely couldn't remember what I did that afternoon. But I knew I hadn't been anywhere near the mountain that day. And I knew I would never hurt Colin. Never. The ludicrous theory Monroe had concocted was nonsense. Utter nonsense. And whoever their eyewitness saw; it wasn't me. I was certain of it. Maybe it was someone who looked like me. But it was not me.

Again, the name *Tracy* echoed in my ears. But I shook it loose.

Adjusting my purse on my shoulder, I stopped. I'd parked opposite a small hair salon. I'd never been inside before but had always admired its bright pink door and its quirky signage. Putting my car keys back into my purse, I pushed on the door. A bell rang, and a woman with long, dark hair and an electric blue fringe looked up at me from behind a reception desk.

"I don't suppose you have any walk-in spots, do you?" I reached up and tugged at my hair. "I'm desperate."

"Well, this must be fate," the woman smiled. "I just had a cancellation. Come on in."

Skye, the salon owner, sat me down in a white leather chair and brought me a cup of coffee. It had been months since I'd been to a salon.

"Wow," said Skye. "What beautiful hair. I'd die for this shade of red."

"I'm getting kind of sick of it, to be honest. I thought about dying it..."

"Oh, gosh, no. I can't let you do that. But if you want a change, we could definitely spice up your style. You have amazing cheek bones. A pixie cut would look *incredible* on you." Skye stood back and grinned at me. "Here, I'll show you." She handed me a stack of magazines, then flicked to a picture of a celebrity I vaguely recognized.

"Okay," I said. "Let's do it."

"Really? Wow. Okay. You're brave. This is great." Skye seemed genuinely excited. "Let me get my scissors, and I'll be right with you."

---

Two hours later, I walked out of the salon, leaving almost two thirds of my hair on Skye's floor. My neck felt naked and exposed, but a cool breeze tickled my skin and made me smile. On the drive home, I tried to think of nothing but my new hair. Which outfits would show it off. What Bryan would say. He probably wouldn't like it; he'd always preferred my hair long. But maybe he'd be pleasantly surprised.

As soon as I pulled up in front of the house, though, my heart sank. I glanced at the dashboard. It was almost 5 p.m. I was supposed to be home hours ago and wasn't in the mood for a family meal or activity.

Inside, I put my keys in the dish on the sideboard near the door and kicked off my pumps. Rubbing my hand on the back of my neck, feeling the short fine hairs, I walked slowly through the living room and the kitchen. Bryan and Colin were nowhere to be seen. But then I heard a playful screech from out back. Following the noise, I walked out onto the decking and waved.

Colin was hiding behind a bush, and Bryan was waving a large water pistol at him. When he saw me, Bryan's face fell. Instantly, he dropped the pistol to his side and crossed the lawn in just a few strides.

"Molly?" He was staring at my hair. His face was ashen. He was not pleasantly surprised. "You cut your hair off? Why?" He shook his head. "You said you needed some time after the police station. But you went and got your hair done?"

I smiled, aware that I probably looked a little crazy but hoping he'd get it once I explained. "I did need time. It was awful, Bryan. They..." I lowered my voice because Colin was peeking out from his hiding spot, watching us. "They asked me so many questions. Awful questions. They think I'm lying about where I was on the day your dad disappeared. They said someone called them. Told them I was in the area. But I wasn't. I mean," I waved my hands in the air and shook my head fervently, "it's madness. Of course, I wasn't."

Bryan rubbed my upper arm, still looking at me as if he was trying to understand the way my face had seemingly changed shape with this new super-short hair. "Well, of course you weren't. You told them you were at the office all day, right?"

"Well..."

Bryan took his hand away and narrowed his eyes. "Molly? You told me you were at work all day."

"Oh, for God's sake, Bryan. Don't start. I've already had Detective Monroe and his sidekick dragging up my past. Throwing my mental health problems in my face as if they were my own doing. As if I'm guilty of something just because I *used* to have issues."

Through gritted teeth, Bryan told me to lower my voice, and ushered me back towards the house. "Molly, calm down. Okay. No one thinks you had anything to do with it. That's crazy." He paused, as if he was trying to pick his words very carefully. "So, where were you? You weren't at work, you were...?"

I closed my eyes and breathed in sharply through my nostrils. "I've been trying to remember. I thought I met up with Carol but..." I shook my head and rubbed at the back of my pixie cut.

"But now you're not sure?"

"They were messing with my head, Bryan." I felt moisture spring into my eyes and was pretty sure I was about to start crying. "I should have called a lawyer, but they said I only needed one if I had something to hide, and I panicked and—"

Bryan finally softened and pulled me towards him. "Okay," he said, kissing my cheek. "Okay. Listen. No more talking to them without proper representation. We'll get someone."

"You don't think it's over?" My heart was hammering in my chest.

Bryan swept his index finger across my cheek and smiled a thin smile. "I'm sure it is. But we'll talk to someone just in case. Yeah? Molly?"

Suddenly, I felt lightheaded. As if I might pass out. "Sorry, I'm just..."

Bryan gestured to the living room. "Go sit down. I'll make you a cup of tea and order takeout for dinner."

I nodded. I was exhausted. All I wanted was to go to sleep. "Bryan?"

"Yeah?"

"You don't think..." I couldn't finish the sentence. But immediately Bryan shook his head.

"Molly, I know you inside out. Sometimes you have trouble telling truth from fiction. And, yeah, there have been dark times. Times when you've been pretty close to the edge. But we fixed it, didn't we? We got you help, and you've been doing so great these past few years." Bryan cupped my face in his hands and pressed his forehead against mine. "I know my wife. And I know she would never hurt another person. Let alone her own family."

Realizing I'd been holding my breath, I let it out in a forceful sigh that left me feeling empty and fragile.

"Now, go sit down. Mexican for dinner?"

"Sure," I said, dazed and a little spaced out. "Whatever you boys want to eat is fine."

"Great. And tomorrow, we'll call a lawyer and get them to give the police a dressing down over the way they've handled this. Okay?"

I nodded, sinking back into the softness of the couch and rubbing at my neck. "Bryan?"

"Yeah?" Bryan turned, phone in hand, already dialing the restaurant.

"Do you like my hair?"

For a moment, Bryan's expression didn't change. But then he smiled. "I'd love you even if you shaved it all off."

## 15

The next morning, I woke feeling like I had a hangover. I'd had a glass of wine with dinner, but not enough that it should have given me such a sore head. Walking heavy-footed over to the dresser, I looked at myself in the mirror and nearly shrieked when I saw my hair. It was *so* short. The kind of cut only movie stars could pull off. What had I been thinking? No wonder Colin had looked at me so strangely all evening.

I was sorting through my drawers, trying to find my strip of pills when Bryan tapped lightly on the door. He was holding a mug of coffee and was clearly trying not to stare at my hair cut.

"Morning. How are you?" He handed me the coffee and sat down on the edge of the bed.

"I feel pretty lousy actually. How much wine did we drink?"

"You barely had a glass." Bryan stood up and held the backs of his fingers to my forehead. "Maybe you're coming down with something."

"I'm fine. I feel fine. I took a sip of coffee, then put the mug down and continued moving things about in my top drawer. "Honey, have you seen my pills? I had three left on this strip, but I can't find them."

"I never touch your pills, Mol, you know that." Bryan stepped up beside me and helped me look. "They're not in here. You must have taken the last one and thrown them away. Where's your new packet?" He started to walk towards the bathroom, where we kept all of our medication out of Colin's reach. Bryan opened the cabinet and frowned. "They're not here, Molly. Didn't you fill your repeat prescription?"

I blinked hard. My head still felt fuzzy, and the coffee didn't seem to be helping. I had a vague recollection of Bryan offering to collect my pills after work. But I couldn't remember when. Maybe it was last month. "I—"

Bryan shook his head and took his phone out of his pocket. "It's okay, I'll call the pharmacy. Oh, that reminds me—Carol called."

"She did?"

"She asked if you'd like to meet for coffee this morning. Might be a good idea. You could take Colin while I try to get hold of a lawyer. We need to figure out what the hell that detective was playing at." Bryan sounded annoyed. Very annoyed. I had been surprised, actually, that he was so calm when I told him how the detective had treated me. Usually, he'd have blown his top. He hated injustice of any kind and rarely stood for it. But maybe he was just waiting until Colin and I were out of the house before he let his feelings show.

"Sure. I'll text her now. Thanks, Bryan."

"You don't need to thank me." Bryan rested his chin on the top of my head—I'd always loved that I fitted perfectly against his chest. It felt like the safest place in the world.

"I know. But I don't want you to think I've forgotten what you're going through. Frank's *your* father. And this is all so horrible." I pulled back and reached up to stroke Bryan's cheek. "You know you can talk to me about it if you need to. I'm not a fan of shrinks, but I think Dr. Robert had a point about that. About us communicating..." I trailed off. It took a lot for Bryan to share his emotions, and the last thing I wanted was to instigate a fight because I was being pushy.

"I'm fine, Molly. Really." His eyes darted towards my hair then settled on my face. "You should go shower and freshen up. And..." he offered me a cheeky smile, "maybe warn Carol about the hair."

———

Carol and I met at our favorite cafe, collected takeout picnic boxes, lemonade, and coffee and headed to the park. I'd packed two big blankets, and we spread them out under a tree near the lake. It was a beautiful day. Warm but with a cool breeze that drifted by every now and then to ensure we didn't get too hot. The park was full of flowers, and the trees were lusciously green. It was perfect. But, deep down, I still felt woozy.

Carol and Colin had always got along great, and they sat beside one another chatting about dinosaurs and Colin's—current—

favorite cartoons. They seemed to change every week, but Carol always managed to keep up and made him feel like she was genuinely fascinated by what he wanted to tell her.

As I nibbled my sandwiches, I tried not to let my mind keep drifting back to the police station. Outside in the fresh air, it seemed like maybe it had all been a bad dream. Frank's disappearance, Kathy's too-long stay as our house guest, Robert Davidson, the police.

Trying to relax, I flicked off my shoes and rubbed at my ankle. As I did, a breeze tickled the back of my neck, reminding me defiantly that it definitely had not been a dream.

After a while, Colin became restless and asked if he could go play ball with some other kids. I nodded and smiled, "Of course. Stay where I can see you though, okay?"

Colin nodded, and I moved up closer to Carol so that I could keep an eye on him.

Plucking a strawberry out of the picnic box and raising an eyebrow at my hair, Carol smiled thinly. "So, are you going to tell me what all this is about? The hair and the spaced-out face?"

I sighed and rubbed at my ankle again. "Actually, before I tell you. First, I wanted to say..." I sat up and looked sideways at her, then back at Colin. "I'm really happy that you've found someone you like. I'm not sure why you didn't tell me about him, and I don't want another argument, I just..." I glanced at her and smiled. "I'm happy for you."

Carol shuffled uncomfortably, stretching out her legs and then tucking them back up again. "I know," she said softly. "I just feel so guilty, Molly. I like Steve, but it feels wrong somehow."

"Carol, it's been two years since Rick died. You have nothing to feel guilty about."

Carol picked at her skirt and nodded slowly. "So—the hair?" Carol wasn't going to let me get away with not talking about it, which was a little ironic considering she'd hidden an entire person from me for months.

I opened my mouth to reply, but before I could speak Colin came running back over to us.

"Auntie Carol, can you come push me on the swings?"

"Oh, sure, honey." Carol started to get up, but I waved at her to stay seated.

"Colin, Auntie Carol's spent a lot of time entertaining you this morning. I'll push you." I stood up and looked over my shoulder. "Are the swings over there?"

"No."

"They're not?" I was sure they were back towards the entrance of the park.

"No. I don't want *you* to push me. I want Auntie Carol." Colin was pouting and speaking very, very loudly. A couple of moms near the group who were playing ball were looking over at us.

"Colin, come on. Mommy wants a turn to play with you too. I miss you." I reached out to ruffle his hair, the way I always did. But he jumped as if I were trying to pinch him.

"No!" He stomped his foot and folded his arms, shouting. "No, get away from me. I don't want *you*. I want Auntie Carol."

Utterly shocked, and crimson with embarrassment, I bent down, took hold of his arm, and through gritted teeth said, "Now, listen here, young man. You do *not* speak to your mother that way in public. Do you understand? It's very, very cruel, and you've made Mommy very upset. How would you feel if Mommy's heart broke into a million pieces? Because that's what you're doing when you act this way. You're breaking Mommy's heart."

Colin's lower lip started to tremble and he pulled away from me, wiping at his eyes with his sleeve and sniffing loudly.

I was wavering, unsure whether to apologize or continue being the bad cop. But then Carol stepped up beside me and ushered Colin back onto the picnic blanket.

"Colin, come here, honey. Have some of this yummy cake. Mommy didn't mean to shout."

"I didn't shout, I—" Carol offered me a withering stare and I stopped mid-sentence.

When I sat back down, she leaned over and whispered, "Molly, what on earth? That was a little harsh, don't you think?"

Colin had reached into his backpack and pulled out his iPad and headphones, shoving them on and curling up as if he wished he was nowhere near me.

I let out a frustrated sigh and buried my head in my hands. When I looked up, Carol was watching me expectantly.

"It's all just getting a bit much, Carol," I said shakily. And then it all came pouring out—all the things I'd been keeping to myself because I didn't want to burden Bryan and hadn't had anyone else to talk to. I told her about Kathy and how awful she was when she stayed with us, how Colin pretty much hadn't spoken to me or come near me since Frank disappeared, how he resisted going anywhere with me, how the police had dragged me in for questioning and made me feel like a criminal. Accused me of... "They said someone told them I was in the area the day Frank disappeared. But I wasn't, I know I wasn't." I shook my head. "And they brought up my diagnosis—the personality disorder—the problems I used to have. They made me feel crazy. They said they spoke to you and asked you if we saw each other..."

"They spoke to me last week, yes. I told them we didn't, but did you say you were with me?" Carol looked worried and moved a little closer so she could put her hand on my shoulder. "Molly, I say this with love, but you do seem a little highly strung right now. Are you sure you're okay?"

"I'm fine!" I said, exasperated that no one seemed to be listening to me.

"Okay, okay. Look, it's a stressful situation. Of course, it is. But you have me and Bryan, and we'll help you through this. Alright?"

I nodded slowly, trying not to let myself cry. Then I leaned over and rested my head on Carol's shoulder. "Please let's never argue ever again, Carol. I can't bear it. I need you."

Carol wrapped her arm around me and squeezed. "I've got you, Molly. I've got you."

# 16

**M**ondays had always been my least favorite day. Spending the weekends with Bryan and Colin, by the time Monday morning rolled around, I dreaded leaving them. So often, I wished that I could just be a housewife. Stay home with Colin all day, baking and doing laundry and making the house nice for when Bryan returned.

Since Frank had disappeared, I'd managed to avoid going in. But Bryan said it wasn't good for me to keep putting it off. So, finally, I was on my way to the office.

Reluctantly, I'd dropped Colin off with Kathy—Bryan thought it was too soon for him to go back to day care as he was still struggling with it all—and I'd stopped to grab coffee and a tray of muffins on the way.

The office of Proctor & Sons had expansive windows filled with glossy pictures of large houses that barely anyone could afford.

Somehow, Ruth and Dean, the younger members of the team, had managed to shift three of these houses *each* in the past few months. But all I'd closed on was a commercial let, a bungalow, and two apartments. I needed to up my game. And I was hoping that muffins might soften Graham up enough to pass me a big fish.

When I pushed open the door, everyone turned to look at me. I'd been expecting it, but I hadn't expected them to look quite so pitying. Self-consciously, I rubbed the short bristly hairs at the base of my skull then waved. Catching my eye, Ruth scurried over, taking my arm and guiding me towards my desk as if I were recovering from an operation. Following her, Dean swiftly brought over plates for the muffins.

"You shouldn't have done this," Ruth said smoothly as she took a coffee and slurped noisily at it while trying not to stare at my hair. "We've missed you. We should be bringing *you* treats."

"I'm sorry for leaving you guys short."

"Oh, it's not a problem," Dean said, shaking his head and talking through a mouthful of muffin. "We've managed just fine. Ruth even closed on that huge place on Fifth yesterday. Didn't you Ruth?"

Ruth nodded, her eyes twinkling. She flicked her hair over her shoulder and smiled. "Well," she said, "I don't like to brag."

Smiling thinly and trying to ignore the way my thighs itched from where the scratches were starting to heal over, I switched on my computer and braced myself for the barrage of emails that would be waiting for me.

"Oh, no need to bother with that," Dean said, dashing over to the printer and returning with a wedge of paperwork. "Graham's out, but he said someone had called and requested you specifically. Not sure who they were referred by." He frowned as he flicked through the papers then handed them to me. "But anyway, she'll be here at nine thirty."

I glanced at the clock, only twenty minutes to get my head back in the game. "Oh, great. Thanks guys."

"No problem." Ruth reached out and patted my hand. "And you just shout if you need anything, okay?"

"I will. Thanks, Ruth."

Just before nine thirty, I leafed through the prospective property details that I'd printed out and counted to five. I felt nervous, which was ridiculous because I was good at my job. I'd been going through a rough sales patch, but there was no reason I couldn't find my way out of it.

I glanced at the clock. Any second now, the doorbell would tingle, and Susan Carmichael would walk in expecting to be wowed by our selection of potential new homes. I looked towards the window. Someone was standing outside looking at the display that Ruth had refreshed that morning. It was a woman. Face obscured, slim legs squeezed into pencil-fit jeans and a pair of strappy red shoes. Her silhouette turned and moved towards the door. Right on cue, it announced that someone was opening it. But as I straightened my blouse, my smile faltered. "Tracy?" My heart leapt up into my chest, and I stood bolt upright. The papers I'd collated dropped to the floor. I looked down at them and when I looked up, the woman who'd entered extended her hand and said, "Hi, Molly? I'm Susan."

For a moment, I couldn't move. Everything about Susan's face felt familiar. The arch of her eyebrows, the sweep of her small, neat nose, the contours of her cheeks. She took her hand back and smiled awkwardly at me. "Sorry, am I late?"

Finally, I snapped myself back into the room. "No. No, you're not late." I bent down and gathered up my paperwork. "I'm sorry." I gestured to the chair opposite. "Do sit down."

Susan obliged and rested her hands in her lap. If she could tell that I was shaking, she didn't let it show on her face.

Reaching for my coffee, I took a large sip then shook my head. "I'm sorry. You just remind me of someone."

"Oh, really?" Susan smiled.

I waved my hand at her and, again, shuffled the papers in front of me. "Apart from the hair," I said quietly. "Your hair's much darker."

Susan's eyebrows tweaked upwards. She patted her smooth almost-black hair, then gestured to my hands. "Are those for me?"

"Of course." I handed over the pile of potential properties and mentally kicked myself. Susan looked like my ideal client. While Ruth knew how to flatter the older, wealthier, male clientele, and Dean was great with commercial properties, my forte was women like me. And on paper, Susan fit the bill. If I played this right, I'd break my spell of bad luck; I couldn't afford to fall apart and let a sure thing slip through my fingers.

"Miss Carmichael. Susan…" I extended my hand and smiled. "Let's start again, shall we? It's lovely to meet you. Can I get you a coffee?"

"Oh, gosh. Yes, please." Susan crossed one leg over the other. She had shoulder length hair, a splash of freckles on her nose, and was wearing a powder blue crew neck that made her eyes pop. Thank God she was friendly and hadn't decided to simply give up and walk out.

Handing her a tall white mug and settling in my leather chair, I slotted my brain back into "work mode" and smiled brightly. "So, Susan, you're new to the area but your parents live here, is that right?"

Susan nodded and took a sip of coffee. "Mm. Yes. I moved away after college, oh, fifteen years ago now. But I just got a job back here, so I'd like to be closer to them." Susan paused and chuckled. "Not *too* close, though."

"I understand completely," I said, nodding and jotting down some notes. "So, you know the area but it's probably changed a little since you were last a resident?"

"Oh, yes. Definitely. New places are springing up all the time."

"When Graham spoke to you, he took down a few details of what you're looking for." I consulted Graham's list, running my finger down it one by one. "A two bed, hardwood floors, outside space, close to some amenities like coffee shops. Subletting for now, is that right?"

Susan nodded. "Yes, absolutely. I'm open to an apartment, but I'd prefer a house. My budget's pretty healthy."

I smiled, trying not to look too excited. "Yes, it is."

Susan laughed and tucked her hair behind her ear. "The new job is paying handsomely, so I decided to splash out. It's a little much, maybe, seeing as it's just me. No kids or husband, or anything. But..." Susan shrugged, as if single women should be living in tiny, cramped bedsits and not well-decorated houses.

"Susan, you work hard for your money, you deserve a lovely place to live. So, did anything in there stand out?" I gestured to the papers in her hands, hoping she'd opt to look at the first two houses because they'd been on the market a while.

"They look great. But I actually wondered..." Susan reached into her purse and took out a small tablet. Turning it to me, she continued, "If we could go look at this place? I just spotted it last night. I know it's an apartment, but it looks pretty nice."

Looking down, I frowned. And then my blood ran cold. "Oh," I said, swallowing hard, "I don't think this is what we're looking for."

"Really?" Susan's face dropped. "Do you know the building?"

My mind faltered. I couldn't think fast enough to give her a reason why not, and so I nodded meekly. "I used to."

"Maybe we could just go take a quick look?" Susan laughed. "I'm hopeless when I get my mind fixed on something. And it hasn't been online that long. I'd hate to miss out."

My mouth felt dry, and I was blinking too quickly. The property Susan wanted to visit was my old foster home. A place I thought I'd never have to set foot in ever again. But now it seemed it had been renovated. And Susan was right, it was precisely what she was looking for. Just four apartments in the building, spacious, on the right side of town, a stroll away from a trendy new area with coffee shops and boutiques, hardwood floors. Listed only a week ago.

"Sure," I said, trying to ignore the queasy feeling that had settled in the pit of my stomach. "Sure."

# 17

S usan slipped into the passenger seat and ran her hands along the dash. "Wow, your car is *clean*." She looked into the back and spotted Colin's booster seat. "And you have a kid? Then I'm extra impressed."

She sat back and smiled at me. I tried to smile back, but my mind was still racing, trying to think of a reason, any reason to call off the visit to Ninety-Five Fitzroy Street and take Susan to any one of the other perfectly good properties I'd found for her.

Fitzroy had memories. Too many memories and, right now, I wasn't sure I could handle them.

But Susan was still holding the iPad, swiping through the pictures and the floor plans, pinching in the screen to examine the hardwood floors.

"It would be great to see some before pictures of this place," she mused as I pulled out of my parking spot and into the throng of traffic. "You think you could request some from the owners? Looks like they've done a heck of a remodeling job."

"Sure. I can ask."

"Do you know why they're subletting it?" Susan finally closed the lid on the iPad and set it down on her lap, placing her hands primly on top of it. She reminded me of someone. Not in the way she looked, just her mannerisms. But then, most single women in their mid-thirties had a similar vibe.

"You don't have kids?" I changed the subject, turning off when the satnav told me to, even though I didn't really need directions.

"No, never met the right guy."

"Plenty of people have kids with the wrong guy," I said quickly, trying to be funny but coming off a little too sarcastic.

"True." Susan laughed, clearly not offended. "I'm an aunt, though. My sister has a little boy."

"Oh, really?"

"Mm. He's adorable. The light of her life." She paused and looked at me. "You must feel that way about your son?"

I smiled, immediately picturing Colin's cheeky grin and shock of auburn hair. The freckles that graced his neck, the same as mine. "Yes. I do."

We were almost there. Another ten minutes and we'd be pulling up in front of the place Carol and I had called home for far too long. I was starting to feel a little shaky. My palms were moist. I gripped the steering wheel tightly and licked my lower lip to try to moisten it.

Reaching over, I flicked on the radio. I tried three different stations, but all of the music was too loud. Too heavy. Too upbeat. And it was making my temples throb.

My purse was sitting on the back seat. Glancing at it in the rearview mirror, I heard myself say, "Oh gosh. Sorry, Susan. I think I hear my phone." Swiftly, I pulled over into a lay by, jumped out, grabbed my cell phone and began to pace up and down, holding it to my ear.

"Oh, oh, dear. Of course. Yes. I'll come right away," I said to no one. Leaning my upper half back into the car, I grimaced and shook my head. Usually, my hair would tickle my shoulders as I made that motion but now, of course, it didn't. It was far too short to even know it was there.

"I'm so sorry, Susan. I hate to do this, it's so unprofessional, but that was my mother-in-law. My son's not well. He was a little peaky when I dropped him off this morning and now he's developed a fever. I'm going to have to go get him."

Susan's face dropped, but she batted at the air with her hand and said, "Oh, sure. Don't worry. Maybe tomorrow?"

"Of course. I'll need to see how Colin's doing, but, yes. We'll reschedule." I glanced back the way we'd come. "I'll drop you back at the office to collect your car."

"Sure. You have my number." Susan patted the iPad. "It'll be hard to resist heading round there myself, though. I'd hate for this one to slip by."

Starting the engine back up, I tried to slow my thundering heart and think of something that would stop Susan from simply going to find another realtor. I *needed* her to be my client. Graham wouldn't let me keep coasting for much longer, and he'd practically set me up with a sure thing. "I tell you what. I'll call the owners tonight and sweet talk them. See if I can't get them to give us first refusal."

"Oh, wow. Thank you." Susan seemed genuinely grateful. "Thank you, so much."

"Not a problem, Susan. I'm just sorry we couldn't see it today." Focusing on the road ahead, I swallowed forcefully. I wasn't going to get out of taking Susan to see Fitzroy Street. Not if I wanted her business. But at least I didn't have to face it today. Maybe tomorrow I'd feel stronger. Maybe tomorrow I'd be able to shut off from the place I knew and look at that big old house as if it held someone else's memories.

Maybe.

---

The next morning, despite promising I'd meet Susan at Fitzroy Street at 10 a.m., I texted and told her that Colin was still sick but that she could call the office and ask for someone else to take her there. I'd spent the whole of the previous evening working up the courage to shrug off my discomfort and take her to see it. But overnight, my bravado had vanished, and I'd woken feeling nauseous and light-headed. No matter how badly I wanted the commission, and Graham's approval, I couldn't go back there. I just couldn't.

It was Bryan's day off, and he'd agreed to look after Colin rather than send him to Kathy's again. So, after texting Susan, I went downstairs and made Bryan a coffee, grabbed the newspaper from the porch, and took them up to him. Colin was still sleeping; he'd

133

had a late night after staying up to watch his favorite superhero movie three times in a row with Bryan. It annoyed me a little, because I was pretty sure if *I* kept Colin up till nine thirty, Bryan would tut at me. But I liked that they enjoyed spending time together, so I didn't chide them for it.

Bryan smiled and sat up on his elbows when I walked in.

"You look nice. Busy day ahead?" He offered me his classic Bryan smile and reached out to take his coffee from me.

"Oh, packed. Yeah. Lots to catch up on." I straightened my skirt and reached for my large leather shoulder bag.

"What've you got in there? The kitchen sink?" Bryan laughed and spread out his newspaper.

Shuffling the bag on my shoulder, I laughed back and rubbed the bristly bits at the bottom of my pixie cut. "Paperwork." I rolled my eyes. "Too much paperwork."

"Well, have a good day." Bryan reached out to grab my hand and pulled me towards him. I landed a little awkwardly on the edge of the bed and almost dropped my bag. Bryan slipped his hand around my waist and kissed my cheek. "That lawyer is calling me back today," he said brightly. "Although, as we haven't heard from the police since Saturday, I'm thinking they've moved on to some actual policing."

Bryan sounded proud of himself, as though by simply contacting a lawyer, he'd managed to stop Detective Monroe from harassing me.

"That's great, honey. Thank you. Oh, did you pick up my pills yesterday?"

"Darn." Bryan's eyes widened and he looked horribly guilty. "I forgot."

"That's okay. I'll get them."

"You sure?" Bryan squeezed my hand. "You skipped yesterday, remember. It's not good for you to do that. If you can't go get them this morning, I'll go. I can drop them by your office."

"No, no. Don't be silly." I got up and rolled my eyes at him. "I'm capable of doing my own errands, Bryan. I'll go on the way to work. I promise." I walked towards the door, then turned and said, "Would you mind cooking dinner tonight? I'll probably be late."

"Sure. Colin and I will go grocery shopping. Just text if there's something specific you want."

Pausing in the doorway, I blew him a kiss. "See you later."

"See you."

At the end of the street, I stopped the car. I'd parked in front of the Joneses' but they both worked at the high school and left super early in the morning. Taking a deep breath in, I took out my phone and dialed the office.

"Hey, Dean? It's Molly. I'm so sorry. Colin's not well. I won't make it in today, but I've let my clients know."

Dean clucked sympathetically, said he'd pass the message to Ruth and Graham, then hung up. My heart was beating ten to the dozen. My skin felt hot and cold and prickly. But at the same time, I wanted to smile. I hadn't had any real alone time since before

Frank's disappearance. And I knew I needed to start taking care of myself.

Usually, I'd have confided in Bryan. But he was going through so much already. I didn't want him to think I couldn't cope. Swiping open my emails, I checked my reservation—Timpson's Day Spa, Indulgence Day for one, nine til six.

Peeking into my shoulder bag, I nudged my bathing suit out of the way and checked that I'd remembered my headphones and a stack of magazines. And then, instead of heading to work, I drove in the complete opposite direction.

---

Carol and I had been to Timpson's once before. A birthday treat from Carol's husband when he was sick. A lovely gesture because he was worried about her and wanted her to relax. But not one that had been particularly welcome.

It wasn't the kind of place Carol and I usually hung out. It was far too fancy. And we'd spent most of the day making fun of the uptight clientele and the smooth-skinned spa attendants, who waltzed around offering tonic water, fresh green apples, and free samples of moisturizer that they knew we could never afford to buy.

Today, though, I decided to pretend I was one of those people. The people who booked in once a month and pampered themselves. The moms who prioritized self-care instead of laundry. The women who always looked glossy and glamorous, not run-down and gray around the edges.

Waiting at the reception desk, I bobbed up and down on the balls of my feet. I could smell the aromatherapy oils drifting in from the pool area. Inside, there were three different steam rooms, a large sauna, and cushioned day beds for lounging on. There were miniature foot spas, hot tubs, and outdoor balconies that looked out on a Japanese garden.

A day inside Timpsons was sure to dislodge all of the stress and tension that had built up over the past two weeks.

"I'll just go and fetch you a robe and a wristband." The receptionist smiled at me. "Help yourself to an apple or a glass of water while you wait."

I smiled and looked over at the pyramid of almost too green apples positioned in the window for passersby to marvel at. I walked over, picking an apple from the top, moved it from one hand to the other, then sniffed its shiny skin.

But as I looked up, I frowned. A silver Audi had pulled up out front and, from where I was standing, the driver looked awfully familiar.

The driver looked like... Frank?

I looked down as my apple thudded on the floor at my feet and rolled away. I moved closer to the window, so that I was almost pressed up against it. The Audi's windows were tinted, but the driver's silhouette oozed the essence of Bryan's father—slim, tall, and his characteristic hooked nose.

Behind me, the receptionist was back and offering me a robe. Shaking my head at her, I rushed outside. And I was about to run right up to the car and yell, *What the hell are you doing here?! Do you know how worried we've all been?!* when someone climbed out of the passenger side and walked around the front of the car.

Shit. Kathy?

The driver rolled down the window and Bryan's mother leaned in, obscuring whoever was inside from view.

I looked back at the spa and then at Kathy, trying desperately to see beyond her and confirm what I was sure that I'd seen—Frank. Alive and well and dropping his wife in town for a spa day.

But I'd told Bryan I was working. If Kathy saw me, she'd tell him. He'd ask why I'd lied to him, and he wouldn't understand that it was a simple matter of needing some alone time, needing to feel free and unbeholden to anyone. He'd say that if I lied about that, I'd lie about anything. That I couldn't possibly have seen his father. And then he'd never believe another word I said. Ever again.

So, feeling sick to my stomach, I fled. I ran around the back of the building, jumped in my car, and drove.

# 18

I spent the rest of the afternoon in my car. I couldn't go to work, and I couldn't go home, so I stopped and got a takeout salad and iced coffee, then sat in the Walmart parking lot, trying to make some kind of sense of what I'd seen.

I'd seen Kathy. I'd definitely seen Kathy. And I'd seen a man who *looked* like Frank.

But it couldn't have been, surely? If Frank was back, I'd have heard about it. And the alternative, that Kathy was somehow *hiding* her husband from us was too ridiculous to be an option. Why would she?

Again and again, I looped back over what I'd seen. The man. Kathy. The man. But none of it made any sense, and as the afternoon wore on, I began to feel sick to my stomach.

At 5 p.m., I finally drove home. I'd told Bryan I'd be late. But when I pushed the front door open at five fifteen, which was actually pretty early for me, he simply seemed pleased to see me.

"Hey," he said, offering me a glass of wine. "Rough day?"

I shook my head and shrugged. "Kinda."

"Well, Colin and I took care of everything today. We've got a fully stocked fridge, and I'm making risotto."

"Risotto?" I leaned back against the counter top and took a large sip of wine, kicking off my shoes and reaching down to rub my ankle.

From the stove, Bryan glanced at my feet, and I thought he was going to ask why my ankle was playing up again. But instead, he wiggled his eyebrows at my shoes and gestured to the hall; he hated it when I forgot to leave them on the shoe rack.

"Sorry," I said, scooping them up.

Usually, Bryan and I would talk shop for a while when I got home from work. He often said he thought it was pretty neat that we were both in the selling trade. Even though he sold cars and I sold houses. We understood the pressures, he said. We got each other.

But tonight, I couldn't do it. I couldn't stand there and make up drama that hadn't happened, and clients I hadn't seen. And I was afraid that at any moment I was going to yell, *Bryan, I saw your father. Right here in town. With your mother.*

So, I asked if I had time for a shower, dropped my shoes into their proper place by the door, and headed upstairs.

Under the hot water, I closed my eyes and tried to think of something else. Anything else. Apart from the question that was whirling round and round in my brain... *Should you tell? Would anyone believe you if you did?*

I stood in the shower for twenty minutes and when I emerged, Bryan was calling me for dinner.

Colin sniffed at the risotto, the way he did when he'd been given a food he wasn't used to, but then decided—by some miracle—to dig in. I tried to smile, but the smell of the parmesan was making my stomach whirl.

I'd felt off all day. Ever since the takeout salad. And it was either food poisoning—unlikely from a salad—or my body's way of telling me that I was not in a good place.

"Did you collect your pills?" Bryan looked up from his risotto, eyebrow arched.

"Yep," I said, smiling through the guilt that was tugging at my stomach because—after what had happened at the spa—the last thing on my mind had been collecting my pills. "I told you I would."

"I know," Bryan replied, waving his hand apologetically. "I wasn't nagging. I was just going to offer to go out to the all-night pharmacy if you'd forgotten."

I smiled thinly. "I remembered."

Lifting a forkful of risotto to my lips, I felt my stomach lurch.

"You're not hungry?" Bryan put his fork down. "Does it need more salt?"

"No, no. Sorry." I reached for the water jug and poured myself a large glass. "I just feel a bit off, that's all."

"What did you have for lunch?"

"A sandwich. Tuna on rye." I almost winced as I spoke. Why not just say that I'd had salad? I bit my lower lip, trying not to listen to the voice in my head yelling, *Here we go again, Molly. Here we go again...*

"I'm sorry," I said, standing up abruptly. "I need to use the bathroom." I pushed my chair back from the table and dashed out of the room, took the stairs two at a time, and ended up in the en suite just in time to dry heave into the toilet bowl.

A few moments later, Bryan tapped on the door.

"Come in," I said, sitting up and resting my back against the cool tiled wall.

"Oh, honey. You look awful. Did you puke?" Bryan bobbed down in front of me and handed me a glass of water.

"Not really."

He reached out and touched my forehead. "Doesn't feel like you have a fever. Why's this come on so suddenly?"

I shook my head. I knew exactly why; I used to feel this way when I first met Bryan. When we were dating, and I was trying to hide so much of my past from him. Every time I panicked and thought someone was watching us, that they'd tracked me down and were going to snatch Colin from me, I had to lie to Bryan about it. I had to tell him I was nervous because Colin's father had been so awful. Or that my experiences in foster care were what had made me so jittery. Or that I was simply exhausted because I was a new mom with a baby. And every time I lied, my stomach would tie itself in knots. In those early days, I barely ate. I lost weight that I'd never managed to put back on, and Bryan had even started talking about me seeing a doctor about my stomach problems. Eventually, when I stopped thinking that Tracy or Andy or their PI was hiding behind every corner, it settled down. But now, for the first time in such a long time, I couldn't tell Bryan the truth. I just couldn't.

"Maybe it's just the stress of work. My sales haven't been great lately. I guess I'm feeling a lot of pressure to—"

To my surprise, Bryan clapped his hands. "Well, why didn't you say? We'll have a good old brainstorm tomorrow. See if we can come up with some ideas to help you get out of the rut. I've been there too. Last year? The dip that lasted three months? It's nothing to worry about, Molly. You're great at your job." Bryan patted my shoulder, smiling, clearly relieved that this was a practical problem with a solution he could get his head around. "Head to bed and try to get some sleep, okay? We'll sort it tomorrow."

I nodded. I still felt sick. "I'll sit here for a couple more minutes. Thanks, Bryan."

As he headed back downstairs to see to Colin and do the dishes, I stayed on the bathroom floor and took my cell phone out of my pocket. If Kathy and I had a different kind of relationship, I could have texted her and casually asked what she'd been up to. To see if she'd tell the truth. But we didn't. I had only ever texted her about Colin.

So, putting my phone back in my pocket, I stood up, took my jar of sleeping pills from the medicine cabinet, and went to bed to drown my thoughts in sleep.

143

Before taking them, I studied the pills in the palm of my hand. I'd first been prescribed them after Jack died. Our foster parents, his *real* parents, had become tired of finding me wandering the hallway crying out for him and so called a doctor who—despite my age—readily provided a prescription. For them, my grief had been an annoyance. But for Carol, it was deeply worrying. And what worried her most was the night I woke her up, shaking her shoulders, grinning, and told her that Jack had come home.

"What are you talking about?" she's said, pushing herself up onto her elbows.

"I saw him, Carol. I saw him from the window. By the tree. Come with me…"

And with that, I'd dragged her down, barefoot, out onto the lawn. Of course, Jack wasn't there. Carol tried to quietly encourage me back inside before we were discovered. But I refused. I searched the entire garden, cutting my feet to pieces scrambling through the brambles. It had started to rain. My nightdress had become sodden with mud and damp. And Carol had stayed, watching me, waiting for me to give up. Until finally I collapsed into her arms and she guided me back to bed.

Closing my eyes, I threw the pills into my mouth and swallowed them down without water. And the last thing I saw before I drifted away was my foster mother's jagged smile as she blew smoke into my face.

# 19

A few days later, having spent endless moments trying to convince myself that while I'd seen Kathy, I couldn't possibly have seen Frank, I agreed to meet her for coffee. Colin had a follow-up appointment with Robert Davidson that morning and even though I didn't think he really needed one, Bryan was worried about him still being quiet and out of sorts, so eventually I had agreed.

Kathy, of course, loved the idea. She was Dr. Robert's biggest fan. She'd even suggested trying another family session, but thankfully, Bryan had agreed with me that it wasn't necessary.

The coffee shop Kathy chose was small and quaint, with white table cloths, expensive looking china, and miniature cakes that left you wanting to go grab a box of Krispy Kremes on the way home because they just weren't quite satisfying enough. She'd taken me there several times before, usually when she wanted to discuss something she thought I wouldn't be happy about.

But today, I had my own plan up my sleeve; I was going to ask her about the spa and, depending how she answered, I'd find a way to bring up Frank too.

We hadn't heard back from the police since they'd first questioned me, but their suspicion was hanging over me. Bryan had been in touch with an attorney who was ready to come with me if I was called in again. And I was determined that if I was, I'd have something to bring to the table. Something that would direct their investigation away from wild theories and towards something tangible —the idea that Frank and Kathy could somehow have been involved in what had happened.

But given that Detective Monroe had already made his mind up about me, I needed something more concrete than simply thinking that I saw my father-in-law somewhere in town. If Kathy was hiding something, she wouldn't reveal it willingly. But I was pretty good at reading people; if she knew something, I'd be able to tell. I was sure of it.

"So, how are you, Kathy?" I wriggled back into the velvet armchair and crossed one leg over the other, trying to get the upper hand by being the one to start the conversation. Immediately, though, Kathy turned it back to me.

"Well, dear, actually, I wanted to talk about how you're doing with all of this. It seems to be taking its toll on you even more than me." She gave me an exaggeratedly worried look and sipped her drink, sticking out her little finger as if we were taking high tea at Buckingham Palace.

"I'm fine, Kathy. Really. I was worried about Colin, but he's doing better now. And we have Dr. Robert on board, don't we?" I looked at her over the rim of my mug, having refused to order tea and instead asked for a double shot cappuccino with extra chocolate.

Kathy pursed her lips. They were painted a bright, harsh shade of red that emphasized their thinness. I'd always thought she would look better in a paler shade. But I remembered her telling me once that Frank liked red lipstick on a woman. "I spoke to Bryan yesterday." She let the sentence hang there, ominously.

I deliberately didn't answer and tried not to shuffle uncomfortably in my chair.

"He says you've been under the weather. Sleeping a lot. Taking pills..." She mouthed the word "pills" as if she didn't want anyone to overhear it.

"They're just sleeping pills, Kathy."

"Bryan also says you've been a little... forgetful."

I blinked hard, trying to interpret her expression. Was she talking about my visit to the police station? Forgetting where I was the afternoon Frank disappeared. "Bryan said that?"

"He's concerned about you, Molly, that's all."

I bristled and bit the inside of my cheek. Bryan hadn't said anything to me. He'd been completely normal. Sure, he'd been a little more attentive than usual. But surely, he knew better than to bring his mother into it?

"Don't be cross with him, Molly. He was reaching out to his mother for support, that's all. Sons rely on their mothers to be there for them in these kinds of situations."

I bit my cheek harder and winced.

"Molly, Bryan is trying to look after you—the way any good father or husband would."

Before I could stop myself, I muttered, "Right, like you'd know what a good father looks like."

For a moment, Kathy didn't move. Her expression didn't change; she just stared at me. I was holding my breath, wondering if, by some miracle, she hadn't heard me. But then she very slowly put her teacup down and leaned forwards. Narrowing her eyes at me, she whispered tightly, "What precisely do you mean by that remark, young lady?"

I was clutching my coffee, trying to find a way to backtrack or smooth over what I'd said; the last thing I wanted was to cause problems for Bryan. His relationship with his father had improved immeasurably over the years, and now wasn't the time to be dragging up the past. But I'd said it—it was out there now, and I couldn't take it back.

Trying to maintain my sense of bravado, I held Kathy's gaze and said softly, "Look, Kathy, you and I both know that Frank hasn't been the perfect father. I know what he said to Bryan after Greg died. I know he told him that it was *his* fault his brother got into the accident. Why do you think Bryan refused to speak to him for so long? Barely saw the pair of you for years? Didn't even tell you about me until we were married and moving back to Portland?"

For a moment, Kathy's mouth hung open. Then she folded her arms, sucked in her cheeks and glared at me. "I hardly think now is the time to bring all of that up, Molly. And, frankly, I can't believe that even *you* would be so insensitive."

148

I was going to let it go. If Kathy had conceded that, yes, Frank's behavior towards Bryan had been less than fatherly at times, then I would have done my best to bite my tongue and change the subject. But she couldn't do it; she couldn't admit that her family was anything other than perfect.

Sitting back and continuing to sip my drink, I wiggled my crossed-over foot and tilted my head at her. "Speaking of what's been going on," I said slowly, "I've been meaning to ask you, Kathy, if there's anything you're not telling us about Frank? Anything that could help the police with their investigation?"

Under different circumstances, this might have seemed like an innocent enough question, but I made sure that my tone remained unsympathetic. If there was something that Kathy was hiding, I wanted her to know that I was on to her.

Looking around the room, as if she was worried that someone might overhear us, Kathy picked up her tea and folded her features into a crumpled, hard-done-by expression. "What on earth do you mean, Molly? Of course, I don't know anything." She was clearly trying to keep her voice low and quiet but wasn't doing a very good job.

"Come on, Kathy." I was waving my hand at her, gesticulating to hammer home my point. In a purposefully loud voice, I added, "I saw you."

Kathy frowned at me, then widened her eyes and shook her head. "I don't know what you're talking about, Molly, I really don't."

Despite the promise I'd made to myself to remain calm, anger and frustration had begun to bubble away inside me; I knew, just knew, from the way she was looking at me that I was right. Kathy was

149

hiding something. "Don't play innocent with me, Kathy." Slowly and in an even louder voice, I added, "I saw you."

With a flick of the wrist, as if she was batting away an annoying mosquito, Kathy rolled her eyes at me.

Behind us, people were glancing furtively in our direction, clearly intrigued by our raised voices. Kathy reached out and tried to gently pat my arm, smiling sweetly, but I sat further back in my chair and simply waited for her to speak.

"It's alright, dear. I know it's hard to keep things straight when you're not feeling well."

As she spoke, our eyes met. She was waiting for me to lose my temper. She expected me to get up, make a scene, yell... make her look like the reasonable one. But a steely resolve had settled in my stomach.

I put my coffee cup down and reached into my purse. Leaving a ten-dollar bill down on the table, I stood up. "I feel perfectly fine, Kathy. Thank you." I shrugged my purse onto my shoulder and started to walk towards the door. Just before I reached it, I turned around and waved. "If you change your mind and want to talk," I called, "I'm always here for you, Kathy. Always."

---

After leaving the coffee shop, I noticed that I was walking with a little more bounce in my step; Kathy was hiding something. I was sure of it now, and I had rattled her. Whatever was going on, she was part of it. I just needed to figure out how it all tied together.

From the coffee shop, I walked slowly towards the park. At the gates, I paused and looked over towards the jewelry store. My reflection was hazy. From this distance, my red hair looked unremarkable and my features could have been anyone's. Smiling a little, I exhaled sharply and nodded my head. Of course, I didn't see Tracy that night; it was absurd. It could have been anyone. Or no one, just my mind playing tricks on me because I was under so much pressure.

Checking my phone, I noticed three missed calls from Susan. She was still desperate to see the property on Fitzroy and, for some reason, didn't want Ruth or Dean to take her round there. Only me. If I didn't pluck up the courage to take her, someone else would snap it up, and I'd be left with a very disappointed client on my books. I was supposed to return to work and see to it, but I needed to sit and think. So, I slipped my cell back into my purse, turned my back on the jewelry store, and pushed open the park gates.

It was a warm day, but not too warm, and the sky was dotted with puffy white clouds providing the perfect amount of shade. As I followed the longer route that wound around the outside of the park, through trees and between beds of perfectly planted flowers, I tried to sift through my brain and put my thoughts in order.

It still didn't make sense—none of it did. Why would someone claim they'd seen me near the hiking trail? Why would Frank collude with Kathy to *fake* a disappearance? They disliked me. I'd always known that. But did they dislike me enough to put Colin at risk by involving him?

I let my fingers trail softly through the tall purple flowers at the side of the path, and I bit my lower lip. Something was going on.

Something I couldn't see. But I was going to figure it out. No matter what it took, I'd figure it out.

After half an hour of wandering, I arrived at the fountain in the center of the park. It was large, with statues of giant fish spurting water from their mouths. I sat down on a bench nearby and turned my face up to the sun. When I looked back, two small children had started to splash in the water. I watched them for a while, smiling.

Colin used to love doing that. When he was little, I'd balance him on the side of the fountain and dip his chubby toes into the water. He'd kick and giggle and laugh as it sprayed him.

I looked down at my watch, wondering whether it was too early in the day to go grab an ice cream. Eleven thirty. I frowned. Something was niggling at me. Eleven thirty...

Shit. Colin!

Springing from the bench so quickly I almost left my purse behind, I raced back towards the big black gates on the south side of the path. I was late. Forty minutes late. How could I have forgotten? How could I just have *forgotten* to go get him?

Tearing back past the coffee shop and praying that Kathy wasn't still there to catch a glimpse of me through the window, I rounded the corner. I looked at my phone—checking for a missed call from Dr. Davidson's office—and then *SMACK,* ran straight into someone.

Whoever it was yelped angrily, and hot liquid sloshed violently onto my chest. I cried out but when I looked up, instead of being sympathetic, the man I'd run into was cursing at me and shaking his now-empty takeaway coffee cup.

"I'm sorry," I said, dodging around him and breaking back into a run, "Sorry."

## 20

By the time I arrived at Robert Davidson's building, a few blocks from the coffee shop, I was red in the face, out of breath, and covered in coffee. My pale blue crew neck had a large stain across the chest and belly. My hair was wild from running, and I felt utterly panic-stricken.

I paused, trying to regain a modicum of composure, but as I worked on steadying my breath, I heard a small, high-pitched wailing noise from inside.

Immediately, I pushed open the door. A bell tinkled. There was no one in the waiting room. "Colin?!"

The crying was coming from Robert Davidson's office. I tapped on the door and pushed it open at the same time. Sticking my head into the room, I followed the sound and saw Colin, sitting on the couch, sobbing.

Dr. Davidson was in the corner of the room, speaking into his cell phone, while his secretary comforted Colin. They both gave me a steely glare as I walked in, and I was sure that the secretary rolled her eyes at me. "It's alright," Dr. Davidson said into the phone. "She's here now. Thank you. Yes. I will."

Ignoring him, and nudging the secretary out of the way, I kneeled down in front of Colin. "I'm so sorry, baby. I had to make a call for work. I lost track of the time." I reached out and stroked his tear-stained cheeks. "It's okay, Col. It's okay. I'm here now."

Colin was still crying. Usually, if he was upset, he would fall into me and let me wrap my arms around him. But this time, he pulled away and buried his face in the secretary's shoulder.

Standing up, I folded my arms and rounded on Dr. Davidson. "Why is he so upset?! I'm only forty minutes late. You're a psychiatrist. You could have kept him calm for *forty minutes*, couldn't you?"

Robert Davidson's expression remained calm and placid as he replied, "I did my best, Mrs. Burke. Colin did very well for a little while, but..." He glanced up at his clock. "It's nearly an hour now since you were due to pick him up. We were getting concerned. I tried your cell phone and got no reply."

I shook my head and reached for my phone. "I don't have any missed calls." I waved it at him, as if I needed to present evidence. "What number do you have for me? Let me check it."

"Molly…"

"Let me check it," I repeated, folding my arms.

Robert walked over to his desk and checked his computer screen. When he read the number, I waved my hand in the air. "Well, there you go. It's wrong. You've written it down wrong."

"Molly, this is the number you—"

"Here," I cut in, leaning forward to scribble on the pad beside his keyboard. "*This* is the correct number."

Standing up and moving back around to my side of the desk, Robert lowered his voice and beckoned me towards him. "I also called your office," he said slowly. "They haven't heard from you. They were expecting you at work after you collected Colin and dropped him back home with your husband."

My heart was beating quickly, too quickly. I felt my breath start to shake in my chest. "I'm sorry. I had a difficult morning, I just went for a walk."

Robert Davidson was watching me very carefully. Gently, as if I were a frightened animal that might bolt, he put his hand on my arm and whispered, "Molly, do you need someone to talk to? I'm worried that some of the issues from your past might be resurfacing."

I opened my mouth to speak, but couldn't find the words to reply with. Behind me, I could hear Colin sniffing loudly and wanted desperately to just leave and take him home and make him see I was sorry.

"I spoke to Kathy. She said you had some worrying things to say when she saw you this morning. If you need to talk to someone, Molly, I can help."

I pulled my arm back and shook my head. "No. I don't need to talk." I stopped and frowned at him. "How do you even know about my past? Have you been looking at my medical records?" I lowered my voice but could hear the venom in it as I spoke. "Because you have no right—"

Dr. Davidson held up his hand and looked towards his desk. "Molly, you signed papers before the family's first session that gave me permission to access your medical history. It's important I have a full picture in order to properly treat your son." He dipped his head to meet my eyes. "Don't you remember signing the papers?"

I felt my cheeks reddening. A hot, pink flush was creeping from my chest to my face, and my skin felt like it was on fire. "No. I don't remember. And I would very much like to see a copy of those papers the next time I'm here." I straightened my shoulders and tried to keep my voice steady. "Now, if you don't mind, I'm going to take my son *home*."

"Of course." Robert Davidson gestured for his secretary, and she nudged Colin off the couch and brought him over to me.

Putting my hands on his shoulders, I steered him away from her and towards the door. When we were safely outside, on the sidewalk, I bobbed down and turned him to face me.

"Colin, Mommy is *so* sorry for being late." I stroked his cheek and brushed his hair from his face—his beautiful, perfect, face.

Colin still looked pale and worried.

"I'll make it up to you, I promise."

He nodded, clearly not convinced.

"Come on," I said, taking hold of his hand. "Let's go."

As we walked, I tried to think of something to say that would make him feel better and nudge him out of his tearful mood. But all that was going round in my brain was Robert Davidson's papers. Papers I didn't remember signing.

Was he lying? Or had I really forgotten them?

---

My eyes were closed. I'd been dreaming. A strange dream. Doctor Robert Davidson and Kathy and Bryan and Frank, all speaking to me in loud, angry voices. Too loud for me to focus on what they were saying.

As the dream faded, I tried to ignore the thud-thud-thud of my heartbeat and ground myself. I was home, in my bed, mine and Bryan's bed, and everything was okay.

I yawned. My head was too heavy on the pillow. I'd pulled a blanket over my legs but my arms, exposed to the air, felt chilled. Finally forcing myself to wake up, I blinked slowly. I was lying on my side, facing the bedroom window. It was open, letting in the cool breeze that had made the skin on my arms prickle. I yawned again but didn't move. It was dark outside.

I squinted at the clock on Bryan's side of the bed. Eight p.m. Rolling onto my back, I stared up at the ceiling, trying to remember when I'd come upstairs. But the last thing I could clearly picture was leaving Robert Davidson's office with Colin.

A noise from outside the bedroom jolted me out of my thoughts— the creak of footsteps. Slowly, the door began to open. I held my breath. Then Bryan's handsome face appeared, and I smiled.

"Molly?" His forehead was creased into a worried frown. "What's going on?"

Pushing myself up onto my elbows, I tried to smile but couldn't shift the sensation that something was wrong. "Bryan?" My eyes felt dry and I rubbed them sleepily, stifling a third yawn. "I was sleeping."

Bryan stepped into the room but didn't close the door. When he spoke, it was with a hushed, urgent voice. "Molly, it's dark out. Colin's downstairs alone."

"No, I... I wouldn't leave him alone."

"He says he fetched his own supper. Potato chips, chocolate biscuits, and soda." Bryan's lips were tight.

Panic fluttered in my chest. "I..."

Bryan walked over to me and sat down on the edge of the bed. "Molly?" He reached out and put his hand on my shoulder, squeezing lightly.

Tears sprang to my eyes, and I pinched the bridge of my nose. "I can't remember," I whispered.

"Can't remember?"

I looked up and reached for Bryan's hands. "Bryan, I remember leaving Dr. Davidson's office. I remember walking with Colin... I think I just came up to have a quick lie-down. That's all."

"But you don't remember?" Bryan looked as if he wasn't sure whether to be mad with me or deeply worried. His usually strong and stoic face was pale, and his eyes were wide.

I shook my head. A clot of anxiety formed in my throat, threatening to turn into full-blown sobs. Twice in one day, I'd let Colin down. Twice in one day, my mind had betrayed me. "Is he alright?" The words came out thin and shaky.

"He's fine." Bryan nodded, but didn't squeeze my hands the way he usually would if he were trying to make me feel better. "I better go and get him ready for bed."

I nodded, folding my arms across my chest. "Bryan, I'm so sorry."

Standing up, Bryan looked down at me. "Just rest, Molly. I'll read Colin a story, then I'll order food and bring you up some tea."

My muscles started to relax, and I breathed out a sigh of relief. "You're not mad at me?"

At the door, Bryan paused and I noticed him bite his lower lip, the way he did when he was trying to figure out what to say. "No," he said slowly. "I'm not mad. But I do need to voice my concerns, Molly." He put his hand on the door handle. "We'll talk it through later. For now, just rest."

---

After Bryan left, I stayed propped up on my pillows, listening to him downstairs with Colin and looping back through my memory. I remembered coffee with Kathy, the park, rushing to get Colin... I looked down at my clothes; there was the coffee stain from the man who I careered into as I sped around the corner.

I remembered talking to Colin on the way home—telling him that I'd make it up to him with a special day tomorrow, that I'd never, ever forget him again.

I remembered walking in the front door... and then it went hazy. Just snippets. As if someone had clipped time into small disjointed scenes in my head. I saw Colin watching TV, saw myself pouring a glass of water, wandering upstairs, looking at the bed and thinking *just a quick lie-down...*

This was the kind of thing that used to happen. When things were really bad. Just before I was diagnosed. Looking back, it was hard to believe that Bryan had ever really wanted to marry me. Right from the beginning, I'd been a mess. In foster care, after Jack died, I struggled. But Carol was always there, and we got through it together. But after I ran away to Chicago with Colin, I had no one. I was utterly alone with my thoughts. Paranoia haunted me every waking minute. And when he was born, it got worse. So much worse. It was only when I met Bryan that I started to see a glimmer of hope. For a while, I managed to hide from him just how bad it was. But then I couldn't do it anymore. He noticed that something was very, very wrong, and he took me to get help.

I was still staring at the coffee stain. Bryan must have noticed it too. Whatever must he think of me? He was so kind, so patient, and not even angry with me. Of course, he was concerned. But in typical Bryan style, all he wanted to do was help me.

Determined to make myself look more presentable and less on the edge of a breakdown, I climbed stiffly out of bed and headed to the bathroom. Under the hot, heavy stream of the shower, I closed my eyes and tried to calm my thoughts.

Whatever was going on, I needed to fix it. The stress of it all; Frank's disappearance, Colin's reluctance to be near me, Kathy's accusations, the police questioning, the spa... it was getting on top of me. But if I wanted to sort through it and figure out what was going on, I needed to stay strong. I couldn't afford to let it over-whelm me. I couldn't allow my mind to let me down. Not again. Not like last time.

After a good few minutes, allowing the hot water to wash away the worry that had lodged itself in my skin, I climbed out of the shower, wrapped myself in a large fluffy towel, and padded back through to the bedroom.

Fresh clothes, tea, food, and a conversation with Bryan would put things right; he always knew what to say.

Opening the top drawer of the dresser, I put my hands in and started to move things around, looking for my sweatpants and a clean white T-shirt—because Bryan always said that white brought out the green of my eyes. I was about to give up and try the laundry basket, when my fingers landed on something unfamiliar.

Shifting some pajamas out of the way, I narrowed my eyes. It was rough and navy—probably something of Bryan's mixed up with mine. I pulled it out, ready to go put it away with the rest of his things. But then stopped.

I swallowed hard. I couldn't move. My hands started to tremble.

I was holding a baseball cap—Frank's baseball cap. It had *Grandpa* stitched on the front in big white letters—a gift from Colin on Frank's last birthday. Slowly, I traced the G with my fingers. There was a small red stain on the tip of the letter. I squinted at it, then realized that it seeped out from the letter and over the top of the cap. I swallowed hard. Blood. It was blood.

## 21

Without thinking, I rushed to the bedroom door and closed it. Then turned around and stared wildly at the room in front of me. I was holding the cap away from me, as if it might burn me if it got too close, and the question, *How did it get here, Molly?* Was reverberating around and around and around in my head.

From the hallway, I heard a creak. Bryan was on the stairs. My heart was thundering in my chest and a sickly heat was spreading through my limbs. I breathed out, forcing myself to count to ten, then rushed to the wardrobe. In the bottom, my sneakers were wrapped in a white plastic bag; they were always getting muddy and Bryan hated the dirt that fell off them, even when I'd cleaned them with a scrubbing brush.

As quickly as I could, I pulled off the plastic bag and shoved Frank's baseball cap into it. Scrunching it up as small as it would go, I reached up and pushed it to the back of the closet's top shelf

—behind a bundle of scarves and gloves that no one ever moved or looked at.

I closed the door just as Bryan entered the room and turned, still wrapped in my towel and damp from the shower.

"That's a sight for sore eyes," he said softly. "Are you feeling better?" He was holding a cup of tea in his hand and reached out to pass it to me.

"Yes, a bit." I took it and smiled shakily at him.

"I ordered pizza. I thought we could eat up here, in bed. Watch a movie? Relax together?" He stepped forward and wrapped his arms around me, kissing the top of my head. "You can talk to me, you know, Molly. Whatever's going on, we can get through it if you just talk to me." He leaned back and gently met my eyes. "We've got to think of Colin, too. If you're struggling—"

I nodded quickly and took hold of his hand. "I know. But I'm okay. I promise. I just needed a rest. I'll be right as rain tomorrow."

Bryan cupped my face in his hands and smiled. "Alright. If you're sure?"

I let him fold me into his arms, and I rested my chin on his shoulder. "I am. Totally sure." But as he held me, and started gently kissing my neck, I couldn't take my eyes away from the closet.

Frank's bloody baseball cap was in *my* dresser. And I had no idea how it got there.

As we ate our pizza, I tried to focus on the movie Bryan had put on his laptop. But my eyes kept flitting back to the closet. Inside, I was counting. *Five, four, three, two, one.* Over and over. But it wasn't working. Every time Bryan moved, I thought he was going to stride over, pull open the doors, grab the cap and shout, "What the hell is this, Molly? What did you do?!"

But he didn't. He just sat beside me, one arm around my shoulders, the other allowing his fingers to dip in and out of the pizza box.

"Molly?"

"Hmm?" I looked at him and frowned.

"I asked if you've had enough? You've only eaten one slice."

"Oh, yes, thanks, I feel a bit queasy, actually."

Pushing the pizza box away, Bryan angled himself towards me and paused the movie. "Molly, is everything alright? You really need to start taking better care of yourself. Everything that's been going on... it's been stressful." He lowered his voice to only just above a whisper, "I don't want you to get sick again. If you need help, we can get you someone to talk to. We can look at your medication." Reaching out to stroke my cheek, he said softly, "You don't have to go through this alone, sweetheart."

I tried to smile, but it was thin and half-hearted. "I know. Thank you." Bryan's kindness was only making me feel worse. "Listen, why don't we finish the movie downstairs? If we keep watching up here, I'll fall asleep."

Bryan glanced at the laptop and looked at me the way he did when he was clearly hoping that things would get romantic. His jaw twitched, and he took his arm back from around my shoulders, but he didn't say anything; he never did. "Sure. You head on down, I'll be there in a minute."

Bryan closed the laptop and picked up the pizza box. "I'll save your slices for Colin. He can have them for lunch tomorrow."

"Sure," I said, trying not to look at the closet. "Good idea."

I waited until Bryan's footsteps got quieter, then went to the door. He was gone. I closed it gently, then tiptoed to the closet and rummaged around until I found the plastic bag containing Frank's bloodied baseball cap. From behind my shoes, I grabbed my brown leather purse—the large slouchy one Bryan had bought me for Christmas—and shoved the cap into it.

Downstairs, Bryan was already settled on the couch ready to resume the movie.

"Hey," I said, lingering in the doorway, trying to sound light and bouncy. "I have a real sweet tooth tonight. I'm going to drive to McDonald's and get us a couple of sundaes."

From the couch, Bryan turned and narrowed his eyes at me. He looked at his watch, then back at me. "It's late, Molly. I'm sure we have ice cream in the freezer."

"I know." I adjusted my purse on my shoulder and picked up the car keys from the dish on the console table. "I just really have a craving for a sundae. Do you want one? Or I can get you something else?"

Bryan paused. His eyes darted to my purse. I held my breath. But then his features relaxed, and he shrugged. "Sure, okay." He turned back to the TV and balanced his ankle on his knee. I was almost at the front door when he called, "Hey, Mol? Extra chocolate on mine, yeah?"

On the porch, as the front door closed behind me, I leaned against it. I was gripping the car keys in my fingers, so tight my knuckles were turning white. Bryan was there. Right there. And I was lying to him, again. What would he say if I told him I'd found his father's bloodied baseball cap in my drawer? Would he accuse me, like the police did? Or would he believe that I had nothing to do with it?

Stepping forward, I looked through the lounge window into our bright, beautiful house. Colin's drawings decorated the walls—not just stuck to the fridge, like in most families, but framed and hung properly because Bryan said he wanted Colin to know how much we treasured them. There were pictures from our wedding, too, and the elaborate couch cushions that Bryan had told me to splurge on because I wanted them so badly.

He was so good to us. But how could I expect him to believe that I hadn't had anything to do with his father's disappearance... when I was starting to doubt it myself?

I turned away from the house and jogged down the front steps. In the car, I placed my purse on the front passenger seat and started the engine.

At least until I figured out what was going on and got my head straight, I needed that cap out of the house. Far away. Somewhere no one would look for it.

As I drove, I could almost feel my purse pulsating on the seat beside me, and I felt sure that if someone stopped me and looked at it, they'd *know* there was something bad inside.

I had no idea where I was going. I'd told Bryan I was going to McDonald's, and promised him a sundae, so I headed towards the drive-thru. It was dark. Pitch dark. The streets in the neighborhood that led away from our house and towards the more industrial side of town seemed unfamiliar and too quiet.

I'd always hated driving at night. And the prickly, nauseating heat of anxiety had started to creep into my skin.

Glancing into the rearview mirror, I noticed a car that looked familiar. Hadn't I seen that car a few blocks back? A Ford Focus. I sat up taller in the driver's seat and adjusted the mirror to see more clearly. My fingers tapped nervously on the steering wheel. Up ahead, a set of traffic lights were turning from green to red.

I pulled to a stop. The car stopped behind me. Keeping my head very, very still, I glanced at the mirror and tried to make out the driver. In the dark, all I could see was a silhouette. Possibly a man, possibly a woman.

When I turned back, the lights were green again and yet, unlike most drivers, the one behind me hadn't sounded his horn or flashed his lights to tell me to move on.

As I put my foot on the accelerator, it felt heavy and cumbersome. McDonald's was up ahead but instead of continuing towards it, I took a left, a right, another left, then pulled over into the parking lot of a large, boarded up warehouse. For a moment, I didn't move. I barely even breathed.

I watched the road. There were no other cars. Everything was quiet.

Finally, I pulled out of the parking lot and drove back the way I'd come. At the junction, I swung into the lane that led towards

McDonald's. I could see it up ahead, its big fluorescent sign screaming at the world that it was open twenty-four seven.

Trying to ignore the increasingly mixed-up thoughts that were swirling around my head, I parked out back, reversing into the space so that I could sit and calm myself down.

The parking lot was busy. There weren't many vacant spaces, so there was bound to be a line inside. I thought about leaving, but I'd promised Bryan a sundae. If I returned without one, he really would think I was losing the plot.

I was about to get out of the car when the silver Ford Focus pulled in and parked up in front of me. Instantly, my breath caught in my chest. I let go of the handle on the driver's side door and slid down in my seat. I still couldn't make out the driver. They weren't moving. They were just sitting there.

With trembling hands, I reached for my purse and pulled it onto my lap. When I looked up, the car door was opening, and the unmistakable figure of Detective Monroe was walking towards me.

I clutched my purse closer. I could feel the shape of Frank's baseball cap inside, and the plastic bag it was wrapped up in rustled as I squeezed it.

I tried to steady my breathing, counting slowly from five down to one. I glanced towards the entrance of the McDonald's. I had two options; get out, act as if I had nothing to hide, and talk to him. Or, leave right away. Just drive. Speed off into the distance. Go somewhere else. Anywhere else.

I drummed my fingers on the steering wheel. I had no choice; leaving now would be suspicious. So, holding my breath, I stepped out of the car.

"Detective?" I asked lightly, adjusting my bag on my shoulder.

"Mrs. Burke," he replied, taking in my hair. Shorter now. Much shorter.

I looked back at the restaurant. "Late night takeout?" I tucked my hair behind my ear and smiled but instead of being a small, polite, normal smile it came out as too big and too forced.

"Actually, I noticed you have a taillight out," he said, gesturing to my car.

"I do?" Was he lying? Was it a coincidence that he was in the exact same place as me at the exact same time? I swallowed hard. My bag felt too conspicuous, as if there were a great big flashing neon sign above it saying, *Ask her what's in the bag! Ask her!* And Monroe was still just staring at me.

"Yes. You do."

"I'll get it seen to."

Monroe nodded curtly then started to walk inside. "My wife's pregnant," he said. "Sent me out for a hamburger and fries, even though she's vegetarian."

I was rooted to the spot. I tried to laugh. "Very chivalrous of you," I replied. Then, realizing that he was waiting for me, I followed him inside.

The line was long. There were six people in front of us, and as we waited to be called up, I bounced impatiently on the balls of my feet. Every now and then, I glanced back towards the door. But Monroe just stared ahead at the big lit-up menu.

"Still no news about Frank?" I asked finally.

"No."

"Will you…" I paused and scuffed my foot against the floor. "Will you want to speak to me again?"

"Perhaps," he replied, still not looking at me.

Finally, we were called forward to order, but Monroe stepped aside and let me go first.

In a hushed and hurried voice, I asked for two chocolate sundaes. Opening my bag, my fingers stiffened. The plastic bag was right there. Frank's baseball cap was right there. And I could feel Monroe watching me. Glancing up at the server, I laughed. "Wallet's in here somewhere," I said, gingerly moving the bag aside and fishing out my bank card. The server nudged my sundaes forward and told me to have a nice evening. I grabbed them, muttered a thank you, then called, "Good night, Detective," and hurried back outside.

In the shadow of the building, I stopped to catch my breath. Beside me, a large metal dumpster was almost overflowing with trash. I tried to steady my breath. If it was super full, it wouldn't be long before it was emptied, and the contents were taken away to landfill or to be incinerated. I could leave the hat. Bury it inside and be rid of it forever. But Monroe wouldn't be far behind me. Any second now, he'd emerge with his paper bag full of food. So, I couldn't risk it.

Like a drunk falling out of a nightclub, dizzy with panic, I stumbled back to my car and climbed inside. *Five, four, three, two, one.*

Glancing into the rearview mirror, I saw Monroe exit the sliding double doors. As he passed me, he nodded, and I quickly reached up to tilt the mirror so that it looked like I was checking my makeup, not sitting there trying not to have a panic attack. Finally, when Monroe's car pulled out of the parking lot and turned left, I sat back and ran my hands through my hair. I shook my arms, trying to release the prickling anxiety in my skin. But when I looked up, my body jolted with surprise. I leaned in, peering at the reflection in the mirror; staring back at me was a woman I barely recognized; gaunt, with gray circles under the eyes and a pale, washed-out complexion. Acne had started to breakout across the bridge of my nose. My hair was scruffy and sticking up in tufts. I looked half-starved and severely sleep deprived.

I reached into my purse and began to shift things around, ignoring the hat. The pills I'd collected were in there. I'd taken one earlier, but when things were at their worst, I was on double the dose. Another might help. Another might stop me from feeling like I was losing my mind.

But they weren't there. I closed my eyes. I could picture walking into the pharmacy and leaving with a white paper bag containing my medication. I took one straight away, because I'd missed my dose, put them into my purse and… I hadn't taken them out. I knew I hadn't. Scraping my fingers through the hair I was beginning to hate, I let out a small feeble growl.

*Five, four, three, two, one.*

*Five, four, three, two, one.*

Why wasn't it working?

# 22

With the chocolate sundaes balanced in the footwell of the passenger seat, and still shaking, I sped out of the McDonald's parking lot and towards the outskirts of town. It was nine thirty. Bryan would be getting worried, but I couldn't go back. Not yet.

I needed to calm down, get rid of Frank's hat, and get my thoughts straight. I couldn't go on like this; spiraling into a whirlpool of confusion, and panic, and hazy memories.

I stopped near the hiking trail that Bryan and I used to take when we first moved back to town and exercise was a key part of my wellness routine. There was a small lookout point with views over the city. Usually, a couple of cars would be parked up. Teenagers, kissing on the backseat. Newlyweds out on dates. Tonight, there were none.

Pulling up, I turned off the engine and reached for the sundaes. Balancing the gray cardboard holder on my lap, I took the long plastic spoon and started scooping chocolate sauce into my mouth. It tasted bland, as if someone had sucked the niceness out of it, but I ate it anyway.

I thought back to that morning, before I dropped Colin at Robert Davidson's office and went to meet Kathy. I didn't remember eating breakfast, but then I couldn't remember the entire drive home either or leaving Colin alone downstairs... or where I was when Frank disappeared.

The woman who'd stared back at me from the rearview mirror was not the woman I was a few weeks ago. She was like a ghost from my past, reminding me that I could very easily slide back to a place I did *not* want to revisit.

I closed my eyes, memories swarming back into my brain. Memories of running away in the dead of the night, clutching at my twenty-four-week pregnancy bump and promising to take care of Colin, no matter what. Memories of arriving in Chicago lost, alone, and terrified. Staying in dirty motels, washing dishes for cash, reality slipping further and further away from me as my lies escalated.

Back then, it was Bryan who fixed me. He caught me in a lie, several lies, too many lies. But instead of turning away from me, instead of walking away from me and Colin, he stayed. He found a doctor who diagnosed me with borderline personality disorder. I got started on my medication and, after not too long, I got better. For years, I'd been in such a good place. Everything was perfect. And I knew I didn't ever want to go back to being that terrified, messed up girl who burned her surrogacy papers and threw them into the ocean.

But now, in just the few short weeks since Frank disappeared, it was all unravelling.

Bryan stuck around the first time. But would he do it again? Would he do it if it turned out that I had something to do with his father going missing? Would he do it if I drove home, showed him his father's bloodied hat, came clean, and told him the truth about my past? Told him I wasn't even sure if I believed myself anymore?

A hot, sticky wave of nausea rushed through me, and I flung open the car door.

I stumbled towards the edge of the lookout point, where the dusty ground gave way to shrubs and grass, leaned over, and put my hands on my thighs. And then I threw up.

Wiping my mouth with the back of my hand, I stood up and tried to stop my head from spinning. Beyond the greenery in front of me, the city lights were twinkling brightly against the calm night sky. It was cool, but not cold. A perfect summer's evening. But the tranquility of it only seemed to amplify the voices in my head and the fear in my gut.

With shaky legs, I turned and fetched my purse from the car. Slowly, I unwrapped Frank's hat from the plastic bag I'd hidden it in, then I pulled back my arm and threw it as hard as I could into the bushes. I was shoving the plastic bag back into my purse when a second car pulled up. A silver Ford Focus. I clutched my stomach. My heart was racing. Monroe followed me. The bastard followed me. The car's engine stopped and the driver's door opened. But it wasn't Monroe; a woman stepped out. Silhouetted by the darkness, she stepped forward, under the glow of the one pale streetlight.

"Susan?"

"Molly?" Susan Carmichael smiled at me, but she looked worried. "Is everything okay? Are you sick?"

Feeling sweaty and wobbly, I shook my head. "Oh, no. I'm fine." I glanced towards the car, hoping she wouldn't spot Bryan's uneaten sundae and my empty one.

"I was just out for a jog. I like running at night. It's so peaceful out here." Susan leaned back against her car and took a long, slow sip from a water bottle she was holding.

"Oh, yes. Me too." I spoke before I had chance to even think about it. "Must have over done it." I glanced towards the bushes. Running could make you vomit, couldn't it? If you overdid it?

"Cool. I didn't know you were a runner." Susan's expression didn't falter, but I shuffled self-consciously. I was wearing jeans that were still damp from scrubbing off the chocolate sundae. Had she really not noticed?

Folding my arms across my chest, I walked closer and rested my lower back on the hood of my car. "Listen, that apartment?" I could barely remember whether we'd arranged for Susan to go alone and check it out or if she was still waiting for me to take her, so I purposefully left the question open-ended.

Susan wrinkled her nose and flicked her long ponytail over her shoulder. "It was grungy. Not for me," she said.

"Sorry. I'll keep looking."

Susan shrugged. "No problem. I'm sure we'll find something." She paused and looked down. She was fiddling with her car keys and when she looked up, she seemed almost nervous. "Listen, Molly— I don't suppose you'd like to..." She trailed off and laughed. "As we both like running late at night, maybe we should do it together some time? I really could use a friend in town."

For a moment, my mouth hung open and Susan quickly backtracked.

"Sorry, inappropriate. We have a working relationship." She shook her head and tucked a loose strand of hair behind her ear. "It's just that I used to go running with my sister Tracy. We'd go on these long, beautiful nighttime runs." She blinked slowly and sighed. "I miss it."

I swallowed hard and wished I was closer to my car so that I could steady myself on the hood. "Tracy?" My voice cracked as I spoke.

"She died." Susan met my eyes. She was speaking slowly, as if she wanted me to really absorb what she was saying. "It was a few years back. She was in a car accident." Susan looked down at her fingernails and added quietly, "It took a lot for me to move back here."

"I'm sure it did." I felt like I might pass out and was suddenly desperate to drive home to Bryan and to not continue this conversation.

Susan tilted her head. She was watching me carefully. "The thing is, so many people tell me they 'get it,' but they don't. There's no way they could."

I nodded. "No. I mean, the loss of a sister—"

"It's not just that. It's the way she died." Susan took a step closer. She was weighing her water bottle up and down in her right hand. She stopped right in front of me, so close I was sure she'd be able to smell the vomit on my breath. Lowering her voice, she whispered, "She died in a car accident because she was out looking for the woman who *stole* my nephew from her." She stood back, her eyes strangely emotionless. "This woman was supposed to be Tracy's surrogate. They'd signed the papers. But she ran away before the baby was born. Tracy went mad with grief. She was out one night, in the rain, searching." Susan paused and looked up at the sky. "It was raining. A thunderstorm. Tracy used to drive around at night looking for women who matched the description. But she was driving too fast. Her car went into a tree." Susan turned her eyes back to me and blinked slowly. "It broke her. Losing her baby."

I felt like I'd been punched in the gut. Tracy? A surrogate? A stolen child? My entire body started to shake. But Susan was still talking.

"She was so excited about the surrogacy. It was everything she'd ever wanted—a baby. A family. And then the surrogate just disappeared. Ran off in the middle of the night and was never seen again."

My lip quivered. It couldn't be. Tracy was alive and living in Rhode Island with Andy. She wasn't dead. She couldn't be. Susan was wiping moisture from her eyes. "What an awful thing for you all to go through." My words came out flat and lifeless.

"Yes," Susan said curtly, folding her arms in front of her. "It was."

"Listen, Susan, I'm sorry, but I have to go. Early start tomorrow. But we'll talk soon? I'll keep an eye out for an apartment for you."

"Sure." Susan didn't take her eyes away from me as I climbed back into the car.

As I drove away, I looked in the rearview mirror. She was still standing there, watching me. And as her shadowy figure grew smaller, I began to cry.

From the lookout point, I drove straight home. Susan's Tracy had to be *my* Tracy, didn't she? The very first time I met Susan, I almost choked on her resemblance to the Tracy I knew. And there couldn't possibly have been two women, with the same name, whose surrogates ran away with their unborn child. But if she was, if Susan was Tracy's sister, then how in the world was it possible that she had turned up on my doorstep and tried to befriend me?

It was too much of a coincidence. And the way Susan looked at me when she spoke about Tracy; it wasn't normal. It was like she was studying every word out of my mouth, every micro expression, every movement.

Back at the house, I walked heavily up the front steps and put my key into the lock. I paused, summoning both strength and energy, and stepped inside.

"Molly?" Bryan rushed into the hallway and grabbed me by the arms. His eyes were wide, and he was holding his cell phone in one hand. "Where the hell have you been? I tried calling. You didn't answer."

I frowned. I hadn't heard my phone ring. "I..."

"It's eleven p.m., Molly. You've been gone two hours." He stood back and let go of me, then waved his arms incredulously. "And where are the sundaes?"

Suddenly, I felt exhausted. Tiredness rushed over me and I grimaced as I brushed my hair from my face. "I bumped into a client. We talked. The sundaes melted."

Bryan shook his head at me. I could see his jaw twitching. "Molly." His voice was deep and measured. "This can't go on. We need to talk about your behavior."

"Bryan, please, not now." I waved him away and pushed past him towards the stairs. "I can't do this now." I was on the verge of tears and needed to be alone.

"Seriously?" Bryan sidestepped in front of me and put his hands on my shoulders. He gave me a little shake. "What is happening here, Molly? You're scaring me."

"It's nothing. I'm fine. I told you what happened. If you don't believe me, go check the car. You can scrape the remnants of your sundae out of the footwell if you're that desperate for a sugar-hit." My voice was so sharp that I barely recognized it.

Bryan stepped back. He was shaking his head and looking at me as if he barely recognized who I was. "We'll talk in the morning," he said darkly. "Go to bed. I'll sleep in the guest room."

I paused at the foot of the stairs. I wanted to turn back, fold myself into his arms, and let him take care of me like he did before.

But I couldn't. Not this time. I had to figure this out alone.

## 23

A t 5:30 a.m., my alarm rang. Bryan always got up at 6:45, so I'd set it to give myself enough time to shower and sneak out of the house.

I hated deceiving him like that. But I couldn't talk to him about what was going on, not until I'd figured it out for myself.

Having barely slept all night, the alarm was completely unnecessary. But it forced me to stick to my plan. I got out of bed, showered, dressed, then folded the sheets and the quilt back, plumped the pillows, and left a note for Bryan:

SORRY. NEED TO BE IN THE OFFICE EARLY. LOTS ON TODAY. WE'LL TALK TONIGHT. LOVE MOLLY XXX

On the landing, I tiptoed past the guest room where Bryan was sleeping and peeped in on Colin. He was fast asleep, mouth open, making the small *eep* sound that he often made when he was dreaming. I let his door close softly behind me, then took the car keys from the hook and left the house.

I had no idea where I was going, or what I was going to do. I just knew I needed to get away from home, and work, and Kathy, and Frank, and *breathe*. Find a space where I could sit and calm my thoughts; try to make sense of what was happening.

As I drove, the sun started to creep up over the horizon. At first, it was a glorious soft orange and, as it grew brighter, the glare made me reach for my sunglasses.

On the outskirts of town, I wound down the windows and let my arm dangle out of the car. The breeze and the sun on my skin made me smile. For a moment, it was as if I was just out for a drive. Nowhere to be. Not a care in the world.

I remembered, briefly, feeling like this when Colin was a baby. In between bouts of confusion and paranoia, I'd found time to go out in the car with him and drive around. In there, in the car, it was safe. Just the two of us. But now, for the first time, he was pulling away from me.

We were always so close. Even when he started to develop a deeper bond with Bryan, when the two of them became this funny little duo, a boys' club I wasn't allowed to be a part of, there was still time for *us*—mother and son. Lately, though, ever since Frank disappeared, there had been no 'us.'

Remembering how tiny he was when he used to ride beside me in his car seat, I sighed and pulled my arm back inside the car. I'd blamed his reaction to my perfume and his reluctance to be near me on the trauma of the attack. But what if it was more than that? What if Colin knew something that I didn't? What if he saw me...?

I shook my head and blinked at the road ahead. For a moment, my eyes had glazed over, and I realized I was drifting into the center of the road. Behind me, a car beeped its horn then, as I pulled back into my lane, overtook. As it sped past, I kept my eyes fixed up ahead. I didn't want to see the driver waving their fist at me or red-faced and swearing.

I drove for over an hour and eventually reached the park where I'd suggested taking Colin canoeing. I pulled up, grabbed my purse, and walked over to the coffee cart. It was always there, come rain or shine, and served pretty terrible coffee. But I purchased a large cappuccino, a blueberry muffin, and a bottle of water. Then I made my way down to the river.

A group of teenagers and an older woman, who looked like she might be their school teacher, were lined up on the shore. An instructor was pointing towards a cluster of canoes, explaining the importance of life jackets and what to do if their boat capsized.

I sat down on a rock nearby and took the lid off my coffee. It was still early, and the air wasn't yet warm. Wisps of steam wound up into the air, and I blew across the drink's frothy surface then took a large sip.

As the caffeine made its way through my veins and I started to feel more awake, I carefully unfolded the paper around the muffin. After a few bites, however, my stomach grumbled, and I returned it to my purse. I was about to zip it back up when I noticed my phone light up. I swallowed hard and cleared my throat.

Up ahead, the teenagers were clambering into the water and screeching at the cold as it came into contact with their flesh.

Gingerly, without taking it out, I angled the phone so that I could see who'd texted me. Bryan. I almost swiped open the message, but it was nearly eight. Ruth and Dean would be in the office at eight thirty. So, ignoring Bryan's text, I dialed the office and told the voicemail machine that I was taking a personal day and would be back in tomorrow.

I expected to feel guilty about it, but I didn't; I needed this. I needed space. I was doing it for my family, so I could get my head straight.

---

I stayed by the river all day. I walked a little. Watched the teenagers and their teacher canoe up and down and play games in the water. I watched a couple playing fetch with their dog. I drank another cup of bad coffee and finished the leftover half of the blueberry muffin.

And I thought about Frank.

My memory lately had been unreliable. That was a fact. When I felt pressured or stressed, my instinct was still to tell an untruth rather than the real truth. That was also a fact. So, it was possible that I'd forgotten something significant, or that I'd lied about it and then forgotten I lied about it.

But what I couldn't get my head around was *why*. Why would I do that? What would I possibly have to gain by hurting Frank and putting my son at risk? What Detective Monroe had said at the station was simply not true. I *hated* the attention that being ill had brought me; I'd never been happier than I had these last few years with Bryan. I would never do anything to ruin it. And I would never hurt my son.

I searched and searched through every crevice of my brain, but no matter how hard I tried, I couldn't land on an explanation. Which left only one plausible truth: that someone was trying to mess with my head.

Momentarily, as I came to this conclusion, I felt relieved. I had clarity. I'd rediscovered some trust in myself.

It wasn't me. It couldn't have been me.

But then a slow, creeping heaviness settled in my limbs; someone was trying to mess with me. Someone had told the police I was at the scene of Frank's disappearance, and they'd planted Frank's bloodied baseball cap in my dresser.

I swallowed hard and wrapped my arms around my torso. My back was starting to ache from sitting on the hard surface of the rocks by the river, and the sun wasn't as warm as I'd expected it to be.

Someone had been in my house. My bedroom. Could Susan have broken in when we were all out? Surely, we'd have noticed. There'd have been a broken window or things out of place. But if it wasn't Susan, the only other person with easy access to our house was Kathy. Kathy who—I was now certain—had been at the spa with Frank that day.

A few days ago, I was convinced Kathy had something to hide. That she and Frank had colluded to make me look like a crazy person, to persuade Bryan away from me, to get Colin and Bryan all to themselves and be rid of me once and for all.

But then there was Susan… Susan, who had shown up out of the blue and confessed to me that her sister Tracy died while she was trying to track down the surrogate mother who ran off with her unborn baby. Surely, it had to be *my* Tracy? And if it was, then Susan's appearance right around the time I was starting to slowly lose my mind seemed like an awfully big coincidence.

Could they be in it together? Colluding to make me look insane because it suited the pair of them? Susan would get revenge for her sister, and Kathy would finally get what she wanted—Colin and Bryan all to herself.

I sighed and reached for my phone. It was getting late, and it was a long drive back to town. Looking down at the screen, I had five missed calls from Bryan and three text message notifications stared back at me. I thought about opening them, or calling him, but I'd decided that the only way through this was to talk to him. Carol was right—Bryan was my rock, the one who'd seen me at my lowest and pulled me through. And I owed it to him to confide in him now.

It might break us. Telling Bryan the truth about Tracy and Andy, and what I did to them might make him hate me so much that he walked out and never came back. But he'd stuck with me so far. He'd loved me no matter how bad things got. And without him, I knew there was no way I'd be able to figure out what was going on.

So, instead of reading the messages, I drove back home reeling through all the things I would say to him to explain what had been going on, and all the ways he would make me feel better.

---

Pulling up in front of the house, I took a deep breath—in through the nose, out through the mouth. *Five, four, three, two,* one. I'd worked out exactly what I'd say to Bryan; I was simply going to tell him everything, calmly, from start to finish. I was going to tell him that I took Colin away because I was afraid Tracy and Andy wouldn't be good parents. I'd tell him that Tracy had appeared with bruises and that they'd argued all the time, and that I did it for Colin. To keep him safe. And then I'd tell him that I was worried I was losing my mind, about Susan and seeing Frank at the spa. And he would listen tentatively, as he always did. He might be mad at first, because I'd kept it from him. But then he'd wrap me in his big strong arms, kiss my forehead, and tell me that we'd fix it *together*—the way we always did.

With a spring in my step, I walked up to the front door and, under my breath, muttered, "You can do this, Molly."

Inside, the house was quiet. The door clicked shut behind me and I strained my ears for sounds from within. Usually, Colin would have the TV blaring by this time, and Bryan would be clattering around in the kitchen preparing supper.

Setting my purse and keys down in the hall, I kicked off my sneakers and padded through to the lounge, the dining room, the kitchen. Then I heard voices out in the backyard.

It was still light outside; maybe Bryan had invited friends over and forgotten to tell me. Brushing down my slightly dusty, day-worn clothes, I headed to the French doors and pushed them open.

First, my eyes landed on Colin. He was sitting in his sandbox, using one of his bright yellow dump trucks to pile sand into one corner. It had been months since he'd played with it, and I'd been starting to think he'd outgrown it, so seeing him crouched down and concentrating hard on the task at hand made me smile.

I was still smiling at him, lost in the memory of the day we bought him the sandbox, when I got the feeling I was being watched. I turned, slowly, as if whoever it was might jump out at me if I moved too quickly.

"Bryan? Kathy?" I put my hand on my chest and laughed a little. "You made me jump. Why are you standing there so quietly?"

The pair of them were staring at me. Kathy's long fingers were resting lightly on Bryan's forearm.

"Where have you been, Molly?" Bryan's face was hard to read. I knew he'd be annoyed that I hadn't called him back, but this was different.

There was no way I was going to tell him the truth with his mother standing there, so, cheerfully, I said, "I've been at work. Didn't you get my note? I had to go into the office early this morning."

"I saw your note." Bryan stepped forward, taking his arm away from his mother. Quietly, he added, "I tried to call you. I texted."

Trying to ignore the heat that was creeping into my cheeks and would soon be making them blush, I rolled my eyes and sighed. "I know. I'm sorry, sweetheart, it's been full-on all day." I glanced at Kathy, then lowered my voice. "But maybe we can talk later? There are some things I want to—"

Before I could finish, as if she couldn't stand listening to me for a moment longer, Kathy stormed forward and waved her hands at me. Looking from me to Bryan, she said to him, "Are you going to let her stand there and lie to you like this? It's unbelievable, Bryan. Unbelievable."

Bryan's forehead was creased into a worried frown. The lines at the corners of his eyes looked more pronounced than normal, and he was scraping his fingers through his hair. When he stopped, he rubbed his temples.

"Bryan?" I ignored Kathy and met his eyes. "What's she talking about?"

"I'm talking about you standing there and telling him barefaced *lies*!" Kathy's voice was louder and higher in pitch. From the sand-box, Colin looked over at us.

"I'm not…"

But Kathy wasn't going to let me speak. She was in full-stride and wasn't going to stop. "I told you not to trust her, Bryan. *We* told you. Right from the start."

"Mom, that's enough." Bryan put his hand on his mother's shoulder and ushered her away from me. "I'll deal with this. It's between me and Molly."

"Bryan—" Kathy tried to protest, looking at me with wild, accusatory eyes, as if the second she was gone, I'd sink my claws back into her son.

"Mom. Seriously. Go home. I'll call you tomorrow."

As Bryan walked Kathy to the door, I stood stock-still. My breathing was shallow, and my legs felt shaky. It felt like time had slipped into another dimension; as if Bryan had been gone hours rather than minutes. And when he returned, instead of feeling relieved, my stomach lurched with dread.

"Bryan…"

He stopped in front of me. His eyes were dark, and his jaw set square and tight. "Not now. When Colin's in bed, we'll talk. He needs calm, not…" Bryan's fingers twitched in my direction, "all this."

"Bryan, please…" I put my hand on his arm, but he shrugged it away.

"I said, not now." Then he turned to Colin and shouted, "Hey, buddy. How about some food?"

Colin looked up and grinned. "Okay, Dad."

And then the two of them went inside, leaving me alone with the fear of what was to come.

# 24

Dinner was re-heated pasta from three nights ago. It was starchy and tasteless, but I forced it down and persuaded Colin to do the same. But, apart from encouraging him to eat, it was as if I wasn't really there. Colin and Bryan chatted easily and conspiratorially, sharing inside jokes and talking about plans for the weekend, while I just sat there and played 'boring Mom.'

Had it always been like this? Had they always pushed me to the outside? Or was this new?

"Mom?" Colin's voice jolted me out of my train of thought, and I scraped my fork loudly across my plate.

"Sorry, Colin, what did you say?"

"He asked if you'd read him a bedtime story?" Bryan was watching me with a pinched, irritated expression on his face; an expression usually reserved for neighbors who parked their car across our drive or TV shows he hated.

"A bedtime story?" My lips spread into a smile; it had been weeks since Colin had asked me to read to him. "Of course. Of course, I'll read to you. Which book?"

---

An hour later, I tucked Colin up in bed, turned out the light, and blew him a kiss.

Outside the door, I paused and looked towards the stairs. A soft light was coming from the lounge, where Bryan was waiting to talk to me. Somehow, my grand plans to sit him down and tell him everything had been hijacked, and now he was the one who had something to say.

Downstairs, I pulled the door closed as I entered the lounge and sat down on the couch at the opposite end to Bryan. He was already leaning forward onto his thighs, fingers laced together, hanging his head as if he was about to say something terrible and needed to pray for the strength to do it.

I swallowed hard and pulled a pillow onto my lap—a habit I'd picked up when I was pregnant with Colin; whenever I felt nervous, I'd reach for a pillow, blanket, or sweater, and hold it in front of me like a form of protection.

Bryan eventually looked up and, when he did, his eyes were moist. "Molly, where were you today?"

The first time he asked me, he'd sounded irritated. Now, he sounded sad. "I told you. I was at work."

As I spoke, Bryan held my gaze with his. And when I finished, he shook his head. "No, Molly. You weren't."

"Yes, I…"

Bryan glanced into the hall. "You went to work wearing sneakers and…" he waved at my outfit, "jeans?"

"They're trying something new—encouraging us to be more casual to attract a different kind of client." The lies tumbled out before I could stop them, the way they always did when I was cornered and felt like I was going to be in trouble for something. It had always been that way; even before I was diagnosed. If I felt threatened, instead of coming clean and telling the truth, I lied. And then I told more lies to make the first lies make sense, and it went on and on and on.

Bryan made an exasperated sound and looked at the house phone, sitting neatly in its cradle near the TV. "I called your office when you didn't answer your cell. I spoke to Graham."

I blinked slowly. I didn't even know he was back from holiday.

"He said you called in sick."

I closed my eyes.

"He said you've been calling in sick a lot." Bryan raised his voice. "Fifteen times in the last six weeks, Molly. *Fifteen times.*"

I shook my head, still keeping my eyes firmly shut. "That's ridiculous…" When I opened them, Bryan was staring at me. His cheeks were flushed, and he was tapping his foot up and down.

Bryan got up and walked over to the dresser in the corner of the room. He opened the top drawer, the one where we kept our paperwork, and took out a wedge of papers. "I didn't believe him. I said you wouldn't do that; you wouldn't lie to me. So, he emailed over the time sheets from the last pay day."

"Bryan, I didn't... fifteen times? No." My head was swimming. I'd called in sick for a few days after Frank's disappearance, the day I went to the spa, and today. Definitely not fifteen. But when Bryan thrust Graham's spreadsheet at me, there it was—fifteen days. My last paycheck had been way smaller than I anticipated, but I thought it was just because I was struggling to bring in new clients.

"Bryan, there's been some kind of misunderstanding. I need to look at these dates, but I'm *sure* I haven't been off sick that often. It's just been a couple of times."

Bryan stared at me for a moment. He was still standing and, in the middle of the room, he looked like an angry statue, glaring down at me and barely moving. "Jesus, Molly!" His voice was suddenly louder. "When are you going to stop this?"

"Stop what? Bryan, I swear." I got up and grabbed his forearms. They were folded and he didn't unfold them. "I promise you, Bryan. I lied today because I needed to get my head straight, because weird things have been happening, and I needed some space to figure out what to do about them. I was going to talk to you about it all. That's what I've been doing all day—thinking about how to tell you—"

"Weird things?" Bryan was still scowling. "What kind of weird things?"

"My memory. I've been forgetting things, foggy-headed, confused. And..." I trailed off. A few hours ago, I'd been convinced that telling Bryan everything was the only way out of whatever the hell was happening. But now... he already thought I was crazy, probably heading for a relapse. Maybe even hospitalization this time. If I told him I'd found his father's bloody baseball cap in my drawer and that I thought someone planted it there, he'd have me committed on the spot.

"Please, Bryan. You have to believe me."

For a moment, I thought he was going to reach out and fold me in his arms. His eyes crinkled at the corners and he shook his head slowly. Then he sighed and took a step back from me. "The thing is, Molly. I don't."

His words hung in the air between us, and I stumbled as if he'd physically kicked me in the stomach. "You've never said that to me before." My voice came out small and hoarse, but it was true. Even when things were at their worst, Bryan never actually said out loud that he didn't believe me.

"You've never behaved like this before. When things were bad, before you were diagnosed, I felt like I could reach you, get through to you. I could tell when you were being untruthful, and I felt like deep down you wanted to be honest with me. But now..." Bryan shook his head. "This is different, Molly."

"Bryan..." I reached up to touch his face, but he pulled away.

"I think some space would be good for both of us. I'd like you to go stay somewhere else tonight."

"Somewhere else? Are you crazy? This is my house, Bryan!"

"I know. And I'm not saying forever. Just for tonight. I need some breathing room. I need to decide what to do... you should under-stand that, Molly. You really should."

I sat down hard on the couch and looked up at him. "But where will I go?"

Bryan shook his head. "How about wherever it is you've been going on all these sick days?"

———

By the time I turned up at Carol's house, my cheeks were stained with tears and I was so exhausted that I thought I might fall down on her driveway.

Gingerly, Carol opened the door. When she saw me, she did a double take, then ushered me inside.

It was late. Outside, everything was dark and eerie, and all I could think about was the fact that my husband and son were alone at home, without me, and that—for the first time in our marriage—I was genuinely afraid Bryan might not let me back in.

"He's never asked me to leave before, Carol." I looked up, hands wrapped tightly around the mug of hot, sweet tea that she'd made me. "He's never doubted me like that. He's always stuck by me, no matter what."

Carol bit her lower lip and tilted her head at me. Gently, she said, "Molly, I know it's hard. I know it's almost impossible when you're having one of your episodes, but I need you to tell me the truth. Have you been lying again? Is it becoming a *problem* again?"

I could feel my legs trembling beneath the table. My foot was jittering up and down, up and down, up and down. I opened my mouth, but I couldn't make the words come, so in the end I just nodded. "I think so." I looked up and met her eyes. "But not about everything. Not about the things he thinks I have…"

"Okay." Carol nodded slowly.

I tried to smile and laugh at myself. "The problem is once you admit you're a liar no one believes a word you say. But if you don't admit it…"

"They still don't believe you." Carol finished my sentence and took hold of my hand. "Molly, listen. It's late. You look like death. Let's go to bed, get a good night's sleep, and then tomorrow you can tell me what's been going on. Okay?"

I breathed in slowly. I really was tired. "Okay. Thank you, Carol."

"Come on then, I'll get you settled in the guest room."

# 25

The next morning, despite promising we'd talk everything through, Carol was halfway out of the door by the time I came downstairs.

"Sorry," she said, wafting a piece of toast at me. "Got to go. Emergency at work. We'll talk tonight, if you're still here." She leaned in and kissed my cheek. "But I hope you're not. Talk to Bryan." She squeezed my shoulder. "Be honest with him."

Sitting down at the breakfast table, I nodded. "I will. I promise."

"Help yourself to anything. Don't forget to lock up when you go to work." Carol paused at the front door and turned back to me. "You are going to work today, aren't you, Molly?"

I looked up at the clock. Seven thirty. Plenty of time. "Yes. Work. Talk to Bryan. Pinky swear." I waved my little finger at her and smiled.

"Good." And then Carol was gone.

In her small, sparse kitchen, I made fresh coffee, fetched a bowl of cereal, then sat down and turned on my phone. This time, there were no messages or missed calls from Bryan—just the screensaver of me and Colin, and about a million unread emails.

I thought about opening them. But I knew at least ten of them would be from Graham, and I didn't want to think about work. I knew I'd have to at some point. But not today. Not now; there were more important things going on.

Whatever was happening with Frank, and Kathy, and Susan, it would have to wait. First, I needed to mend my marriage and find a way to show Bryan that he could trust me. I needed to get a grip, get control of myself, and prove to him that I was still a good mother. A good wife.

So, after using Carol's shower, I straightened the bed in her guest room, washed up my mug and cereal bowl, and headed for the grocery store.

---

A few hours later, I returned home with two big bags of groceries. Bryan's car wasn't on the driveway. He'd gone to work, which meant Colin would be with Kathy. As I pictured her fussing over him, kissing him with her thin red lips and stroking his hair with her talon-like fingers, I gritted my teeth and tried to ignore the voice inside me that was whispering, *If she wasn't so involved in Bryan's life, none of this would be happening.*

Even though I'd been gone less than twenty-four hours, the hallway felt foreign. Empty. Bigger than normal.

Bryan was much tidier than I was, and he'd taken the opportunity of me being out of the way to organize our shoes and coats on the rack by the front door. Now, Colin's shoes were lined up on the shelf up top. Bryan's spare work shoes, sneakers, and summer espadrilles were on the bottom shelf. Mine were in the middle, and he'd polished my favorite pair for me.

I smiled and let out a small sigh; a man who polishes his wife's shoes, surely, wasn't preparing to kick her out of the house permanently. Probably, when he got home he'd be full of remorse. He'd kiss my forehead, and we'd both apologize, and everything would go back to normal. Especially when he saw that I truly was making an effort.

In the kitchen, I unloaded the grocery bags. I'd bought ingredients for Bryan's favorite muffins, the chili that both he and Colin loved, and the DVD that Colin had been pestering me for. It was going to be a family evening, just like the ones we used to have.

I tapped the countertop and brushed my hands on my jeans. It was nearly midday. They'd be home at five—plenty of time.

I started with the chili, chopped the ingredients, fried them a little, then put them into the slow cooker so that by the time the boys arrived home, the house would be full of the heavenly smell of their favorite food. Then, the muffins. Cherry and dark chocolate. I'd made them almost every day for Bryan when we first got married. I smiled to myself as I folded the chocolate pieces into the batter. There was no way Bryan could stay mad at me if I presented him with these.

After cleaning up the kitchen, with the muffins safely out of the oven and cooling on a wire rack by the sink, and the chili bubbling away in the slow cooker, I swept through the house plumping pillows, straightening picture frames, and dusting. Bryan had cleaned up last night, and the house was never particularly untidy anyway, but these were gestures that he would notice; the kinds of things I never usually did.

About an hour and a half before they were due home, I ran a long, hot bath, soaked for half an hour, then put on the green dress Bryan always complimented me on and a smattering of subtle makeup. I brushed my hair, even though it didn't really need brushing now that it was so short, and stood back from the mirror. I still looked thin and tired, but it was clear I was trying.

Downstairs, at four forty-five, I settled at the dining table and tried to decide on a posture that said, *Welcome home, look how hard I'm trying.*

I wanted Bryan to walk in and smile from ear to ear when he saw me. I wanted him to instantly know that I'd thought about what he'd said, and that things were going to be different. I reached for my phone and tapped it. The screen lit up. Four fifty. Any minute now, I'd hear the car pull up outside, footsteps on the decking, keys in the door.

I glanced into the hallway. The shoes Bryan had polished were just visible around the doorframe. I looked down at my feet, then smiled. Hurriedly, I left the table and kicked off the pumps I was wearing. I'd just replaced them with the leather kitten heels, the ones that Bryan had polished for me, when I heard Colin's voice floating in from outside.

"What's for dinner?" he was saying.

"Not sure, buddy. We'll have a look at what's in the fridge."

I smiled to myself. They were going to be so pleased.

There wasn't time to make it back to the dining table, so I positioned myself in the middle of the hall. I was trying to decide whether to put my hand on my hip or leave it dangling at my side, when the door opened.

"Mommy?" Colin stood in the doorway. Bryan's hands were on his shoulders.

"Hi, sweetheart. I'm home." I smiled at him, but Colin simply frowned, then looked up at Bryan.

"Go on through to the lounge, bud. I'll be there in a minute."

As Colin rushed past me, I reached out and tried to pat his head, but he ducked and I missed. I laughed and looked at Bryan. "Has he had a good day with your mom?"

Bryan closed the door, locked it, and put the keys in the dish on the console table. He stopped in front of me, a few feet away, and folded his arms. "What are you doing here, Molly?"

"Can you smell the chili? I made chili, and your favorite muffins…" I waved my arms at the hallway. "And I tidied up. Can you tell?"

Bryan was looking at me strangely. "Yeah. I can tell."

I smoothed my dress and tilted my head at him, trying to remind him that it was the one I usually wore on our anniversaries. Looking down, I wiggled my foot at him. "Thank you for polishing my shoes. That was really kind."

Bryan frowned, as if he had no idea what I was talking about. "Your shoes?"

"I mean, even after everything that happened last night, you took the time to tidy and polish my shoes. Who does that?" I stepped towards him and tucked my hands under his arms, trying to loop them around his back.

Bryan unfolded his arms and let them hang loosely by his side. "Molly, I didn't polish your shoes…" He put his hands on my arms and lightly pushed on them.

I let go of him and stepped back, tucking a short strand of hair behind my ear.

"Molly, what's going on? You're dressed up like we're going on a date. You've been cooking… when did you get home?"

"I've been doing it all afternoon," I replied, smiling. "I wanted to show you, Bryan, that I'm doing better. That I listened to what you said, and I know things need to change."

Bryan sighed and pushed his fingers through his hair. In the lounge, Colin was watching TV, and I could just make out the top of his head as he bobbed along to the soundtrack of his favorite show.

"I thought we could have a family evening. I got that movie Colin wanted to watch, and—"

"Molly… stop. Please, just stop."

A slow, creeping sense of dread settled in the pit of my stomach, and I felt my smile start to fade. Something was wrong. This wasn't how it was supposed to go. "Bryan?"

"Did you go to work today?" The question was blunt and direct, and he stared at me while he waited for my answer.

"I…" Suddenly, I felt ridiculous. Standing there, dressed up, in my high heels.

"If you wanted to prove to me that you're getting a handle on this, you should have gone to work!" Bryan was losing his temper. It hardly ever happened, but I could see his face changing color.

"Bryan…" I tried to reach for him, but he pushed me away. "You know what? I can't do this." He was shaking his head and his eyes had changed; instead of angry, he looked sad. "I need some space. Are you capable of staying here and watching Colin?"

I nodded, blinking back tears. "Of course, I am."

"Good. Then I'll see you later."

And then he was gone.

## 26

I stood in the hallway for a long time after Bryan left, staring at the door and feeling incredibly stupid. Of course, I should have gone to work. Of course, the best way to prove to Bryan that things were normal was to be... normal. But, once again, I'd got it wrong. Messed it up, like I always did.

I was fighting the urge to run upstairs and sob into my pillow, when Colin's voice drifted in from the lounge. "Mommy? I'm hungry."

Taking a deep breath in, I kicked off my shoes and padded barefoot to the couch. "I made chilli. Is that okay?"

Colin looked up at me and nodded. A flicker of a smile danced on his lips; at least someone was pleased with me.

"I also got that movie you wanted." I smiled, trying to shake myself out of the Bryan-induced daze I was in.

Colin bunched up his fists and grinned. "Really?"

"Ah ha." I handed it to him. "How about we have a TV dinner? We'll put the movie on and eat in our pajamas."

Colin nodded slowly, then a little quicker. "I'll go change," he said, jumping up from the couch.

As he ran up the stairs, I leaned back onto the arm of the couch and sighed. I might have messed things up with Bryan, but at least I could still try to fix them with my son. When Colin came back, he looked me up and down and said sternly, "You said pajamas, Mom."

I glanced down at my outfit. "Right. Sorry. Okay, you put in the DVD, I'll be back in a minute."

Upstairs, I grabbed my gray sweatpants and matching sweater, wriggled my feet into a pair of fluffy pink slipper socks, then ducked into Colin's room and took the quilt from his bed. When he saw me return, he grinned. A genuine, pleased to see me grin that made the anxious twittering in my chest start to fade.

I tossed the quilt at him and smiled. "Get settled, bud. I'll grab our food."

And when I presented him with a large bowl of steaming hot chili, with tortilla chips to dip into it, and guacamole on the side, I saw him sigh. He wriggled down beside me and, for the first time in weeks, didn't flinch when I cuddled up to him.

"This is nice," I whispered.

"Shhh," he replied. "The movie's starting."

A couple of hours later, after making our way through two bowls of chili and a muffin each, Colin yawned and said he was ready for bed. It was late, almost eight and way past the time when I usually started getting him bathed and into his pajamas.

"No bath tonight, Col. You're already in your PJs, so let's go straight to bed, yeah?"

Colin nodded and tried to fight an enormous yawn. "Okay."

Together, we dragged his quilt back upstairs, straightened it out on his bed, and read three bedtime stories. By the time I reached the end of the third, his eyes were heavy, and he looked like he was about to fall asleep on my shoulder.

I kissed the top of his head and wriggled down on the bed. "I love you, Col."

"Love you too, Mommy."

I wanted to ask him if he was still scared of me, if getting rid of the perfume had helped, if he was ready for us to be friends again. But I didn't want to ruin it. He was there, and he was all mine, and he was perfect.

I kissed him again, then slid out of the bed and tucked him in. "I'll always, always protect you, you know that?"

But Colin was already asleep.

Back downstairs, I tidied away the dishes and straightened the couch cushions. It was eight thirty. Bryan had been gone for hours and hadn't told me where he was going. My chest fluttered. What if he'd left? What if he wasn't going to come back?

I picked up my phone and scrolled to my messages.

*BRYAN, WHEN WILL YOU BE BACK? I'D REALLY LIKE THE CHANCE TO TALK TO YOU.*

No reply.

I called three times. No reply. I tried to watch TV, swiped through social media feeds on my phone, drank two strong cups of coffee. But by ten o'clock, I was becoming frantic.

Convinced that Bryan had run away and that I'd never see him again, I did what I swore I'd never do… I opened up the Locate My Phone app on my iPad. I knew Bryan's password; it was always the same one—my birthday, Colin's, and his.

As I waited for the page to load, I held my breath. Then there it was, a little blinking dot. I squinted at the screen… Bryan was at a restaurant. *Our* restaurant. The one we always visited on special occasions.

---

It was usually a fifteen-minute drive to Arancini's, but I made it in ten. I was pretty sure that I ran a red light but didn't care.

A few paces away, I stopped and pulled over into a vacant space at the side of the road. I gripped the steering wheel and took a deep breath. All the way over, I'd been trying to convince myself that Bryan was eating alone. That he'd simply wanted some time to himself and had gone somewhere familiar. But, suddenly, my stomach was twisting with doubt.

What if Bryan had finally had enough of me? What if he'd found someone else? Someone reliable, normal, undamaged…

Finally, I forced myself to get out of the car. I walked past three other restaurants and a late-night coffee bar, then there it was. Our place. Mine and Bryan's.

I stopped outside the window and looked past my reflection into the main dining room. There were smaller spaces out back, but Bryan and I always chose a booth over by the windows on the right-hand side. My breath caught in my chest and I reached out to steady myself; Bryan was in our booth. And he wasn't alone.

My palm had landed flat against the glass window. It was cool to the touch, and I couldn't seem to make myself take it away. A couple sitting on the other side of the glass were staring at me. They called a waiter over. The waiter stuck his head out of the door and in a hushed voice, asked, "Ma'am? Is everything alright?"

Blinking quickly, shaking my head to bring myself back to reality, I turned around slowly. "My husband is inside."

"Okay." The waiter glanced back into the restaurant. "Would you like to come in and talk to him?"

I looked back down the street. I could just get back in the car and go home and pretend I hadn't seen the back of a dark-haired woman's head sitting opposite my husband. But then I sucked my breath in forcefully, straightened my shoulders, and said, "Yes. I would."

Inside, the waiter and the couple from behind the window watched me as I walked purposefully over to Bryan's booth. His hand was outstretched, his index finger gently stroking the hand of the woman he was sitting opposite. He left it there for a moment, then he reached up and touched her cheek. He said something and smiled. She started to laugh. Then he did too. She tossed her shiny dark hair back over her shoulder and reached for her wineglass.

"Susan?" I was standing beside the table. They both looked up at me, smiles frozen on their faces.

Susan paused with her wineglass half-way to her lips. "Molly?" She wrinkled her forehead at me, then looked at Bryan.

"Molly, what are you doing here?" Bryan stood up and ushered me into the booth beside him, trapping me in the corner as if it might prevent me from making a scene.

"Me?" I looked from Bryan to Susan. "What am I doing here? What are *you* doing here? With *her*?"

Susan had put her wineglass down and folded her hands neatly into her lap. She looked confused, but not alarmed, as she said, "Bryan? How do you know Molly?"

It was taking every ounce of willpower in my body to stay calm, but as she spoke to Bryan as if *I* was the intruder, anger bubbled over. Loudly, so loudly that all around the restaurant heads turned to stare at us, I shouted, "How does he know me? He knows me because I'm his *wife*!"

Bryan put his hand on my forearm and in a hushed voice said, "Molly, please. You're making a scene."

"You think that's a scene... if you want a scene, I'll give you a scene..." I was about to get up and throw something—water, maybe, or the leftover food on their plates—but Bryan took hold of my hand and squeezed.

"Susan is a colleague, Molly. She's just joined the company. I offered to talk her through how it all works, who's who... she's new in town. She doesn't know anyone just yet." He softened his voice and met my eyes. "I would have told you. She was going to come to the house but when I got home, you were..." He stopped and glanced at Susan, then shook his head and sat back in his seat. "We're colleagues. That's all."

Susan who, until now, had been quiet, reached her hand out across the table. Resting it just in front of me, she patted the white cloth with her neatly manicured fingers. "He's telling the truth, Molly."

I shook my head. I felt like I was underwater. All around the room, I could feel people staring at me. I looked down at my clothes and shuddered. I was still wearing my gray sweatpants and sweatshirt. There was a chili stain on the front of the pants, and the cuffs of the sweatshirt were wet from where I'd let them get soaked in the washing-up bowl. "Oh God," I muttered.

When I looked up, Bryan was exchanging a look with Susan that said, *I'm so sorry, I'm so embarrassed of my wife.*

Feeling like I might vomit, I flapped my hands and started nudging him along the bench. "Bryan, can you move? I'm so sorry. I need to go. Susan, I'm sorry."

Bryan did as I'd asked and stood up to let me out. "I'll walk Molly back to her car."

When we reached it, I leaned against the driver's side door and hung my head. "Bryan, I...'"

"Molly, where's Colin?" Bryan was looking into the car as if he'd expected him to be there.

Colin....

I sucked in my cheeks. My knees were threatening to buckle. "He's at home," I said defiantly, trying to force down the nausea that was almost choking me. *You forgot your own son. You left him alone. What kind of mother are you?* Vicious taunts started to circle in my head.

Bryan's eyes widened. "Home? He's at home?"

"With Carol." The words came out all on their own, but as soon as I'd said them, I nodded. "I called Carol to sit with him." I reached for my phone. "You can call her and check if you'd like."

Bryan held out his hand. He was about to take it, then he shook his head and put his hand into his pocket instead.

"I wouldn't do anything to put him at risk, Bryan, you know that. I was just... scared. I needed to see you."

Bryan sighed and pursed his lips. Then, as if it was taking a great deal of effort to be nice to me, he pulled me in to lean on his chest and wrapped his arms around me. Kissing the top of my head, he said, "Go home, Molly. I'll say goodbye to Susan, and we'll talk when I get home."

## 27

I waited for Bryan for what felt like forever. When he finally arrived home, I stood up from the couch, then sat down again, then stood up and lingered beside it.

As he walked in, I smiled. "Would you like a cup of tea?"

Bryan breathed in slowly and walked over to the couch. He sat down and gestured for me to join him.

"Bryan…" I sighed and shook my head. "I'm so sorry. All of this. The whole day, it's been a mess. I was so desperate to show you that everything could go back to normal, but I've just messed it up." I paused, waiting for him to smile and tell me I hadn't; that it was okay. That he understood.

"Molly." Bryan looked at me. His eyes were scanning my face, and his jaw was set into a pained expression. "I called Carol."

I swallowed hard. I looked up to the ceiling. Colin was okay. I'd checked on him as soon as I got home and he was sleeping like an angel, in the exact position he'd been in when I tucked him up.

"She couldn't hear me because she was at a gig with her new boyfriend." Bryan let his words sink in and watched me carefully, as if he was waiting for the slightest twitch in my features to give away what I was thinking.

I bit the inside of my cheek. A tumble of fresh explanations were threatening to pile out of my mouth.

"I'm going to ask you a very simple question and I want a yes or no answer." Bryan put his hands in his lap and looped his fingers together. "Did you leave our son alone here tonight, Molly?"

I stood up. I couldn't sit still. Nervous energy was coursing through my veins, and I began pacing up and down. I let out a small, weak, grunting sound, as if the effort of telling the truth was a physical test rather than a mental one. "Yes." Finally, I said it. "Yes, I did." I'd been staring out of the window and turned back to Bryan. "But—"

Bryan put his hand up to stop me from speaking. "That's all I needed to know." He got up and walked to the kitchen, took a glass from the cupboard above the sink and poured himself a large whiskey. No ice.

When he returned, he looked at me as if I were a stranger. He stood in front of me and took a large sip from his glass. "I can't do this."

"Bryan..."

He shook his head and took another sip. "I can't do it, Molly. I stood by you before—the first time—but this is different. I never thought you'd put Colin at risk. But..." He breathed in shakily and blinked as if he was in danger of starting to cry. "I don't know what is going on here. I don't know what's happening, but something is happening. And if you don't trust me enough to share it with me, then I don't know what's next for us."

Stepping forward, I tried to grab his arms, but he pulled away. I wanted to tell him that I'd been trying—trying to find a way to talk to him about it and tell him all of the horrible secrets from my past.

"I know you've suffered a lot of heartache in the past, Molly. But I always thought that I was the one person you were honest with. Small lies, yes. Little white lies. I've always known about those. But not this." He had walked over to the dresser and was tracing the edge of a photo frame with his index finger. He picked it up and turned it to me. It was a family portrait, the three of us, grinning at the camera as if we didn't have a single care in the world. "I honestly never thought you'd put Colin at risk. I didn't believe a word the police said when they called you in for questioning, I stuck up for you when my mother accused you of being unhinged... I never betrayed you, Molly, not once." Bryan thrust the frame into my hands. "But you betrayed us tonight. And all the other times you lied. When you said you were at work. When you said you couldn't remember where you were the day my father disappeared..."

"Bryan, I don't remember. I promise you—"

For a moment, Bryan didn't move. Then he hung his head and said in a low voice, "The thing is, your promises don't mean anything, Molly. Not anymore."

Bryan swigged the last of his drink, then poured another. "Listen, whatever is going on, my priority right now is Colin. He's my son, and it's my job to make sure nothing happens to him. I've let him down lately. I was too wrapped up in trying to help you figure out what was going on with you." Bryan breathed in deeply then shook his head. "Well, no more." He set his whiskey glass down on the dresser and turned to face me. "I'm going to take him to my mother's while you figure out if you still want to be in this family."

My head started to swim, and my eyes momentarily glazed over as Bryan's words sank in. "Of course, I do…"

"Then you need to prove it, Molly. You need to sort yourself out. Because, if you don't…"

I narrowed my eyes at him. A short, sharp laugh escaped my lips. "Then, what? You'll divorce me?"

Bryan blinked slowly.

"Bryan… you wouldn't."

"I'd do anything to keep Colin safe."

Throwing my arms in the air, I started pacing up and down the living room floor. Then anger bubbled up inside my stomach, and I whirled around to face him. "Is this to do with Susan? Is it all an excuse so you can run off together? Is that it?"

Bryan stared at me for a moment, his mouth hanging open in disbelief.

"Because I don't remember her listing the showroom as her place of work when I filled out her background information." I folded my arms and started tapping my foot, as if I'd figured him out and was waiting for him to confess.

"Susan is a colleague. A work colleague. I don't know what information she gave you, Molly, and quite frankly, I'd be surprised if you could even remember. Now, I'm going to go upstairs and fetch my son. And when we're gone, you need to figure out how the hell you're going to turn this around."

As Bryan walked into the hall, I started after him. Then stopped. Surely, this wasn't really happening? Surely, it was all a dream? A horrible dream? My husband wasn't about to leave in the middle of the night. He wasn't about to take my son and leave me...

A few minutes later, tears streaming down my face, I looked up as Bryan appeared in the hallway. Colin was cradled sleepily in his arms, draped in Bryan's jacket.

At the front door he paused and looked me up and down as if he didn't even recognize me anymore. "Please, Molly. I love you. Sort yourself out. Talk to someone. Talk to Dr. Davidson. Someone. Anyone. Just fix this." He turned to the door, then looked back. "Everyone goes through shitty times, but as parents it's our duty to protect our child. When you feel ready to do that, call me."

## 28

After Bryan left, I finished his bottle of whiskey and passed out on the couch. I woke to the sound of the doorbell ringing. It splintered through my brain and made my skull pound.

I rubbed my temples, dragging my eyes open, and looked up at the ceiling. Slowly, I forced my feet to the floor and stood up to peer through the blinds.

It was Carol. She was standing on the porch, checking her phone. BANG BANG BANG. Now she was thumping her fist on the door. "Molly. I need to talk to you. Is everything okay?"

I sat back down and hung my head in my hands. I felt like I might vomit. Nausea was swirling in my stomach, and a flood of memories from last night was battering my brain. Again and again, I saw myself, an eerie, quivering reflection in the glass of the restaurant, standing there like a crazy woman, yelling at Bryan, lying to him, leaving Colin alone...

I started to wretch and ran to the kitchen sink. Gripping the sides, I hurled up an acid mixture of bile, alcohol, and partially digested chili.

Standing up, I wiped my mouth with the back of my hand and drank several big gulps of water straight from the tap. The banging on the front door had stopped. Carol had gone.

Slowly, I slid down to the kitchen floor and leaned against the cupboards below the sink. My phone was in my pocket. The battery was almost dead. I'd called Bryan at least one hundred times last night and left so many voicemails that I'd run out of things to say, except, "I'm sorry," and, "Please come home."

Tucking my knees up under my chin, I wrapped my arms around them and rested my forehead on top. I was on the verge of tears again, but I'd spent so many last night that I probably didn't have any left.

Everything had fallen apart. My whole life. I swallowed hard and let out a small, low, groan. Bryan had taken Colin and, if I didn't sort myself out, it might turn from a temporary situation to a permanent one.

I was still trying to gather the strength to stand up when my phone vibrated. I looked down at it. A message from Bryan.

*Molly, I hope you're okay. I meant what I said last night—sort yourself out, and we can talk about getting back to normal. But I need to know you're serious about making a change before I let you see Colin.*

I held the phone in my hand, gripping it so tightly that my knuckles began to turn white. I swallowed hard and let my thumbs linger above the keyboard. Then, I took a deep breath, turned the phone off and pulled myself to my feet.

I'd fought for Colin once before, and I would do it again. No matter what, I was going to find out what the hell was going on and prove to Bryan, once and for all, that I was a good mother.

---

Determined that by the end of the day I'd have started to find some answers, I jumped quickly into the shower, washed away the smell of whiskey, and dressed in jeans and a loose white blouse. I styled my hair, put on makeup, then headed to the office.

As I pulled up outside, my heart fluttered in my chest, but I bit back my nerves and strode confidently up to the door. When I entered, Ruth and Dean looked up from their desks, open-mouthed, as if they were seeing a real-life ghost.

"Is Graham here?" I asked loudly.

Ruth nodded.

"Thanks," I replied, striding towards his office. I tapped on the door and waited for him to usher me inside. When he saw me, his eyebrows tweaked upwards.

"Molly?" He was wearing an ill-fitting black suit and a shirt that was too tight across the stomach.

"Graham," I walked in and sat down. With my hands in my lap, I pursed my lips and breathed in slowly. "I have an apology to make. I am *so* sorry for letting you down. I've been going through... something. But I'm sorting it out now."

"That's good to hear, Molly, but—"

"I know I've had a lot of time off—actually, I want to talk to you about that because I'm really not sure it was quite the amount of days you mentioned, and I'm not entirely happy about you sharing information with my husband..." I shook my head and tried to focus. "But we can talk about that another time. I just need a couple more days, and then I'll be back. Right as rain."

Graham leaned forward onto his desk and looped his fingers together. Gently, he said, "Molly, don't you remember our conversation?"

I frowned at him. "Conversation?"

Graham sighed and shook his head. "Molly, I can't keep doing this."

From the main body of the office, I could feel Ruth and Dean staring at me through the half-open blinds. "Doing what?"

Graham pursed his lips and tapped his fingers up and down on the table. "Molly, I'm sorry. We parted ways. I had to make arrangements; I can't run the business partially staffed." He stood up and gestured to the door. "Your replacement is due to start this morning. We've boxed up your things. They're by your desk."

For a moment, I stayed seated. I felt sick, as if the room was swaying from side to side. My hangover was still gripping my skull, and I was desperately trying to remember Graham's texts.

He cleared his throat and walked around to my side of the desk.

I stood up and he placed his hand on my back, guiding me towards the door. He stayed beside me all the way to my desk, as if I was a crazy person who might start trashing the place, then he handed me my box, and held the front door open.

"I am sorry, Molly. And I wish you the best of luck with... everything."

Gingerly, I stepped out onto the sidewalk and blinked up at the sun. Graham replaced me? Without even talking to me about it?

I was on the verge of caving in, collapsing into a heap of tears and running back home. But I couldn't. I had to keep going—for Colin. So, I climbed into my car, started the engine, and drove without really thinking about where I was going. This all started when Frank went missing, so perhaps the only way to figure out what was going on was to find out where the hell he was.

I'd spent most of the previous evening going over and over his disappearance in my head. Someone said they'd seen me near the hiking trail. Frank's bloody cap was in my dresser, and Colin had been afraid of me for weeks after it had happened.

But I still had absolutely no memory of where I was that day.

I'd gone over it and over it, but still couldn't remember. The only thing I knew for sure was that I wouldn't have hurt him. I had no reason to. And, no matter what I'd been through in the past, I'd never actually physically hurt anyone...

Eventually, I arrived at the hiking trail. I wasn't sure whether I'd meant to go there, or if it had happened by accident, but it seemed like as good a place to start as any. Perhaps something would jog my memory. Perhaps I had been there; perhaps I'd been looking for Frank and Colin, couldn't find them, and went home.

I climbed out of the car and pulled a baseball cap onto my head. I reached back to loop my ponytail through the hole at the back, forgetting that my hair was no longer there. Then, watching every footstep as if I might see something that revealed the truth about what happened, I walked slowly towards the spot where Colin had been found.

Bryan had described it to me; right by the big signpost with a map of the hiking trails, between two tall, twisty trees. When I reached the spot, I crouched down and looked up. None of it seemed familiar. I examined the sign, the trees, tried closing my eyes and picturing Colin and Frank walking side-by-side...

Nothing. It didn't trigger a single thing.

With heavy legs, I trudged back to the car and climbed in. I sat back and closed my eyes. Okay, so if I didn't remember being there, then I needed to assume that I never was. And if I wasn't, then I was back to my original theory; that someone was messing with me. Someone else had attacked Frank and was trying to make it look like I was involved.

I opened my eyes and put my hands on the steering wheel. "Kathy," I whispered under my breath, "Let's start with Kathy."

As I drove into Kathy and Frank's neighborhood, I slowed down, watching carefully at the cars that passed, trying to recognize the one that had been at the spa, with the driver who looked just like Frank.

I was drawing closer to Kathy's house when I did a double take. There on the sidewalk, coming out of one of the houses, was Susan.

Quickly, I pulled up on the opposite side of the road then, waving, jogged over to her.

When Susan saw me, her eyes widened, and she stepped back as if I were about to start accusing her of sleeping with my husband. "Molly," she said, glancing at the realtor standing beside her. "What are you doing here?"

"My in-laws live nearby."

Susan nodded and folded her arms uncomfortably in front of her chest. "I see."

"So," I said, trying to smile but watching her closely, "you found a place?" I glanced sideways at the agent beside her. I recognized him. Sneaky bastard, stealing my client when she was technically still on my books.

Susan cleared her throat and nodded. "I did. Yes." Then she stepped forward and said, "Molly, is everything okay? Bryan told me what happened when he got home. I'm so sorry…"

I sucked in my cheeks. "He told you?" I leaned in, close to her face. "Why is it that you're in such close contact with my husband?"

Susan's eyes widened, and she glanced at the agent. "I…"

He stepped in and smiled, taking Susan's arm. "I think it's probably time for us to go sign that contract now." He looked at me and nodded. "Molly, nice to see you."

"Just one moment." Susan gestured for him to go back inside without her, and he raised his eyes as if to ask, *Are you sure?* Susan nodded and repeated the gesture. Then she turned to me. "Molly,

I'm not sure what's going on. But if you could use someone to talk to…"

I gritted my teeth.

"I know what it's like to lose something. I can't imagine how you must feel—being without your son." She was so close that I could feel her breath on my cheek, and she was looking me straight in the eyes. "When my sister's baby was taken, she was broken." Susan paused. "And if I *ever* found out who hurt her like that, I'd make them pay."

My mouth opened, but before I could speak, Susan shrugged and stepped back.

"I know it's not the same. You'll be back with Bryan and Colin soon, I'm sure of it. But me? I'll never see Tracy again."

I looked back at the car, desperate to leave.

"Did I ever show you a picture of her?" Susan was reaching into her purse. When she looked up at me, she was holding an old crumpled photograph. "Here." She handed it to me. "Wasn't she beautiful?"

I swallowed hard, examining the face of the woman in the picture. Could that be *my* Tracy? She was young, so young that it was hard to tell, and she was in elaborate fancy dress—a pink wig and large sunglasses. But it was possible. Definitely possible.

"That was her eighteenth birthday." Taking back the photograph, Susan smiled at me, then took out a cigarette and lit it. "Would you like to go for a coffee and chat?"

As she puffed smoke in my direction, I coughed and wafted it away, the familiar trickle of panic starting to run down my spine. "No.

225

Thank you." Part of me wanted to reach into her purse and snatch the photograph, take it away, and examine it up close. But another part wanted to run and get as far away from this woman as possible.

"Okay, well, you know where I am if you need a friend."

## 29

From Susan's house, I drove a couple of blocks then stopped. I'd started the day with a resolve to fix everything, and yet every step I took seemed to make things worse. I thought that by just trying hard, trying really hard, I'd figure out what was going on. But—I picked up my phone and returned to the messages from Graham—I was still forgetting things. Huge chunks of time. Things were happening that I had no explanation for.

I sighed and gripped the steering wheel; I couldn't trust myself. I couldn't trust my own mind. So, I took out my phone and dialed the one person I had left—Carol.

"Hello?" She sounded pissed.

"It's me." My voice was shaky.

"I called around this morning. You didn't answer the door."

"I know. I'm sorry."

"Bryan told me what happened. He called me last night. You told him I was sitting with Colin?"

I breathed in and pinched the bridge of my nose. "Yes, I did."

"Well, I wasn't. So, who was?" Carol's voice was clipped and irritated.

"No one," I said quietly.

For a moment, Carol didn't speak. Then she sighed and muttered, "Jesus, Molly. You left him alone?"

"Carol, please. I need help. I feel like I'm going mad, but a bigger part of me thinks I'm not."

"I'm sorry, Molly, but first of all, have you noticed that you only ever call me when *you* need something? And second of all, I don't know what you're trying to say. What's going on?"

I let out a frustrated groan. Was she right? Did I only pick up then phone when I needed something from her? "Carol, I'm sorry. But I think someone's messing with me. Things keep happening, things I don't remember afterwards."

"Like what?"

"Like Graham says we had a conversation… a conversation that led to me being *fired*, but I don't remember it."

"Molly?" Carol was audibly shocked. "You got fired?"

"Yes. No. I don't know." It was too much. Tears started to fall, and I buried my head in my hands.

"Listen, if you think there was a misunderstanding, call him. And as for the other stuff—we need to talk properly. I'll come over tonight. Okay? We'll talk it through."

Shakily, I nodded. "Really?"

"Yes. Really." Carol sounded annoyed, but that didn't matter. If I could just sit down with someone and go through it all, I might find some answers.

"Thank you."

"I'll see you later."

Hanging up the phone, I held it in my hands and stared at it. Then I took a deep breath and called Graham After three rings, he picked up, but he didn't sound happy about it.

"Molly?"

"Graham, listen, I'm not going to make trouble. I just need to ask you... when you fired me, was it on the phone? Because I don't remember..."

There was a pause, then Graham replied, "Molly, I didn't fire you. You texted me and said you were going through a hard time. I said we could try to think of something. But you quit."

"Quit?"

"Yes."

"By text?"

"Yes."

"Okay. Thank you."

I hung up. Graham was still talking, but I'd heard everything I needed to.

Opening up my messages again, I scrolled through the entire list. There was nothing from Graham. I bit the corner of my lip. Then navigated to Google and typed *Retrieve deleted messages.*

---

Back home, I opened up my laptop, plugged in my phone, and followed the Google instructions to reset it from its last backup. It was set to automatically back up every night, so I should be able to just pick a date and go back in time.

Graham said we texted on Thursday, so I chose the date from the list of backups, then waited while my phone turned itself off then on again.

This time, when I opened up my messages, they were different. Right there, at the top, was a conversation with Graham.

Nervously, I pressed it with my thumb. And, just as he'd said, there it was… messages from me saying that I quit.

I narrowed my eyes at it.

I stared at the date. Thursday. Where had I been that day? What had I been doing?

Walking aimlessly to the kitchen with my phone clutched in my hand, I filled the kettle and put it on the stove then leaned back against the countertop. Then it hit me—that was the night I drove to McDonald's. The night I found Frank's baseball cap in my drawer. The night I ran into Susan...

My hand flew to my mouth, stifling a gasp. She could have gotten hold of my phone. I reeled back over my memories of the evening. We'd talked beside our cars. She'd mentioned Tracy and then she'd left. No, I'd left. Did she have a chance to sneakily send texts from my phone? Looking down, I examined the times. Late. Eleven forty-five. I was sleeping then. I was definitely sleeping.

A violent shiver shook my arms and legs, and I gripped the side of the counter. Susan *had* to be connected to what was going on, and to Tracy. And if all this started when Frank disappeared, then she was probably connected to that too.

With a dry mouth and a tight throat, I poured myself a cup of black coffee, piled in three large spoonfuls of sugar, and texted Carol.

*Are you still coming over tonight? Really need to talk. I can order takeout?*

Carol replied almost straight away. *Sure. Seven?*

I told her *Okay*, then took my coffee and my phone back to my laptop.

Paranoid that the messages between Graham and I would mysteriously disappear, I printed them out, three copies. I put one in my desk drawer, one in a pale blue folder, and shoved one into my handbag.

Then I Googled Susan's name. *Susan Carmichael*. Nothing. I navigated to Bryan's salesroom's website and scrolled through the staff pages. She wasn't there. But they were always slow to update things. I tapped my fingers impatiently on the desk. Where did Susan say she'd lived before moving back to town? My head was fuzzy. I tried to recall our first meeting, but all I could remember was the way I felt when I saw her—like I was looking at a reincarnation of Tracy. Different. But the same.

Finally, I gave up. Susan Carmichael—at least, this Susan Carmichael—didn't exist in Maine.

I went to the kitchen and made another coffee, limping slightly as my ankle began to throb. When I returned to the computer, instead of typing in Susan's name, I tried Tracy's. *Tracy Williams—Maine.* As always, nothing came up. *Tracy Williams, Rhode Island.* Nothing there either. Two social media accounts, but both old women in their sixties who were clearly *not* the Tracy I was looking for. I tried Andy's name too, even though I had no idea what he looked like. I tried the name of Tracy's store, to see if she'd opened one in a different city or state. But still, there was nothing that fit the couple who I had promised a baby.

I swallowed hard and rubbed at the back of my neck. The fine hairs at the base of my skull had already grown a little and were more prickly than before. My fingers lingered above the keyboard. Momentarily, I thought about slamming the lid shut and walking away. But I had to try.

*Tracy Williams. Rhode Island. Car accident.*

And there it was. Top of the page. A local news headline.

My palms were sweating. I reached for my coffee but couldn't bring myself to drink it. Finally, I clicked. And a big, bright, shining image of Tracy sprang up in front of me. My eyes were frozen on her face. Eventually, I tore them away and scanned the words below.

*Tragic accident... late at night... raining... dark... lost control of her car.*

Again, I looked at her photograph. She was standing outside some-where, maybe a park. There were trees in the background, and someone's arm was looped around her shoulder. A woman's arm. But whoever it was had been cropped out.

———

By 6 p.m., my eyes were sore and my back was aching from sitting at the laptop all day. I'd printed out everything I could find to do with Tracy and Susan, and had scrawled a timeline of events on one of Colin's large pieces of drawing paper.

Now, the timeline sat in the center of the dining table. Beside it, my blue folder of printouts about Susan. I stood back, resting my hands in the groove at the base of my spine and rocking from side-to-side to ease the ache.

If I was going to persuade people that Susan was up to something, and that I wasn't simply losing my mind, I needed to be methodi-cal. I needed to present them with hard evidence. If I told Bryan that his new colleague was an infiltrator from my old life, that she'd hacked my phone, texted my boss, deleted messages, and conspired to make me look crazy, he would probably turn his back on me forever.

But if I presented him with proof—if he could see the pieces for himself—then he'd finally believe me. He'd have to.

In the hallway, I called the local Italian restaurant and ordered mine and Carol's favorite dishes. Then I waited impatiently in the hallway for her to arrive.

At seven, bang on time, her noisy old station wagon pulled up outside. Peering through the peephole in the door, I saw her pause, smooth her clothes, and take a deep breath—as if she was preparing herself for something she didn't really want to be doing.

I opened the door before she had a chance to ring the bell and threw my arms around her.

"Thank you for coming." I squeezed tightly, and Carol patted my back—just between my shoulder blades.

When she stood back, she frowned at me but then corrected herself and tried to smile. "Molly, are you okay?"

Tucking my too-short hair behind my ear, I stood back and gestured for her to come inside. I felt jittery and nervous as I waited for her to hang her purse and jacket on the hook near the door.

"I ordered food. It'll be here soon."

Carol nodded. She was still looking at me strangely, so I suggested we head through to the living room. "Wine?"

Carol folded her arms in front of her chest. "Maybe we should stick with coffee?"

I laughed, a little too loudly. "It's okay. I can have one glass without losing my shit." I walked to the kitchen and took two large glasses from the cupboard beside the sink. I'd have one glass. Just one. When I turned back, Carol was standing beside the dining table peering at the large piece of drawing paper that was covered in my scrawled, hurried handwriting.

"Molly?" She looked up at me. "What is this?"

Shaking my head, I passed over her wineglass and gestured to the folder and the timeline that I'd spent all day putting together. "It's evidence."

"Evidence?" Carol was biting her lower lip.

"I called Graham. Like you told me to." I leaned in and lowered my voice. "It turns out, I quit. Apparently, I texted him and told him I didn't want the job anymore."

Carol breathed in sharply and sipped her wine. "Molly. Really? You quit?"

"That's just it. I didn't."

"I'm sorry, I don't understand."

"It wasn't me; it was—" I was about to launch into the story of Susan and Tracy when the doorbell rang. I smiled. "That'll be the food."

# 30

When I returned to the living room, Carol was sitting on the couch and had put her wineglass down on the coffee table. She smiled as I handed her the bag of takeout, then began to pile her spaghetti into one of the bowls that I'd already set out.

As we began to eat, I caught her looking up at me, and beyond me to the table. Eventually, she sat back, balanced her bowl in her lap, and said purposefully, "Molly, what's going on?"

Wiping my mouth with the back of my hand, I hurriedly chewed and swallowed my mouthful of pasta. Carol was the only one who knew the truth about Tracy. She was the only one who knew what I did. So, if anyone was going to believe me, surely it would be her.

Lowering my voice, even though there was no one else there to hear us, I nudged closer and set my bowl down on the coffee table. "Do you remember Tracy?"

"The woman who was supposed to adopt Colin?" Carol whispered, clearly shocked because I had forbidden her from ever talking about what happened. "Of course, how could I forget?"

"Well, a couple of weeks ago, a woman showed up. She looked creepily similar to Tracy, but I didn't think anything of it. She came to my office, said she was moving back to town and wanted help finding somewhere to live."

Carol was watching me carefully and had stopped eating.

"I saw her a couple of times. The second time she mentioned that she'd had a sister called Tracy who *died*."

Carol swallowed hard. "Okay. But..."

"No, no, no. Wait." I shook my head and waved my hands at her. "Her sister Tracy—she died when she was trying to hunt down the woman who had run away with her son. The *surrogate* who'd run away with her son."

For a moment, Carol didn't move. But then she sat back against the couch cushions and, under her breath, said, "Shit."

"Right? I kept telling myself it had to be a coincidence. But how could it be? And the thing is, Susan showed up right around the time Frank went missing. Right around the time my whole life started to fall apart." I was speaking loudly, gesticulating too much, but I was desperate to make Carol see what I was seeing. "I mean, I thought I was imagining it. People following me. Her resemblance to Tracy. But—"

"So, you think that Susan—"

"I think she's messing with me. I think she tracked me down, and she knows my history, and she's been playing games to try to drive me insane. For revenge."

Carol's face creased into something resembling a wince, as if I'd suddenly gone too far.

I got up and grabbed my folder from the table. "Here. Look. This is everything I've found out about her. But the most important thing is..." I took out the sheet of text messages between Graham and I. "The night I was supposed to have sent these messages to Graham quitting my job? I was asleep. It couldn't have been me. I ran into Susan late. I'd been to McDonald's and—" I shook my head. "That's not important. What's important is that she could have sent them." I paused and widened my eyes. "She must have sent them then *deleted* them."

Carol took the piece of paper from me and narrowed her eyes at the messages. "Molly, how did she send them? Did she take your phone? And if she deleted them, how do you have them now?"

"My phone backs up automatically every night. She must have deleted them after they were backed up. I restored it and BOOM, there they were." I was standing in front of Carol with my arms folded, waiting for her to stand up and shout, *Jesus, you're right. She's out to get you. What do we do?!* But she didn't.

Slowly, Carol got up and went over to the table. She put down the printout of texts that I didn't send and leaned forward to look at the timetable I'd written out. When she looked back at me, she spoke softly and gently. "So, you think that Susan came here to get revenge for what happened to her sister? And..." Carol waved at the giant sheet of paper. "And Frank's disappearance was part of that?"

238

I paused. I was tapping my foot. I pinched the bridge of my nose. "I'm not sure. That's where it gets murky. Maybe it's totally unconnected, but Susan found out about it and decided to try to frame me? Maybe she's the one who called the police and said she'd seen me there?"

Carol nodded and made a *mmm* sound at the back of her throat. "But, Molly, the compulsive lying. Leaving Colin alone? Accusing Bryan of having an affair?"

"With Susan! An affair with Susan!"

"What?" Carol was frowning at me.

"*Susan* was the woman Bryan met at the restaurant last night. Apparently, she works at the dealership with him now. I mean, come on, Carol. Surely, you can see that something about this *stinks*. It's not just me."

"No. It's not. Of course not. But, Molly, you've been lying again. To all of us. And a few days ago, you thought it was Kathy who was conspiring against you. Perhaps..." Carol sighed and shook her head. "Perhaps Susan came here to confront you. But perhaps she doesn't have a clue who you are, and all this is just..."

"What?" My voice came out sharper and more clipped than I'd intended. "All in my head?"

"I didn't say that. I just think that maybe we should talk this through with someone."

"Exactly. So do I. First thing tomorrow, I'm taking this to the police."

"The police?" Carol's eyes widened. "Molly, I'm not sure that's a good idea."

"I have evidence, Carol."

Carol paused, sighed, bit her lip, then took a step towards me and gripped my upper arms. "Molly, what you have here is not evidence. The fact the messages were deleted doesn't mean that Susan sent them. I mean, think about it, how would she even get hold of your phone for long enough to have a conversation with Graham? And I thought you said your phone backs up every night? Did she keep your phone overnight? Send the texts, go to sleep, delete them in the morning and then sneak your phone back into the house... all without you noticing?"

Carol was watching me closely. I could feel my mouth hanging open, and I was desperately trying to slow my brain down enough to take in what she was saying. "She still could have..." I trailed off and looked down at my hands.

"Molly," Carol said slowly, "what you've got here is some print-outs of people called Susan Carmichael and Tracy Williams who have *nothing* to do with the two women we're talking about, an article about a horrible road accident, and a list of muddled-up dates written in a child's crayon."

I flinched. I looked at the table and stared at the dates. They looked muddled because I'd written notes beside them, but it was all there. It all made complete sense if you just read it properly. "But the woman in the article is *my* Tracy. Just like Susan said..." My voice came out tiny and childlike.

"Let's call someone. A therapist. Maybe they can help you sort through all of this."

I blinked several times without speaking. Carol's usually harsh features had softened.

"Molly, are you taking your medication?"

I let out a *pah!* Sound and waved my hands in the air. "Seriously? You don't believe me? After everything I've just told you. You honestly think it's a coincidence that Susan showed up at exactly the same time all this started to happen?"

"Honestly?" Carol's eyes were glistening, and she was struggling to look at me. "Right now, Molly, I don't know whether I believe that Susan even exists."

I stumbled backwards as if Carol had physically punched me in the gut. "How can you say that?"

Carol was holding out her hands like she was trying to coax me out of a trap. "Molly, you know what happened after Jack died. You—"

"Yes! You're right. I fell apart. I saw him everywhere. His ghost. Haunting me. Every single day for weeks and months." I was yelling and tears were streaming down my face. Carol was crying too. "But this isn't the same thing, Carol. This is different."

"Is it?" Carol ducked her head to catch my eyes. "Is it really?"

---

It was raining. Huge, plump droplets were snaking their way down the window pane and settling in the rivets at the bottom of the frame. I pressed my hand to the glass. It was cold. Looking past my fingers, suddenly, the sky began to clear. Sunlight burst through the clouds and flooded the garden.

Wiping away the condensation, I began to smile. There he was.

"Jack!"

He looked up from the swing beneath the big old oak tree and grinned at me. Even from where I was standing, I could see the sparkle in his deep brown eyes and the freckles across the bridge of his nose. He gestured for me to join him. My feet were bare, but I didn't bother to search for shoes.

As I moved through the house, it was like I was walking through a bright white tunnel. A whooshing noise filled my ears and as I turned my head, nothing was in focus. All I could see was Jack.

Out on the decking, a splinter pierced the skin of my heel, but I ignored it. I started to run. When I reached the tree, Jack stood up, and I flung my arms around him. He picked me up, kissed me, and set me down on the swing. Standing behind me, he began to push.

As I stretched out my legs, blood began to drip from my foot. I pointed at it, but Jack just laughed and kept pushing me. Soon, I was flying through the air. As I swung backwards and forwards, my long red braids whipped across my face. I looked down at the ground. A puddle of blood was pooling beneath me and with each swing it got wider and deeper. I shouted for Jack to stop.

"Why?" he called. "We're having such fun."

"My foot, Jack, my foot." There was panic in my voice.

Finally, he tugged on the metal chains and I slowed to a stop. Stepping in front of me, he leaned in and playfully nibbled the end of my nose. "What's up, little rabbit?"

"My foot," I whispered. But when I looked down, the blood was gone. Laughter bubbled up into my chest.

"Silly old thing," Jack chided, reaching out a hand. "Come on. Follow me."

"Where are we going?"

Already tugging me across the lawn, Jack turned and held his index finger to the side of his nose. "You'll see."

As we trotted towards the house, Jack's grip tightened around my fingers and my heart began to flutter. But then, instead of going up the steps to the back door, he pointed down. At our feet was a small dirty window, half obscured by grass.

"No, Jack. I don't like it down there."

"It's just a spooky old cellar, Mol. Nothing to be afraid of."

I pulled on his hand. "Please, let's go back." But my voice was too small, and Jack was already leaning down to open the window. Gently at first, he pressed it. But it didn't move. So, pulling his sleeve down over his hand, he thrust his fist through the middle of it. The noise of splintering glass filled my ears. "Jack, don't."

"Come on, Molly." He was climbing through, beckoning me to follow him. For a moment, I couldn't move. But when I turned to look at the swing, the sunshine was gone and dark clouds were swirling in the sky, threatening to bring back the rain.

My bare feet landed with a slap on the cold concrete floor of the cellar and I winced, expecting to feel shards of glass from the broken window. I wriggled my toes. Nothing.

In the darkness, I heard Jack fumbling in his pockets. And then the sharp scratch of a match being lit. Jack turned and held it in front of him. I looked down. Again, there was blood beneath my feet. But still no glass.

"Jack," I whispered.

"Molly," he whispered back.

When I looked up, his face was pale. "I think I hurt my hand," he said, then staggered, swaying, and dropped the match.

"Jack?" I shouted into the darkness. Dropping to my hands and knees, I snaked my fingers across the floor, through hot sticky wetness, over Jack's feet and legs, until finally I found the match-box. With trembling hands, I opened it and after one, two, three tries managed to light a match.

Turning to Jack, I slammed my hand over my mouth and stifled a scream. There was blood. Too much blood. I threw the match to the floor, but it stayed alight. I grabbed Jack's hands in mine, pushed his sleeves up... and this time I couldn't stop the scream that came. It tore through my bones and ricocheted off the cellar walls. And by the time it stopped, he was gone.

I put my bloodied hands on Jack's face and begged him to wake up. I shook him, trying not to look at the deep vertical gashes on his wrists. But he didn't move.

"Jack, please. Don't leave me. Don't leave me here."

After a long time, I sat back and wrapped my arms around my knees. Burying my head, I began to rock backwards and forwards.

*Five, four, three, two, one.*

*Wake up, Molly. Wake up.*

# 31

When the nightmare ended, I held my eyes shut and tried to breathe. My entire body was shaking, and I was covered in a film of cold nighttime sweat. The bedsheets were bunched between my fists. If Bryan had been there, he would have woken me, and I wouldn't have seen it. But he was gone. And so, the whole gory theater had—for the first time in so many years—played itself out the way it had every single night for countless nights after Jack's death.

Finally, terrified that somehow I'd be back there in the cellar, I opened my eyes and reached for the lamp beside the bed. As light filled our large, cream, neatly decorated bedroom, I released my grip on the sheets and sat up. I was on Bryan's side of the bed—a habit I'd picked up since he left—and as always, it was disorientating.

Standing up, I threw open the drapes and unlatched the window. Cold air trickled in, calming my red-hot cheeks. Downstairs, the remnants of my investigations into Susan and Tracy were still scattered across the floor. After throwing Carol out, I went through them again. And again. And again. Until my eyes were so sore they could barely see any more.

And I drank. A lot.

By the bed, an empty bottle of red wine had leaked droplets onto the cream carpet that Bryan took so much pride in keeping spotless. In a daze, I went to the bathroom, fetched some stain remover, and began to scrub. Then I went downstairs and threw the bottle in the trash. It clinked merrily as it made contact with another. But remembering how much I'd consumed brought a rush of nausea to my throat.

I stood there, swaying on my tired, still-drunk legs. And then I rushed to the bathroom, braced my hands on the shiny porcelain sides of the toilet, and made myself hurl up every last ounce of alcohol that I'd consumed that evening.

Staggering back from the sink, I wiped my mouth with the back of my hand and shuddered. The family bathroom was large with bright blue tiles on the walls. It had always been the coldest room in the house, so whenever Colin had a bath, I made sure to warm his towel on the radiator in the hall. Now, it was hanging neatly on the hook behind the door—pale gray with whales and flamingos and sandcastles on it.

I reached for it and as I walked back to the bedroom, I patted it across my forehead, then my lips, then my hands. In mine and Bryan's too-quiet room, desperate to fall back into bed and close my eyes, I grabbed the tumbler from my dressing table and turned to go fill it with water.

But then I stopped stock still. I was standing in front of the wardrobe. And its full-length mirrored doors projected back a ghost. My hair was shorter. But the rest… it was how I used to look. When Colin was a baby. Before Bryan found me and saved me from myself.

I stepped closer and raised my hand to my face. Still clutching Colin's bath towel, I was wearing black underwear and a gray vest top with an ugly red wine stain on the front of it. From beneath the bottom edge of the vest, my hip bones protruded more sharply than normal. My face was gray at the edges, its skin stretched tight across my cheekbones. I reached up to touch my hair and heard a sob escape from my lips.

*What the fuck happened to you, Molly? What the fuck happened?*

---

Three days later, pulling up in front of Kathy and Frank's house, I straightened my shirt then checked my reflection in the rearview mirror. I'd managed to cover the gray shadows beneath my eyes with concealer, and I'd washed my hair that morning.

I was wearing a smattering of makeup, a new perfume—nothing like the one I used to wear—and clothes that were smart but casual.

After my dream about Jack, I'd spent the following twenty-four hours in meltdown. I'd ignored Carol's calls, ignored Bryan's calls, ignored everything. I had paced up and down, read through my reams of paper, torn up my timeline and rewritten it. And finally, when I was certain—absolutely one hundred percent certain—that I wasn't making it all up, a sense of calm had settled over me.

It didn't matter if Carol believed me. It didn't matter if she thought I was having some kind of breakdown. I knew, deep in my heart, that I was right about Susan. Something was going on. But I hadn't forgotten about Kathy *or* the man who looked exactly like my father-in-law who'd dropped her off at the spa that day.

So, in an effort to prove to Bryan that I was doing *okay*—and so that I could, once and for all, get to the bottom of whether Kathy was involved in plotting my downfall, I had arranged to go over to her house for coffee and a supervised visit with Colin.

The fact that Kathy and Bryan were insisting I was supervised with my own son made my blood boil and my jaw clench so tight that my teeth started to grate. But the alternative—that Bryan would walk away from me and take Colin with him—was not an option.

Stepping out of the car and plastering my best "I'm fine" smile on my face, I walked up to Kathy's shiny front door with, what I hoped was, an energetic bounce in my step. After knocking, I stood back and allowed my hands to linger at my sides. For a moment, I left them there. But then I raised them and crossed my arms before putting them back where they were and trying to ignore how awkward I felt.

Probably deliberately, Kathy took a long time to answer. When she did, she smiled thinly at me and waved me inside without any of her usual pleasantries.

"Kathy, thank you for doing this," I said, unsure whether I should shake her hand, hug her, or just stand there.

"Of course. Colin will be pleased to see you."

"Is he here?" My heart fluttered in my chest as I looked through the open doorways that led off from Kathy's large, shiny entrance hall.

"He's in the garden. Shall we head out?"

"Sure." I nodded, trying not to look too desperate. But as we passed through the large French doors and onto Kathy's immaculate patio out back, I was unable to control myself; I shrieked, rushed forward, and wrapped Colin in my arms. He smelled so good. His hair, his skin, his clothes. They all smelled familiar, and as I pulled him close and felt his small body fold into mine, tears sprang to my eyes. "Oh, baby boy. I missed you," I whispered, breathing in his scent.

For a moment, Colin was stiff and unresponsive. But then, finally, he hugged me back. "Missed you too, Mommy."

When I sat back, he was crying too and, although I hated to see him upset, a part of me felt like doing cartwheels; if he missed me, he wouldn't let Bryan take him away. If he missed me, it was only a matter of time before we were all back together.

Behind me, Kathy was watching us with a narrow stare. Her arms were folded in front of her chest. She was wearing a smart pencil skirt and a pale pink blouse, and she looked unnaturally smooth-faced. "Will you two be alright while I go make coffee?" She glanced back at the house. Perhaps she was considering calling for Bryan.

I followed her gaze. At first, I'd been so taken up with the idea of seeing Colin that I'd almost forgotten about Bryan. But now, suddenly, the knowledge that he was in the house somewhere and hadn't come out to see me yet made my heart hurt. Trying to maintain my smile, I sat down in the sandpit beside Colin and told Kathy we'd be just fine. "You can watch us from the window," I offered, without a hint of irony or sarcasm.

Kathy nodded briskly and went inside to make the drinks, returning before I'd managed to coax any real conversation out of my son. "Molly," she called, sitting down in a large wooden chair on the patio and gesturing for me to join her. "Coffee."

"Be back in a minute," I said to Colin, kissing the top of his head. He smiled, and I felt him watching me as I walked over to sit with his grandmother. Taking the coffee from Kathy, I wrapped my fingers around the mug and smiled at her. "Thank you for this."

Kathy nodded, sipped her own drink, and waved a finger towards Colin. "He's been doing remarkably well, despite all the upheaval."

"Yes. He looks well. Thank you, Kathy."

I caught Kathy blinking at me slowly, as if she was surprised I'd offered her any thanks. With pursed lips, she gave the tiniest nod and said simply, "I'd do anything for Colin. You know that."

For a moment, neither of us spoke. But then, eventually, I managed to work up the courage to say, "Has there been any news?"

Kathy swallowed hard but managed to keep her expression neutral. "No. There hasn't."

"The police…" I was choosing my words carefully, trying to show concern but not raise Kathy's heckles.

"The police are useless. They say that soon they'll have to downgrade the search. Not enough evidence, something like that." Kathy sniffed loudly and took a tissue from her sleeve. Gently, she dabbed it at her nostrils then tucked it back where it had come from and continued to drink her coffee—conversation over.

Trying not to let my mouth twitch into a smile at the knowledge that Detective Monroe had gotten no further with his witch hunt, I changed the subject. "Is Bryan here?"

Kathy didn't look at me; she just stared straight ahead at Colin, who was lining up his diggers and tractors in the sandpit. "Yes, he's here."

I looked up towards the guest room that Bryan and I had stayed in a couple of times in the past. Was he there? Was he watching me? The idea of it made me blush a little, and I crossed my legs at the ankles; if he *was* watching, I wanted him to see me being polite to his mother, attentive to Colin, smiling, acting like my old self.

"He thinks it's best if you two maintain some distance for a while. But he's happy for you to keep seeing Colin," Kathy waved her hands at the garden, "like this. With me."

I swallowed hard. Kathy would be waiting for me to react, for my voice to raise in pitch, and for my cheeks to become flame red with anger. But I pushed it down. I pushed down the urge to yell at her and instead I said, "I understand. I have a lot to prove to him."

Setting down her coffee cup on the small table beside her, Kathy laced her fingers together in her lap. "Have you given any more thought to the idea of speaking with Robert? I know Bryan raised the issue with you before he left."

If Kathy was trying to push all my buttons, it was working. The idea that Bryan had discussed me needing psychiatric help made me want to upend the table and send her coffee flying all over her pristine pink blouse. But I didn't. "I've thought about it, yes." I shuffled in my chair and waved at Colin as he looked in my direction. Then, putting my coffee cup down beside Kathy's, I angled myself towards her and said, "Kathy, I was wondering whether you and I could take a walk together? Being completely honest, I need someone to talk to, and I don't feel comfortable doing it when Colin is close by."

As Kathy scrutinized my face, I held my nerve. I waited, with wide eyes, until finally she nodded and said, "Alright. I'll ask Bryan to watch Colin. It's probably best if you wait out front."

---

When Kathy finally joined me on the driveway, she had changed into flat walking pumps and was wearing a ridiculously large pair of sunglasses. Stepping into line beside me, she remained silent. Further down the street, just as we were about to reach the crossroads, Kathy began to veer right. A small pathway led between some trees and down towards the local park. But I stopped and waved at the crossroads. "I thought we could go around the block."

Kathy looked in the direction of the park. If I could read minds, I'd have put bets on the fact that she was wondering what the hell I was up to. But instead of objecting, she shrugged, waved at the sidewalk ahead of us, and said, "As you wish."

We were about half a block away from Susan's house when Kathy said—from the corner of her mouth— "So, what is all this about, Molly?"

Without breaking my stride, I tipped my head at her and smiled. "About?"

"You said you wanted to talk to me away from the house. So..."

I hadn't actually thought that far ahead. I'd simply wanted an excuse to get her out of the house and, ironically, for once I was struggling to think on my feet. I was about to mutter something about wanting her advice about what I could do to get Bryan back, when finally we reached my *real* reason for asking Kathy on a walk—Susan's house. The one she'd rented from a realtor who *wasn't* me. The one that, coincidentally, was just a few minutes' walk from my in-law's house. The house where Bryan was now living.

Stopping and looking up at it, I smiled. "Lovely, isn't it?"

Kathy paused beside me, looking distinctly like someone who did *not* want to stop and admire the scenery. "It's a nice house, yes."

"One of my clients lives here."

"Really?" Kathy removed her sunglasses and began to chew the tip of them.

I walked forward. "It's lovely. Do you want to take a look?"

Kathy laughed nervously. "A look? Molly, this is someone's home."

"Oh, but Susan is such a doll. She won't mind if we take a look around. The backyard is great. Come on..." I gestured for Kathy to follow me. As we approached the passage that led down the side of Susan's property, I looked back. Was Kathy resisting because it was an odd thing to go snooping around someone else's house? Or was I right? Was she resisting because she knew exactly who lived here and was worried that I was finally on to them?

With a fizz of adrenaline in my chest, I stepped into the passage and strode towards the garden. Behind me, Kathy called, "Molly, I'm not comfortable with this. Come back."

I was almost in the garden, picturing whirling around and demanding that Kathy tell me the truth about her obvious connection to Susan, when something caught my eye—movement. Something had moved. There, beside the shed.

I stopped, reaching out to brace my hand on the wall beside me. I narrowed my eyes, then let out a small muffled screech—there, by the shed, was a silhouette. A man's silhouette.

Whirling around, I ran back down the passage and stumbled out onto the grass. I stopped. Kathy was no longer there. I stepped forward, heart beating fast, and stood on the sidewalk. I looked up and down the street. But she was gone.

---

I caught up with Kathy just a few houses down from hers. She was walking briskly with her arms swinging by her side and her neatly styled hair bobbing up and down. When she heard me running to catch up with her, she rolled her eyes and snapped, "Really, Molly. I don't know what that was about, but it was *highly* unprofessional. You don't take people to your clients' houses. It's just..." She looked at me, offered an exasperated frown, then trailed off.

"I know. I'm sorry, I was just trying to show you that I'm doing better. That I helped a client find a lovely house. That's all." I smiled shakily, trying to convince myself that what I was saying was true so that it would sound more convincing.

We had reached Kathy's house. She stopped beside my car and, for a moment, I thought she was going to suggest I get in and go home. But instead she sighed, looked up at her front door, and said, "Listen, I know that you and I haven't always seen eye to eye. But my son loves you and..." She paused, as if what she was about to say was physically hard for her. "And despite everything, on the whole, you've been a good mother to Colin."

I opened my mouth to reply, but Kathy waved her hand at me.

"Come in and we'll finish our talk."

# 32

Sitting on a stool at the granite-topped island in the middle of Kathy's sparkling kitchen, I watched her take the cake she'd made out of a tin and place it on a stand. Ceremoniously, she brought it over to me, cut us each a slice and lifted them onto small china plates. Then she handed me a cake fork and poured two cups of tea.

Instead of sitting down, she stood opposite me and broke off a piece of cake with the tip of her fork. "It's almond," she said. "You're okay with almonds, aren't you?"

I studied her face but she seemed sincere. "I'm fine with almonds, Kathy. Thank you for checking." I paused, my fork lingering above the peaks of the creamy-looking frosting.

"You know…" She was raising her cup to her lips, sticking out her little finger the way she always did. "I think, Molly, that you should just go ahead and say whatever it is you've been wanting to say. There's clearly something on your mind. Is it Bryan? Are you hoping I'll step in and convince him to move back home?" She sipped her tea, watching me over the rim of the cup.

I put down my fork and let my elbows rest on the cool granite top. "It's not Bryan." Then I breathed in deeply and said, "I actually wanted to ask about Frank."

Kathy put her teacup down and folded her arms. "There's been no news, you know that, Molly. You already asked me."

"I know. But that's not what I wanted to ask about." I breathed in. This was it. As soon as I told her what I'd seen at the spa, I'd know from the look on her face whether it really had been him, whether this was all some kind of elaborate deception. "I saw you with him at the spa." I let the words slip out slowly and casually, picking up my fork and waving a bit-sized piece of cake as I spoke.

"The spa?" Kathy raised an eyebrow and laughed. "Well, yes, we've been to the spa together. I go once a month and Frank drives me."

"You're admitting it?" My eyes widened and my mouth fell open in surprise.

Again, Kathy laughed. "Why wouldn't I?"

"So, it was him? A few weeks ago?"

Kathy stopped laughing and frowned at me. "A few weeks ago?" Kathy started to speak more slowly, "Molly, a few weeks ago, Frank was missing. I hired a cab."

I rolled my eyes and leaned forward. "Come on, Kathy, I saw you. It wasn't a cab, it was an Audi. Just like the one Frank drives."

Kathy pursed her lips and shook her head at me. "Molly, are you seriously suggesting… what? That all of this—that Frank's disappearance is just one big game?"

I folded my arms, trying to interpret the look in her eyes. "Is it? I heard what you said to each other, the night of Colin's adoption. I heard what you said about me." My voice was getting louder and, despite knowing that Colin and Bryan were in the house somewhere and that I should be trying to stay calm, I couldn't stop myself. "You've always thought I wasn't good enough for Bryan. So, perhaps all this is—" I waved my hand in the air, searching for the word. "Well, I don't know what it's about. But I know something is going on. And I know what I saw at the spa. I saw Frank. And you. Together."

Kathy's expression had changed. Usually, I saw contempt or dislike or frustration when she looked at me. But now there was something different there. She looked… worried. "Molly," she said quietly, "Frank is *missing*. His car is sitting in our garage. Go check if you like. But either you're playing some kind of game, in which case I think it's very cruel of you to be doing this, or you're in far more need of help than I imagined."

"I saw you!" The words came out loudly, a shout verging on a scream. "I saw you, Kathy. Was Susan in on it? How does she fit in? Tell me, for fuck's sake!" I slammed my fork down then picked it up again."

"Molly, I have no idea who you're talking about. I don't know anyone called Susan. But the Audi that dropped me off at the spa was a private cab," she replied tentatively, looking past me into the hall as if she was wondering whether to call for Bryan. "But why were you at the spa? Were you following me, Molly? Because—"

"Forget it," I snapped. "I should have known you wouldn't admit to it." Gripping the counter with one hand, I used the other to shovel in the piece of cake that I'd been wafting around and waited for the sugar-hit to clear my head. Kathy was still watching me and looked like she might be about to go call Robert Davidson herself and beg him for help.

I cleared my throat. It was tight. I cleared it again, but it didn't help. A slow, creeping heat was spreading through my chest. I coughed. My breath caught and when I breathed in, I could barely suck in enough air to keep my head from going dizzy. Something wasn't right…

I stood up and waved my hands at my throat. Kathy was still watching me.

"Walnuts…" I spluttered, barely audible above my gasps for air.

Kathy's eyes widened. She shook her head, turned to the cupboard behind her and, in comically slow motion, moved things around until she found a bag of flour. She presented it to me, as if seeing the word "almond" on the packet would enable me to breathe again. "It's almond, Molly. You're fine. Unless you're allergic to almonds too?"

I stood up. The stool scraped against the tiled floor. I was gasping, and the room was starting to become hazy. Then I heard something… a voice. Colin's voice. "Mommy? Is Mommy okay?" He started to sob.

And then Bryan was there, grabbing hold of me. He'd handed Colin to Kathy and was asking me where my purse was.

"It's in the hallway," Kathy answered for me.

Bryan dashed to the hall and just seconds later, although it felt like hours, he was back. He guided me onto the stool and something sharp bit into my upper thigh. My EpiPen. He always made sure I had one with me.

"It's okay, Molly. It's okay." Bryan was cupping my face with his hands, staring into my eyes. He looked worried. My breath started to return to normal, but my heart was still beating ten to the dozen. He told Kathy to get me a glass of water, then told Colin that it was okay. I was okay.

"What happened?" he asked, as my breath returned and my shaking stopped.

I shook my head. I was looking down at my lap. But then Kathy muttered, "She needs help, Bryan. Psychological help," and I couldn't stop myself.

My eyes snapped upwards and, through gritted teeth, I yelled, "She tried to kill me! That's what happened! I was asking questions, questions she didn't like. She knows I'm getting close to the truth. She tried to poison me, Bryan." I turned to Bryan and gripped his forearms, willing him to see what I saw, willing him to see that this wasn't me having some kind of episode. It was real.

"Molly, please…" Bryan's eyes looked misty. He glanced at Colin, who was staring at me and nuzzling into his grandmother.

"Bryan, can't you see? It's her. It's all her." I paused. "Her and Susan. They're conspiring to—"

"Susan?" Bryan's expression crumpled, and he rubbed the bridge of his nose with his thumb and forefinger. "Jesus, Molly." He lowered his voice and stepped closer to me, looking deep into my eyes. "You need help, Molly. Please. Please listen to me."

For a moment, I didn't move. But then I let out a guffaw. A huge, loud, burst of a laugh, because there was so much energy inside me and so much frustration that I didn't know what else to do with it. "Bryan, why can't you see it?! Your mother is a psychopath. She's been hiding your father. You know that? I saw them together!"

Beside Kathy, Colin was crying. Big, salty tears were streaming down his cheeks, and he'd started to make gulping noises as he sobbed.

"Colin, honey, there's no need to cry." I tried to soothe him, but when his crying got worse, I gritted my teeth and raised my voice. "Seriously, Col. Stop crying! I'm the one who should be crying, because your grandma is trying to kill me, and your father has abandoned me."

Suddenly, Bryan's face changed. It set into something tight and angry, and he muttered to Kathy that she should take Colin upstairs and out of the way. As they left the room, he stepped back from me. His jaw was twitching. "Now, listen to me very carefully, Molly. All this…" He waved his hand at the discarded EpiPen. "Blaming my mother for what was *clearly* an accident. It's got to stop. It's more than just the lies now, and if you can't see that you need help, then I don't know what more I can do. If you don't do something—right now—today to prove to me that you're willing to talk to someone about what's going on, then I'll have no choice."

I frowned at him. My stomach felt heavy and my skin was cold. "No choice? What are you talking about?"

"I'm talking about a divorce, Molly. For Colin's sake. Because we can't carry on like this."

A few blocks away from Kathy's house, I pulled over and screamed at the top of my lungs. I screamed, and thumped the steering wheel, and let tears stream down my cheeks. I stayed there for over an hour. And then, finally, I picked up the phone.

"Dr. Davidson? Robert? I need to see you. It's Molly Burke."

"Molly? Hi. What seems to be—"

"I need you to tell me if I'm going crazy."

## 33

R obert Davidson extended his hand to shake mine. I let him grip my fingers tightly but couldn't return the gesture; it had taken every ounce of strength inside me to make it to his office.

"Can I offer you a drink? Coffee? Tea? Water?" He had ushered me in and was standing beside his neat black desk.

"Tea. Thank you." I swept my fingers through my hair, still surprised when it came to an end at the base of my skull. It was shiny and soft. I'd washed it that morning, styled it with a blow dryer and one of those big, round bristle brushes that hairdressers use. But it still didn't have the same finish to it that Skye at the salon had achieved. Instead, it looked like I'd simply woken up one day and decided to hack it off myself.

Dr. Davidson handed me an oddly square white mug and gestured for us to sit down. This time, as it was just the two of us, I chose the armchair.

"So, Molly…" He sipped his tea and wriggled his shoulders into the back of his chair as if we were friends sitting down for a catch up. "Why don't you start by telling me exactly what made you call the other day?" He waved his hand and took another sip of tea. "Take your time."

Crossing one leg over the other, I released a shaky breath. I was tapping my fingers on the side of my mug but when Dr. Davidson's eyes flickered towards them, I stopped. "Bryan threatened to divorce me."

I waited for a look of surprise or empathy to cross his face. But it didn't, he simply nodded and said, "I see."

"Since his father disappeared, I've been… struggling. The issues I had in the past seem to be—" I stopped short, unsure how to describe what had been happening.

"Resurfacing?" Robert said kindly.

I nodded. Tears sprang to my eyes, and I tried to blink them back. "I thought I was holding it together. But I'm not." And then there weren't just a few tears, there were floods. Floods and floods of them. Dr. Davidson took my mug, placed it gently on the coffee table, and handed me a packet of tissues. Then he sat and waited.

A few minutes later, eyes red and sore, nose dripping, I finally stopped.

"Talk me through what's been happening. From the beginning."

I sighed and looked up at the clock. Trying to muster a wry smile, I replied, "I'm not sure we have time."

"Well," he said, smiling back, "as much as you can."

I breathed in, crossed my legs the other way and reached down to rub at my ankle. "When Colin and Frank were attacked, I started to have bad dreams. The kind I haven't had in years. I thought someone was following me. I've been forgetting things, chunks of time, things I've done, things I've said." I was scratching at my ankle. I could feel my nails against the paper-thin skin. Soon, they would break through.

"Molly..." Robert Davidson reached out and put his hand over mine. "How did you hurt your ankle?"

I blinked at him. No one had ever asked me that question. Not even Bryan.

Picking up a light brown folder from the table beside him, Dr. Davidson leafed through it. "I've read your notes, Molly. I've read about everything you went through after Colin was born. Originally, they thought it was a form of postnatal depression but then diagnosed you with borderline personality disorder, is that right?"

I nodded, sitting on my hands so that I didn't return to the ankle injury.

"But you had a very specific fear, didn't you? A fear that seemed to trigger everything?"

Again, I nodded, weaker this time.

"You were scared that Colin would be taken from you."

*Five. Four. Three. Two. One.* "Yes."

"Can you tell me why that is, Molly?"

Looking at Robert Davidson, it was as if he knew. Only, how could he? No one knew. Even Detective Monroe hadn't managed to find out. "Because I took him from someone else."

———

At first, Robert's expression remained completely neutral. But then it darkened. He reached for his notepad and nodded gravely. "Molly, are you telling me that Colin is not your child?"

Almost springing up out of my chair, I waved my arms and shook my head. "No. It's not like that. He is my child." I breathed in and gripped the arm of the chair. "But I was a surrogate. My eggs were fertilized with someone else's sperm. I signed papers promising Colin to another couple." I rubbed at my thighs, the spot where the scratches had been. "You have to understand, though, that what I did was legal. In Maine, with surrogacy like that, you're allowed to back out. It said so in my contract. But..." I trailed off, trying desperately to shift Tracy's face from my mind. "I didn't tell them what I was doing. I just left."

Relaxing slightly, but still with a furrowed brow, Dr. Davidson said, "I see. And you've never told anyone about this?"

"Only my sister Carol."

"Bryan doesn't know?"

"I met Bryan when Colin was six months old. I told him that Colin's father was abusive." I was scratching my nails against the fabric of the armchair. "I was a mess. I needed to explain—"

"Why you were so nervous?"

I nodded. "Bryan took care of me. We dated for a few months, and then he started to realize that something wasn't right. My lies were getting out of control and I'd started to forget things. When I forgot, I didn't want to admit it, so I'd lie. When anyone asked about Colin's father, I'd lie. Soon, there were so many lies I couldn't remember what I'd said and what I hadn't said."

"And that was when Bryan got you some help?"

"He took me to a doctor in Chicago." I waved at the file in Robert's lap. "It's all in there."

"Molly," Dr. Davidson said softly, leaning forwards in his chair. "It's absolutely no wonder that you're struggling after what happened to Colin and your father-in-law. By not telling your doctors in Chicago about Colin's history, you stifled an essential part of your treatment. And the fear of thinking that Colin was missing, and the residual worry about what's happened to Frank, must have been a *huge* trigger for you."

"But my medication—"

"Medication is very useful, Molly, but without talking therapy and some true coping strategies in place, you were bound to relapse. I'm just amazed it's taken this long." His eyes were kind. Deep and kind, and they made me want to cry again. "Are you still taking your medication?" He flicked back through his paperwork to find my prescription.

"Sometimes," I offered meekly.

Robert nodded. "Okay, well, the first thing we're going to do is get you back on your meds. I'll suggest a slightly higher dose for now, until we get you on an even keel again. Does that sound okay?"

"Yes. Thank you."

Looking up, he continued, "Tell me, Molly, if it was legal to take custody of Colin, why didn't you tell the adoptive parents that you'd changed your mind?"

I sighed and re-crossed my legs. "I've asked myself that question so many times. But they wouldn't have let me go. And I couldn't risk Colin being brought up like that."

"How do you mean, Molly?"

"The way I was." My eyes were wide, and my cheeks were flushed. "Andy, Colin's biological father, was abusive. He beat his wife—Tracy. I saw the bruises."

Dr. Davidson closed his eyes briefly and nodded as if it was all becoming clear. "I see."

"I grew up in foster care. Carol and I saw things that children shouldn't ever see. I couldn't let my baby go through that." I was scratching my ankle again and looked up to meet Dr. Davidson's eyes. "It's an old injury. It only bothers me when I'm stressed." I stopped scratching and told him about the diner. Jumping over the fence. Ending up in hospital. "That was the first time I ever spoke to a psychiatrist. But I didn't want to admit back then that there was anything wrong with me."

Robert was scribbling something in his notebook. When he looked up at me, he said, "And now you think there is something wrong?

I breathed in and almost chuckled. "Yes. There has to be. It's like before, but worse. I'm losing chunks of time, lying even when I don't need to, lying when I shouldn't. I accused Bryan of having an affair. I accused Kathy of trying to kill me, and—" I stopped.

"And?"

"The woman I thought Bryan was having an affair with, I think she's Tracy's sister. I think she's here to punish me for what I did. And I think that somehow it's all wrapped up with Frank and my missing text messages and Kathy and... I mean. I'm crazy. Aren't I? It's the only explanation."

Dr. Davidson held up his palm in the universal gesture for whoa, stop there. "Okay, Molly. First of all, I'd never tell you that you're *crazy* or *mad*—we don't use those words in this room—but perhaps what we need to do is try to sort fact from fiction. Often, when someone suffers from a compulsion to lie, those lies become ingrained in their psyche. So much so that they begin to believe they're true. It's almost as if you create a false memory for yourself. Does that sound familiar?"

"Yes," I whispered. "Sometimes, I tell a lie and then it appears in my head. I can see it. And then I start to wonder if it really was a lie in the first place." I wiped a tear from my cheek and looked up at the ceiling.

"Molly, it's okay. I can help you."

"Really?" I rubbed the back of my neck and released a long, shaky breath.

"There is a lot that we need to work through. Are you sure you're ready?"

"Yes," I replied without hesitating. "I am. I can't lose my husband or my son. So, I'm ready."

# 34

---

*THREE WEEKS LATER*

Any moment, Bryan would be arriving with Colin. For three weeks, they'd been staying at Kathy's house, and I'd been home alone trying to fix myself. For twenty-one days I hadn't seen my son. But now, Bryan was giving me a chance. A chance to prove I was getting better.

Unlike the day I went to see him at Kathy's, I hadn't gone over-the-top trying to make an effort. I was just… normal. Or as close to normal as I could manage.

The house was clean, I was wearing jeans, my favorite "mom" crew neck, and yellow pumps. Colin's room was just as he'd left it —I'd resisted the urge to move things around and look like I was trying too hard—and there was a reasonable amount of food in the fridge.

As soon as I saw Bryan's car, my heart started to flutter. We'd spoken just a couple of times since the episode at his mother's house. But then a few days ago, he'd called and offered to bring Colin to stay with me on the weekend.

I'd wanted to ask what had prompted his change of heart—I'd purposefully been refraining from texting him or calling him to tell him how I was doing. Instead, I'd just quietly carried on. I'd taken a new position as a freelance realtor with an agency in town. Not my ideal position, but they were busy and needed help. And, in the back of my mind, I thought that if Graham heard I was back in the circuit and doing *okay*, then he might call and ask me back.

I'd also had six sessions with Dr. Davidson. *Six.* Two per week. Bryan must have known I was going, as the charge would be showing up on our joint account, but he hadn't mentioned it.

Perhaps the fact I was simply "getting on" with things was what had spurred him to bring Colin over for a visit.

The car pulled up and Bryan climbed out of the driver's seat. Somehow, he was even more handsome than I remembered. And, waving casually, I felt the way I had when we first met—nervous, like a schoolgirl with a giant crush.

Bryan returned my wave but didn't smile. He opened the back passenger door, leaned in to unbuckle Colin, then walked up to the porch holding his hand. As they approached me, Colin stepped behind Bryan and hid his face in Bryan's arm.

"Hey, guys," I said, trying not to be overly enthusiastic. "How are you doing?"

"Colin's a little nervous," Bryan said, offering a small lopsided smile.

I nodded, brushed my hands on the front of my jeans, then bobbed down in front of him and tried to remember what Dr. Davidson had told me. Stay in the moment. Focus on the here and now.

"Colin, I understand that you're a bit nervous. Mommy wasn't feeling very well last time you saw her. But I'm doing much better now, and I'm excited to spend the weekend with you." I took a deep breath and looked up and Bryan, then added, "*But* if you feel upset or want your dad—anytime—that's okay. You just tell me, and I'll take you straight back to Grandma's. Or we can call him. Whatever you want."

Colin looked up at Bryan, who was watching me carefully. His eyes had softened. His mouth twitched into a smile, and he patted Colin's head. "See, buddy. I told you Mom was doing better."

Gingerly, Colin stepped forward and into the hallway. He glanced towards the stairs.

"Your room's just as you left it. Go see." I smiled.

Colin nodded, kicked off his shoes, and tore off to go rediscover his room. I turned back to Bryan and leaned against the doorframe. "Would you like to come in? I could make some coffee."

His body twitched, as if he was fighting the urge to step inside. He looked at his watch. "Sorry, Molly. I better not. I'm picking up the keys to a new apartment."

"A new...?" My mouth felt suddenly dry; living at his mom's was one thing, moving to a new place with our son was something totally different.

"Colin and I need our own space. It's only a rental."

I nodded and licked my lower lip. "I see. But I thought…" I was tapping my fingernails on the wooden frame of the door. "I'm really trying, Bryan. Can't you stay at your mom's a bit longer? Then we can talk about—"

"I just think it will take the pressure off if there's no rush. And you know that Mom can be a little… overbearing." Bryan didn't seem mad, or like he was trying to punish me, but he did seem like his mind was already made up.

"Where is it?" I asked. "The place you've found?"

"Fitzroy Street. A big old house turned into apartments. It's nice. You'd like it." A smile almost started to show at the corner of Bryan's mouth, as if somehow he'd chosen the apartment because he knew I'd approve of it.

"Fitzroy?" I felt like I'd been punched in the gut. Hadn't I told him the address of my old foster home? When we moved back here? Hadn't I mentioned it and insisted we didn't buy a house anywhere near it?

"Susan recommended it. She said she looked around there but went for something different in the end. It's a rolling monthly lease, so it seemed a good option."

For three weeks, I'd managed not to let thoughts of Susan take over my brain. But now, all of a sudden, she was back. I'd let myself forget the fact that she worked with Bryan. I hadn't thought about them seeing one another every day or about her using him to get her revenge on me. But now here she was—telling Bryan about the *one* place I couldn't stand the thought of him moving into.

"What is it, Molly?" Bryan's tone had sharpened. Clearly, he thought I was about to kick off about him speaking to Susan.

I swallowed hard. "Bryan, bad things happen in that place. Please don't go there. Anywhere else... just pick anywhere else but there."

Bryan looked like he was trying not to lose his temper.

Slowly, as calmly as I could, I said, "This isn't me losing my mind, Bryan. That apartment block is my old foster home. And it doesn't have good memories for me. You know that. You know what happened to Jack."

For a moment, Bryan just blinked at me. But then he brushed his fingers through his hair and said, "I didn't know it was the same place. But I'm sorry, Molly. It's a good apartment. Good price. Close to work. You don't have to visit us there, I'll bring Colin here to see you. If this weekend goes well." He breathed in, letting what he'd said just sit there in the air between us for a moment, then reached out and put his hand on my forearm. Gently, he added, "These are the kind of things you have to learn to let go of. Talk to Dr. Davidson about it. He seems to be helping."

I was still standing there, speechless, when Bryan told me he had to go and returned to his car.

The Bryan I was married to a few months ago would have pulled me close and told me that of course he wouldn't go near the place if it upset me. *This* Bryan had somehow become cool and distant. Surely, it wasn't unreasonable that the thought of him and my son living in my old foster home—the place where such awful things had happened—wasn't something that sat easy with me?

As he drove away, I stood rooted to the spot. I watched his car until it was out of sight, then noticed that small, silent tears were rolling down my cheeks. All of a sudden, I felt further away from Bryan than ever.

"Mom?" From inside, Colin's voice called for my attention.

I wiped my eyes with the back of my hand and headed in. "Yes, buddy?"

"Can we go for ice cream?"

I leaned back against the door and smiled. At least I still had Colin; I'd *always* have Colin. "Of course, we can. Let's go."

In Colin's favorite ice cream parlor, I took out my phone and called Carol. When she answered, her voice was tight. But at least she answered.

"Hey," I said, before she could start to speak. "I'm with Colin. Bryan brought him over for the weekend."

"Oh." She sounded surprised.

"Are you busy tonight? Colin wanted to ask you over for pizza and movies." I lowered my voice and turned away from Colin. "And I wanted to apologize. For last time. And for not being a very good sister to you." I trailed off and let my sentence just hang there for a moment.

I heard Carol breathe in sharply. But then she said, "Okay. I'll come by after work. Tell Colin I want a Hawaiian."

"Will do." As I hung up, I spun back around to Colin and grinned at him. "She said yes."

Colin nodded, looking far too grown up, and thrust his spoon into his ice cream sundae. "Cool."

Later, after we'd filled ourselves with ice cream and then walked it off in the park, we returned home and set about choosing a movie for our evening with Aunt Carol. At six thirty, I called the pizza place to order our usual.

"Sorry, ma'am, we're only doing collection tonight. Our delivery guy's off sick."

I glanced at the clock. "Okay, no problem. We'll come collect them."

Ignoring Colin's groans of protest, I bundled him back into the car and set off for the pizza parlor a few blocks away. Glancing in the rearview mirror, I saw him start to yawn—the sugar high from the ice cream clearly wearing off and, by the time we got there, he was fast asleep.

Leaving him in the car, I hopped out, rushed inside, paid, then drove home at just above the speed limit so that we'd get there before Carol. I was lifting the pizza boxes from the passenger seat and balancing them in my arms when I saw her car at the end of the street.

"Darn." I ran to unlock the front door. My sheets of research papers about Susan were still stacked beside the computer, and I'd meant to throw them in the trash in case Carol saw them. I'd only just finished shoving them into the trash can beneath the sink when she appeared in the doorway.

"Hey," she said, smiling hesitantly at me. "You already got the pizzas?"

"Oh. Yeah." I nodded at the boxes. "Delivery guy's off sick so we went to collect them." I turned and switched on the oven so that I could warm them. "Coffee?"

"Yes please." Carol sat down on one of the stools in front of the breakfast bar and sighed.

"Long day?"

"Long *week*," Carol replied, almost smiling at me as she looked around the living room.

I poured us each a coffee and was rustling in the cupboard for some cookies when Carol said, "Molly, where's Colin? Is he upstairs?"

"Colin? Shit!" Dropping the cookies, I ran full-pelt to the front door, threw it open, and raced down the steps. Inside the car, Colin was crying and pulling at his seat belt.

I flung the door open. It hadn't been locked. I was shaking as I pulled him out and wrapped my arms around him. "Colin, I'm so sorry. I was only inside with Aunt Carol. You weren't out here long, buddy. It wasn't long."

"It was. It was long." Colin was sobbing and, once again, a heavy sensation of dread and guilt was settling in my stomach.

On the porch, Carol was watching us. As I walked up the steps, still holding Colin in my arms, she widened her eyes at me. "Molly? What the…"

I shook my head at her, concentrating on making Colin feel better, and took him inside. Setting him down on the couch, I told him to pick the movie he wanted to watch while I got the pizza warmed up.

An hour later, with Colin tucked up in bed, Carol turned to me and put her hands firmly on top of mine. "Molly... you need to tell Bryan what happened."

"No. Carol, it was an accident. Anyone could have done it. Moms do that kind of thing all the time. It's nothing to do with what's been going on." I looked at her pleadingly. "I'm taking my meds, I've been seeing a psychiatrist. I'm doing okay, Carol."

Carol nodded slowly. "But you still need to tell Bryan. If Colin mentions it... It'll be better coming from you. And a chance to show him you're doing better."

I reached down and scratched at my ankle; it hadn't bothered me for weeks but was starting to throb again. Finally, I stood up. "Okay. I'll call him."

## 35

"I was staying in a motel," I said, screwing my eyes shut as memories of sticky floors and mold-covered walls washed over me. "I'd been doing dishes in the kitchen to pay my rent, but they found someone permanent and wanted me out."

Dr. Davidson nodded sympathetically and scribbled something on his notepad. "And how pregnant were you at this time?"

"Nine months. Colin was due any minute."

"That must have been very frightening."

"Carol and her husband Rick had been sending me money. She'd tried to persuade me to come home, but I couldn't. I couldn't risk Tracy and Andy finding me."

"Where were you planning to live?"

I tapped my fingernails lightly on the side of the doctor's customary square white cup and shrugged. "I didn't have a plan. I had a car. Before I started to look really pregnant, I'd got some work and saved enough to buy an old Civic. Like the one I left behind."

Robert pursed his lips, as if he could see exactly where this was leading.

"I packed my bags and loaded everything into the car. Then I just drove. I was looking for somewhere quiet where I could park without being noticed, but half-way down the freeway the cramps started. I looked down and—" I stared down at my lap, remembering the moment my navy-blue sweatpants became sodden with water. The moment I knew it was finally happening. "So, I drove straight to the hospital."

"And did you tell them your real name?"

I nodded. "Yes." I frowned and scraped my fingers through my hair to give them something to do. "I'm not sure why. I don't think I was thinking clearly."

"Was the birth straightforward?" Robert asked, crossing his ankle over his knee and letting it balance there.

"Relatively," I said. "I don't remember much. It lasted a long time. Over twenty-four hours, so by the time Colin arrived I was exhausted." I picked at my jeans and swallowed hard. "There was some sort of problem with his airway, so they hurried him off out of the room. I saw them take him away in this tiny little plastic bassinet. But I was so high on the drugs they'd given me that I could barely speak. They told me to keep still. I needed stitches. And then I think I fell asleep."

"Seeing him wheeled away must have been very traumatic for you."

"At the time, I don't think I took it in. But when I woke up, I panicked. I was in this empty room, all alone, on the bed. Colin wasn't there, and when I tried to call for a nurse, it took them forever to come to me. When they came, they said that Colin was somewhere else being treated. And I freaked out." I shook my head as a vision of a small, dark-haired girl with bright red roots and frightened eyes danced in front of me. "I remember getting out of bed and running down the corridor in my hospital gown, banging on doors, looking for him." I tried to laugh, but it came out too loud and too coarse. "I'm lucky they didn't section me."

"Not at all," Robert replied. "For any new mother to wake up without her child would be extremely distressing."

"Eventually, they took me to him. And I refused to leave his side." I reached shakily for the coffee table, set down my mug, and poured a glass of water. "They kept me in for a few days. I think they knew I was homeless and were waiting for me to come clean."

"And did you?"

I nodded. "I told them what I told Bryan—that Colin's father was abusive and that I'd run away and had nowhere to go. They were very kind. They put me in touch with a charity who found me a place in a group home. A hostel for new moms. And it was nice." I smiled. "There were some nice women there…"

"But…?"

I let my smile drop and took a large sip of water. "I felt like a fraud. They'd all been through something truly awful. They were afraid for their lives. And the more they asked me about my story, the worse I felt." I shifted in my chair and tried to resist the urge to lift my leg and scratch at my ankle. "They ran a day care program, so that the women there could get back to work. When Colin was six months old, I started waitressing at a diner." I smiled. A real smile this time. "And that's where I met Bryan. They gave us staff discount, so I often ate there on my days off. Took Colin. I walked in one day and dropped my things all over the floor. Bryan helped me pick them up."

"And the two of you started dating?"

I nodded.

"But you never told Bryan about your past?"

"No. He doesn't know."

Robert paused and looked down at his notes. "Moving back here. That was Bryan's idea?"

"Yes. He wanted to reconcile with his family."

"And you agreed?" He sounded surprised.

"At first, I said no. But I wanted Colin to have a family. A real family. Here, we've got Bryan's mom and dad." My throat constricted and I corrected myself. "At least, we *had* his dad until…"

"Of course." Robert tapped his pen on his notepad.

"And Carol's here. Her husband was sick at the time and, although I don't think I was a particularly good sister to her, at least I was here. In town."

"I see. And you weren't worried about Tracy and Andy finding you?"

"I checked her name and the bookstore she owed had passed to someone else. I couldn't find any record of them here in Maine, so I assumed they were back in Rhode Island. That was where they lived. Tracy commuted here at weekends to run the store, but because of Andy's job, they couldn't move." I tried to relax my shoulders and looked Robert Davidson straight in the eyes. "Besides, with Bryan I felt safe. I can't explain it, really. But he always made me feel as if nothing bad could happen when he was around. You know?"

Robert smiled, as if it was nice to hear someone talking so positively about their spouse. "Molly, it's clear that you and Bryan have something very special." He leaned forward onto his elbows. "So, do you think maybe it's time you told Bryan the truth?"

After leaving Dr. Davidson's office, I drove round the block five times before finally heading home. Pulling into Maple Drive, the sun was setting at the end of the street, and I felt like if I just kept going, I might reach the center of it. I parked the car and sat there for a moment, fingers gripping the steering wheel, pulse throbbing loudly in my ears.

The very thought of telling Bryan the truth made me feel sick to my stomach. But I'd agreed to it. I'd said yes. I'd ask Bryan to go with me to my next session and, there, I would finally bare my soul —tell him all of it. Every single, awful, detail of what I did to Andy and Tracy. The truth about Colin's father.

Behind me, the Davieses' front door clattered shut and I jumped, twirling round as if it were a gunshot or an explosion. To one of the lower branches of the big green maple tree, Arthur Davies had tied a red child's swing. His daughter was sitting on it, rocking her legs back and forth in a gentle rhythm. I looked away.

Climbing out of the car, I kicked off my shoes and walked barefoot to the front door. For some reason, naked feet often jolted my brain into gear—as if the cold on my soles sent a shockwave up my spine and woke everything up. Today, though, it had no effect.

Inside, I dumped my purse by the door, allowed my shoes to clatter onto the rack, and walked mindlessly through to the kitchen. There, I poured a large glass of white wine and set it down on the counter-top. Studying the stem, and marveling at how something so thin and delicate could support something so weighty, I spun it slowly around and watched the wine slosh gently up the sides of the glass.

Lifting it to my nose, I took a long deep breath and let the scent of the grapes settle in my nostrils. Then I put it back down and shrugged off my jacket. It was still warm outside, but for some reason whenever I visited Dr. Davidson, I felt the need to wear a jacket. As if having something to pull tightly around me on the way in and out somehow softened whatever was said in the room.

Slowly, I returned to the hall and hung my jacket on the hook by the door. When I turned back, I leaned against it and flicked on the hall light. It wasn't dark outside, but it was approaching late after-noon and the sun was at the back of the house. Now, the hallway was brighter. And it hurt my eyes.

Blinking, I took it all in—the life that Bryan and I had crafted so carefully together. The pictures from our wedding in Chicago—a small but beautiful day, where Colin wore a baby tuxedo and we had ice cream to celebrate. The shoe rack Bryan built. The rug that matched the drapes. The polished hardwood floors, and the brushed chrome ceiling lights that complemented our door handles.

Like a ghost, I floated from the door to the stairs and up to Colin's room. For the first time in months, I closed the door, lay down on his bed, and flicked on his moon and stars nightlight. As the fuzzy white galaxy that Bryan had bought for our son swirled across the ceiling, I reached up and placed a hand on my forehead. Robert Davidson was right. Bryan deserved to know the truth. And now that the decision was made, all I could do was pray he could find it in him to understand and to see that if I hadn't done what I did, we wouldn't have Colin. He'd be someone else's child. Some other couple's pride and joy. And that wasn't something I could even bear to think about.

# 36

With my fingers laced together and my leg jittering nervously beneath the table, I glanced out of the window and searched the parking lot for Bryan.

I was waiting for him at our favorite roadside diner. It had always reminded us of the place we first met, when Colin was a chubby pink newborn and Bryan was a handsome stranger who came to my rescue when I dropped my diaper bag and sent the contents flying across the floor.

I could almost see myself—so young, so nervous that I was being followed. When Bryan had approached me and put his hand on my arm to ask if I was okay, I'd flinched as if he'd waved a knife at me. I just couldn't believe that anyone would be so *kind*. But, right away, he and Colin had formed a bond.

Usually Colin, who'd suffered from terrible croup, would cry and cry for hours. But Bryan seemed to have an innate knack for settling him. He settled me too. He didn't seem to mind that I was twitchy and always looking over my shoulder. He had just gotten to know me and, slowly, his calm exterior had started to brush off on me.

Back then, I'd never have believed it if someone had told me that I would let myself get so low that I'd almost lose both Bryan *and* Colin. But he'd been surprisingly kind after I told him about leaving Colin in the car.

I could tell he wanted to be mad, but he'd taken a deep breath and said, "I appreciate you being honest, Molly. It's a big step." Afterwards, I'd texted him and asked whether he'd go to a session with me—with Dr. Davidson; I needed to prove to him that I was doing better and that leaving Colin like that was genuinely the kind of thing that could happen to any mother. I'd held my breath almost the entire ten minutes I waited for his reply. But, eventually, it came: *Okay. Let me know when the appointment is. I'll be there.*

So, there I was. Waiting at the diner so we could have breakfast together before going to see my psychiatrist.

Finally, I spotted Bryan's tall frame crossing the parking lot. The doorbell tingled as he crossed the threshold and, when he saw me, he nodded. I wished he'd smile at me. I wished he'd look at me the way he used to, but the fact he was no longer seething with anger would have to do.

"Molly." He sat down on the red leather bench seat opposite me and reached instinctively for a menu.

"Thank you for doing this," I said, mimicking him even though I had absolutely no appetite.

Bryan put the menu down and placed his palms on top of it. "Telling me the truth about Colin was a big step. I appreciate you being honest." He smiled—the smallest flicker of a smile.

"I'm trying," I said quietly.

Before he could answer me, a waitress arrived and—without asking what I wanted—Bryan ordered our usual. "And coffee," he added.

The waitress nodded and, a few moments later, returned with a coffee pot and poured us a mug each.

After taking a long, slow drink, I looked up and tried to make my body relax into my chair. "When we speak to Dr. Davidson, he'll tell you how well I'm doing."

Bryan nodded and smiled thinly. "I hope so."

I picked at the table with my fingernail. It was a little sticky and made me want to go grab a cloth and wipe it down.

"Molly…" Bryan paused, as if he wasn't quite sure how to phrase what he was about to say. "Now that you're doing better… all that stuff—about Susan and my mother and people conspiring to frame you for my father's disappearance—is that…?" He looked at me with wide, questioning eyes, as if he was praying that my irrational thoughts had disappeared.

I shifted and cleared my throat. "You want me to be honest?" I looked up at him. I wanted so badly to lie. It was on the tip of my tongue—yeah, yeah, I'm fine, I've forgotten all about it. But I couldn't. If I wanted to keep Colin in my life, I needed to at least try to be open with my husband.

"I really do."

I breathed in and then exhaled loudly. "I still feel that there is something strange going on. But Dr. Davidson is helping me to come to terms with the idea that it might all be a reaction to..." I stopped and looked away. "To my past."

"The personality disorder?" Bryan dipped his head to catch my eyes.

"The stuff that happened before that. Before we met."

Bryan put down his coffee cup and lowered his voice to a soft whisper. "Molly, you can tell me anything. Is this about foster care? Or before? I know you had a bad time of it with Colin's father, but you've never really told me what happened..."

I swallowed hard and when I spoke, my voice came out shakier than I'd expected. "I want to tell you. I promise, I do. But Dr. Davidson suggested I do it in our session. So that it's a safe space."

Bryan sat back and picked up his coffee again. Was he hurt that I didn't feel safe enough to tell him now? If he was, he didn't show it. And, before I could ask him, the waitress arrived with our food.

While Bryan tucked in, I moved my pancakes around my plate and struggled to eat even a few mouthfuls. Eventually, I gave up and put my fork down. Bryan noticed, but didn't say anything.

"You remember when we first met?" The question left my lips before I could stop it.

Bryan put his fork down too and looked around the room. "It was a diner just like this one. A weekend. I was having breakfast and reading the paper before my Saturday shift." He gestured to the door. "The door jingled. I looked up... and there you were. The most beautiful woman I'd ever seen." Bryan smiled and reached out to brush the tips of his fingers against mine; he had told me this story before. I loved it. I made him recite it every birthday, anniversary, and Christmas because it was like something from a fairy tale and because his eyes sparkled as he spoke. "The second I looked at you, I knew I had to talk to you. But then I spotted Colin balanced on your hip, this red-headed, podgy-looking baby. And I remember thinking 'Of course, she's already married. Has a kid. A perfect life.' But then—n"

"Then I dropped Colin's diapers all over the floor." I laughed and put my hand on top of Bryan's, trying desperately to make him remember the way we'd both felt in that moment.

"There was this huge clatter and all your things went everywhere. Colin's bottles, your ratty old wallet, your cell phone, diapers, diaper cream. The lot."

"But you rushed over and helped me scoop it up."

"And you were so flustered, and Colin was crying. So, I ushered you over to a booth—"

"And you bought me breakfast."

"And the rest is history."

I smiled and squeezed his hand. "I love you, Bryan. And I'm so sorry for what I've put you and Colin through. But I'm getting better. And when we see Dr. Davidson, I'm going to be honest with you. Finally. I'm going to tell you all about my horrid past and," I breathed in and took my hand back, then added solemnly, "and if you still want to be with me after that, then I'll do everything in my power to be the best wife you could have for the rest of our life."

# 37

D r. Davidson passed me a glass of water and closed his notebook. "So, you see, Molly's been doing really well. And I think you'll agree, Bryan, that the fact she told you the truth about what happened with Colin and the car… well, that's a *huge* improvement."

Bryan smiled at me, but he still looked apprehensive.

"The thing is, sometimes Molly lies so convincingly to herself that she starts to believe what she says. It's like it becomes her reality. So, we've been doing a lot of work on staying present in the moment, focusing on being grounded in the here and now, and looking logically at a situation."

"Basically," I added, trying to inject a little lightness to the room, "if everyone else is seeing lemons but I see limes, I need to tell my brain that they're lemons."

Bryan nodded. "I see. And what about…" He cleared his throat. He was sitting opposite me, and I wished he'd chosen the seat beside me so that I could pat his leg or hold his hand. "Molly said she wants to talk to me about her past. I know about foster care. Her friend Jack dying so tragically." Bryan cleared his throat and looked at me, holding my gaze. "It was part of what drew us together. I was still dealing with my brother's death, and Molly had never processed what happened to Jack." Bryan let Jack's name hang in the air for a moment, then said, "And I know Colin's father abandoning you like that took its toll." He raised his eyebrows. "So, what else is there? What don't I know?"

I glanced at Dr. Davidson. When we first met, I worried that he was on Kathy's side and out to get me. But over the past few weeks, with our twice-weekly two-hour sessions, I'd come to trust him. He was a good man. He knew Kathy, but he certainly wasn't "on her side." He'd even agreed with me that it would be best for Bryan and I to have some distance from her for a while.

Robert nodded. "I think it's time, Molly. Remember, this is a safe space. What you say between these walls, stays between these walls."

Suddenly, I was trembling. I'd repeated my story to Bryan so many times that I'd started to believe it myself. But the truth was very different.

"I wasn't honest with you about Colin's father." I blurted the words out then tried to slow myself down. "But Dr. Davidson has helped me to see that the trauma of thinking I'd lost Colin, the day he and your father disappeared, triggered emotions that I never dealt with. And everything that happened before I was diagnosed with my personality disorder… it came back ten times worse."

Bryan looked petrified. He must have been going through hundreds of terrible scenarios in his head. "Jesus, Molly. What is it?" He leaned forward, resting his elbows on his knees and lacing his fingers together.

I looked over at Dr. Davidson. He nodded gently. "Colin's father didn't beat me or abandon me. Bryan, I was a surrogate. I was young, in debt, working in this crappy diner. This woman I met, Tracy, she was amazing. So kind, so warm. She and her partner Andy were desperate to start a family, but she'd had a hysterectomy and there was no way they could ever have a child of their own. They'd started to look for a surrogate. Except, they couldn't find anyone they liked. She knew I was struggling for money, and they liked that I had red hair like she did." I stopped and closed my eyes, trying to shift the image of Tracy's face from my mind. "When she first suggested it, I said no. But then I thought about it, and it just felt right. I saw Tracy on the phone to Andy every day, and they were always laughing and joking. I thought he was a good guy. I thought they were a good couple."

"What do you mean? You *thought* he was a good guy?" Bryan's eyes flashed with something that almost looked like anger, but his face remained expressionless.

"Tracy said he was on board. I guess I should have pressed—asked to meet him in person. But she said he was working back in Rhode Island and it didn't feel..." I trailed off, embarrassment burning in my cheeks; I'd been so young, so tempted by the idea of a way out of the poverty I'd found myself in, that I hadn't once thought it was odd Tracy didn't want me to meet her partner.

"Wait. You're saying that Colin is..." Bryan trailed off, then stood up and looped his fingers together at the base of his neck. "He's not *yours?*"

"Yes, yes, he is. He is mine. They used my eggs and Andy's sperm."

"But, this couple?"

"They were going to adopt him. But I started hearing them argue on the phone. All the time. Horrible rows. And then Tracy kept turning up with these bruises on her face. She lied to me about how she got them. I could tell." I paused and shrugged a little. "I guess when you've told as many lies as I have, you can recognize it in another person." I met Bryan's eyes. "And I know fear, Bryan. She was scared of Andy. Terrified. I couldn't let my son grow up the way I did."

"So, you…" Bryan scraped his fingers through his hair and took off his glasses. He pinched the bridge of his nose, then finally looked at me. "You stole their baby?"

"No. I didn't steal him. I left to keep him safe." I was still looking deep into Bryan's eyes, willing him to see it the way I did.

"Colin's real father is out there somewhere searching for his son?"

I shook my head. My cheeks were flame-red and my hands were shaking. Dr. Davidson motioned to me to calm down. "No. Bryan, Colin has no *real* father. I carried him. I grew him. I gave birth to him. He's *mine*. He's always been mine." I stood up and walked over to Bryan. "And now he's *ours*. You're the only father he's ever needed."

"You *stole* him!" Bryan whispered. Then, as the words settled in, he almost visibly recoiled from me. "Were you having an episode? Was that it?" He shook his head. "Fuck, Molly. No wonder you were so screwed up when I met you. You were on the run with someone else's baby?!"

I waved my hands and tried to stop my voice from climbing even higher. "No, it wasn't like that." I glanced back at the couch. "Please sit down and let me explain."

Bryan lingered in the middle of the room. For a moment, I thought he was going to walk out and that I'd never see him again. His complexion was almost gray. Slowly, he nodded. And without speaking he sat down. This time on the couch, so that I could sit beside him.

I angled myself so that I could face him and reached for his hand. He didn't squeeze back, but he didn't pull away either. "I started having doubts about Tracy and Andy's relationship. To start with, she told me he was working out of state and that was why we had to start everything off without him. But then, as time went on, she just kept coming up with excuses not to introduce us. Then I started to hear them arguing on the phone. All those loving phone calls turned to fights. Constant yelling. And then..." I sucked air past my front teeth, remembering the day as clearly as if it was yesterday. "Then I saw her one day, and she had a black eye. She told me it was an accident. The car door. But I *knew*. I knew it wasn't."

Bryan breathed out loudly but still didn't take his hand away.

"That *same* day, I felt Colin kick for the first time." I felt my eyes getting misty and blinked back the moisture, trying desperately to keep some composure and not let the memories overwhelm me. "And I knew then that I couldn't give him to them."

"But he was *their* baby, Molly. Not yours. You stole that poor couple's *baby*."

"No, Bryan, he wasn't theirs. I was only twenty-four weeks pregnant. I had the right to change my mind."

Bryan's mouth dropped open as if he didn't know what to say.

"You think I should have gone through with it? Given birth to my perfect little boy and then handed him over? Left him there, with them? Let him get beat up, or worse."

"I'm saying, you made a promise. And you don't know what goes on behind closed doors." Bryan's lips set into a thin line. He was glowering at me as if it was taking every ounce of willpower he had not to walk out. Finally, he turned to Dr. Davidson. "How do I know she's telling the truth about this?"

As his words sank in, I clutched my stomach. I felt like I'd been punched in the guts.

"Bryan, Molly has just told you something very real. What she's talking about is the *root* of all her recent behavior. She suffered some problems after Jack died, but what happened when she was pregnant was the trigger for her personality disorder. Her compulsion to lie started after Colin was born. Didn't it, Molly?"

I nodded and wiped my eyes with my sleeve. "After I ran away, I was convinced people were following me. I had no idea what Andy looked like, so every time a strange man got too close, I freaked out. I had to lie to people about Colin's father. Everyone asked about it. And I guess the lying..."

"It bled into other parts of her life," Dr. Davidson finished. "But she's trying to correct things, Bryan. What Molly has done today is a huge step."

Bryan buried his head in his hands and let out a groan. When he looked up, his eyes were moist. "Somewhere out there, two parents are missing their child. Don't you feel bad about that?"

I breathed in sharply and held the air in my chest. I knew what Bryan wanted me to say. But I also knew the truth. "I did what I thought was best for Colin. And, Bryan, *we're* his parents."

Bryan opened his mouth, then closed it, then laughed dolefully and waved his hand. "So, all this with my father? It *triggered* feelings about the abduction?"

I flinched at the word "abduction." It seemed like a deliberate attempt to hurt my feelings, but Bryan wasn't usually so callous. "Yes," I said meekly. "When I thought he was missing, I guess all those old fears about him being taken from me came back up."

"And that's when you started to take time off work, lie to me about where you were, accuse my mother of all kinds of crazy shit, accuse me of having an *affair*?"

I blinked and made a small choked-up sound in the back of my throat.

"Bryan, let's try to keep our language calm and blame-free. Molly is trying very hard to be open with you so that you can move forward as a family."

I waited for Bryan to soften. I waited for him to tell me he understood and that we'd work through it all together. But he didn't.

Standing up, he looked down at me and shook his head. "Molly, you stole someone else's child. How am I ever supposed to trust you again?"

# 38

I stayed in Dr. Davidson's office, sobbing, for over an hour after Bryan walked out. He told me that Bryan needed time. He told me I'd done the right thing in confessing, and then he said, "Maybe, Molly, you should consider tracking down Tracy and her husband?"

Instantly, my blood ran cold. "What?"

Dr. Davidson held up his palms at me. "It could give you closure."

"They could take Colin away."

"That's unlikely, given the circumstances."

I shook my head. How could he possibly know what was likely in this kind of situation? "No. I can't."

"Okay, well, just think about it? We can discuss it at our next session."

I nodded, feeling as if I'd been hit by a truck, and stood up. "Okay."

"Molly?" he called as I reached the door. "Remember what we talked about—live in the moment. Confront your past, but don't dwell on things."

---

Outside, I blinked as the bright sunlight hit my eyes. The street was busy. There were people, cars... nothing was any different to how it had been when I walked into Robert Davidson's office an hour ago. And, yet, everything had changed.

I'd finally told Bryan my deepest truth. I hadn't expected him to just shrug and laugh it off, but I hadn't expected the venom in his voice or the steely darkness in his eyes. He was disappointed in me. Worse, even, *disgusted* by me.

I shuddered, despite the sunshine, and wrapped my arms around myself. Bryan would be on his way to collect Colin from Kathy's, and I was praying that he wouldn't tell her what I'd said. I leaned back against the brick wall behind me and closed my eyes. I was picturing Bryan scooping Colin up and hugging him tight, re-evaluating our entire life, thinking of it all so differently now he knew the truth.

I breathed in deeply and tried to remember what Dr. Davidson had said—don't dwell. *Don't dwell.*

I reached into my purse and took out a small black notebook that he had asked me to bring to our sessions. Last week, we'd made a list—a list of all the people I'd grown suspicious of, so that we could re-evaluate it when I was feeling stronger and see whether I was still having those feelings or whether I was thinking more clearly.

I knew what he was trying to do. And on one level it was working; I felt less manic, less forgetful, calmer. But my thoughts about Kathy, and Frank, and Susan hadn't changed. They were there, in the back of my mind, nibbling away and refusing to be silenced.

I sighed and looked at my list. Dr. Davidson was helping. But he was working under the assumption that everything I'd felt about Frank's disappearance, and Susan, and people being "out to get me." was a reaction to my past—a fabrication. A lie concocted by my own brain.

I wanted to believe him. I wanted to just slip back into the way I'd felt before all this started. But, deep down, I didn't. I didn't believe that I'd made it all up. It felt real. And now I was trapped in a place where I had no one to confide in. If I admitted to Dr. Davidson that I still believed Kathy and Susan were conspiring to drive me mad, and that they were somehow involved in Frank's disappearance, he'd probably have me committed. If I told Bryan, he'd divorce me. Even Carol was at her wit's end with me.

I had no one. And the realization that I was suddenly completely alone, and that I couldn't even trust my own mind, hit me like a tidal wave.

I was breathing heavily, panting, on the verge of a panic attack.

I stumbled away from Dr. Davidson's office and back towards my car.

Inside, I gripped the steering wheel and tried to slow my heart rate back to normal. All I could see was Colin's face. He was slipping away from me. I was going to lose him. Finally, after all these years of keeping him safe, he was going to be taken from me and it was all my fault. My own, twisted, fault.

I breathed out shakily and rolled down the window to let some air into the car. *If everyone is telling you it's a lemon, but you see a lime, maybe you need to accept that it's a lemon.*

For years, I'd been tricking my brain into believing the little lies that I told on a daily basis. So, perhaps now, for Colin, I needed to make myself believe that all the paranoid thoughts and feelings in my brain weren't real.

If I behaved as if they weren't, and did all the things that someone would do if they had realized they were wrong about something, then maybe eventually it would sink in.

So, straightening my shoulders and wiping the last few tears from my cheeks, I started the engine and drove towards Susan's house.

When I pulled up, Susan's car wasn't in the driveway. I looked at the clock on the dash. It was just after midday, so she could be at work. I could return home and come back later, but if I did that I might lose my nerve. So, instead, I got out of the car and walked up to the front door. I was peering through the window, trying to spot some signs that would indicate whether she was home, when a sharp clattering sound made me stand up straight and strain my ears.

It seemed as if it was coming from out back. Remembering the day that I brought Kathy here and thought I saw someone in Susan's garden, I shook my hands to release some tension and headed towards the passage at the side of Susan's house.

There it was again. A low, clattering sound. Like someone moving things around.

I stepped into the passageway and followed it down towards the garden. Susan's shed was visible. It was blue and had small plastic windows. And the door was open...

I held my breath. It could be Susan, out back, doing some gardening. But I knew it wasn't.

Quietly, I padded onto the lawn and around the back of the shed. I stopped and listened. But whatever I'd heard from out front was no longer making any sound. For a moment, I paused, leaning back against the grainy wood of the shed and looking up at the sky, which had started powder blue but was now a tepid shade of gray. I should leave. I should get back in my car, go home, and carry on my sessions with Dr. Davidson. But as I walked towards the front of the shed, I stopped. Gingerly, I peered in through the window, cupping my hands around my face. At first, all I could see was garden equipment hanging on the walls. But as my eyes moved down, there, pressed up against the back wall of the shed, was a small fold-out camp bed. A bed that looked like it had been slept in.

Dipping back down, I walked around to the open door and stepped inside. The floorboards creaked beneath my feet, causing nervous goose bumps to break out on my arms. There was no one there. But on top of the bed sat a crumpled sleeping bag, some discarded beer cans and... I moved closer and reached out to pick up the magazine that was sitting beside the sleeping bag. *Super Car Extra*. My thoughts tripped over one another. Frank's all-time favorite magazine was in Susan's shed, beside a clearly used sleeping bag. *Frank*'s favorite magazine. I turned it over, looking for an address label on the back—we'd bought a subscription for him as a gift last Christmas—but this was a store-bought version. A new edition, well-thumbed, corners turned down to mark interesting pages. I moved towards the camp bed and nudged the sleeping bag to one side. Was Frank *sleeping* in Susan's backyard?

Glancing behind me, I bobbed down to look under the bed, searching for a backpack, a wallet… proof that I could photograph and take straight to the police station so that when I yelled at Detective Monroe, "See! I'm not crazy!" he'd immediately acquiesce and apologize. I was reaching into the dark crevice between the bed and the floorboards when I heard something behind me. I turned. Someone was there, silhouetted in the doorway. I tried to stand up. The silhouette raised its arm. I held my hands out in front of me, but something struck the side of my head. Pain ricocheted through my temples. And then everything went black.

My eyelids were heavy. As if they were made of concrete. My fingers brushed against a tough, scratchy fabric. When I opened my eyes, I was looking at a wooden ceiling. Wearily, I tried to push myself up. I was still in Susan's shed, on the camp bed.

Someone was standing beside me. They stepped out of the shadow, and my heart began to thunder in my chest. "Frank?"

Bryan's father was skinny and had a rough, wiry beard. He looked like a homeless person. "Molly, take it easy." He held his hands out, and I scrambled backwards on the camp bed.

303

"Don't come near me!" I yelled, reaching behind me onto the shelves above the bed, desperately searching for something I could use as a weapon.

Frank stepped forward. "Molly, please. Be quiet."

"I'll scream!" I shouted, still trembling.

Frank sat down on the camp bed and reached for me. He gripped my arms, and I tried to pull away from him. He forced his hand over my mouth, but I bit it. Hard. He yelped and stood up, backing away from me but still asking me to be quiet and to listen.

I stopped searching for something sharp and started to throw things. Anything. Any object I could find. I needed to disarm him enough so that I could get out. Get out and run. Call a neighbor. Call the police.

Finally, I grabbed a pair of garden shears and jutted them out in front of me. "Step back," I said tightly.

Frank had been shielding his face but lowered his arms. "Molly..."

"I said, step back."

Frank looked over his shoulder. Then lowered his eyes and stepped back, away from the door. My stomach fluttered triumphantly, and I held the shears out towards him as I stepped slowly forwards. I was almost at the door. The second my foot was on the grass, I would run. I'd run to the nearest house and get them to call the police, come with me to Susan's before Frank had a chance to disappear. Finally, I'd have proof. Of what, I wasn't sure. But proof that at least I wasn't crazy.

The floor of the shed creaked. "I don't know what this is," I said to Frank, "but you'll pay for this, Frank. You'll pay for what you've done."

"I don't think so."

My blood ran cold. It wasn't Frank speaking. It was a woman. The doorway had darkened. I barely dared look, but then I did. And there she was—Susan. Except now, she had fiery red hair just like Tracy's. And she was holding a gun.

## 39

Susan waved the gun at Frank. "Bring her inside. We can't talk out here." Then she looked at me. Her eyes landed purposefully on the shears. I let them drop heavily from my hand and clatter onto the floor. Susan nodded, and Frank stepped behind me. He put his hand firmly on my back and nudged me forward.

Inside the house, Susan led the way to her large, sparse living room. It was empty, except for a small gray couch and two wooden chairs. Frank guided me to the couch and sat down beside me, while Susan pulled over a chair and set it down in front of me.

Weighing the gun up and down in her hands, she said slowly, "I'm not going to hurt you, Molly. I just need you to listen."

I shifted away from Frank. "What the hell is this?" I reached up and felt the side of my head. It was still pounding from where Frank had knocked me out.

Susan crossed one leg over the other and narrowed her eyes at me. "Do you know who I am, Molly?"

My throat constricted, and my mouth felt suddenly dry.

"You do, don't you? I was hardly subtle about it."

My voice came out small and croaky. "You're... Tracy's sister."

Susan nodded slowly, reaching up to stroke her hair. "You saw the resemblance, didn't you? Even with the wig."

I breathed out a long, shaky breath and tried to steady my trembling hands. I glanced at Frank. It still didn't fit. Susan and Tracy and Frank's disappearance. How did one thing have anything to do with the other?

"You ruined my sister's life." Susan was speaking calmly, looking me directly in the eyes. "You stole her baby, and she couldn't live with it."

"She..."

"They said it was a car accident. They said she was mad with grief, driving too fast in the rain. But we, her family, knew better."

"You think she...?" I couldn't even bear to say it out loud.

"She killed herself." Susan was looking deep into my eyes. She said the words loudly and let them hang there, suspended in the too-quiet air between us.

I reached out and gripped the arm of the couch. The newspaper article said it was an accident. I felt as if the room was swaying, closing in on me, opening up beneath me all at once. "I never meant..." When I looked up, Susan was wiping tears from her cheeks with one hand and trying to hold the gun steady with the

307

other. "Susan, I'm so sorry. I liked Tracy. I wanted to help her. I never meant to hurt her."

"Then *why* did you do it? Are you really so self-centered that you'd enter into a contract to give someone a child and then just disappear in the night without thinking twice about how it would affect them? Not even *talk* to them about it?" Susan's tone had changed from forceful anger to something more melancholic, and she looked away from me.

I moved my hands to my thighs and pressed down hard, trying to ground myself. "Andy," I croaked.

"Andy?" Susan narrowed her eyes at me. "What about him?"

"He was violent. Beating her up. I couldn't let Colin grow up like that."

Something flickered in Susan's eyes. "Violent?"

"That's why I ran." I edged closer and wrung my hands together, suddenly desperate for Susan to see that I never intended to hurt Tracy. Never. "He hit her. She came to the bookstore with a black eye, more than once, and they were always fighting, horrible fights. I know what it's like to grow up like that, and I wasn't going to do that to my baby." I sat up a little straighter and slowly said, "I did it to keep him safe."

In Susan's hands, the gun began to dip. What I'd said had caught something inside her—some tiny speck of truth. I could see it quivering in her eyes. "Andy was..." She shook her head. "No. He couldn't have been. She'd have told me."

"Would she?"

"She was my sister," Susan said loudly.

"Yes. But people don't always speak up when they're afraid."

As I watched Susan take in what I was saying, finally she lowered the gun into her lap. "Afraid," she whispered.

"Susan?" Frank's voice made me jump. "You don't think?"

Susan looked at him. "Do you?"

Frank breathed out heavily but before I could try to figure out what Susan had just asked him, she picked the gun back up and said, "Even if I believe you. Even if Andy was... the guy you say he was. What about Tracy? You didn't think about keeping *her* safe?"

I hung my head. No. I hadn't. I hadn't given Tracy a second thought. All I wanted was to make sure the baby growing inside me was safe. For a moment, no one spoke. Then I looked up and wiped my eyes with the back of my hand. "I'm sorry."

Suddenly, and unexpectedly, Susan laughed. She stood up and grabbed two fistfuls of hair, now holding the gun perilously close to her own skull, and let out an anguished roar. "For fuck's sake! I wanted to hate you, Molly. All these years, I've hated you."

I looked at Frank but he was watching Susan. "We need to tell her," he said softly. "Whatever she did in the past, we need to—"

"I know!" Susan cut him off. Then, quieter, "I know." Turning around, she sat back down and leaned forwards. "These last few weeks, everything has unraveled, hasn't it?"

"Yes," I whispered, thick, heavy dread forming in my stomach.

Slowly, Susan reached into her pocket and took out her cell phone. She handed it to me, and when I looked down at the screen, I almost laughed. "What is this?" I looked at Frank then back at

Susan. I was staring at a picture of Bryan, my husband, beside Tracy. He was kissing her cheek. They were smiling. I frowned at it. Bryan looked younger. "What is this?" I repeated, barely even a whisper.

"Have you ever asked Bryan what his middle name is?" Susan gestured to the phone.

"No…" I shook my head, squeezing my eyes shut and scrabbling back through memories of when Bryan and I first met before adding, "he doesn't *have* a middle name. He told me he doesn't–"

"It's Andrew." Frank cut in, his voice low and quiet. But then he looked up and met my eyes as I tentatively opened them. "Bryan's middle name is Andrew. When he moved away, after college, he started calling himself Andy."

"Andy…" A hot wave of nausea washed over me. I stood up. I was still gripping Susan's phone. I started to swipe through her photos. There were more. Tracy and Andy on a beach. At Tracy's book-store. By a lake. Clutching a twenty-week scan picture and waving it at the camera.

I dropped the phone. My breath was coming quick and shallow.

Susan stood up and handed me a bottle of water. "Here. Sit down."

I did as she said. Beside me, Frank's eyes looked full of tears. The room was spinning. Shakily, I lifted the water to my lips. But it was no use. As the water hit my stomach it gurgled back up, and I vomited onto the floor. Again and again until there was nothing left to come up.

Panting and wiping my mouth with the back of my hand, I pressed myself against the back of the couch as if somehow I might be able to crawl through it and disappear from whatever hell I'd found myself in. "What the *fuck* is going on here?" I looked from Frank to Susan. "What is going on?!"

Gently, Frank reached out and patted my leg, but I was numb; I could barely feel it. "I'm sorry, Molly. I never meant for it to go this far. I didn't know, at first. I didn't even know Tracy. We weren't talking back then and..." Frank sighed. He looked like an utterly broken man, as if he barely had an ounce of energy left inside him. Meeting my eyes, he said carefully, "Bryan isn't the man you think he is. He was Tracy's partner. After you ran away with the baby and the surrogacy fell through, she became very depressed. She started searching for you. Going on midnight drives." Frank glanced at Susan then back at me. "He says that it was raining, and she had an accident while she was out looking for you. Susan thinks she may have been depressed and that it was deliberate. But whatever the reason, afterwards, Bryan went mad with grief." Frank paused and bit his lower lip. "He tracked you down, Molly. He married you so that he could get his son back."

I blinked at Frank. My brain had stalled. His words were circulating, round and round, but they didn't seem to mean anything. They couldn't be real. I laughed and shook my head. "That's nonsense. It can't be true. It's..." I trailed off. Then with tears in my eyes I looked at Frank. "I don't understand."

Opposite where I was, Susan was still standing and staring at me. But now she looked almost sorry for me. "Everything that's happened over the last few weeks, it was all Bryan's idea. I hadn't spoken to him since Tracy died. After the funeral, he disappeared and stopped answering my calls. But a few months ago he emailed me and said he'd tracked you down. He told me he'd found Colin. That he was okay but that you were..." Susan paused, searching for the word. "Unhinged. He said he needed help to really prove it. To make sure that he could get custody and do what Tracy would have wanted."

"And you didn't think it was strange that he'd *married* me?!"

Susan blinked slowly. "No. Not at the time. I was so angry with you. And Bryan…"

"He's manipulative," Frank added. "He knows how to get people to do what he wants."

"So, both of you… this whole time? Everything that's happened was Bryan trying to make me think I was going crazy? Trying to make other people think I was going crazy?"

Frank nodded. "Yes," he whispered. "When he told me who you were, and about Tracy and Colin, and that he wanted to get custody, I begged him to stop and do things right—call a lawyer, get custody of Colin the *right* way." Frank sighed heavily. "But he wouldn't listen. We met. The three of us, a few weeks before I took Colin hiking. Bryan said that all I had to do was fake my disappearance and lie low for a few weeks while he and Susan—"

"Started playing with my head?"

Frank made a *hmmm* sound and scraped his hands through his hair.

Gripping my water bottle, my throat was so tight I could barely speak. "Why would you agree to it? I almost understand Susan going along with it. But Frank… why?"

Beside me, Frank began to cry. "Because I'm a terrible father, Molly. I treated Bryan so badly after his brother died. I never did anything to help him. Not his whole life."

"And this is how you thought you'd make it up to him? Did Kathy know?"

Instantly, Frank shook his head. "No. Never. She doesn't know anything. None of it."

I lowered my head into my hands. I felt dizzy. I wanted Bryan. *My* Bryan. But my Bryan didn't exist. He was gone. And in his place was a monster. "We've been married for three years," I whispered. "We met when Colin was a baby. How could he keep pretending all this time?"

When I looked up, Susan was watching me. The gun was still in her hand.

"I still don't understand," I said, unsure whether I was asking her or Frank or just thinking out loud. "He could have just taken Colin. I trusted him completely, we were a *family*. He could have run away years ago and—"

Frank cleared his throat. His eyes were still watery. "It wasn't just Colin he wanted, Molly. He wanted you to suffer. He wanted revenge."

"And he didn't want to be on the run his whole life. He wanted to make sure that no one could question his right to take custody of Colin," Susan added.

"And he did it…" I said, letting the truth sink hard into my gut. "Right now, I look totally unstable. I'm a compulsive liar. I'm seeing a psychiatrist. I lost my job. I accused my mother-in-law of trying to kill me with a walnut cake." I laughed, because it was so ludicrous it was almost funny.

313

Susan was still staring at me when Frank added, "No, Molly. That's not true. He hasn't done it. Not yet. And..." he glanced at Susan.

Susan closed her eyes, and when she opened them she was no longer holding the gun. "And we're going to help you get your son back."

# 40

"I did this for Colin, and for my sister." Susan was pacing up and down the room.

I nodded, sensing that she wanted me to say I understood.

"But Bryan isn't sticking to the rules."

"What do you mean?" My stomach tightened.

Frank sat back down beside me and laced his fingers together tightly. "Colin was never supposed to get hurt. I never agreed with what Bryan was trying to do to you, but it was supposed to be about protecting Colin. He was *never* supposed to get hurt."

A wave of hot, prickly nausea washed over me but Frank continued.

"I was supposed to take Colin on a hike, leave him somewhere safe where I could see him, then hide out in the bushes and stage my disappearance. Bryan told me he'd be safe the whole time. I'd lie low for a few weeks, then Susan would arrive back in town around about the same time everything was starting to get a little crazy for you."

Susan interrupted. "Bryan knew that if I started dropping hints about Tracy, on top of everything else, you'd soon start to crumble."

"Everything else?"

"Making you think you'd forgotten things. Messing with your medication so that you were either taking too much or not enough. The bloody baseball cap. Texting your boss and quitting your job for you." She raised her eyebrows as if she was waiting for the pieces of the jigsaw to finally slot into place.

I blinked hard. I felt like the room was swaying beneath my feet. I *knew* something wasn't right. But hearing it out loud—confirmation that I wasn't losing my mind, but that someone was taking it from me—was something I couldn't quite absorb.

I frowned, remembering the day Frank went missing, and how scared I'd been, and how Colin… "Colin had a head injury." I looked up at Frank. There was a large almost-faded bruise on the side of his face. "Did Bryan…?" I pinched the skin on my upper thigh to try to stop myself from hyperventilating.

"Exactly. Bryan told me Colin would be safe. I *never* would have gone along with it if I'd known."

"Neither would I," Susan added quietly. "I had no idea what Bryan had done until Frank called me and begged for help."

"He attacked us. It was supposed to be staged, but he attacked us." Frank's eyes were wide, and his voice was almost a whisper.

"When I woke up, I was in the middle of a forest on the other side of town. I had no idea where I was. It took me days to find my way out, and then I didn't know what to do. I didn't know how much Susan had to do with what had happened, so I hid."

"You *hid*? Why didn't you stop it?! Why didn't you go to the police?!"

Frank stood up and started pacing up and down the room. "He's always been... quick to anger."

Tracy's bruised face flashed in front of me and I shook it away.

"When his brother died, he changed. He got into fights, was downright cruel to his mother. But she didn't want to see it. Besides, it sounds crazy, doesn't it? The whole thing sounds crazy. And if Bryan could do that—if he could hurt Colin—I just didn't know what else he was capable of. What if he framed *me*? Had me locked up and then Colin was left with no one to protect him?" Frank was speaking quickly, rubbing his fingers through his hair. He stopped beside the bay window and leaned against the wall with one outstretched hand. "Eventually, I called Susan and I told her what happened."

"I didn't believe him at first." Susan paused and looked up at the ceiling as if she was trying to recalibrate her thoughts, and then she offered me a wry smile. "I suppose when you've spent so long believing something, focusing all your energy on it, it's hard to let go."

I swallowed hard.

"I *hated* you, Molly. But when Frank told me what happened – when I *saw* him – well, I guess I started to question things. I put Frank up in a motel for a few days while I tried to clear my head and then when I moved in here I put him out back in case Bryan came over."

Susan stood up and walked over to Frank. She put her hand on his shoulder, and he reached up to squeeze it. "I wanted revenge for Tracy," she said quietly. "When Bryan first told me about you, I was so angry. I was sick with rage. I couldn't eat. I couldn't sleep. All I wanted was to keep Colin safe. Because that's what Tracy would have wanted. But I didn't think it would go this far." She stepped forward and folded her arms in front of her stomach. "As soon as I met you, I knew in my gut that something wasn't right. What Bryan said about you didn't match up with what I saw and I should have acted on it–"

"So, why didn't you? Why didn't you question him and what he was telling you to do?" I met her eyes, searching to see if she was telling me the truth or if this was just another game.

Susan hugged herself a little tighter and looked down at the floor. When she looked up, her eyes were watery. "I wanted to, but I didn't know how." She stepped closer. "I was wrong. But I did this to save Colin, not to hurt him. I would never hurt him."

Suddenly, without warning, a burst of laughter escaped my lips and I waved my hands in the air. Susan and Frank turned to look at me. "You did this to *save* Colin?!" Susan had left her gun on the chair. She saw me look at it but couldn't move quick enough. I grabbed it and raised it up in front of me. Both of them stepped back, pressing themselves against the wall. "*I* saved Colin. Bryan—Andy—whatever the fuck his name is. He was *beating* Tracy. I got Colin away from him. And now you—the pair of you—have put him in danger."

Susan's expression changed. She swallowed hard and, when she spoke, her voice was quieter than before. "You really believe he hurt Tracy?"

"He hit her. I saw the bruises. And then he chased me down, *married* me, and lived a complete lie for three years so that he could slowly drive me insane and steal his child back. He attacked his own father. He attacked Colin! I wouldn't be surprised if *he* was the reason Tracy died." I looked at Frank. "After everything he's done, tell me you don't think he's capable of hurting her. Tell me!"

Frank shook his head then looked at Susan. "She's right. You know she's right. My son is dangerous. And we started this, so we need to stop it."

My hands were starting to shake, but I didn't dare lower the gun.

After what felt like a lifetime, Susan's steely expression finally crumpled, and she whispered, "I know. But how?"

---

Susan's eyes were wide, and she'd turned very, very pale. Reaching up, she tugged at her ponytail and shook her head. "I must have been crazy to let this happen." She looked at me, then quickly looked away. Walking over to the bay window, she stared out at the street. Her shoulders started to shake. Frank was beside her and gingerly reached out to touch her arm.

"He's good at getting people to do what he wants," Frank whispered. "You were grieving. He took advantage of that."

Suddenly, it felt ridiculous to still be holding the gun. Part of me wanted to put it down. It was heavy in my hand, and I wouldn't know how to use it even if I wanted to. But a small voice inside me was whispering, *Can you even trust these people?*

Turning away from Susan and Frank, I tried to slow the thoughts in my head and sort them into a logical order. I looped back over everything that had happened since the day Colin and Frank didn't return home on time. I tried to re-frame it. I pictured Bryan. I tried to make his face merge with the one I'd conjured up for Tracy's husband Andy all those years ago. But my brain couldn't make it fit.

My breathing was getting quicker. My skin was hot and cold at the same time. Trembling, I put the gun down on the counter that separated the lounge from the kitchen and reached for the water Susan had given me.

I sipped it, barely managing to keep still enough to swallow.

Then Susan's voice cut through my panic. "Molly, did you hear what I said?"

I blinked quickly and turned around. "What?"

Susan's cheeks were red. She wiped at them with the back of her hand and sniffed. "I called Bryan yesterday. I tried to talk to him, but he was so…" She shook her head. "I told him this wasn't what I'd signed up for, that the idea was to do what was necessary to secure Bryan's custody of Colin. It was supposed to be to protect him. He wasn't supposed to get hurt."

"And what did he say?" Fear settled my stomach. Every fiber of my body wanted to run to Colin, pull him close to me, and never let him go.

Susan breathed out slowly. "He said he'd do whatever it took to make you suffer."

I swallowed hard and sat back down on the couch.

"I told him I was out. I told him I wanted no part in it. I tried to make him step back, take a breather, think about Colin, but…"

"What?"

"He said it was too late. He said he no longer wants to fight for custody." Susan stepped closer to me and glanced over at Frank.

In a low, exhausted, voice, Frank added, "He's taking him out of the country, Molly. Tomorrow morning."

---

I needed to keep my composure… if I had any composure left to keep. I needed to think clearly. Now was not the time to fall apart. Just like the night I fled with Colin when he was still growing inside me, I couldn't panic. I couldn't give in to the sickening nerves that were swarming through my body.

"Where is he taking him?" When I finally spoke, somehow, my voice came out slow and measured.

"He said Europe. He didn't say where. All I know is that the flight is early." Susan looked up at the clock. It was seven thirty. It would be dark soon. Colin would be getting ready for bed, totally unaware that his father was going to wake him in the early hours of the morning and steal him away from everything he knew.

"Then we have to stop him." I stood up and shook my hands and arms, trying to free myself from the tension that was threatening to paralyze my body. "We have to stop him." I looked from Susan to Frank. Frank nodded, but Susan turned away.

Stepping around her and grabbing her by the elbows, I let my fingers press hard into her skin. "Susan, you've spent years hating me. I get that. What I did to Tracy was unforgivable. But I did it for Colin. And everything you did was for Colin too. We both want him safe." I paused and looked deep into her eyes. "Do you really still believe that he's safer with Bryan than with me?"

Susan held my gaze. Her eyes were flickering with thoughts that I couldn't interpret. Finally, she whispered, "No, I don't."

Until she answered me, I hadn't realized that I was holding my breath and, suddenly, it whooshed out in a sigh that made my lips quiver. "Okay. So, what do we do? Do we call the police?" I looked at Frank. "If the two of you back me up—"

Frank inhaled sharply. "I don't know, Molly. Bryan's clever. He could have laid a trail to cover his own ass, and we'd know nothing about it."

Susan exhaled shakily and looked at the clock. "Their flight is at two a.m., so they'll probably leave for the airport around eleven. If we go now, we'll catch him off guard. That's our best shot. He thinks he's winning. He thinks you're ready to crumble, Molly." Susan gripped my arms in return. "If you turn up at his door and distract him, I'll get in and get Colin. I'll sneak him out and take him to Kathy and Frank's."

I nodded slowly. "When he realizes Colin is gone…" Images of Bryan brandishing a kitchen knife or wrapping his hands around my neck and choking the life out of me rushed through my brain.

"I'll pull the fire alarm on the way out. Cops and the fire department will turn up. He won't be able to hurt you, Molly."

I closed my eyes and counted to ten. When I opened them, I bit my lower lip and said, "Okay. As long as you promise me, Susan, that Colin will be safe. No matter what, you keep him safe and you don't let him see anything..." My words stuck in my throat. Images from my childhood raced in front of my eyes. "You don't let him see anything bad. Okay?"

Susan nodded. "I promise."

Beside us, Frank cleared his throat and brushed his fingers through his hair. "I'll go talk to Kathy. I'll..." He sounded like he was going to stumble over the words. "I'll tell her everything. If Bryan does get away with Colin then, maybe, just maybe, she'll be able to talk him out of it."

# 41

As we pulled up outside Bryan's apartment, my blood ran cold. Beside me, Susan took out a cigarette and wound down her window. She was leaning out of it, but the smoke began to filter back in. I wafted it away. But it came back and as I closed my eyes, I saw Jack. Beside me. Hiding under the bed.

We were holding hands, and he was pressing his finger firmly against my lip. I was so afraid that I could barely breathe. Beyond the bed, it was dark. But then the door creaked open and a slither of light crept into the room. Heavy footsteps on the landing made me squeeze Jack's hand, and he squeezed back. We were so close that I could feel the sweat breaking out on his skin. I screwed my eyes shut and started counting under my breath. But the rancid smell of cigarette smoke made me splutter and cough. I slammed my hands over my mouth and when I opened my eyes, Jack was staring at me and shaking his head.

The light disappeared. Someone was blocking it. Then my foster mother's thick calloused hands appeared from nowhere, snaking beneath the bed, searching for us. Jack pushed me back and wriggled forward. I tried to say, "No, Jack," but the words wouldn't come out. Her fingers found his tiny, thin wrists and began to drag him away from me.

Jack didn't make a sound. Just walked silently in front of her as I lay there, trembling, letting him go.

"That was the last time I saw him," I whispered.

"Molly?" Susan was lightly shaking my arm and when I opened my eyes, I was surprised to see a look of concern on her face.

Turning from her, I looked up at the building in front of us. Huge. Gray. Silhouetted against a sky that was turning angry and gray, swollen with rain clouds the weather station hadn't predicted. I tried to focus on the here and now. Just like Robert had said. But all I could see was my foster father. Lighting his cigarette, standing over me, blowing smoke into my face as his lips curled into an angry grin. "Now that Jack's gone, you and Carol will have to take his place." His voice rattled with phlegm.

"Molly?" As Susan spoke, the remnants of her now-extinguished cigarette wafted into my nostrils, and I began to feel like I was choking. Suddenly, I couldn't breathe. My chest was tight. A panic attack was about to take hold of my body, and I couldn't stop it. Tears sprang to my eyes and I began to give into it. Even as I thought about Colin, inside, about to be whisked away from me forever. Just like when I let Jack go, I was too weak.

Then Susan grabbed my hand. "Molly. Breathe."

She'd thrown her cigarette out of the window. The smell was disappearing. Turning away from the house, I pried open my eyes and tried to focus on Susan's face.

"It's going to be okay."

"It's…" I was panting, struggling to speak. "It's this place."

Susan looked past me, at the house. "This is the place I asked you to take me to when we first met."

I nodded.

Quietly, Susan replied, "Bryan told me to ask you to show me around here." She frowned and looked back at me. "And now he's moved in here… what is this place? What does it mean to you?"

"I don't know how Bryan found out. I never told him exactly where… maybe he asked Carol." I shook my head and began to pick at my jeans, rubbing my fingernail against a rough thread, trying to focus on the feeling of it rather than the memories that were pounding in my head. "It's my old foster home. Bad things happened here."

"So, he chose it because he knew it would have a bad effect on you."

I nodded. I was trying to breathe, trying to think, but it wasn't working.

"Molly." Susan grabbed my hands and her touch made me flinch. Sharply, she asked, "Can you do this? Because Colin's in there and we're running out of time."

I turned to the house and wound down my window. I gripped the side of it and breathed the fresh, almost-nighttime air. Without the cigarette smell, the sight of the house was easier to bear. "My very first boyfriend died in that house," I whispered. It had been years since I'd said it out loud. Carol and I barely spoke about it, and all I'd told Bryan was that it hadn't been a nice place to grow up in.

Susan narrowed her eyes, and I thought she was going to tell me to get a grip. But then her shoulders dipped and the corners of her mouth softened. "What happened?"

"I can't. Not now." I shook my head and moved to open the door, but Susan pressed the locks and sealed us in.

"Yes. Now. You need to focus, Molly. So, if something's eating you up inside, you better get it out. And quickly."

Leaning forward, I braced both hands on the glove compartment as if we were still moving and about to career off the road. Above us, a crack of thunder rumbled through the air. This was not how I'd imagined confronting Jack's death. After the nightmares came back, I'd pictured finally telling the story to Robert Davidson, one day soon, when I felt strong enough. We'd sit in the cozy confines of his office, and he'd give me tea and tissues and tell me it wasn't my fault.

I sat up and looked at Susan. She was waiting for me to speak, but it was out of necessity, not sympathy. I paused and sucked in my cheeks.

"Jack killed himself. My foster parents were his real parents. And they abused him. Beat him. It was..." I closed my eyes and pictured his face... kind, smiling Jack. The first boy I ever loved. "He couldn't take it anymore. He went down into the cellar and..." My fingers went to my wrist and stroked it gently. "I found him. He'd been missing for days."

When I turned to look at Susan, she was very, very pale. She swept her hand over her hair and bit her lower lip. "It wasn't your fault."

I blinked at her. "You don't understand, I wasn't brave enough. He always stuck up for me, protected me. When they came for us, he always kept me safe." My words caught in my throat as my foster mother's heavy shoes beat a throbbing pulse in my ears. *Thud. Thud. Thud.*

Susan reached over and grabbed my upper arms. There was no kindness in her eyes, but as she spoke, there was a force in her words that I hadn't expected. "Molly, you were a child. It was *not* your fault."

For a moment, I wavered beneath her hands. And then I began to cry. Huge, quivering sobs shook my body. And Susan quietly watched me. Finally, when there were no tears left, she reached into her purse and handed me a tissue. With tight lips, she said, "Bryan knew, didn't he? He knew what happened here, and he wanted to use it against you."

I nodded, still shaking but no longer crying. "I never told him the details. But he must have found out."

"And that's why he wanted Frank and Colin to disappear. To set off the trauma you felt when Jack first went missing." Susan swallowed hard and then waved her hand towards the house. "And what happened to you here is why you took Colin from Tracy. Because…"

"Because I couldn't let Colin grow up the way I did. I couldn't let him see the things I saw," I said, wide-eyed, praying she finally understood.

Susan's skin was gray around the edges, and she looked like she might vomit. "Molly, I swear," she whispered. "I had no idea what he was really like. I had no idea he was violent to my sister. Tracy never said. Never even hinted…" Shaking her head, she continued darkly, "I thought this was about getting Tracy's son back. I thought I was doing the right thing." She put her hand over her mouth and choked back a sob. When she finally took it away and spoke, her voice was hoarse. "Listen, what happened to you, it's awful. What happened *here* is awful. And everything Bryan has done to you is… well, it's unspeakable. But if we don't get out of this car and go inside, that man is going to take Colin and we'll never see him again. So, you need to be strong now, okay? Fight the panic you're feeling and go in there. For Colin."

Slowly, I bunched my fingers into two tight fists and let my nails dig into my palms. "That house took everything from me," I said as thunder rolled over head. "I'm not going to let it happen again."

## 42

As I walked slowly up the front steps, I tried not to look towards the oak tree where the swing used to be. I could see its upper branches peeking out from behind the porch that wrapped around the outside of the building. But I knew that if I took it in— really took it in—the memories would swallow me whole.

At the door, Susan stood beside me. "Bryan Burke, 2A," she muttered." Then reached out and pressed every other buzzer except Bryan's. After a moment's pause, the door clicked and someone let us inside. Susan pushed the door and it swung gently open. I paused, my feet unwilling to move. But she grabbed my hand and pulled me forwards.

Standing beneath the large glass chandelier in the wide wood-floored hall, I shuddered. "It smells the same," I whispered, rubbing my index finger across my nose as if it would wipe out the scent of the past.

"But it's not the same," Susan said sharply. "Look." She gestured to the doors on either side of us. "Those aren't the rooms you remember, they're totally different. They're people's homes now, Molly. This *isn't* the same place. It can't hurt you."

I nodded and forced myself to look at the stairs—a large sweeping staircase that curved around and led to the landing where Jack, Carol, and I spent so many nights peeking out from between the wooden banister rails, listening for signs of our foster parents' drinking or arguing. For belts being loosened and cigarettes being lit.

"You can do this, Molly." Susan pressed her hand into the small of my back and nudged me forward. "I'm right behind you."

---

Climbing the stairs, I glanced back and saw Susan lingering at the bottom. My purse was slung over my shoulder, but I was holding my credit card in my hand. *When he lets you in, you turn and take off your jacket, drop something, and wedge the card in the door-frame so it doesn't close. Right?* That's what she'd said. That was the plan. In the car, it had sounded easy. But now, my heart felt like it was going to burst right out of my chest. If Bryan caught me, then Susan wouldn't be able to get into the apartment.

Turning back, I whispered loudly, "If I don't manage to do it, you'll call the police?"

Susan nodded gravely. We had agreed that if I went to the police and told them what Bryan was planning, they would never believe a word I said; he had set everything up so that I was the world's most unreliable witness. They *might* believe Susan and Frank, but none of us had any evidence. It was our word against Bryan's. And if they asked Colin... well, he'd say that his daddy was the best daddy in the world, and that he'd never do anything to harm him.

I breathed in and turned away from her. "Okay."

At the top of the stairs, I tucked my hair behind my ear, moistened my lips, and tried to look the way I always looked. When I reached out to knock on the door, my hand began to tremble.

*Five, four, three, two, one.*

Then I rapped my knuckles three times on the dark green door and stood back.

I could feel Susan's presence, but didn't dare look behind me. She was there, out of sight. But as I waited for Bryan to answer and strained my ears for sounds of movement inside, I felt an over-whelming sense of dread; what if he'd already gone? What if he'd lied to Susan and was already on a transatlantic flight with my son? With Colin...

"Molly?" Bryan's deep voice jolted me back into the hall, and I blinked at him as if he were a figment of my imagination. He smiled, adjusting his glasses on the bridge of his nose with his index finger. Yesterday, I'd have found that smile endearing. Today, it made me want to vomit. "What are you doing here? It's late." He was frowning now.

"I..." My mouth was dry and my tongue felt too big, stuck behind my teeth, not letting the words out. "I came to apologize." I breathed out, tried to slip into character and believe what I was saying, the way I had a million times before. "And to talk about what I told you in our session."

"Why didn't you call?" Bryan was standing in the doorway, his frame blocking the apartment from my view, and he wasn't making any signs of letting me inside. Stepping forward a little, he pulled the door behind him. "You should have called, Molly. We can't disrupt Colin like this; it's not fair."

"I know, I just…" I trailed off. *Think, Molly. Think.* "I needed to see your face. I needed to explain. And…" I breathed in and shook my head. "I promise that if you still feel you can't trust me after I've done that, then I'll give you space. I'll stay away for as long as you want me to, so that I can prove to you I've changed." With all the willpower I could muster, I made myself step forward and reach for Bryan's hands. I smiled up at him. The way I had so many times in the past, as if he was my sun and my moon and everything in between. "Please, Bryan." I looked around at the hallway and shuddered. "It's hard for me to be here. Could we talk inside? Just for a moment? I won't wake Colin, I promise."

For a long, painful moment Bryan just stared at me. His eyes flitted to the hallway behind me then rested back on my face. A flicker of a smile that, now, sent a shock of fear to my stomach crossed his face. He stood back and ushered me inside.

Barely through the doorway, I stumbled and dropped my purse. It fell to the floor and, as I'd hoped, the contents spilled over the threshold. "Oh God, I'm sorry, Bryan," I whispered as I bent down and began to scoop my things back in. Turning to the door, as I shoved my wallet back into my purse, I quickly slipped my credit card into the wedge of the almost-closed door.

When I stood up, Bryan was behind me. Close. So close that I could smell his cologne. So close that I could feel the warmth of his body vibrating towards me. "Molly…" I was trying to interpret the look on his face, but his features were utterly foreign to me. He was a stranger. A stranger who, this morning, I'd been desperately in love with. He reached for me. My entire body tensed. His fingers wrapped around my wrist. "It's okay," he said softly. "It's not the same place it used to be." He glanced towards the large open-plan living room. "Come see."

I followed Bryan through to the lounge. It was large and looked utterly unfamiliar. The open-plan kitchen was shiny and new. All of it barely even lived in. Scanning the room, I looked for any sign that Bryan was about to escape with my child. Suitcases, a passport lying on the countertop. But, of course, there was nothing.

"They've done a good job," I said quietly as he filled the kettle.

"They sure have. I'm glad Susan recommended it to me. Colin loves it." He softened his expression and turned to me. "Don't worry, I told him it's like a holiday. Some father and son time while Mommy gets better."

As he handed me a cup of coffee, in my head, I was screaming, *Liar, liar, liar!* But I tried to keep my face neutral. A little shaky. Because he wanted me to be shaky. But neutral.

"So..." Bryan leaned back against the kitchen counter. The hallway was in his eyeline. I needed him to move. Susan was waiting outside and in exactly five minutes she would attempt to sneak in. I glanced at the couch. There was one thing guaranteed to distract him, but the thought of it made my stomach churn.

"Can we sit?" I asked.

Bryan narrowed his eyes at me, but then nodded and gestured for me to go sit down.

Usually, I would sit close to him out of choice. Because ever since we met, I'd wanted to be near him. I'd felt safe with him. Protected. As if nothing could ever hurt me. But now, as Bryan edged up beside me, every muscle in my body wanted to recoil backwards.

"I'm sorry I chose to tell you everything at Dr. Davidson's office. You know him. He's your childhood friend. I didn't think about how it would feel to hear that in front of him." I tried to laugh and shrugged. "I mean, I should have told you when we met, of course I should. But—"

Bryan placed a firm hand on my thigh and squeezed. "I get it, Molly. You don't have to apologize. I'm sorry for reacting the way I did. It was just such a shock."

I nodded fervently. "I get that. I'm sorry, Bryan. But you have to believe me when I tell you that I did it because I thought it was best for Colin. All I've ever wanted is to keep him safe." My voice started to tremble. I wanted to jump up and run for Colin. I wanted to tip my boiling hot coffee into Bryan's lap, run to my son, grab him, and leave.

But I needed to do this right. I needed to stay calm.

Bryan was nodding thoughtfully. "I can't say it's going to be easy to wrap my head around what you did. I mean, I feel so guilty, Molly. For that couple. That poor couple. You know, when I came back here after our session with Robert, I almost looked them up online. I almost started googling them, looking for surrogates who ran off with babies around the time Colin was born."

"Bryan…"

"I thought about finding them, calling them, letting them come meet Colin."

Tears were starting to build behind my eyes. I was gripping my coffee cup so tightly that the heat was making my hands sting. *Liar, liar, liar!*

"But then I thought… they'd take him. Wouldn't they? They'd take him from us. From *you*. I mean, they might agree to shared custody with me. But they wouldn't want you anywhere near him. No judge would allow it. And then Colin would lose the only mother he's ever known."

Even though I knew Bryan's words were designed to cause me pain, my heart stung with every beat. "So, you're not going to try to find them?" I said weakly.

"No." Bryan suddenly stood up. "No, I'm not."

I let go of the breath I'd been holding and reached out to put my coffee cup down on the table. Then I moved closer. Bryan was still clutching his drink, but I put my hands on top of his and as his brow furrowed, he allowed me to take it from him.

After setting it down beside mine, I allowed a coy smile to dart across my lips and tried to remember how I felt the first time Bryan kissed me. Shoving aside the swirling anger in my gut, and the panic, and the nausea, I stroked the side of his face and whispered, "I miss you, Bryan. I know we can't fix things overnight. But I'm trying. I really am."

Bryan closed his eyes and leaned into my touch. "Molly, this isn't a good idea. If Colin…" He moved his shoulders as if he was going to turn to look in the direction of Colin's room, but I shuffled closer and forced my other hand to grace his thigh.

336

"I won't stay the night," I said softly. And then I pressed my lips to his and let him pull me close.

# 43

As Bryan's large, strong hands settled on my waist, my heart began to race. He was nuzzling into my neck, his stubbled chin scraping roughly across my skin when, finally, Susan appeared. She had taken off her shoes and was tiptoeing across the hall. Bryan lifted his head, but I pushed my fingers through his hair and said hoarsely, "Don't stop."

Willing Susan to hurry, I straddled Bryan's lap and started to unbutton his shirt. He was breathing heavily, and my entire body was trembling. Then there she was. She had Colin in her arms. She ran across the hall, not making a single sound. And as I watched her reach the door, I released a long heavy breath.

*Click.*

Bryan stopped kissing me.

"Bryan? What's wrong?" I whispered, barely daring to breathe. Surely, he didn't hear the door? He couldn't have. I tried to remove myself from his lap. "You know, you're right. Maybe we shouldn't —" But my words were cut off by a short sharp squeal as Bryan grabbed a fistful of my hair and pulled. My neck snapped back. He shoved me down onto the couch and moved so that he was towering above me.

"What the fuck is this, Molly?" he growled. "Do you think I'm stupid?"

I shook my head, grabbing at his hands as he pulled tighter and tighter on my hair. "No, Bryan. Of course not. What do you mean?"

Standing up and almost tossing me to the floor, Bryan stalked towards the window. And then the fire alarm began to sound. Whirling around, he looked from me to the hallway, then broke into a run.

I stood up, my legs shaking so much they could barely carry me, and I stumbled towards the door. From Colin's bedroom, at the same time that a bolt of lightning sliced through the sky outside, Bryan released a thunderous roar.

I was at the door. My fingers were trembling, grappling for the handle. But then I heard him. Footsteps. *Thud, thud, thud.* Swirling around, I saw my purse sitting on the kitchen counter. I ran for it and thrust my hands inside. And when Bryan appeared in the hallway, his once sparkling eyes now black with rage, I pulled out Susan's gun and thrust it forwards.

"Don't come any closer," I spat.

Bryan stopped and looked me up and down as if he was wondering whether he could charge forward and rip the gun from my hands before I pulled the trigger.

"I mean it, Bryan. The police and the fire department will be here any second. They'll search the building."

A slow, sharp smirk broke across Bryan's face, and he swept his hand across his forehead. "Molly." He shook his head and laughed. "Dear Molly, what have you done?"

The gun felt heavy in my hands, but I held it still. All I needed to do was keep him there until the police arrived. That's all.

"Conspiring with some stranger to steal your son away? And now a gun? Don't you think you've gone a bit far this time?"

I glanced furtively towards the window, praying that Susan was already on the way to Kathy and Frank's and taking Colin far, far away from this place.

Slowly, Bryan began to walk towards me. "Maybe you should give that to me, sweetheart. This won't look good in court. Will it? Turning a gun on your own husband."

"You're not my husband," I spat, stepping back and jolting as I came into contact with the glass edge of the coffee table. "You're a *monster*."

Bryan was still inching closer and still smiling. "I don't know what you're talking about."

"Yes, you do!" I cried, all the rage and frustration and fear from the last few months bubbling up inside my chest.

"Tell me, then, Molly. Tell me what you believe is going on." Bryan stopped and crossed his arms in front of his chest.

"You're him. You're Andy. Colin's father. You beat your wife."

"Tracy wasn't my wife," he cut in gently. "We were never married. But carry on…"

"She killed herself, and you came after me for revenge. You married me. You built a life with me, Bryan, and it was all a lie." My voice began to crack. "How could you do that? How could anyone do that to another person?"

Bryan shrugged and took off his glasses, letting them drop to the floor beside him. "You tell me, Molly. You seem to find lying remarkably easy. You've lied to everyone your entire life."

I opened my mouth to speak, but nothing came out.

"Think about it, Molly. Who are the cops going to believe?" Bryan had started moving again, but I had nowhere to go. The coffee table was behind me, so I began to inch sideways towards the window. "Me? A stand-up guy whose parents will testify that he's a dutiful, loving father to his adoptive son. Or you? A crazy woman who stopped taking her meds, accused her own mother-in-law of murder, *attacked* her father-in-law and her son in broad daylight. A woman who quit her job, who has a history of being a compulsive liar, and whose own sister thinks she's unhinged."

I screwed my eyes shut, shaking my head. *Thud, thud, thud.* Bryan was coming closer. "That's not what happened."

"Isn't it?" When I opened my eyes, Bryan had tilted his head at me and was Bryan again. Wide-eyed, concerned. "That's what Dr. Davidson thinks happened. That's what everyone else thinks happened."

"No!" I shouted, waving the gun. "Not everyone. Susan knows the truth. Your father too. He never agreed to Colin getting hurt. He never agreed to what you did. They're on *my* side now, Bryan."

For a moment, Bryan's smile wavered. And then he furrowed his brow. "Are they?"

I looked towards the window.

"Was Susan helping you rescue Colin? Or was she helping *me* get Colin away from *you*?"

Darting to the window, I looked down. Susan's car was still there. Why was it there? That wasn't what we'd agreed. My head was swimming, swirling. I reached up and grabbed at my hair, letting out a long, low growl.

The fire alarm was still ringing. The gun felt like lead in my hand. But I wasn't going to let him win. Not now. Behind me, on the window ledge, was Bryan's one solitary ornament. A large gold clock that I recognized from Kathy's house. I began to tremble. Slowly, I lowered the gun. "Bryan," I whispered, and when I looked up, he was watching me.

"Yes?"

"Please help me. I think I'm very, very ill." I held out the gun and Bryan nodded.

"Good girl," he said, nodding. "Good girl." Moving forward, he held his hand out and I returned the gesture, offering him the gun and allowing tears to tumble down my cheeks. As he wrapped his hand around mine, he kept my eyes locked in his gaze. I loosened my grip and let him take it. But before he could retreat, or turn it on me, or shoot me dead, I brought my left arm forward, brandishing the big heavy clock, and smacking it into his temple.

Bryan staggered backwards, still gripping the gun. With his other hand, he reached for his temple. A dark trickle of blood was running down the side of his face, but I didn't stop for breath, I launched forward and hit him again. And this time, he fell.

*Thud.*

---

Hurtling downstairs, I skidded into the hall and bolted for the front door. Behind me, the door to Bryan's apartment was open on its hinges, but the wail of the fire alarm drowned out any noise from within. On the windows beside the door, thick heavy raindrops began to trickle down and pool in the ridge between the glass and the frame. I shuddered. Closing my eyes against the memory of the day Jack went missing, I shook myself free from it and reached for the keypad.

Pressing the exit button, I heard a faint *buzz*. The door clunked, the lock releasing itself so that I could finally burst out of this Godforsaken building. But as my hand settled on the handle, everything went quiet. The alarm stopped. For a split-second it was silent. And then the lights went out.

I tugged at the door, but it didn't move. I pushed it, leaning the weight of my shoulder into the solid unwavering wood. Outside, the rain was beating down on the patio and the windows. Bryan's neighbors were gathered on the sidewalk, huddled together, but none of them seemed to see me. Again, thunder rumbled through the sky and, seconds later, lightning struck.

"The eye of the storm," I whispered. Stepping back from the door, I glanced at the window, then turned, desperately searching for something I could use to break through. There was nothing. I ran at it, jutting my elbow out, trying to pierce through and not caring if it cut my skin to pieces. But it didn't fracture.

My ears were still vibrating with the ghost of the fire alarm and as I moved, my head felt thick and heavy. I was exhausted. And for a moment, just one small moment, I wondered what would happen if I just sank down to the floor and stopped fighting.

When I looked up, the neighbors parted and I could see Susan's car, still parked out front. What was she waiting for? I pressed my palm flat against the window and peered out. As I watched, the interior light of the car flickered on and suddenly Colin's beautiful face was illuminated at the window. I waved frantically, unsure whether he could see me in the dark. Reaching for my phone, I dialed Susan's number.

"Molly, what's happening?"

"I think the power's out. I can't unlock the door."

"Shit."

"Is Colin…?"

"He's fine, just fine."

"Why didn't you leave, Susan? Why are you still here?"

"I wanted to wait for you. Frank's on his way with Kathy." She paused then in a low voice asked, "Molly, where's Bryan?"

"I hit him. He fell." I looked up at the stairs and in the silence before Susan spoke again, I heard the smallest, faintest, creak of a floorboard.

"Is there somewhere you can hide until the police get here? Somewhere safe?"

"Yes. Shit. Susan, I think he's awake."

"Okay, go. Molly, run. Hide."

"I…" I was frozen to the spot. Colin was right there, just beyond the door and I couldn't get to him. If only I could break the glass.

"Go! Now! And if he comes for you, Molly, get him to confess."

"Confess?" My brain couldn't keep up. I was too tired. It was too much.

"Record it. It's the only way we'll prove what he did."

Proof… the word circled my head, around and around. If I had proof, he'd never be able to take Colin from me. Never.

Without thinking, I started to run. Holding my phone out in front of me to light the way, I bolted to the door below the stairs. I knew exactly where it led and prayed with every breath in my body that it wasn't locked.

As my fingers met the cold door handle, I stopped and breathed in. Jack's face was floating in front of my eyes but when I pressed down, and the door swung open, it disappeared.

Taking one last look behind me, I stepped down into the cellar. The door closed with a light click. In front of me, the stairwell and the room below were pitch black, illuminated only by the glow of my cell phone as I held it out like a torch.

At the bottom of the familiar concrete steps, I braced my hand on the wall and fought the urge to let out a whimper. The last time I was in that cellar, standing on that step, Jack's cold, dead body lay in front of me, slumped in a pool of his own blood.

He'd been missing for days. After supper one evening, we had gone to bed as usual and when Carol and I woke the next morning, he was gone. At first, we thought our foster parents had done something to him. We were terrified. Too terrified to search for him. Perhaps if we had, we'd have found him in time to help him. But we didn't. We were twelve years old and paralyzed with fear.

On the third day, finally, we summoned the courage to search. A storm was raging outside then, too, and our parents were not home. Carol had gone to search the woods out back, and I'd taken the house. I'd looked in cupboards, in the attic, in every tiny hiding place I could think of. And then I went to the cellar.

We'd been down there only once; it was out of bounds, and when they caught us playing amongst the old empty wine bottles and the piled-up boxes, they beat Jack so badly that he missed three days of school afterwards. Halfway down the stairs, I'd almost stopped and turned around. It was too spooky, and I knew Jack wouldn't want me to scare myself searching for him. But something had made me continue. And when I flicked on the bright fluorescent light, there he was. With a kitchen knife in his hand, his wrists wide-open and his eyes closed. In a way, it looked as if he were sleeping. But his face was leeched of every ounce of color and when I reached for his hand, his body was stiff and ice cold.

Carol found me two hours later, still clinging to his body, our parents in tow. And without Jack to protect us, it was me who took the beating that day.

"I'm sorry, Jack," I whispered. But as the words left my lips, the door behind me began to open. Shoving my phone into my pocket, I darted forward. A sliver of light was sneaking in through the window that led out onto the back of the house, and I inched around it, heading for the piled up and discarded building materials in the corner of the room. Ducking down behind them, I held my phone out in front of me, reduced its brightness, switched on the recorder, slipped it back into my pocket, and waited.

## 44

"Come out, come out, wherever you are…" Bryan's voice sent a shockwave of panic rattling through my bones. "Molly," he said softly, "I can help you, sweetheart. Just come out and talk to me."

Bunching my hands into fists, I pressed my back against the wall and held my breath.

*It's the only way to prove what he did…*

Susan's words echoed in my ears. So, just as Bryan stepped into the eerie light of the window, I stood up.

"I'm here, Bryan."

The blunt edges of his lips spread into a smile. "Ah, Molly. There you are." He was still holding the gun and when he turned into the light, the side of his face was covered in blood.

Holding my hands up to show I wasn't holding any kind of weapon, I edged slowly out from my hiding place. "Let's stop this, Bryan. It's gone too far."

Bryan weighed the gun up and down in his hand, as if it were a plaything, then raised it and pointed it directly at my chest. "It certainly has." He tweaked the barrel of the gun to indicate that I should move further into the room. I did. "That's it. Right there," he said, still smiling. "Is that where you found him?"

Glancing behind me at the wooden post in the center of the cellar, I nodded. "How did you know?"

"Your nightmares, mostly. When we first met, you'd say his name over and over. *Jack, no. Jack, I'm sorry.*" Bryan laughed. A coarse crackling laugh that reverberated through the room. "I asked Carol about it a while ago, made out that I was worried you were having an affair. And, of course, she told me the whole ugly story. I mean, why wouldn't she? I'm your *loving* husband."

At the word *husband* I shuddered violently and wrapped my arms around myself.

"Ah, ah, ah." Bryan waved the gun at me. "Hands where I can see them please, Mrs. Burke." He gestured for me to sit down, then looked around the room. In front of where I'd been hiding, a large pile of plastic blue rope had been discarded along with some old ceiling panels, radiators, and kitchen cupboards. "Good job the builders were a bit slap-dash in their clean-up." Bryan smirked, reaching for the rope.

As he wound it round me, tying me to the spot where Jack took his last breath, I closed my eyes and prayed that he wouldn't think to search my pockets. "There," he said, pulling it tight and stepping back.

"How will you explain this?" I asked, narrowing my eyes at him as the rope bit into my arms and wrists.

"I restrained you for your own good, Molly." Bryan reached up to touch the drying blood on his forehead. "You attacked me in my own home. Persuaded Susan to take Colin from me." He shook his head and looked around the room. "It's no surprise really, given what you went through here. That kind of a start in life is bound to drive anyone a little," he reached up and twirled his finger at the side of his skull, "*crazy.*"

"But I'm not crazy, though, am I?" I said, sharply, willing Bryan to take this one last slice of glory.

For a moment, he didn't move. And then he tipped his head back and laughed. A deep, booming laugh. When he looked at me again, he shook his head. "No, my dearest wife. You're not crazy."

*Five, four, three, two, one.* "I knew it."

"Did you? Did you figure it all out? I'd be truly surprised if you did." Bryan reached for a nearby stool and sat down, leaning forward to put his elbows on his knees. "Did you figure out that I married you for revenge? That I spent three and a half years plotting exactly how to ruin your life and take *my* son back? Did you figure out that it was all me? My father's disappearance, Susan showing up to haunt you, the bloodied baseball cap in your drawer?" He stood up and waved the gun in the air. "It was actually quite a lot of fun in the end," he said, grinning at me. "Seeing just how many of your buttons I could push. And, of course, the fact that you're a diagnosed compulsive liar, with a childhood sweet-heart who slit his own wrists, well, that was just too perfect to be true."

I closed my eyes. "So, you set it up to look like I was a terrible mother."

"Not just a terrible mother. A dangerous mother," Bryan said solemnly. "I need the courts to believe without a shadow of a doubt that *I'm* what's best for Colin."

With tears streaming down my cheeks, I latched onto the heat of my phone, sitting there in my pocket, recording every last word out of his sinful mouth. "What else did you do to me, Bryan? What else?!" I yelled, struggling against the rope. "You might as well tell me now, seeing as when we get out of here you'll deny it and send me to a psychiatric hospital!"

Bryan paused, then tilted his head to the side and shrugged as if I was right. "Molly, there's too much to say and not enough time."

"My medication? Did you switch it?"

"No," he said thoughtfully. "I just hid it. Told you you'd forgotten to pick it up. Made sure you skipped a few days here and there. I did lace my mother's cake with walnuts, though. Not the first time. That was an honest mistake, but the second time, while you were out on your walk…"

I breathed in shakily and bit the inside of my cheek. *Stay focused, Molly.* "And Graham? My job?"

Bryan smiled, his eyes twinkling. "Ah, you found the deleted messages, did you? That's a shame. But, yes, I texted him. Pretended to be you." His smile wavered, and he sat back down, his features settling into something different. Something darker. "But you know *why*, don't you, Molly?"

"To punish me," I whispered.

"To punish you for stealing *my* child." He waved the gun. "And for destroying my beautiful Tracy."

"I never meant to hurt her, Bryan. Or you. I just wanted what was best for Colin."

Shouting now, above the roar of the storm outside, Bryan yelled, "*We* were best for him. Me and Tracy. But you broke her heart. And then she broke mine." He stood up, inching closer. "She killed herself because you stole her child." He raised the gun and pointed it at me. "You ruined our life."

"Bryan…" I was waiting for him to pull the trigger, shoot me right in the heart. But he stopped. Then stepped back, turned the barrel, and pressed it against his thigh. "What are you—"

*BANG!*

Bryan staggered backwards and slumped down onto the stool, gripping his leg.

"Bryan?! What are you doing?!"

Leaning down and pressing the full force of his weight onto the wound in his thigh, he grimaced. "I can't believe you shot me, Molly," he said, wide-eyed, looking around as if someone was there to hear him.

Behind my back, my hands flopped down, and I stopped struggling against the ropes. "Wow," I whispered. "You've won."

Bryan was still smiling at me, wincing as he tried to stop the blood gushing from his leg.

"Except…" I paused, tilting my head at him. "How did I shoot you when you'd already tied me up?"

Bryan's lips quivered and his smile dropped. "What?"

"I mean, I know you're strong, Bryan. But even you couldn't wrestle a gun from me and tie me up after just being shot in the leg, surely? And me? I'd either run or shoot you again, finish the job, not hang around for a chat and give you a chance to overpower me."

Bryan's hand began to shake. The gun was at his side and I could see it trembling in his fingers. Quickly, he stood up, dragged himself over to me and began to unwind the rope. Tugging at it, pulling, grunting as he struggled to undo the knots he'd tied.

"You're not as clever as you think you are," I whispered as a sliver of light appeared at the door at the top of the stairs. "And you'll never, ever get your hands on my son, Bryan. That, I can promise you. I'd rather die—"

"Rather die, would you?!" he yelled, raising the gun to my temple and pushing it so hard against my skull that I could already feel the bruise. "Fine. You crazy bitch. Fine!"

"Drop the gun! Put your hands above your head and drop the gun!"

Behind Bryan, two armed police officers and Detective Monroe were all pointing their weapons at his back. Bryan met my eyes with his, gave me one last smile, then smashed the gun into my face.

Blood was trickling down the bridge of my nose. Some of it was in my eyes. But I couldn't reach it. My hands were still tied. As the two uniformed officers dragged Bryan out of the cellar, Detective Monroe untied the ropes and pulled me to him. Wrapping his arm around me, he guided me up into the light.

"The power's back," I whispered, blinking up at the chandelier in the hallway.

"It's okay, Molly, there's an ambulance out front. They'll get you checked over." Detective Monroe passed me to a smiling paramedic who wrapped me in a crispy silver blanket and ushered me onto the back step of a parked ambulance.

"Any other injuries?" she asked, gently, dabbing at my forehead.

I shook my head and winced as pain shot from my temples to my eyebrows. "No. Just my head."

"The storm's over," the paramedic smiled, looking up at the sky.

"Is it?" I replied.

She had barely finished cleaning the blood from my face when the shrill voice of Kathy Burke shattered the haze of the front lawn. Looking up, I saw her banging on the window of the police car. "Bryan! Wait! This has to be some kind of misunderstanding!" She turned away from Bryan, calling to Detective Monroe but he ignored her. Then she saw me. Storming over, with Frank at her heels, she slammed her hands onto her hips. "Molly, tell them. Tell them to let him go."

The paramedic stepped between us and held up her hand. "Excuse me, ma'am, but Mrs. Burke has a head injury. If you don't calm down, I'll have those officers over there escort you somewhere else." She nodded at Officer Daniels and the policeman standing next to her.

Kathy swallowed hard. Her features dropped. Beside her, Frank reached for her hand and squeezed. "I've told her everything," he said to me in a croaky voice. "But she's having a little trouble—"

"I'm sorry, Kathy." I shook my head. "Bryan isn't who you think he is. He isn't who any of us thought he was." I was about to continue, to tell her about the ropes and the lies and the gun in my face, when the sound of car door opening made me turn away. The paramedic tried to get me to turn back, but I waved my hands at her and stood up.

Susan was on the sidewalk with her hands on Colin's shoulders. He was crying, slow silent tears, but when I crouched down and opened my arms, he hurtled towards me and buried his face in my shoulder. Barely able to stay on my feet, I grabbed hold of him and stroked his beautiful red hair. "I'm so sorry, buddy. I'm so, so sorry." Holding his face between my hands, I ducked to meet his eyes. "Are you okay?"

Colin nodded. "Are you?" He was looking at my head.

"I'm just fine." I smiled. "Just fine." I stood up and took hold of his hand. "Come with me. I'm not letting you out of my sight. We'll finish up here, then we'll go home and get cleaned up and drink huge steaming mugs of hot chocolate. Okay, buddy?"

"Daddy too?" Colin looked towards the police car where, thankfully, Bryan's face was obscured by a crowd of neighbors who were being herded out of the way.

"Perhaps not right now, Col," I said quietly.

In front of us, the paramedic was waving for me to return. Susan put her hand between my shoulder blades and gently guided me back. It was cold. The whisper of rain was still hanging in the air and the warmth of Susan's hand on my back made me realize how chilled I was. I shuddered, still gripping tightly to Colin's tiny warm hand. But Kathy wasn't going to give up. "Molly," she said, wide-eyed. "Please, tell me. What the hell happened here?"

Glancing at Susan as the paramedic began to stitch the wound on my head, I reached into my pocket then handed Kathy my phone. "Press play," I said. "It's all there. Just don't let Colin hear it."

---

Halfway through the recording, Kathy started to cry. Walking slowly back towards me, her heels clapping against the slick sidewalk, she swept her hair from her face and tried to compose herself. "I don't want to hear any more," she said hoarsely, handing the phone back to me.

Frank, who had been trailing behind her, tried to put his hand on her arm, but she pulled away from him. "I'll wait in the car."

Frank hung his head and, as Kathy walked away, he whispered, "All this is my fault." Beside him, Susan shook her head. "I'm just as much to blame as you are, Frank. We both—"

356

"No," he said forcefully. "It started way before all this." Reaching for my hands, he squeezed them tight. His eyes were watery, and his features looked almost broken in two from the pain of what he was thinking. "Bryan's brother Greg died when Bryan was ten years old. Greg was my favorite. I know you shouldn't have favorites, but I did. He was such a beautiful boy. Bright, happy, confident. A joy to be around. And Bryan was always such a sullen child. When Greg drowned, I blamed Bryan. Greg was off on his own, and I told Bryan he should have been with him, looking out for him, the way big brothers are supposed to."

I wrapped my arms around myself. Inside, a small part of me was wondering whether we'd ever really know the *truth* about Greg's death. Or Tracy's. If Bryan was willing to go to such lengths to take Colin from me, surely he could…

"Frank, that's in the past. Bryan's actions are his own," Susan said, putting her arm on Frank's shoulder and squeezing lightly. "A dark past can't excuse what he did." She looked up at the house. "No matter how bad it was."

# 45

In soft autumnal daylight, 95 Fitzroy Street looked like any other house. Large windows, a quaint wraparound porch. Friendly. Welcoming.

I had been standing outside since sunrise, watching the lights in the windows flicker on and off as the people living in their brand-new, shiny apartments got ready for work, and school, and life.

I'd watched them start to filter out onto the sidewalk, travel mugs of coffee in hand, somehow still totally in love with their home despite knowing what horrors had taken place there. Bryan's apartment was empty, of course, but the others were just as they were before it had all happened.

Behind the house, the oak tree's upper branches stuck up like a crown above one of the ground floor apartments, which used to be the dining room. Adjusting my purse on my shoulder, I walked towards it. I skirted around the side of the building, past the white wooden railings that stood like soldiers guarding the patio, and towards the garden where Carol, Jack, and I had spent so much of our childhood. Out there, we were happy. Out there, we were free. Inside was where the badness happened.

The swing that Jack had made me was no longer there. So, I stood for a moment beneath the lower branches, closed my eyes, and pretended that it was. I pretended that I was flying through the air and that he was standing behind me. And when my feet finally touched the ground, he put his hand on my shoulder and whispered, "Everything's going to be alright, Molly. Just tell them the truth."

Opening my eyes, I sighed, longing to see his face one last time. I'd had countless therapy sessions with Dr. Davidson since the attack, but while his main purpose was to try to coax me to remember where I was on the day Frank disappeared, for some reason I kept diverting the conversation back to Jack. It was as if now it was out of its box, I needed to talk about what happened. I needed to say his name and relive the day I found him, and to be told again and again that none of it was my fault.

Eventually, the court asked another psychiatrist to try. But still, those hours when I was supposed to be at work, and when Colin and Frank were attacked, were blank.

"I'm so sorry," I'd said to the prosecutor when we met for our final briefing before court.

"It's really not a problem, Mrs. Burke," he'd replied. "We have your father-in-law's testimony that it wasn't you who attacked him, and Susan O'Connor has admitted to calling the police with the fake tip of you being in the area. Where you were is inconsequential. Bryan's lawyers might like it to mean something. But it doesn't. And after what you've been through, it's no wonder that your memory is shaky." He was a surprisingly kindly man, the prosecuting attorney, and I'd smiled at him gratefully.

I looked at my watch. Only an hour to go.

Taking one last look at the house, I left the shadow of the tree and walked away from it for the very last time.

---

## FIVE HOURS LATER

As Carol and I stepped out into the sunlight, I pulled my sunglasses down and smiled. Behind us, the courthouse and its large white pillars were silhouetted against a powder blue sky. A hand caught hold of my elbow and I turned.

"Mrs. Burke." Detective Monroe put his hands into his pockets and nodded at me. "I don't often make apologies—"

I raised my hand at him. "Let me stop you there, Detective. This chapter of my life is over. And there is nothing that I need to hear from you." Slipping my arm through Carol's, I turned away from him. On the sidewalk, a cluster of reporters flashed their cameras at me and thrust microphones in my direction.

*"Mrs. Burke, are you pleased with the verdict?"*

*"Mrs. Burke, will you be keeping your last name?"*

*"Mrs. Burke. Do you feel guilty about what you did to Tracy O'Connor?"*

I brushed my way past, ignoring them but keeping my head held high, focusing on the tap-tap of my heels against the sidewalk.

Opposite the courthouse, I hugged Carol goodbye, hailed a cab and slid into the back, pulling my purse close to my side and removing my glasses. In the rearview mirror, the cab driver looked at me, and I noticed his eyebrows tweak upwards as he realized who I was. These days, my face was famous. The story of Bryan Burke and what he did had been splashed over every newspaper and every media outlet for months. I glanced at my watch. Later that afternoon, I had an interview lined up. A chance to get my side of the story across. A chance to get them to stop focusing on Jack and Tracy and shine a spotlight on the monstrosities that Bryan put me through.

The cab drove slowly, stopping every now and then at a stop sign or a crosswalk. "Can we go a little faster?" I asked, shifting impatiently in my seat and peeling my bare legs away from the leather cushion beneath me.

"Not really," the driver replied gruffly, waving a hand at the traffic in front.

Finally, a few blocks away, he stopped, and I climbed out, tugging my skirt down and straightening my blouse.

It was autumn. A crisp breeze was in the air and all around the trees were turning from green to orange and gold. Entering the park, I stopped to look at the jewelry store opposite. After the divorce settlement, I'd be able to afford anything I wanted from that shop. But, of course, I wouldn't spend it that way; I'd spend it getting Colin as far away from Maine as possible.

Susan, Frank, and Kathy were waiting to meet me. Frank had been at court most days, but Kathy couldn't bear it, and Susan said she didn't think she'd be able to stop herself from screaming at Bryan across the court room. So, on the final day they'd stayed away.

I walked down the grass-lined path and around the fountain until I saw them, sitting on a dark green bench watching Colin kick a football.

When they saw me, they stood up in unison. "We got coffee," Susan offered, holding out a cardboard cup full of hot sweet cappuccino. I took it from her and smiled.

Beside Frank, Kathy was silent. Her lips were tight, no longer coated in coral red lipstick and, these days, gray circles were a permanent feature beneath her eyes. Frank looked better. In the months awaiting Bryan's trial, he'd put some weight back on and regained some of the strength he'd lost while he was wandering around in the wilderness hiding from Bryan. But his eyes were still full of so much sadness that it was hard to look at them.

"Well?" he asked, quietly. "What was the verdict?"

"Guilty. Aggravated attempted murder." Frank's hands were thrust deep into his pockets, but I reached out and squeezed his elbow. "I'm afraid Bryan won't be coming home for a very, very long time."

Silently, Kathy pressed her hand to her chest and turned away, sitting back on the bench with a quiet thud.

"I'm sorry," I offered, even though I didn't mean it. "It was the tape recording that did it," I said quietly, lowering my voice so that Kathy didn't have to listen.

"You told them about Tracy and the adoption?" Frank asked.

"I did. Bryan's lawyers tried to turn the tables, of course, but essentially what I did wasn't illegal and," I glanced at Susan, "as much as I wish I'd done it differently, Bryan had other options to get access to his son. After tracking me down, he could have asked for joint custody. Or at least visitation. He didn't have to do what he did. And after Frank testified that it was Bryan who attacked him…"

Susan's lips were pursed, but she reached out to squeeze my arm. "Thank you for keeping our role in everything out of the proceedings. You'd have been perfectly within your rights—"

"You were as much victims of Bryan's madness as I was, Susan. There's no way that you should be punished."

She nodded gratefully, and turned towards Colin. "What are you going to do now?"

I shrugged and took a sip of coffee. "I'm not sure yet. Graham offered me my job back, but I can't stay here. Not after everything that's happened."

On the bench, Kathy gripped its side and her shoulders began to shake. Stepping around Susan and Frank, I crouched down in front of her and put my hand lightly on her leg. "Kathy, you'll still be able to see Colin. I'd never want him not to see his grandparents."

Kathy took a tissue from her sleeve and dabbed at her eyes. "Why?"

"I'm sorry?"

"Why would you be so kind after everything we…"

I shook my head at her and stood up, then said firmly, "Listen, all of us want what's best for Colin. Of course, you all believed Bryan. You had no reason not to. But you had every reason to doubt me."

Kathy began to protest but I waved my hand at her.

"It's true, Kathy. With my past, I'd have doubted me too."

Brusquely, she patted my hand, then stood up and walked over to give Colin a hug. Tucking his football under his arm, he let her squeeze him tight, then hurtled over to me and asked to go play on the swings.

"Of course, buddy, but don't be long. We have a couple of places to be this afternoon."

I was about to tell Kathy and Frank that I'd let them know when we were settled somewhere new so that they could come visit, but Kathy began to walk away.

"Molly," Frank said darkly, "after everything that's happened, we've decided that staying in touch with Colin will be too painful for us."

I felt my mouth drop open a little and looked at Susan, who was frowning as if she couldn't believe what she was hearing, then back at Frank. "Too painful?"

Frank looked towards Kathy. She was standing with her back towards us, still as a statue, waiting for him to join her. "Kathy needs a clean break. A fresh start. Obviously, we'd like to know how the boy's doing. But…" He let his voice trail away. "I hope you understand."

I nodded quickly as Frank reached out to shake my hand. "Of course," I whispered, fighting back tears. "Goodbye, Frank."

---

After saying goodbye to Kathy and Frank, Susan and I sat for a while, side by side. "I was wondering," she said, eventually, "if maybe you'd come and visit Tracy's grave with me one day. Bring Colin." She paused and sucked in her breath. "It would mean a lot."

"Of course," I said, balancing my coffee cup on the arm of the bench. "I'd like that. I'd like a chance to say sorry."

"You know, I still can't believe it," she muttered. "I can't believe I missed the signs."

"So did I, Susan. When I agreed to be their surrogate, I had no idea what Bryan was doing to Tracy. She seemed happy."

"In court, he denied it," she said meekly.

"Of course, he did." I tapped my fingers on the side of the cup.

Susan pursed her lips. "Why couldn't he just admit it and say he was sorry?"

I exhaled a long, deep breath, then looked up at Colin. "I can't believe Kathy and Frank don't want to stay in touch with their grandson."

"At least it severs ties with Bryan," Susan offered.

"That's true. I suppose otherwise, I would always worry that he'd find us."

---

At home, Carol opened the door and smiled, despite the worry etched on her face. "Pasta's in the oven," she said.

I leaned into her for a hug and sighed. "Thank you."

Inside, we settled Colin in front of the TV, and I followed her into the kitchen. "Everything okay?" she asked, pouring me a glass of wine.

There was a lot that I wanted to say, but I couldn't say any of it in front of Colin, so I just smiled and took a sip from my glass. "Fine. Just fine." Later, though, after Colin had trudged sleepily up to bed and we'd almost polished off an entire bottle, I turned to her and whispered. "Carol?"

"Mmm?" she said, tucking her feet up beneath her in the armchair next to the bay window.

"Seeing Bryan's smug smile shatter as he was led away to prison was one of the best moments of my life."

Carol nodded knowingly.

"Right up to the second the judge gave the verdict; it was written all over Bryan's face that he thought he would get away with it. He thought the court would find him not guilty, and that he'd be home in time for dinner."

"Well, the bastard was wrong. Wasn't he?"

"He certainly was."

"Is he contesting the divorce?"

I shook my head. "No. In sixty days, I'll be a free woman. Totally free."

Carol smiled and chinked her empty glass with mine. "Then we'd better finish off your packing, hadn't we?"

I looked around the room. Already, the pictures of me and Bryan were gone. Standing up, I took one of Colin's drawings down from the wall. "These are the only things I want to take," I said.

"What about the rest?"

"All this?" I asked, brushing my hand against the arm of the couch and then waving at the TV and the coffee table and the expensive drapes. "It's just stuff. Stuff from a life that wasn't really mine. And I don't need it anymore."

# EPILOGUE

*TEN YEARS LATER*

I t was late in the afternoon. My favorite time of day to be in the forest. Through the trees, lazy sunlight dappled the well-trodden path in front of me and, from up ahead, Colin shouted—n in his deep, almost-broken voice, "Mom, hurry up!"

Quickening my pace, I jogged up behind him and wrapped my arms around his shoulders. Taller than me now, but still sporting the same fire-red hair, he squirmed away and started to laugh. Momentarily, my smile dropped. His laugh never failed to remind me of his father. But I pushed the thought away and patted his back. "What do you want for dinner, birthday boy?"

Colin shrugged. "Can we drive to the store?"

I looked at my watch. "Not right now, Col. It's getting late." The nearest store was twenty miles away and, although Colin didn't know it, his birthday surprise would be arriving at any minute.

368

At three o'clock on the dot, the doorbell rang. Wiping my hands on my jeans and smoothing down my emerald green blouse, I checked my makeup in the hall mirror.

"Carol!" I cried, barely able to contain my excitement as I opened the door.

"Molly!" Carol threw herself at me and pulled me tight to her chest. Since we last saw one another, she'd lost weight, and I'd managed to gain some. So, now, we were almost an equal size. "I missed you," I whispered, squeezing her tight and breathing in her familiar scent.

Finally, we let each other go and Carol stepped aside, blushing. "Molly," she said, "this is Kevin." From behind her, a short, muscly man with a beard and glasses waved a polite hello then extended his hand.

"It's great to meet you, Molly. Carol has told me so much about you guys."

I let Kevin shake my hand and smiled. "She's told me a lot about you too. Come in, come in." And, standing back, I ushered them inside.

"Where is he? The birthday boy?" Carol asked, stepping inside and heading immediately for the kitchen.

"Out back," I said, following them through to the kitchen.

"Wow." Kevin stopped in front of the large kitchen window. "What an amazing backyard. The river and the trees? Every young boy's dream."

I grinned and hugged my arms around myself. "I know. It's beautiful, isn't it? The house is small," I said, waving at our surroundings. "But it's the location that swayed me."

I was about to offer him a tour, when the backdoor swung open and Colin's gangly teenage frame entered the room. "Mom?" he said, eyes on his phone rather than what was in front of him. But when he looked up, he froze.

Carol grinned at him and waved her arms in the air.

"Aunt Carol?" Colin jumped forward, letting her embrace him and tousle his hair. "What are you doing here?" His voice squeaked with excitement and he coughed loudly to clear his throat.

"Well," Carol stepped back and slipped her arm through Kevin's, "I wanted to introduce you to Kevin. *And* someone told me it's your birthday around about now?"

Colin grinned and bunched his fists, a gesture leftover from his childhood that always made me smile. "Sure is," he replied.

"Then we better get the presents out of the car, hadn't we?" Carol replied, gesturing for Kevin to see to it.

"Yes, ma'am," he replied, kissing her on the cheek. "Anything you say."

---

Later that evening, with the sun now resting safely behind the mountain and stars twinkling brightly in the sky, I sat back in my chair on the wooden deck behind our house and sighed.

Beside me, Carol threaded her fingers together behind her head and smiled at me. "What a wonderful afternoon," she said.

"Colin loved his gifts," I replied. "And he sure is a big fan of Kevin." Down by the river, Colin was teaching Kevin how to skip stones across the surface of the water. And Kevin was doing terribly at it.

"Everyone's a fan of Kevin," Carol replied. "I don't know how I got so lucky."

"Because you deserve to be happy," I said sincerely.

"Well," Carol turned to look at me, "so do you, Mol." She wiggled her eyebrows. "So, is there anyone on the horizon... any local guys caught your eye?"

I shook my head quickly and reached for my wine. Taking a large sip, I crossed one leg over the other. "No. I've had quite enough of men, thank you."

"But, Molly..." Carol's voice had changed and was becoming more big sisterly. "You can't be alone out here for the rest of your life. At some point, Colin will have to go to school, college..."

I sat up straighter and bit my lower lip. "Truth is, Carol, I don't know how I'd ever trust someone like that ever again. Not after Bryan."

Carol sighed and reached out to squeeze my hand. "I understand that. But not all men are like Bryan."

"I know," I whispered, watching Kevin as he play-punched Colin's arm for taking one of the best stones. "But how can you tell? From the outside, Bryan and Tracy looked like the perfect couple. There was never even the smallest sign that something was wrong. But look at what was going on behind the scenes."

Carol nodded and sipped her drink. But then she frowned and turned towards me. "They seemed perfect?"

"Mm hmm," I said, pulling my sweater a little closer around my shoulders. "The perfect couple."

Carol cleared her throat and when I looked at her, she was pale, and her eyes were wide.

"What is it?" I said, leaning over the arm of the chair to put my hand on her forearm. "Are you alright?"

"I thought you said that Bryan was beating Tracy? You said you saw bruises?" Carol's voice was a little shaky.

My mind tripped on itself and my tongue felt suddenly too thick for my mouth. "Yes, I did."

"But you just said—"

I laughed and took back my hand. "Come on, Carol. You know what I meant. They were perfect *before*."

"Before?" Carol was watching me closely, and she had put down her wineglass.

"Before I started seeing the bruises," I said, fixing my eyes on her, letting my words linger in the air between us. "When I signed the surrogacy papers, everything seemed normal. But *after* I started to notice things." I shook my head and took another sip of wine. "Honestly, Carol, I've been through ten years of therapy and I take my pills like clockwork, and you're still looking for inconsistencies in what I say?" I let a flicker of hurt dart across my face.

For a moment, Carol didn't move. But then she let her sternness drop and rubbed her hands across her face. "Jesus, Mol. I'm sorry. It's been a long day."

"It's okay."

"No, it's not. You don't deserve to be constantly questioned."

"Really, Carol, it's okay. After everything that happened, I get that you're still wary of me."

"I'm not wary of you."

"But you still think I'd lie to you?" I was watching her closely.

Carol paused, scratching at a loose thread of wool in her thick gray sweater. "No," she said. "Of course not."

"Good." I stood up and gestured for her to join me. "Because you're my sister, Carol. And I'd never lie to my sister."

# END OF MOTHERS DON'T LIE

Do you love psychological thrillers? Keep reading to discover an exclusive extract from Jo's *A Perfect Mother.*

# THANK YOU!

Thank you so much for reading my book. I really hope you enjoyed this psychological thriller. If you did enjoy this book, please remember to leave a review.

You can leave a review on:

Amazon:
www.amazon.com/Jo-Crow/e/B0781194Q5

Goodreads:
www.goodreads.com/authorjocrow

# ABOUT JO

Jo Crow gave ten years of her life to the corporate world of finance, rising to be one of the youngest VPs around. She carved writing time into her commute to the city, but never shared her stories, assuming they were too dark for any publishing house. But when a nosy publishing exec read the initial pages of her latest story over her shoulder, his albeit unsolicited advice made her think twice.

A month later, she took the leap, quit her job, and sat down for weeks with pen to paper. The words for her first manuscript just flew from her. Now she spends her days reading and writing, dreaming up new ideas for domestic noir fans, and drawing from her own experiences in the cut-throat commercial sector.

Not one to look back, Jo is all in, and can't wait for her next book to begin. *You can contact Jo at:* authorjocrow@gmail.com

facebook.com/authorjocrow

goodreads.com/authorjocrow

bookbub.com/authors/jo-crow

amazon.com/author/jocrow

# MAILING LIST

If you enjoyed my book and would like to read more of my work please sign up to my mailing list at:
www.JoCrow.com/MailingList

Not only can I notify you of my next release, but there will be special giveaways and I may even be on the hunt for some pre-release readers to get feedback before I publish my next book!

## BLURB

**A picture is worth a thousand words—and every one is a lie in this gripping psychological suspense thriller.**

Laurie Miller is left in utter shock when her husband vanishes without a trace, leaving her with a stack of bills she can't pay. As the lonely days stretch into weeks with no reappearance or body resurfacing, the stay-at-home mom accepts a photography job from a former sorority sister, and current Instagram sensation, and returns to her Milwaukee roots—and the trauma she thought she'd escaped.

Her college days left her with scars no camera can capture, and Laurie's old OCD coping mechanisms creep in as she navigates the frightening new life of single motherhood. But becoming a personal photographer to a popular Instagram-Mom is helping Laurie provide for her daughter like any good mother should. She just never expected her daughter to become the center of so much attention.

As the world of celebrity influencers feed her insecurities, Laurie realizes she's not only lost her husband but now is losing the love of her only child. Arguments ensue. Accidental injuries surface. Allegations of neglect and endangerment are flung her way. But when Laurie's daughter goes missing, a twisted scheme thrusts the past into the glaring light of the present.

And this time, her daughter's life is at stake.

Get your copy of **A Perfect Mother** at www.jocrow.com

---

## EXCERPT

**Chapter One**

After what felt like forever, I finally made it to the car and slid in behind the steering wheel, heart jittering, hands clammy, skin prickling with the sensation of being watched. Beside me, on the passenger seat, I set down my purse, my camera, and my keys.

The darkness outside was pressing up against the windows of the car, bringing with it a chill that made me shiver. The college parking lot was badly lit and although in the distance I could see the muted light of the classrooms, the space in between was filled with nothing but darkness. With the tip of my elbow, I pushed the interior lock until it clunked loudly and sealed me in.

Safe. I was safe.

Taking some long, slow breaths—in through the nose, out through the mouth—I reached into the inside zip pocket of my purse and took out a small unlabeled plastic bottle. From it, I shook a quarter-sized dollop of hand sanitizer into my palm. Slowly, I rubbed it into my fingers and then carefully wiped the steering wheel. It was the good stuff; the kind used in hospitals and commercial kitchens. It was fragrance-free and left my hands papery, raw, and looking older than they should have done. But it did the job.

After I'd cleaned the steering wheel, I started on my camera, carefully wiping the body and the controls then dusting the lens six times counter clockwise with the brush Ben bought me for my birthday. Midway through the seventh swipe, a vicious tap-tap-tap on the window shook my concentration. My breath caught in my throat, my heart thundered, my mouth instantly dried up. But then Jenna's face was pressed up against the glass and she was smiling at me, laughing, gesturing for me to open the door.

I didn't. But I did wind down the window.

"Jenna? Did I leave something behind in class?"

"No, silly. We wondered if you wanted to join us for a drink. Every week you say, 'Maybe next time.' But next week's the last class, so…" she trailed off and shrugged, glancing back at the others who were watching us expectantly.

My fingers tightened around the body of the camera in my lap, my knuckles whitening with the pressure. "I'm so sorry. I can't. Next week, though, I promise."

"Sure," Jenna replied, clearly not buying it. "See you."

I opened my mouth to add an explanation. But I couldn't think of one, and she was already walking away.

Sitting back and trying to steady my breathing, I watched Jenna's silhouette disappear. The interruption meant I had to start my ritual all over again. Hands. Steering wheel. Camera. And by the time I'd finished, everyone else from the evening class had left, mostly on foot. A couple of times, I'd thought about saying yes when they'd asked me to join them. But then I'd pictured myself in a crowded bar with bodies I didn't know jostling up against me, and too much noise, and floors sticky with who-knows-what, and every time I'd said, "No, thanks. Maybe next time."

The same thing happened when I thought about walking to class and back. It was only a few blocks from home, but now that the evenings were closing in and there were ominous shadows and dark corners to contend with, I couldn't make myself do it. Plus, it was the one night of the week I had sole use of the car, and I wasn't going to give that up.

More often than not, the class, or the car, or both, caused a row between Ben and I, and tonight had been no exception. Ben said he needed to 'take care of something' at work and wanted the Honda, and before I knew it, I was waving my arms and raising my voice, even though our daughter, Fay, was right there staring at me with her big watery eyes.

"Ben, you work late every night of the week. This photography class is the only thing I have that's for me. You know how important it is."

"I'm not telling you to stay home. My mom will—"

"I don't want her round here all the time."

"It's not all the time, Laurie. It's one night."

"I need the car."

"Can't you walk?"

"No, Ben. I can't. You're staying home. End of discussion." And with that, I'd grabbed the car keys from the hook, slung my camera over my shoulder, and slammed the door triumphantly on my way out.

Now, though, my bravado had faded, and I was starting to wish I didn't have to return home. Maybe I should have said 'yes' to the drink? At least it would have drawn the evening out a bit, made Ben wonder where I was, given him time to miss me. But I didn't. As usual, I simply couldn't let myself be free. So, I had no choice. I had to go back.

Heading away from the college, I noticed Jenna and the others up ahead. They were laughing. Probably at me. I didn't look at them as I drove past, just stared straight ahead and pretended they weren't there. And soon enough, I was pulling into our neat little street with its neat little houses—the white picket fences, and the porch swings, and the gabled roofs that had made me fall in love with Arlington all those years ago—and I knew I was going to have to apologize to Ben.

I'd overreacted; I shouldn't have yelled, especially not in front of Fay, but lately Ben and I just couldn't seem to be around each other without arguing, and it was always me who ended up looking like the irrational one. Somehow, he managed to stay calm even when he was angry. He kept his voice measured and soft, never yelled, never cried or stormed out. Me, on the other hand... my emotions were too quick to escalate, and my thoughts too jittery to put into any sensible kind of order. Even if I knew what I wanted to say, it never came out the way I intended it to. And afterwards, no matter how convinced I'd been at the time, I'd start doubting myself and wishing I'd handled things differently.

Walking up the four stone steps that led to our front door, I inhaled deeply through my nose and let the air expand in my chest. I held it there for a moment, counting slowly from ten all the way down to one, then reached into my purse for the house keys. My fingers snaked through its insides—wallet, compact, phone—but couldn't locate the keys, so I turned back to the street and angled myself towards the light coming from next door's porch. Our own porch light went out weeks ago. Ben said it looked like kids had broken it because he'd found shattered glass and a couple of small round stones not far from our welcome mat. But neither of us had gotten around to fixing it.

As I finally found the keys, a car pulled into the street. It had a loud engine, dimmed headlights, and it slowed as it approached me. Something about it made me wrap my arms around myself. I narrowed my eyes, but the driver was just a blurry silhouette, obscured by tinted windows.

The car stopped, lingering in the middle of the road. Then, as I turned back towards the house, I felt it start to move again. I glanced over my shoulder. This time it parked right in front of our Honda. Almost directly in front of our house. The headlights went out. The engine stopped. But the door didn't open. And then, just as I was about to run inside to fetch Ben and tell him something weird was going on, it jumped back to life and sped off.

Clutching my purse and camera close, I tutted at myself. If I mentioned it to Ben, he'd tell me it was nothing. I was always suspicious of new cars on the street, and nine times out of ten they were simply lost and looking at the house numbers. It was the dark that was making me nervous. I always felt on edge when I was out at night, but starting to rant about strange cars watching the house would only cause another argument.

*Pull yourself together, Laurie,* I whispered, reaching out and unlocking the front door.

Inside, the house was still and dark—quieter than normal. Ben would usually be slumped on the couch with the TV blaring, half-asleep with his laptop open and paperwork all over the floor, but the lounge was empty.

I set my camera down on the kitchen worktop and flicked on the coffee machine. Perhaps Ben was in bed. Sometimes, he crashed out in the basement—his 'creative lair,' where he came up with new ideas for the bakery and pored over business plans and cash-flow forecasts. But when he did, there was always a telltale sliver of light bleeding out from the gaps around the doorframe.

With the absence of any such light, I sighed, and scraped my hair back. I hated it when Ben was in bed before me because it meant I had to simply wash, change, and crawl into bed, rather than giving the bathroom a quick once-over with the steam mop and some bleach. Still, at least it would delay any confrontation until morning. Maybe by then I'd have figured out how to say what I wanted to say: *I miss you. I'm lonely. You work too much, and you don't share things with me anymore.*

The green light on the coffee machine started blinking, releasing a piping hot stream of extra-strong espresso into a short white cup and nudging me out of my tangle of thoughts. I always did it this way—a short sharp hit of caffeine that would keep me awake long enough to tackle the shots I'd taken—because if I didn't edit them straight away after class, life would get in the way and they'd be resigned to a permanent 'to do' list. Coffee in hand, I took my camera to the nook under the stairs that had become my workspace and plugged it into the computer. Scrolling through the photographs I'd taken in class, I pinged a few Instagram-worthy shots over to my phone and—not for the first time—wished I'd drummed up enough freelance photography work to pay for one of the models that linked seamlessly with your social media profiles and editing software.

Perhaps I'd ask Ben about it. If he was working all these hours, things at the bakery must be going well. Mustn't they?

I stayed in my nook for a little over an hour, playing with the post-production lighting effects we'd been learning about and, as always happened when I was engrossed in my photography, I managed to forget everything else and just… be.

Eventually, I glanced at the clock in the corner of the screen. It was getting late and the espresso was wearing off, so I tidied my desk, washed up my coffee cup, tucked my shoes neatly onto the rack in the hall, and padded up the stairs towards mine and Ben's bedroom.

Fay's room was on the left, opposite the family bathroom. She was a light sleeper, so I almost didn't dare nudge the door open to check on her, but something told me I needed to.

The door creaked as I pushed it back far enough for me to stick the upper half of my body into the room. My eyes slowly adjusted to the darkness. I scanned Fay's bed for the familiar bundle of legs and arms cocooned beneath the covers. She had a habit of sliding right down into the middle of the mattress, burying herself so it was almost impossible to tell which bumps were her and which were bundled up blankets. But there was always a foot or an elbow that gave her away.

I blinked. The covers were flatter than normal, smoother. There was no lump in the middle. No leg protruding to the side or crop of messy hair peeking out of the top. I grappled for the light switch. A dim orange glow illuminated the room. Fay was not there. Her bed was empty.

Get your copy of **A Perfect Mother** at www.jocrow.com

# WANT MORE?

WWW.JOCROW.COM

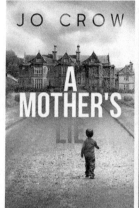
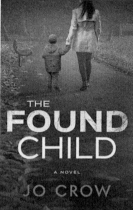
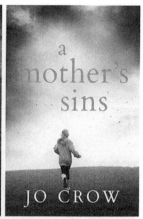

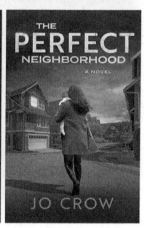